THE JAGGED CIRCLE

Jockey Girl

Jockey Girl
The Jagged Circle

THE JAGGED CIRCLE

SHELLEY PETERSON

A Jockey Girl Book

DUNDURN
TORONTO

Publisher: Scott Fraser | Acquisitions editor: Kathryn Lane | Editor: Catharine Chen
Cover designer: Sophie Paas-Lang
Cover image: istock.com/rhyman007
Illustrations: Marybeth Drake
Printer: Marquis Book Printing Inc.

Library and Archives Canada Cataloguing in Publication

Title: The jagged circle / Shelley Peterson.
Names: Peterson, Shelley, 1952- author.
Description: "A Jockey Girl book."
Identifiers: Canadiana (print) 20200269216 | Canadiana (ebook) 20200269224 | ISBN 9781459746947 (softcover) | ISBN 9781459746954 (PDF) | ISBN 9781459746961 (EPUB)
Classification: LCC PS8581.E8417 J34 2020 | DDC jC813/.54—dc23

We acknowledge the support of the Canada Council for the Arts and the Ontario Arts Council for our publishing program. We also acknowledge the financial support of the Government of Ontario, through the Ontario Book Publishing Tax Credit and Ontario Creates, and the Government of Canada.

Care has been taken to trace the ownership of copyright material used in this book. The author and the publisher welcome any information enabling them to rectify any references or credits in subsequent editions.

The publisher is not responsible for websites or their content unless they are owned by the publisher.

Printed and bound in Canada.

VISIT US AT

dundurn.com | @dundurnpress | dundurnpress | dundurnpress

Dundurn
3 Church Street, Suite 500
Toronto, Ontario, Canada
M5E 1M2

We all need family —
if not the one we have,
we'll find another,
for better or for worse.

Things we face fade away.
Things we flee follow us.

Calm Before the Storm

Life isn't about waiting for the storm to pass. It's about learning to dance in the rain.

— Vivien Greene

Evangeline Gibb's spirits were low. It was Monday of the spring break, and all her friends were away with family, either skiing down snowy slopes in faraway lands or sunbathing on romantic beaches. And here she was, mucking stalls in her grandmother Mary Parson's four-stall wooden barn. Sixteen-year-old Evie envisioned a lonely week of boredom.

The snow should have melted by now, she brooded. *Flowers should be shooting up. Birds should be singing. Leaves should be sprouting. But no.* The tree branches were stark and budless against the grey, unsettled sky, and she was bundled up in her old winter jacket with her blue knitted toque pulled over her long red hair. When she exhaled, she could see her breath. The water tap was stiff with frost, and she'd had to use the hairdryer on it to get the water running.

At least the pipes weren't frozen, she thought begrudgingly. She switched on the old barn radio beside the telephone.

"*Good morning this Monday, March twelfth, at two minutes to eight. The current temperature is minus four, but good news, folks! By two this afternoon we'll hit plus seven. You heard right! Our wintery weather will be moving down to New York. Might as well ... they blame us anyway.*"

Dumb joke, Evie moped, as she put down her pitchfork to empty the wheelbarrow. The very idea of a spring thaw seemed like a distant dream.

Followed by her tall black dog, Magpie, Evie pushed the heaped cart over icy ruts to the manure spreader. In her irritation, she shoved it harder than necessary up the slippery ramp, and the whole thing tipped over, spilling horse manure and urine-soaked wood chips onto the ground.

"Arghhh!" she yelled. "Shh-shoot!"

Magpie scampered for cover, and Evie stomped back into the barn to retrieve her pitchfork. Angrily, she forked up the mess and refilled the barrow. "I can't stand this!" she muttered aloud.

The winter had been especially long and harsh. With intense storms, high winds, and frequent power outages, it had been so bad that her grandmother had finally invested in a generator. Evie was glad, since no power meant no water, and no water meant driving miles away to haul it back for the horses to drink. And they drank a lot of water.

She dumped the twice-handled load in the spreader and carefully backed the wheelbarrow down the slick ramp. This time she managed to keep the front wheel from sliding off.

"Calm down, you jerk," she told herself. She was acting like a spoiled brat, and she knew it. Being on a horse farm surrounded by beautiful countryside wasn't a bad way to live. She filled her lungs with fresh air and counted to ten.

She gazed over the sloping fields and winding driveway fenced with ancient cedar split rails. The property had been in the Parson family for years, and from the first time she'd laid eyes on it, Evie had thought it was totally charming. As she stood at the barn door, to her right the lane curved up to the yellow Victorian farmhouse with a white wraparound porch. To her left, the lane ran down to the gravel road and across a meandering stream by way of the quaint wooden bridge that gave the farm its name, Parson's Bridge.

Her spirits lifted further as her gaze landed on the four horses in the big paddock out front, munching on the round bale of hay that Glen Judge had dropped off the day before. Each horse was attractive in its own way, Evie decided, from tall and thin to short and curvy. And all with such different personalities. She took pleasure in how pretty they looked against the white snow.

Each horse wore a different coloured blanket. Calm and collected Paragon was a lanky bay, and his blanket was bright green. He'd been Gran Mary's show hunter and was still elegant and in surprisingly good shape. The retired old chestnut racehorse, Bendigo, who'd won half a million dollars in his career and was still feisty, wore burnt orange. Christieloo, Gran Mary's cheerful, willing hacking horse, was a palomino. Her deep-blue rug contrasted perfectly with her coat.

Last — *but certainly not least*, Evie thought — was her horse, No Justice. He was a sleek black and very nicely suited up in his blanket of crimson red. She called him Kazzam.

Her eyes rested on him. He belonged to her, she reflected, but really, *she* belonged to *him*. Kazzam's bad temper was legendary, but Evie understood what angered him and why, and she felt he usually had good reason. She loved him for his distinctive personality. He returned that love by trusting her and allowing her to ride him. Together, they made a great team.

How proud she was to have a horse like him! A smile slowly brightened her freckled face as she thought about the ebony gelding. His ear tips almost touched together when pricked forward, and he had a crisp white heart on his forehead. His alert eyes shone with intelligence, and his profile was patrician, lending him a regal bearing and an air of confidence. He was small but mighty, standing only fifteen hands, but he possessed powerful speed. He was a Thoroughbred, bred for stamina and swiftness.

Nine months earlier, against all odds, Kazzam had won an upset victory at Canada's most prestigious Thoroughbred race, the Queen's Plate. Evie had been the rider. She'd just turned sixteen and had barely made apprentice jockey in time. It sometimes felt like it had all been a dream.

A training injury had sidelined their plans that year, and Evie worried about further damage being done to the gelding if they raced again. She was contemplating what other career might suit him best. For the past few months, when the weather permitted, she'd been training Kazzam to jump. It had begun as a strengthening exercise, but the small black horse had such an aptitude for the sport and was so eager to work that Evie had expanded their training schedule. She'd found the book *How to Train Your Jumper* at BookLore in Orangeville, and Gran Mary helped her pace out the proper striding.

They did gymnastics and triples and bounces and oxers. Evie dragged out old lawn furniture for Kazzam to jump, and an old blue tarp from the barn became a water hazard. She admired his talent and his brains. He learned very quickly, and once he figured something out, he never forgot. Plus, they were having lots of fun.

She stretched out her arms and shoulders, noticing how the sun was trying hard to break through the clouds. The day was starting to look promising.

Normally on school mornings, she would get to the barn by six o'clock. She'd feed the horses their grain and blanket them while they were eating. After turning them out into the field, she'd scoot back to the farmhouse for a shower and a bowl of oatmeal before catching the school bus at seven-thirty. She mucked the stalls after school, unless Gran Mary had time to do it.

But today was a school holiday, and Evie could take her sweet time. *Like mucking stalls is a holiday*, she thought wryly. To be honest, though, she really didn't mind because where there's manure, there has to be horses.

She imagined a *real* holiday: a lazy walk along a sandy beach in a turquoise bikini. Her toenails and fingernails would be painted the same bright blue, and her dull winter hair would come alive as sunlight sparkled on its vibrant red hues and warm breezes billowed it around her face as if she were a model. Her pasty-white, freckled skin would magically transform to be smooth and tanned. She'd casually stoop to pick up a shark's tooth or a pretty pink shell at whim. The soundtrack of her daydream was jazzy and sexy and cool — "The Girl From Ipanema," a song she'd heard on one of Gran Mary's old cassettes.

She began to sway and hum the tune. *La dee la, and laa dee la-la, the la de la-pa-la-la de la-la, and la de la-la de la de la-la goes Ahhhh ...*

From his paddock, Kazzam looked up and caught her eye. He shook his mane and pawed three times with his front right hoof. Evie laughed aloud, startling Magpie, who'd been watching her with anxious eyes ever since the wheelbarrow debacle.

"It's okay, Mags," said Evie as she rubbed the dog's silky ears. "Just me, being snapped out of a beach fantasy by a smartass horse."

Magpie's deep-brown eyes stared up at Evie intently, and she made a gulping sound deep in her throat. Evie loved her dog's strange little noises. She reminisced about how they'd found each other. Back when Evie was still living with her father, she had overheard him ordering that Kazzam be euthanized for insurance money, so she'd stolen Kazzam in the night and run away. She and her horse had found shelter in a deserted shed, and the next morning she'd awoken with a stray dog curled up beside her, asleep — black, with a white splash on her chest and white speckles on her toe tips. Evie had named the dog Magpie.

Evie patted Magpie's head fondly. Her long skinny tail wagged happily, as if she were sharing those memories. Evie laughed. "We've had a lot of adventures, haven't we?"

Kazzam turned his attention back to the hay and resumed eating, and Evie pushed the empty barrow back into the barn with Magpie at her heels. The dog promptly curled up on her bed of old horse blankets.

There was one stall left to clean. As she lifted the manure and dug out the pee spot, Evie mulled over her options for the rest of the day. She had some reading to do for history before the end of the break, plus a manageable pile of French grammar exercises.

Her most time-consuming assignment was an essay on the novel *Lord of the Flies* by William Golding. *Easy*, thought Evie. *Stranded boys on an island can't get their act together, and in a winner-takes-all power struggle, death ensues.* She was certain that a plane full of *girls* would have figured out how to live peacefully until help arrived. She'd write the essay from a feminist point of view.

The thought of sitting inside doing schoolwork was not appealing. The sky was brightening up, and if the forecast was true, a hack through the woods with Kazzam seemed like a much better idea. She'd have tons of time for homework over the coming week.

Suddenly, Magpie jumped up. The ruff on her neck rose straight up as she raced outside, barking. Evie looked out to see horse trainer Jerry Johnston, or J.J., driving his new white truck up the lane — too fast, as always.

Evie's grandmother was still asleep. She had a bad cold, and yesterday she had worked late into the night to meet a deadline for her latest book. Evie did not want Jerry to wake her.

She ran out, waving her arms. "Jerry! Jerry!"

His gaze was focused on the house, and he looked right past her. Evie scooped up some snow, quickly formed a snowball, and, with perfect aim, landed it on the windshield. Jerry slammed on the brakes and skidded to a halt.

His eyes were wide as he got out. "Are you trying to kill me?" He stood beside the truck with the door open.

"I'm trying to save your life," Evie answered coolly. "Gran Mary will murder you if you wake her up."

"It's after eight. I've been up for hours."

"She worked 'til three this morning. Give her a break."

Jerry pursed his mouth. "You scared me with that little stunt."

"I'll tell her you stopped by."

"This can't wait. I need to talk to her now."

Evie studied him. "You have your racing face on."

Jerry's gaze shifted. "I always have my racing face on."

"You want Kazzam to race this season," Evie guessed, "and his paperwork has to be signed and approved pronto."

"You call him Kazzam, but he'll always be No Justice to me." Jerry took on an air of importance. "I'd like to talk this over with Mary before it becomes an open discussion."

"Seriously, Jerry? Kazzam is *my* horse, remember?"

"Yes, yes." He looked surprised.

"You actually forgot? After all we went through?" Evie was angry. "He's *my* horse and *I* am the one to talk to!"

"You're right, of course." Jerry shook his head slightly and spoke with affection. "How could I forget? Winning the Queen's Plate, well, that was the biggest moment of my life to date."

Evie's defences came tumbling down. "Mine, too. I was just thinking about it. It's still hard to believe we did it."

"You're the one who did it. Chet Reynolds called you 'Jockey Girl' in his book." He chuckled. "Nobody else could stay on that darned horse. He scared them all."

"You believed in Kazzam, Jerry."

"Always."

8

"More than you believed in me." Her eyes twinkled as she subtly reminded him that she'd been his last choice of jockey.

"You can't blame me for that!" Jerry sputtered. "He was a true outlaw, a wild one. He dumped experienced jocks! And you weren't even an apprentice then. Mary and I had to make that happen."

"Yeah, but it was *me* who had to prove Kazzam wasn't a danger to other horses and show the Jockey Club I could ride."

"Let's not quarrel, Evie. Yes, I want No Justice to race again. He's the best there is — with you aboard, I admit. None of the jockeys will touch him. But hey, if luck had been with us last year, he could've won the Triple Crown."

Evie had to agree. Kazzam was a fighter. He was always the smallest horse at the starting gate and had a frustrating habit of being the last to leave the gate. But once he made his move, his speed was unmatched.

Jerry continued. "He would've made a meal of the Prince of Wales Stakes if he hadn't stripped his heel. Shame."

Evie nodded. In a training run, Kazzam had overreached with a hind foot and gouged a piece of flesh from the heel of his left fore. The wound had been slow to heal, but luckily infection hadn't set in. "Thymetofly won it, though, and that was good," she said.

"Yup, and he won the Breeder's Stakes, too, 'cause No Justice wasn't fitted up." Jerry waved off that thought with a flick of his wrist. "Spilt milk. He'll be back in prime form in no time at all. We'll show them."

Evie hesitated. The truth was, she'd already decided Kazzam's racing career was over. "I've been training him to jump."

"He's a racehorse, for crying out loud. He should be racing!" Jerry's palms were open and his face was full of hope.

"But he's more than that to me. When he injured himself, it gave me time to think."

"Don't think too long. It may feel like January, but it's the middle of March. Training should start right away."

"Look, Jerry, I want to try other things! He's a legend and he should retire from racing a winner."

"Do you want a winning racehorse or a mediocre jumper?"

"You don't know he'll be mediocre. He's got a great jump, and he's quick and careful."

"He's too small. Jumpers are seventeen hands!"

"People said he was too small to be a racehorse, too. They wrote him off, and you know it."

"This is exactly why I need to talk to Mary. She'll talk some sense into you."

"I repeat! He's *my* horse! *I* should be the one —"

"Gotta go," Jerry interrupted. "He's got to get training soon." He climbed back into his truck and put it in gear. "Like this week."

"It's *my* decision!" Evie called.

"I'm going up to the house. One cup of coffee."

"You'll wake her up and she'll be mad."

"I'll come back later if she's not astir." Jerry said, unrelenting.

Evie threw up her hands. "You wake her, you deal with her."

"I've never met a woman I couldn't charm." Jerry smiled broadly and slammed the truck door shut.

"You're delusional," Evie declared, hands on her hips.

The window rolled down. "Did you say, 'You're cool, as usual'?" Jerry gave her the thumbs up and waved.

Evie shouted, "No! I said you're delusional!"

The truck's tires skidded on the ice as Jerry gunned the engine and drove up to the farmhouse.

Evie watched with pursed lips and waited. Mary's Labrador retrievers, Simon and Garfunkel, were lying on the back porch. On cue, they began to bark an urgent intruder alert. Evie frowned. They'd wake up her grandmother for sure. The noise stopped as soon as they recognized Jerry, but it was likely too late.

At least she'd tried.

Evie went back inside the barn to finish her chores, muttering to herself about Jerry's nerve going over her head about Kazzam.

Her cellphone pinged. A text message. She rummaged through her pocket for her phone and took a look. Mark! Her boyfriend, Mark Sellers, was in Florida with his family. She pulled off her right glove, swiped the bottom of the screen, and eagerly read the message.

Beach, surf, sunshine, and freshly squeezed orange juice don't make up for being here without you. Miss you! ☹

Evie's heart rate elevated with joy. Am I supposed to feel sorry for you? A *swoosh* sounded as she pressed Send.

A few seconds passed before she heard another *ping*. No. Can I call later?

Time? *Swoosh*.

Ping. 6?

Okey-doke. *Swoosh*.

Ping. Gotta go. ☺

Deep-sea fishing? Scuba diving? Sunbathing? *Swoosh*.

Ping. Grocery shopping. Jealous?

Don't forget the freshly squeezed. ☺ *Swoosh*.

Ping. Xoxo

Evie put her phone back in her pocket, happiness filling her entire body. Mark was totally dreamy, with his light-brown hair and matching eyes. And his delicious smile! She couldn't wait to see him after the break.

She'd be glad to see her girlfriends, too. Things were pretty dull with everybody away, and she already missed hanging out with Brinda, Rebecca, and Hilary. Amelia — well, she was another story. They used to be friends, but Amelia had a crush on Mark and was jealous of Evie, so she had written nasty things about them on social media. Evie didn't expect their relationship to improve in the near future.

The music on the radio paused for a news update. Again, they reported that winter was leaving and spring was arriving. *That settles it*, Evie thought. *Homework can wait. I'm going for a hack.*

She went back to work, and soon the stalls were clean and bedded down. She breathed in the smell of the new wood shavings with satisfaction. She scrubbed the feed and water buckets and began to sweep the aisle. When Jerry had run Maple Mills Stables, the Thoroughbred racing estate where she'd grown up, he'd always said you could tell a lot about a person by the way they swept a barn. Evie always made sure to do it well.

The property at Maple Mills was gorgeous, with its rolling pastures and pristine white fences. The house was grand, the stables immaculate, the landscaping exceptional. But Evie would take living with Gran Mary in the cozy warmth and humble tidiness of Parson's Bridge over Maple Mills any day of the week.

As she swept, her mind drifted back to Maple Mills and the tumultuous events of the previous summer. Her mouth tightened. There'd been a lot of drama, including the arrest and conviction of her father, Grayson Gibb. The horses had all been shipped out, including the champion, Thymetofly, and all the staff were let go.

Her father would be behind bars a long time. *That's a good thing*, thought Evie with an involuntary shudder. He'd tried every possible way to prevent Kazzam from entering the Queen's Plate. Evie had managed to overcome each of his hurdles and had been ready to race. But the night before the race, Grayson had bribed a security guard to kill Kazzam. If not for the last-minute help of Gran Mary and Yolanda Schmits, their groom and friend, there would've been a very different ending.

Evie still had a hard time accepting it. Why had her father done that? Was it because he'd wanted Thymetofly to win? Was it to protect Evie from possibly having an accident, as he'd claimed? Or was it to prove his point that Evie must obey his orders or pay the consequences? She felt conflicted. She wanted to believe that he loved her, but why? And was he even capable of love? Thinking about him, she felt like she'd been punched in the stomach. She would never understand the mind of her father. Not in a million years.

He'd sure messed up her mother.

Evie's mother was Angela Parson Gibb. All her life, Evie had thought her mother was dead. That was what her father had told her. Until she'd met Gran Mary and learned the truth.

Angela had become addicted to OxyContin after a serious riding accident. When Evie was three years old, Angela had disappeared. Convinced that she was a worthless addict and that her little daughter was better off without her, Angela left Evie at Maple Mills with her father.

She fell deeply into addiction and wasted twelve years of her life living on the streets of Toronto.

Now, Angela was in rehab at the Quest, a drug rehabilitation facility with an excellent record of success. She'd been there for four months and was doing well, but Evie had no illusions about how difficult rehab was. Angela hadn't been able to kick her habit before, and Evie didn't want to presuppose her chances this time.

Because her mother had regressed before, visitors were not allowed, nor was she permitted to make phone calls. Evie sighed. She'd have to wait until Angela got home to see her.

Grayson Gibb had remarried soon after Angela left. His new wife, Paulina, had a daughter from a previous marriage named Beatrice, or Beebee. Together, they had Jordie, Evie's half-brother.

With Grayson in jail, Evie had moved in with Gran Mary, and Paulina and her kids had moved to Newmarket to live with her new boyfriend, horse trainer Kerry Goodham.

Then, Angela had put Maple Mills Stables on the market. Contrary to popular belief, it was Angela, not Grayson, who owned it. There'd been no interest in the property for eight months, not even one serious inquiry. But just recently, someone had seen it and made an offer on the spot, and it had sold almost overnight. Gran Mary had handled the paperwork for Angela. Evie was curious to learn about the people who'd bought it.

A bulletin interrupted her thoughts.

"*This is an Amber Alert. Fourteen-year-old Stacey Linn from Newmarket was last seen on March eighth, dressed in black jeans and a black hoodie. She was hitch-hiking west with an unidentified girl along Highway 9, west of Highway 400. If anyone has seen Stacey Linn or knows of her whereabouts, call 911 immediately."*

Newmarket. That got Evie's attention. Newmarket was where Beebee and Jordie lived. And Beebee and the missing girl were the same age. Evie wondered if they might know each other.

Chores done, she turned off the radio and began walking up to the house with Magpie. The air felt decidedly warmer. She stuffed her hat and gloves into her pocket. When she unzipped her coat, the zipper pull came off in her hand.

"Rats. But with any luck I won't need this old thing anymore this year," she mumbled to herself, enjoying the feel of the sun on her face. She gaily sang, "*La dee la, and laa dee la-la* ..."

Jerry's truck stopped beside her on his way out. He rolled down his window. "You were right," he said. "Mary was not at her finest."

Evie shrugged. "I tried."

"You did. By the way, what are your neighbours asking for their farm?"

"The Malverns?"

"I guess. Just south of you. Twenty-five scenic acres. I saw the sign."

"I don't know. Gran Mary says the farmhouse and barn need a ton of work. The fences, too."

"Nice views, though, and good neighbours." He smiled angelically. "My winnings from the Plate are burning a hole in my pocket. I'd love to live next door."

"Trying to get in my good books? He's *my* horse, Jerry."

"Yeah, yeah. Oh, speaking of real estate, I heard something interesting. People moved into Maple Mills last week."

"That was quick. Who are they?"

"Rich people," chuckled Jerry. "I'll drop by and see if they need a trainer." He winked at Evie and waved as he drove down the lane toward the road.

2

A Grisly Discovery

*The greatest mistake you can make in life is to be contin-
ually fearing you will make one.*

— Elbert Hubbard

Evie continued walking up to the house, planning to
creep in without waking Gran Mary and change into her
riding clothes to take Kazzam out to the trails. She felt
tingles of excitement as she imagined galloping across the
neighbour's meadow through the snow and along the
paths in the backwoods between the concession roads.
She could almost feel the breeze on her face.

Inside the mudroom door, she kicked off her work-
boots and let in the dogs, drying them off before allowing them into the rest of the house. Then, she hung up
her old coat and hat.

I'm glad winter is almost over, she thought. *I'm sick
of all these winter things.*

"Hi, dear," said a muffled voice from the next room.

"Gran Mary! I didn't want to disturb you."

"You didn't. I'm up. I'm here on the couch."

Evie found her lying down in the kitchen sitting
area, bundled up in a blanket. Her nose was swollen

and the skin around her bloodshot eyes sagged. She looked awful.

"Can you bring me the box of tissues beside the phone?" Mary asked, then sneezed. "I feel rotten."

"You look worse. No offence." Evie brought the box and offered it to her before setting it on the coffee table.

Mary pulled out a few tissues and gingerly blew her sore-looking nose. "That man! I'd just woken up and fallen back asleep for the hundredth time and he came knocking." She sniffed. "The dogs made a terrible racket."

"I told him not to wake you."

"He said you threw a snowball at his windshield. Did you?"

Oops. "Yes, but ..."

"Good girl." A wobbly smile appeared on Gran Mary's face. "I hope it landed."

Evie was relieved. "It did! Exactly where I aimed."

"I told him to go away." Mary pulled out another tissue.

"He'll call later. You know Jerry. I'm taking Kazzam out for a ride, okay? Can you go back to bed and sleep a little longer?"

Mary's smile slid off her face. "I was about to do that when the phone rang."

"And?"

"Angela tried to run away from the Quest last night. She got as far as the stone wall behind the orchard."

Evie plunked down in a wooden kitchen chair. "But why?"

Mary shrugged. "She'd been doing so well. The doctors and staff were so pleased with her progress. She would've been discharged in a few weeks."

Evie felt let down. Now her mother would have to stay in treatment much longer. "Why would she do that? Was she looking for drugs?" She dreaded the answer.

Mary rubbed her forehead. "It's happened before, but nobody knows for sure. It came as a shock to everyone. Angela has been a model patient. They'll have to keep a very close eye on her." She frowned. "And they're moving her back to the secure wing."

"Oh, no. She hates it there."

"I know, but if she goes back to the streets, it'll be impossible to find her. You know how it works. She'll hide and none of her friends will rat her out. Been there before." Mary shook her head sadly.

Evie's heart ached for her grandmother. Angela was Evie's mother, and that was hard enough, but she was also Mary's daughter. There was a lot of guilt mixed into that emotional soup.

Mary brightened somewhat. "The good news is that they want us to come for a visit."

"Good," said Evie, "maybe we'll find out why she tried to run away. She *must* have had another reason besides giving up and needing a fix."

"Agreed. Let's hope she doesn't try it again."

"Or at least if she does, that she comes here and not back to Toronto."

Mary and Evie sat silently for a few minutes, each deep in her own thoughts.

A sharp thump on the kitchen door startled them both.

Evie jumped up so quickly that her chair tipped over and hit the floor with a smack. She half expected to see her mother's face, but no one was visible through the door window.

The dogs were at the mudroom door, barking but also wagging their tails. She opened it.

Her half-brother, Jordie, stood on the stoop. His round eyes looked up into hers. He tried to smile, then began to cry.

Evie bent down and hugged the eight-year-old tightly. "Jordie! Come in! You're shivering!"

Immediately, the three dogs swarmed him.

Mary got off the couch and hastened to the kitchen. "Dear boy! Get your wet things off and Evie will cuddle you up in the plaid blanket. Evie, dear, you forgot to close the door."

Evie slammed the door shut. The legs of Jordie's snow pants were soggy from the knees down, and she called the dogs away so he could pull them off.

"Don't shoo them!" Jordie protested. He rubbed their ears and put his arms around their necks. "Good boys, Simon and Garfunkel! Good girl, Magpie!" The dogs wiggled with glee and licked his face. He began to smile.

"How did you get here?" Evie asked as she helped him pull off his outerwear. Newmarket was more than sixty kilometres away, and it was only eight-thirty in the morning.

"You know Brent? The farrier who shoes Lord Percy? Well, he lives near us, and he shoes the new horses at Maple Mills."

Lord Percy was a handsome show horse that belonged to Jordie's mother, Paulina. "The new owners moved their horses to Maple Mills already?" asked Evie.

"Yeah. Last week. They moved from Newmarket, and Brent worked for them there."

"So, Brent drove you here?"

"Yeah. Um, so anyway, I'd asked if he could give me a ride to visit my sister, that's you, next time he was going. So he did. He dropped me off at the lane when we saw you were home."

Mary joined them with warm cocoa and muffins. Her face was gentle as she asked, "Did you forget to call us first?"

Jordie held his cocoa carefully with both hands and took a sip. "Yum. This is really, really good."

"Did you?"

"It happened really fast. Brent saw me taking out the garbage this morning. I forgot to do it last night. It's my job."

"Go on," prompted Evie.

"Um, I was in my pyjamas? And he said he was coming here, so I got my snowsuit on as fast as I could and got in his truck."

Evie smiled. Jordie was still wearing his pyjamas. Superman pyjamas.

Mary sat down beside him. "But what if we hadn't been home?"

"I would've stayed with Brent all day. He said I could. But we saw your truck and the dogs. Evie was going in the back door."

Mary smiled. "Good detective work."

"Brent told me to tell Mom before we left, and I said that I did." He looked down. "I tried, but she wouldn't wake up."

"So she doesn't know where you are?" asked Mary.

"Well, um, no. But she was really, really asleep."

Mary nodded thoughtfully and passed him the muffin plate. "They're cranberry. Does Beebee know you're here? Or Kerry?"

"Kerry was already gone. He teaches all day." Jordie looked uncomfortable.

"And Beebee? Was she asleep, too?" Evie persisted.

"So, about Beebee? You need to know something."

Mary and Evie waited for Jordie to finish his mouthful of muffin. He'd taken an enormous bite, so it took some time. As she watched him chew, Evie considered how dull life had seemed earlier that morning. Her greatest concern had been boredom and frozen taps. Things had suddenly gotten serious.

Finally, Jordie swallowed. He wiped his mouth on his pyjama sleeve. "Yum. I sure am hungry," he said. "I didn't have breakfast. And you know what's funny? These muffins are cranberry and your name is Gran Mary. Cran Berry. Gran Mary. See? It rhymes." He grinned. "Isn't that funny?"

Mary and Evie chuckled. "I've missed you and your crazy sense of humour," Evie said. Jordie opened his mouth wide to take another bite, but Evie stopped him. "Hey, first tell us about Beebee."

Jordie put down the muffin, but eyed it longingly. "She's never home. And she's weird. Kerry says teenagers always get weird, but she's really weird."

Mary asked, "Why do you say that?"

Jordie looked puzzled. "Because she is?"

Evie tried another approach. "Name one weird thing."

"She *looks* different. Her hair is weird and all black and she has black eyes and black lips and her face is white. And she yells at Mom and me a lot. And when she's not yelling, she talks so, I don't know, um, *weird*. Like she says *like* all the time, and her voice is sort of like baby talk in a scratchy voice." He mimicked her in a high, whiny voice. "She sow-unds sor-ta like thi-i-is."

Evie smiled at his effort. "Does she have friends?"

"Yeah." He mimed putting his finger down his throat and retching.

"Is she going to school?"

"Um. I *think* so. Sometimes."

"Does she have a boyfriend?"

Again, he mimed putting his finger down his throat. "Dunno."

"Is she still swimming? Dancing?"

"Um. Dunno. Don't think so. Can I eat the rest?" Jordie's hand was stretching out toward the plate.

Mary smiled at him. "You go ahead." She stood, crossed the room to the phone, and picked it up. "I'll just make sure your mother isn't worrying about you."

Jordie spat out half his mouthful. "Don't make me go back! Can I stay here? With Evie?" The boy stared at Evie with round, pleading eyes. "I don't eat much, mostly, and I'm mostly quiet. Please?"

Something's very wrong at home, thought Evie.

Mary set the receiver back in its charger. She sat down on the couch beside the young boy and looked at him seriously. "What else is going on, honey?"

Jordie shoved the rest of the muffin into his mouth. When he spoke, crumbs and saliva dribbled down his chin. "I just need to stay with Evie. And you. That's all." He crossed his arms and sat back in an effort to look defiant.

Both Mary and Evie took their cue from him. They sat silently and waited.

He couldn't keep quiet for long. "Kerry's really nice. He doesn't, um, know anything, you know, about kids? Like, he lets us do anything we want. He's not around much, anyway."

Mary prodded a little. "Is he good to you? And to Beebee?"

"Oh, yeah," grinned Jordie. "He orders pizza. Extra cheese."

"Delicious," agreed Evie. "And your mom? How are things with Paulina?"

"Great!" Jordie answered with enthusiasm. *A bit too much enthusiasm*, Evie thought. She watched him checking their faces for signs of skepticism.

"That's wonderful," said Mary. "Then I'll give her a call."

"No. She's not great." Jordie's face crumpled. "She really likes her wine. And all her 'Mother's helpers.'"

Mary and Evie glanced at each other. Did he mean that Paulina was taking pills? What kind? Was that why Jordie hadn't been able to rouse her that morning?

"Beebee has these weird friends and she's acting all crazy, but Mom doesn't notice or even *care*. She hasn't been home in ages, even to sleep! But Mom doesn't even know if we go to *school*! She only cares about Kerry and her dresses and her wine. And shopping."

Evie sat closer and gave her little brother a hug. She remembered all too well what her stepmother was like. It seemed that Paulina hadn't changed a bit since they'd moved. Evie had hoped that leaving Grayson and being with Kerry, who was a kind man, would help. "I'm so sorry. You must feel all alone."

Jordie rested his forehead on Evie's chest and accepted her hug. His shoulders shook.

"Never mind. You can stay here," Evie said, and then looked at Mary, silently pleading for confirmation.

Mary nodded. "You can stay, at least for now, but I do need to call your mother."

"Okay." Jordie's sobs subsided slightly as he clung to Evie.

Poor little boy, thought Evie. *Paulina needs a kick in the butt.*

Mary pressed the numbers and waited. Evie and Jordie listened as she left a message. "Hello, Paulina. This is Mary Parson. Don't worry about Jordie. He's here and wants to stay for a visit. I'd love to have him. Can you give me a call, please?'

As Mary was leaving her contact numbers, Jordie whispered, "Evie? She got it all wrong. I don't want to *visit*. I want to *live* here. Can I? Please?"

"Let's see what your mom says, okay?" Evie said quietly. "And what about Beebee? She'd be upset if you left."

Jordie shook his head vigorously. "Are you crazy? She won't care one bit. I told you, she's never home. She'll be happy I'm gone."

Evie knew how he felt. Beebee had never exactly been a warm and fuzzy person, even before she got "weird." But she cared about her brother more than she let on, Evie felt certain. "Where does Beebee go when she's not at home?"

"I don't know. Her friends', I guess. She doesn't talk to me."

Evie gave his shoulder an extra squeeze. "It'll be okay."

Mary said, "Jordie, come with me. You need a hot bath, and then we'll find you some clothes. You can't spend your life wearing pyjamas, and Newmarket is too far to pick up your things. Evie, throw his snowsuit into the dryer. Do you want to come shopping with us?"

"If it's okay, I'd rather take Kazzam out for a hack. Unless you want me to come?"

"No, we can do this ourselves. Right, Jordie?"

Jordie grinned. "Right!"

Gran Mary always rose to the occasion, thought Evie with admiration. Even when sleep deprived and sick with a cold, she pulled herself together when she was needed.

"Are you sure you don't need my fashion advice?" Evie asked.

Jordie took in Evie's old barn clothes, from the torn and faded blue sweatshirt to her paint-stained old jeans and her striped socks with holes in the toes. He said with great gravity, "Yes. Cran Berry and I are quite sure we don't need your fashion advice."

All three laughed. Evie was glad that her little brother had regained his sunny disposition.

She changed into her riding clothes quickly and grabbed her old coat on her way out. She paused, remembering the zipper was broken. Gran Mary had given her a new red coat for Christmas, lightweight but warm. She put the new coat on and smiled as she left the house. She could make an effort to look fashionable, despite what Jordie thought.

Evie was in a hurry to get out on the trails and enjoy the day with her horse and her dog. It was the best way she knew to feel totally connected with the world. She couldn't describe it in words, but her entire spirit grew larger and fuller and happier when she was out riding.

She filled her lungs with fresh, cool air, and detected a faint under-smell of earth. Could the forecast be right? *Spring might actually replace this endless, cold winter*, she thought.

Magpie's long black body shot ahead with the speed of a greyhound. Her exact breeding was a mystery, but sometimes, like now, Evie thought she must be mixed with sighthound.

Halter and lead shank in hand, Evie walked out to the field.

Kazzam's head shot up from his hay, and he watched her approach as he chewed. She noted the line of his glossy black neck with approval, taking pleasure, as always, in his handsomeness and his aura of intelligence and confidence.

She looked into his questioning eyes. "Yes, we're going for a ride. Right now." She rubbed his ears and slipped the halter over the heart-shaped white marking on his forehead. Together they walked into the barn, where she brushed him and tacked him up, attaching the green-flannel quarter sheet behind his saddle to keep his kidneys warm.

She'd just strapped on her helmet and stepped onto the mounting block when Gran Mary's truck appeared. Mary rolled down her window as she slowed and called, "Have a good ride, dear!"

"I will!" Evie put her left foot in the stirrup and mounted. "Happy shopping!"

Jordie's smile was very broad as he madly waved to her.

Evie settled into the saddle and guided Kazzam past the back of the barn and along the hayfield toward the woods. They picked up a trot. Magpie raced past too closely, and Kazzam playfully shot a hind hoof out at her. It missed by a mile, but Evie gave him a firm half-halt.

"Not on, Kazzam. You know the rules." She chuckled as Kazzam reacted with a wary backward glance.

They continued trotting until they got to a wide wooden plank over a small stream. The rudimentary bridge was covered with shiny ice that was melting in the sun. Should they attempt to step on it and risk slipping?

She slowed Kazzam and asked him to slide down into the ditch instead. The horse's hooves broke through the thin ice and sank into deep mud. He plodded through and then jumped up onto the other bank.

Magpie leapt in and out in two strides. She ran in circles with glee, which made Evie laugh aloud.

It was eleven o'clock, and the sun had gathered strength, just as the radio predicted. Evie unzipped her new jacket as they trotted through the bright meadow and into the dark woods.

The pine-needled forest floor was soft and dry, and they accelerated to a collected canter. Glorious minutes passed as horse and rider covered the ground through the tranquil pines. Evie called this place the Cathedral. She felt at peace here, on the back of her horse and in the company of her dog.

She noticed something looming on the path ahead and slowed Kazzam to take a good look. Fallen trees blocked the path.

These old pines must have tumbled down over the winter, Evie guessed. They were able to walk around the first one, but just ahead were two more trees that had fallen at steep angles. Evie estimated the low side to be two feet high and the high side about four, with roughly twenty feet between the two trees.

She patted Kazzam's neck. They'd jumped lots of jumps in the ring, but never with dead branches sticking out randomly, which looked very odd and a little treacherous. "Well, boy, no time like the present. Let's go."

Kazzam acted like he'd done this all his life. At her request, he trotted quietly to the first log and leapt high. He stretched his neck out, lifted his front knees smartly, and landed softly in a gentle canter. Steadily, she kept her leg on, and they sailed over the next one, missing the dead branches without effort or anxiety.

"Good boy!" she praised. "If Jerry could see you now!" Her little black horse could do anything. "Mediocre, my foot."

On they cantered for a few more minutes, until they emerged into a small, sunny clearing surrounded by scrub brush and pines. The snow had melted in spots, exposing rough grass.

Evie slowed Kazzam and stroked his neck. "We're in heaven, boy," she said. Exhilarated, she threw her head back to give thanks to the universe. "Dear Lord of creatures great and small, thank you, *thank you*, for this beautiful day, my wonderful horse, and for my sweet, sweet dog."

Suddenly, Evie heard Magpie howling. She couldn't see the dog, but her cries were close by and intense.

Kazzam's neck arched and his ears pricked forward intently. His body tensed. He spun around to face the opposite direction and began to quiver. He snorted loudly.

Evie looked around for Magpie, but saw nothing. She heard her again, now whimpering softly. Something was definitely wrong.

"Magpie! Come, girl!"

The dog continued to whine and bay from wherever she was. The hairs on Evie's neck bristled. The yowling echoed off the trees, making it difficult for Evie to locate it.

Confusing her further, there were several paths leading out of the clearing, each going in a different direction. When she searched the ground for Magpie's paw prints, she noticed tire tracks made by some kind of small tractor-like vehicle.

She urged Kazzam closer to investigate.

The horse snorted again, refusing to go. He jogged on the spot and tossed his head. Evie stroked his neck. "It's okay, Kazzam. We've gotta find Mags." She squeezed her legs and tried to turn him around.

The gelding shook his head sharply, and with a downward thrust, pulled the reins from Evie's hands. He put his nose to the ground and ran straight along the path going south, in the exact opposite direction to where Evie had wanted him to go.

Then Kazzam stopped abruptly in a shaded brushy section. He had led her directly to Magpie. Evie took a closer look.

The poor dog was shaking, and her whine had intensified into a howl that chilled Evie to the bone. With stricken eyes, Magpie stared up at Evie, then back at something on the ground.

Evie gasped. Her stomach flipped. Beside Magpie was the form of a young girl lying face down in the snow.

Emergency

You don't overcome challenges by making them smaller but by making yourself bigger.

— John C. Maxwell

The girl lay motionless well off the path, obscured by scrubby brush. She was extremely slender and wore jeans and a black bomber jacket over a black hoodie. Strands of long purple hair made an octopus pattern around her head. One boot was missing, revealing a purple-and-pink striped sock.

Was she alive, or was she dead? Evie's stomach heaved. She commanded herself not to vomit and pulled herself together. If the girl was alive, she needed help, and fast. *How did she get here?* Evie wondered. More importantly, was she breathing?

Evie slid down from Kazzam's back and secured the reins through a stirrup in case he bolted, so he wouldn't trip on the dangling reins.

Summoning all her courage and ignoring her squeamishness, Evie knelt beside the girl and peered at what she could see of the face. The girl's skin was bluish white. Streaks of black mascara were smudged around a closed eye. There was no sign of melted snow under her nose and mouth to indicate she was breathing.

Gently, Evie turned the girl's head a little to the side. She wet her hand and held it to the girl's mouth and nose. No breath. Then she placed her hands on the girl's back to detect any movement. Nothing at all.

The body was totally without life. Evie picked up the girl's slender, ungloved hand. It was limp and stone cold.

As she placed the hand back on the ground, Evie noticed a mark on the inside of the wrist. She rotated it so she could take a look, and saw a tattoo. It was a jagged black circle, about the size of a toonie. The outline was rough, as though it was supposed to be barbed wire or it had been done by an amateur. And the skin was swollen and red, which made Evie suspect it had been done recently.

Abruptly, Evie recalled the Amber Alert on the radio. This could be the missing girl! She looked about fourteen. She was wearing black. Unbidden, fragments of instructions from crime shows and murder mysteries filled her brain. She must call for help. She must not move the body. She must not disturb the crime scene. She must stay here until the police arrived.

Evie stood quickly and reached into her pocket for her phone. It wasn't there. She checked all her pockets frantically. Then she remembered. She was wearing her new riding coat. Her phone was in the pocket of her old barn coat, hanging on the hook in the mudroom. Back at Parson's Bridge.

Her brain was spinning. The girl was dead and didn't need an ambulance, but the police had to be notified, plus the girl's parents and family. *How horrible*, she thought with a shudder.

Evie knew, too, that before too long, the coyotes and turkey vultures would start tearing at the body. It had to be moved.

She heard drums beating and looked around. It was a few seconds before she realized that the sound was her own heartbeat pounding in her ears. She felt dizzy and more than a little sick. *This is not the time to faint*, she scolded herself. *This is the time for courage.* She dropped her head between her knees and breathed in and out as slowly and as deeply as she could manage.

Magpie looked at her with a tilted head and a cocked ear, awaiting instructions. Kazzam stood respectfully, uncertain, but apparently not inclined to run home.

Her animals had faith that she knew what to do, and she was not about to let them down.

"All right," Evie said aloud. "I'll cover the body with your quarter sheet, Kazzam. The scent of humans might keep predators away for a while." She unfastened the girth buckles and slid the thick flannel blanket out from under his saddle, then buckled the girth again. She gingerly covered the body from head to toe.

"Now, we go home and call the police. We'll lead them back here, as close as they can get." She felt a bit better now that she had a plan. She mounted Kazzam from the ground. "Mags? Let's go!"

There was a direct route back to Parson's Bridge, and Evie took it. They trotted briskly through the forested trails, then down a wide lane, around a locked gate, and onto the gravel road.

They picked up speed toward home. She wanted to race the whole way, but with a kilometre to go, she forced herself to slow Kazzam to a trot, then to a walk so he could get his breathing back to normal. The girl was already past help. There was no reason to hurt her horse, and his heart was pounding.

Evie rode Kazzam right up to the farmhouse and jumped off at the mudroom door. She opened it, letting Gran Mary's dogs out to join Magpie. She threw the reins over Kazzam's head, reached in through the door, and grabbed her phone from her barn coat pocket. Exactly where she'd left it.

She punched in 911.

A woman answered. She gave Evie the option of connecting to the police, the fire department, or an ambulance. Evie chose police. Within seconds, a man's voice came on the line. Evie calmly explained that she had found a body and described where it was. She was told that an officer would arrive as soon as possible, likely within five minutes. Evie politely asked that the officer come to the barn because she needed to put her horse away.

Evie pressed End, very pleased with her calm and presence of mind. All the while, Kazzam stood quietly.

Then, without warning, her knees gave out. She found herself sitting in the snow holding her phone in one hand and Kazzam's reins in the other.

Magpie rushed to her side and licked her face. With her hands full, Evie submitted. Then she yelled harshly, "Enough!"

Magpie sat back, surprised.

"I'm sorry, I'm sorry," muttered Evie. "I've never found a body before." She rubbed the dog's head affectionately with her elbow. "I guess you haven't, either. At least not a human one."

She staggered to her feet and led Kazzam down the slight incline into the barn. As she removed his tack, she noticed how sweaty he was. Too wet to put outside. She covered him with a light blanket, filled his water bucket, and gave him some hay.

An Ontario Provincial Police cruiser drove up the driveway followed by an ambulance, both with lights flashing. Evie felt a sudden tightness in her chest.

"Mags, stay here with Simon and Garfunkel," she commanded. "I'll be back." Magpie slithered away with her tail between her legs. She shot Evie a wounded look and disappeared into an empty stall. Evie shut the barn door behind her.

However much she loathed the idea, she had to lead the police to the corpse in the woods.

The two emergency vehicles had stopped in front of the barn. A police officer stepped out of the cruiser. She was tall with an upright posture and a very serious face. Probably in her thirties, Evie guessed. Maybe forties. Evie had a hard time with adults' ages. Especially when they wore dark sunglasses, like this one did.

"Evangeline Gibb?" the officer asked.

"Yes."

"Did you call 911?"

"Yes."

"You found a body in the woods?"

"Yes."

"Can you show us the way?"

"Yes."

"Good. Come with me." The woman opened the passenger door of the cruiser. She closed it when Evie sat down.

Evie buckled her seat belt. Then she remembered Gran Mary. "Um, I need to call my grandmother. She'll wonder where I am when she gets home."

"Go ahead." The officer looked at her. "Where to?"

"Turn left at the road. The lane is a few kilometres on the left. I'll tell you when."

The cruiser led the way, with the ambulance right behind.

Evie's hands were beginning to shake, but she managed to press Gran Mary's contact. It rang once and she left her message. "Gran Mary, it's Evie. I found a body in the woods and I'm taking the police there now. Please put Kazzam out when he's dry. I left all the d-d-dogs in the b-barn."

The police officer gave her a sideways look. "You're shaking so hard the car is rocking. Are you okay?"

Evie nodded. She didn't trust her mouth to form words.

Very quickly, they arrived at the lane.

"H-h-here," said Evie. It was closed off with a rusty gate, held shut with a chain and lock. A horse could get around it easily, but not the cruiser or the ambulance.

The officer braked. She popped open the trunk, stepped out, strode to the rear of the car and fetched a pair of bolt cutters. She tossed a navy-blue blanket to Evie as she marched past, and after one deft snip, the chain dropped. She lifted the end of the gate and swung it open for the emergency vehicles to pass through.

Evie was impressed with the officer's matter-of-fact confidence. She did everything efficiently, without a wasted movement. Evie nestled into the navy blanket and watched the woman get back into the car and put it in gear with one fluid motion.

"How far?" the officer asked, driving along the rutted lane.

"All the w-w-way to the end."

They bumped and slid and sped along until the lane came to a dead end. The trails from this point were too narrow for a car, but an all-terrain vehicle could get through, Evie reflected, thinking of the tire tracks.

As soon as they'd stopped, the paramedics jumped out of their vehicle and swiftly removed a stretcher.

The police officer looked hard at Evie. "Will you be able to walk? I can see you're in shock."

"I'm not in sh-sh-shock!" Evie exclaimed, indignant. She opened the car door and promptly fell out into the wet snow.

Maybe I am, she reconsidered. *If this is what shock's like.*

With effort, she got her legs underneath her and pulled herself up. Her teeth were chattering and she could do nothing to stop it. She tried to walk, but her left knee collapsed. She fell again.

The officer grabbed the blanket from the seat and wrapped it around Evie's shoulders. She helped Evie up and sat her back down in the car. "Point in the general direction. We'll find her."

So embarrassing. Evie tried to think how to explain where they should go. It was hard, with so many trails going in all directions. She really had to pull herself together. They'd never find the body without her.

She struggled to get out of the car. Again, she fell out. This time, with her arms restricted by the blanket, she fell nose first into the slush.

Magpie showed up just then, muddy and breathing hard.

"Mags! H-h-how did you …?" The dog must have escaped from the barn and followed them along the road. *Smart dog!* Evie involuntarily made a snorting *hee-haw* noise and began to laugh. She couldn't stop. She thought she might start to cry.

Magpie shoved her long snout into Evie's face and nudged her, hard.

"Ouch!" Evie yelled. But it did the trick. She stopped laughing. She dragged herself up to the seat of the cruiser and pointed into the woods.

"Find the girl," she ordered Magpie. The dog looked in the direction Evie was pointing, looked back for confirmation, and began to run.

Evie looked into the officer's startled face and said, "Follow the d-d-dog."

The officer opened her mouth to speak, but changed her mind and took off after Magpie, accompanied by the paramedics.

Evie's body was still shaking. She pushed herself to her feet and tried out her legs. They felt rubbery, but this time they held her up. Step by careful step, she followed them into the woods, trying to keep her eye on Magpie as the dog darted in and out of the brush with her nose to the ground.

Within a few minutes, Evie caught up to them at a small clearing. Magpie was whining and staring at them, and the officer was intently searching for clues.

Evie stared at the ground. The same tire tracks as before. "Tracks! Good girl, Mags."

"Is this where you found the girl?" asked the officer.

"No. It's farther on." Evie pointed north.

"Then why is the dog whining?"

"Because she's on the girl's trail and she wants us to follow," answered Evie. It seemed obvious to her.

The officer knelt to study the ground. "Huh." She stood. "Keep away from these tracks. Describe the girl."

"She was wearing a black hoodie and black jeans, and she had dyed purple hair. She had one boot, and the other was missing. I put my quarter sheet over her."

"What's that?" asked the officer.

"It's sort of a small blanket for my horse. It's green."

The officer nodded as she inspected the ground. All Evie saw was melting snow, mud, slush, and tire tracks. She noticed that Magpie had disappeared into the woods.

Then, a little way off, Magpie began to howl in the same doleful way she had earlier, when she'd found the girl.

Evie ran.

"Wait!" commanded the officer.

"Follow me! Magpie found her!" Disregarding the officer's order, Evie tracked Magpie up the path to the north. The prints circled toward a small creek. Over a knoll on the far side, she saw a long black tail wagging. The expectant face of her dog popped up.

"Good girl!" panted Evie. She climbed the knoll and looked down. There lay the girl, exactly as Evie had left her.

The officer and paramedics were right behind.

"Step aside," ordered the officer sternly. Evie promptly did as she was told.

The paramedics rushed to the girl. Evie watched as they threw off the quarter sheet and pushed on her chest with quick, firm thumps. They breathed into her mouth. To Evie, the girl looked totally unresponsive.

The medics placed the girl on the stretcher and strapped her in. They signalled to each other, lifted the stretcher in one synchronized movement, then retraced their steps through the brush to the ambulance as quickly and smoothly as was humanly possible. It all took less than a minute. Evie stood in awe.

The ambulance siren started up. It sounded shockingly loud in the woods, but grew fainter as the vehicle raced away.

The officer and Evie walked back wordlessly. As they approached the cruiser, the officer stopped, faced Evie, and scowled slightly. "Kids play games. They don't realize how serious things are. If a real emergency happens while services are engaged in a prank, people die."

Evie nodded in agreement. "That makes sense."

"Do you know this girl? Think carefully before you answer."

"No, I don't." Evie became confused. "Why?"

"I warn you, I hope for your sake that this is not a prank."

A *prank*? It began to sink in. Did the officer think that she'd made all this up? With a friend playing dead, or something?

"That would be a really sick thing to do!" Evie exclaimed.

The officer marked the path with yellow police tape and then opened the passenger door of the cruiser for Evie. Sternly, she stood waiting.

Evie didn't get in.

"Do you want to walk home?"

"Not really. But I'd rather walk than ride if you think I'm the kind of kid who pranks the police." Evie's blood was boiling. "I did my civic duty here, and you accuse me of making this up?"

"Are you?"

"No! I don't know that poor girl. I found her, just like I told you. And I have a lot more important things to do with my time."

The officer frowned in thought. Then she nodded, as if she'd come to a decision. "I believe you. There's something I'll share with you. Get in." She slammed the car door after Evie sat down, then she walked around to the driver's side.

Evie reopened her door to let Magpie in. The dog wagged her muddy tail and sat on the floor at Evie's feet.

The officer smiled for the first time. "That's a good dog you have. We might not have found the girl without her."

Evie nodded and patted Magpie's wet head.

"My name is Officer Katrina Summers."

"Nice to meet you," said Evie automatically, then added, "I guess." The woman certainly hadn't been too friendly so far.

Officer Summers backed the cruiser down the lane past the rusted gate, got out, and tied yellow tape across the lane. Then she resumed her place behind the wheel. "So. Let me explain. We have reason to believe that something strange is going on, and it involves a group of young girls. I had to be sure you weren't one of them."

Evie was curious. "Okay?"

Officer Summers put the car in reverse, backed onto the road, and began to drive south. "Three weeks ago the body of a young girl was discovered in the bushes just west of the town of Newmarket. You might've heard it on the news. She was found in the same condition."

"Newmarket?" Evie was startled. "I heard an Amber Alert this morning about —"

"Yes. A girl named Stacey Linn is missing."

"And she's from Newmarket. Is this girl Stacey?"

"Don't jump to conclusions. Follow the clues and pay heed only to facts."

Evie considered this. "Tell me more about the dead girl. The one who was found three weeks ago."

"She was comatose at the scene and died in hospital. The OPP sent the particulars to every jurisdiction in the province. The exact circumstances of her death remain a mystery."

"How old was she?"

"Fourteen."

"So, the girl we just found who might or might not be Stacey Linn and the dead girl were both about fourteen."

Officer Summers glanced a warning at her. "You're doing it again."

"Sorry. You said the two girls were found in the same condition. What do you mean?"

"Face down in the snow, appearing lifeless."

"*Appearing* lifeless?"

"The other girl had a faint heartbeat, almost undetectable. This one did as well."

Evie wasn't sure she'd heard correctly. "She's alive?"

"Yes. At least for now."

"Will she make it?"

"Hard to say. The other girl didn't."

Evie looked out the window and saw that they were already turning up her lane. She noticed that Kazzam was not outside. Gran Mary and Jordie must not be back yet. "Who would do this?"

The officer grimaced. "We'll find out. We'll follow the clues. That's what we do."

Evie nodded. Her head was spinning. "Can you let me out at the barn?"

"Sure thing."

"I wish ..." Evie had to get something off her chest. "I ... I thought she was dead, so we didn't gallop home.

I didn't have my phone with me. I wish I'd gotten help for her sooner."

"You did your best."

"But still, if she dies, it might be because of that."

"We couldn't have gotten to her much sooner. Really. Thanks for your help, Evangeline."

The officer stopped the cruiser at the barn door. Evie opened the car door and Magpie jumped out. In a rush of concern Evie asked, "Can you let me know? If she lives, I mean? Or dies?"

Officer Summers handed her a business card. "Yes. That's the least we can do. I'm heading back to the woods now to meet the forensic team. Call me later."

Evie got out of the car. "I will."

"And call me if you think of anything helpful to this case, or if you learn anything. Gossip, anything odd around here."

Evie nodded and watched the cruiser drive down the lane. She stood for a minute, deep in thought. *That poor girl.* Someone had almost killed her, then driven her into the woods and dumped her. Who would do that? And why?

4

Missing Person

Happiness is not a station you arrive at, but a manner of travelling.

— Margaret Lee Burbank

Evie watched the police cruiser turn left at the road to return to the scene of the crime.

The upper half of the barn's Dutch door was wide open. It was clear that Magpie had somehow unlatched it and jumped out. Evie marvelled at how the dog had tracked them and found them in the woods.

She heard Kazzam's angry nicker, so she hastened into the barn. Simon and Garfunkel wagged their tails, happy to see her, while Kazzam glared impatiently at her over his stall door.

"In a rush to go outside, by any chance?" He tossed his head with his ears pinned. "You made your point. You don't scare me." She removed his cooler and checked that he was dry before she put on his halter and snapped on the lead shank. They walked out of the barn into the sunlight, closely followed by Magpie and the two Labs.

As soon as Evie let Kazzam loose in the field, he punched his hind legs up to the sky and bucked three times before trotting over to the round bale to greet the other horses. He then promptly dropped to the ground and had a good roll.

"That's my boy," said Evie softly.

She inhaled deeply and made a fervent wish that the girl she'd found in the woods would live. The memory of the unconcious girl in the snow appeared vividly in her head. Her throat constricted and her tears filled her eyes.

She walked into the field. For the millionth time, her heart swelled with gratitude to be living with these majestic and graceful creatures. Even in the darkest times — and finding a body in the woods certainly counted as dark — being with horses filled her soul.

The day had warmed up, so she removed the blankets from Christieloo, Bendigo, and Paragon. As she did, each one lay down and rolled, giving its back an intense scratch. Winter hair from each horse — black, brown, chestnut, and palomino — made patches on the melting snow.

With a last glance, Evie strode up to the house and deposited her coat and boots in the mudroom.

As she was plugging in the kettle for a cup of tea, Jordie burst into the house, quivering with energy. Gran Mary followed much more slowly. She dropped into a kitchen chair. "The new mall. What an adventure."

"We went shopping!" enthused Jordie, "and got the coolest things ever!" His face glowed as he opened a bag to show Evie.

Evie gave him a hug. "You'll look so cool."

Gran Mary looked exhausted. Evie remembered how little her grandmother had slept the night before, and how sick she still was. "Can I make you a coffee?" Evie asked.

"Wonderful. You're a dear. Thank you."

"And we saw an ambulance," Jordie yelled, unaware of his volume. "And police cars and everything! On this road!"

"You must have heard them," said Mary. "They went right past. I wonder what's going on."

"You didn't get my message?" asked Evie, surprised.

Mary looked at her with confusion. "What message?"

"I left a message on your phone."

"I didn't hear it ring." Mary reached into her purse and turned on her phone. Without waiting for Evie to explain, she played the message.

"*Gran Mary, it's Evie. I found a body in the woods and I'm taking the police there now. Please put Kazzam out when he's dry. I left all the d-d-dogs in the b-barn.*"

"Why are you stuttering?" asked Jordie. "You don't stutter. My friend Albert at school does. He takes lessons to fix it."

Mary stared at Evie. "You found a body?"

"Yes. Well, I thought so, but it turned out she wasn't dead. They rushed her to the hospital."

"Oh, my." Mary looked stunned. "This all happened while we were gone?" Evie nodded. "Well, I'll be. Where did you find her?"

"In the clearing on the other side of the McCreaths'."

"How old is she?"

"I guess around fourteen?"

"My dear. I'm so sorry. Such a shock. Are you okay?"

"I'm fine now. But I *was* in shock. My knees gave out."

"Goodness. No wonder you were stuttering." Mary got up from her chair. "You sit right down, Evie. I can make my own coffee, and I'm going to make you a nice cup of tea. Now, while I do that, tell us everything. Start at the beginning."

Evie felt her throat tightening again, and tears began to fall down her cheeks.

"My dear," Mary said. She put her arms around Evie and held her tightly. "I can't imagine. It must've been awful."

"It was. But I'm fine," said Evie hoarsely. "Really." She hugged her grandmother, grateful for her comfort.

Mary chuckled. "I can see that."

Evie blinked back her tears. "Can't fool you, can I?" She wiped her cheeks. "I feel kind of stupid. I keep crying."

Mary looked her in the eye. "I'm very proud of you, Evie. You're a strong and good person. And strong, good people cry. Only a heartless person wouldn't be affected by something like this, and you have a big, loving heart."

"Thanks, Gran Mary." And she meant it. Mary's compassion helped remove the hollow feeling Evie had been carrying ever since finding the girl in the woods.

Jordie was checking the cupboards for something to eat. "Hey, there's a blinking light over here. What is it?"

"It's called an answering machine, and it's old-fashioned, like me," said Mary. "Just press the button that's blinking."

"*You have four new messages,*" the machine declared. "*Message one.*"

Paulina's voice came on, sounding groggy. "Hello. Ah, just got this. Sure, Jordie can visit. Sure. Ah, it's March break, isn't it? Um, Kerry and I are going to Wellington to look at horses. I'll call when we get back? Next week sometime?"

"*End of message.*"

Just like always, Evie thought, *Paulina thinks of herself and nobody else.* She hadn't made any plans for Jordie while they were away for an entire week.

"*Message two.*"

"Brent Keir here. I left Jordie at your driveway. Saw Evie and the truck and didn't come up. I'll swing by around three to drive him home. It's 519-873-0897. Thanks."

"*End of message.*"

"But I don't want to go back!" cried Jordie in a panic.

"No, no," said Evie, "you're staying here. We'll call him."

"*Message three.*"

"Hi, you guys. It's Yoyo. Got a new job! I'll tell you all about it when I can. Mystery location!"

"*End of message.*"

Yolanda had been looking for permanent work since Maple Mills closed down. "Mystery location? That's intriguing," said Evie.

"Good for her," added Mary.

"*Message four.*"

"Hi, Mary. Paulina again. Can Beatrice stay with you, too? That would solve another problem. Thanks so much! I'll have someone drive her over later today. Toodle-oo!"

"*End of messages.*"

Evie sighed. Paulina hadn't thought about either of her kids during March break. She sounded a whole lot perkier in the second message. Either she'd had a coffee or two, or she was just nicer when she was asking for a favour.

"No-o!" cried Jordie. "I don't want Beebee here! She'll wreck everything!"

"Come here, Jordie," said Mary softly.

The boy reluctantly came around the counter and stood beside her chair. "What."

"Let's have some lunch. We're all hungry. And let's hear all about what happened to Evie while you and I were shopping our hearts out."

Jordie slowly began to smile. He wiped his nose and wet cheeks on his sleeve. Through trembling lips he said, "Okay. I'm glad I'm here with you and Evie, Cran Berry."

He threw his arms around Mary's neck and squeezed. Mary hugged him back and didn't let go until he released his clutch.

By the time they finished lunch it was a little after two, and Evie had told them all the details about finding the girl. As Mary had predicted, they all felt better with food in their stomachs.

"Can I show you my new clothes now, Evie?" asked Jordie.

"I'd love to see them."

"Spread them out on the table," directed Mary. She sneezed and lay down on the couch. "And let Evie see how good you're going to look."

Evie watched the little boy eagerly empty out the bag. "Are these March break clothes or school clothes?" she asked.

"These are Jordie Gibb clothes! I'll wear them forever!"

"Three shirts, cool pants, a nice sweater, and underwear and socks. Nice. I like the colours you've chosen."

"Only one colour. Everything is blue, my favourite."

Evie pointed from one piece of clothing to the next. "But all different shades of blue. See? And they look great together."

"Blue is blue, Evie."

"Except when it's blue-green or blue-red or blue-grey or dark blue or light blue."

"It's still blue!"

"Okay, kids, enough chatter. My head hurts." Mary lifted her head wearily. "Jordie, take your blue clothes upstairs and put them away. The same room you had last time." She put her feet on the floor and sat up. "Evie, I'm going up to bed. Can you bring in the horses and feed them at four?"

"Sure. I hope you feel better."

"Thanks, dear." Mary slowly climbed the stairs and disappeared into her room.

"She sure is old," said Jordie.

"She's got a cold, that's all."

"Is she going to die?" Jordie looked worried.

"No, Jordie. She's sick but she'll get better."

"Good. Can I help with the horses later?"

Evie chortled at how quickly his mind jumped from one thing to another. "What's so funny?"

"I'm just happy you're here." And she was. She wanted her brother to stay at Parson's Bridge, at least until they knew what was going on at home. Just how bad was it?

"Why is your face all wrinkled up?"

"I'm thinking. I guess my face does things I don't know about."

Jordie made a circling motion around his ear. "Cuckoo!" He swept up his purchases and ran up the stairs. "I'll put all my new blue clothes away!" he called.

"Shh! Gran Mary is trying to rest!"

There was a knock at the kitchen door. Evie spun around to see the face of Brent Keir at the window.

She opened the door. "Brent! I got your message and meant to call, but I forgot. Sorry."

"I got finished a lot sooner than I thought. Is Jordie ready?"

"There's been a change of plans. Jordie's going to stay here for a while." Evie paused. "But I'd love to hear about the new people at Maple Mills. Do you have time?"

"Sure. I'm running early. Is there any coffee made?"

"No, but it's easy. Sit down. How about some lunch?"

"Don't worry about it. I'll get something on the road."

"Ham and cheese sandwich? PB and J?"

"If you insist, ham and cheese, thanks. Better wash my hands first. They're pretty grimy."

Evie directed him to the bathroom off the hall, then prepared the sandwich and some coffee. Brent sat down just as she placed them on the table. "Milk and sugar?"

"Double. Thanks, Evie."

"So, how many horses are there at Maple Mills?" Brent's mouth was full, so he showed her with his fingers. "Eight? There are twenty-four stalls."

"More are coming," he answered after swallowing. "And you know who'll be starting work there later this week?" Evie shook her head. "Here's a clue. She's cute and blond."

"I don't know who you consider cute, Brent. Tell me."

"Yolanda Schmits."

"Yoyo! That's great." Evie grinned. "So, that's the 'mystery location' she mentioned. She left a message."

"All the grooms are sworn to secrecy."

"Seriously?"

Brent rolled his eyes. "Strange but true."

51

"Weird. Will they still call it Maple Mills Stables?"

"No. They shortened it to M.M.S., same as the initials of the new owner. Doctor Manfred Maris-Stapleton."

"How much of a coincidence is that? Those letters are on the gates and over the barn doors."

Brent smiled. "Saves on replacing them. Maybe that's why he bought the place." He snorted at the possibility.

Evie sat down across the table from him. "The name is familiar. Is he famous for something?"

"Yeah. He's a heart surgeon, and he invented something — I forget what. It was in the news. He's a big deal."

Evie shook her head. "Not ringing a bell."

"Every spring he has a big fundraiser in Newmarket for the Heart and Stroke Foundation. A steeplechase, tents, everything. Like a fall fair. Maybe they'll do it in Caledon. I went one year and it was fun."

"That's it. That's where I've heard of him." The fundraiser sounded interesting to Evie. "I hope he does it here, too. Why does he have horses? Does he ride?"

"His daughter does," said Brent. "She's looking for another one in Florida, at the big horse show in Wellington." He kept eating. "A fancy one, too."

"How many does she have?"

"A few." He chewed thoughtfully. "She has a problem keeping her horses sound."

"Why?" Evie sensed that Brent wasn't telling her everything.

"Nothing. She's had bad luck."

"Brent, my imagination is worse than the truth."

He laughed. "I've been their farrier for a long time, and I've never seen anybody go through more horses than Cynthia. There's always something. It's bad luck."

Evie nodded but still wasn't satisfied. "Who's her coach?"

"I thought you knew. Kerry Goodham."

Evie's eyes widened. "Kerry and Paulina are on their way to Wellington right now to check out a horse. Is it for her?"

Brent nodded. "Yeah. Only the best for little Cynthia." He raised his eyebrows. "Oh, she's a handful. Glad I had sons."

"You think girls are harder to raise?"

"This one is."

Before Evie could ask what Brent was talking about, Jordie came down the stairs and saw him. His brow furrowed with suspicion. He whispered to Evie, "Did you tell him?"

"Yeah."

"Hey, buddy, what's up?" asked Brent.

"My mother wants me to stay here."

"Sure, no problem." Brent ate the last bite of sandwich and drank down his coffee. He stood up to go. "Thanks, Evie. That was exactly what I needed."

"Sorry I didn't call you. Could've saved you a trip."

"And miss lunch?" He smiled and tousled Jordie's hair. "See you around, big fella."

Jordie looked uncertain. "You won't actually see me around in Newmarket. But thanks. I mean, for bringing me here."

Brent winked at the boy and put on his coat. "Right you are."

Evie walked him outside and shut the door behind them to be sure that Jordie couldn't hear. "Is everything okay with Beebee?"

"Why?"

"You're a neighbour. You see them around. Jordie thinks Beebee's getting into trouble, but Paulina doesn't notice."

Brent shrugged. "Paulina doesn't notice much. Never has." He opened the door to his truck and climbed in. "Beebee's a good kid. She'll be okay once she gets away from that crowd."

"What crowd?"

"Spoiled teenage brats. You know the type."

Evie shrugged. "I guess."

"Cynthia's one of them. She's a troublemaker. Good thing she moved away."

"Beebee and Cynthia are friends?" asked Evie.

"Kerry coaches them both."

Makes sense, Evie thought. She said, "Small world."

Brent shut the truck door and nodded. Evie turned back to the house. Brent didn't seem worried. Maybe she shouldn't be worried, either.

Just as she re-entered the kitchen, the phone rang. Evie pounced on it so it wouldn't wake Gran Mary. "Hello?" she said.

"Who's that?" asked a female voice.

"It's Evie. Who's this?"

"Paulina. We've boarded. The plane is taking off. You'll have to deal with Beatrice."

"Yeah, okay, but … where is she?"

"How should I know? She's not answering her phone."

"What do you want me to do?"

"She'll have to stay with you. Nobody's home at our house."

"Where's Sella?"

"The kids are too old for a nanny."

"But, does Beebee have a key?"

"I wouldn't trust her with a key! The house'd be full of her horrible friends. Hey, the stupid stewardess is grabbing my —"

"Paulina? Wait!" No response. The phone was dead.

Jordie shook her arm. "What's wrong? Your face is all funny again!"

Evie plopped down in a kitchen chair. "Beebee's supposed to stay here, but she doesn't know that, and your mother doesn't know where she is."

"So? She never knows where Beebee is."

"But she and Kerry are on a plane to Florida, and Beebee doesn't have a key to your house."

Jordie shrugged. "Then she'll sleep wherever she usually sleeps. She hasn't been home in a week."

There really is a problem, Evie realized. "Do you know any of her friends? Or how to reach them?"

Jordie shook his head. "No. I've only ever seen them from my window and they all look the same."

"And how's that?"

"Black hoodies, white faces, black lips, black eyes."

Just like the girl in the woods. Evie felt shivers travel up her spine and down her arms. There were too many similarities to ignore. The Newmarket connection, the group of bad friends, and now Beebee was missing. Was this the kind of gossip that Officer Summers had been talking about?

Evie went to the phone. She pulled the OPP card out of her pocket and punched in the numbers. It rang a few times, then went to voice mail.

She left a message. "Hello, it's Evangeline Gibb. I just learned that my fourteen-year-old stepsister is missing. She lives in Newmarket. It might be related, so call me back. Please."

She put the receiver in the holder and stood in thought.

"What's wrong?" asked Jordie. "Tell me!"

"I called a police officer to help us find Beebee, that's all." Evie reassured her brother with a hug. "She'll call me back."

"Okay, but ..." Jordie didn't look satisfied.

"But what?"

"You won't be able to find her if she doesn't want to be found."

"We have to try, Jordie." Evie had an idea. "Hey! The police officer I called is right up the road with the forensic team. I'll go talk to her now."

"I want to come!"

"Good idea. I'm taking Kazzam. You ride Christieloo."

Jordie looked skeptical. "Can't you drive?"

"Not yet. It's on my list."

"Then can I stay here and watch a movie?"

"I guess, but don't wake up Gran Mary. You choose."

"Yay! I want to watch the one about training a dragon!"

Evie set up the old DVD player and tucked Jordie in with a blanket on the couch. "I'll have my phone, so call me," she said. "And tell Gran Mary where I am."

"Okay. I love this movie! I know most of the words."

Evie put on her new riding coat and made sure she had her phone. She left the house with Magpie at her side.

To save time, Evie brought the saddle and bridle out to the field and quickly tacked up Kazzam. The horse gave her an inquiring look.

"I know, I know. You've been ridden already today. I'll have you back before you know it."

Kazzam sighed and took a long last look at the round bale.

Evie led him outside the paddock gate and hopped up onto his back. They trotted briskly up the road to the lane with Magpie following behind.

The lane was roped off with yellow police tape, but there was another way in through the bushes. Evie was certain that Officer Summers would understand once she heard that Beebee was missing. Kazzam stepped out easily as they travelled into the woods.

A cruiser was parked at the end of the lane beside the narrow trail, and a large policeman stepped out of it. He stretched out his right hand, his palm facing Evie. "Stop right there!"

"Hello, sir. I'm Evangeline Gibb." She smiled pleasantly. "I'm the one who found the girl. I need to speak to Officer Summers."

"No one is allowed to be here except authorized personnel."

"Yes, but —"

"Are you aware that you crossed police tape? That's an offence."

"I have new information to share with Officer Summers."

The way the man's mouth disappeared into his chin made Evie wonder if the act of thinking was difficult for him. She simplified her message. "Is Officer Katrina Summers here?"

"No. She left. Forensics is almost finished, too."

"Oh. I called and left a message."

"If she feels it's important, she'll call you back. Now, get away from the scene. We don't need more horse tracks messing things up." He glared at Magpie. "Or dog prints."

Evie turned Kazzam around, disappointed. She'd have to go home and wait for the officer's call. But her stepsister was missing, and time was of the essence. She had a bad feeling that she couldn't shake.

Beebee could be anywhere. She might be with friends in Newmarket, but she could also be in trouble. What if she came to Caledon? This Cynthia person had moved here, and Stacey Linn had hitchhiked here.

Evie knew she was jumping to conclusions, which Officer Summers had warned against. *Follow the facts*, she told herself.

They were halfway down the lane to the road when she remembered the tire tracks. The girl in the woods had been transported from somewhere on an all-terrain vehicle. Where was that somewhere? If Beebee was involved, those tire tracks might lead right to her. *Follow the trail!*

"Simple. We'll follow them backwards to where they begin," she murmured. "Mags! Come, girl."

Making sure that they were out of the police officer's line of sight, Evie ducked Kazzam off the path and onto a small trail that fishtailed back to just behind the roped-off crime scene. The bare branches made it difficult to keep out of sight.

The forensics team was packing up. Horse, dog, and girl quietly watched them trudge back to their vehicle, loaded with metal cases.

As soon as all the vehicles were gone, Evie searched the ground for the ATV tire tracks. She thought she knew where she'd seen them earlier, but the snow had continued to melt and now she couldn't find them in the scrubby bushes and choppy terrain. Not as simple as she'd thought.

"Tracks," she said to Magpie. "Tire tracks?"

The dog whined and tilted her head. She stared intently into Evie's eyes and whined again uncertainly.

"Tracks," Evie repeated. "Good girl!"

Her eyes brightened when she recognized the praise. Her tail began to thump on the melting snow, and she started to work. Within seconds, she had found them.

"Good girl!" exclaimed Evie again. "You're so smart!"

Now, she could make out where the tracks led into the woods to where the girl was dumped. With luck, Beebee would be at the opposite end.

Kazzam and Evie stayed behind Magpie as the dog led them through the bushes and over the hillocks. Evie was able to see the tracks in the receding snow and mud, but they disappeared in the coarse, long grass. Without Magpie's nose, Evie knew they'd have been lost, for sure.

The path ended at a gravel road. Magpie didn't falter. Nose down, she crossed the road and entered a wooded path that Evie didn't recognize. They continued on between fields of grazing cows and farrow fields waiting for spring planting.

I must remember how to find this path, Evie thought. It was quite a nice place to ride. She noted how Kazzam trotted with confidence, as if he knew where they were going.

Then, it occurred to Evie. *He does know!* They were heading back toward Maple Mills Stables, where Kazzam had lived most of his life.

5

Nuisance

They may forget what you said, but they will never forget how you made them feel.

— Carl W. Buehner

When Evie, Kazzam, and Magpie arrived at the next concession road, it was a little after three-thirty. It would take just over thirty minutes to get back to Parson's Bridge. *We should head home now to bring in the horses*, Evie thought. But, if she reckoned correctly, this was the last concession before the highway.

Evie made herself a deal. If they didn't get to the end of the tracks before they reached the highway, she'd turn around and start out again the next morning. She didn't want to risk crossing six lanes of speeding traffic on her horse, especially not with her dog.

Decision made, she said aloud, "The horses won't die if we're a little late." They had water and a round bale of hay to eat, and the weather was perfect.

Her phone rang. She fumbled in her pocket and answered just before it went to voice mail. "Hello?"

"Officer Katrina Summers here." The officer sounded rushed. "You called. Something about your sister?"

"Yes! Thanks for calling me back." Evie spoke as she and Kazzam followed Magpie along the winding trails toward the highway. "My stepsister is missing. She's fourteen, and she lives in Newmarket."

"How long has she been gone?"

"Hard to say. She doesn't always keep in touch."

"Has it been reported yet?"

"No. I only found out about an hour ago. My stepmother doesn't know where she is. They left for Florida and we're supposed to babysit her."

"Does she go missing often?"

Evie took a deep breath. "Okay, yes, but here's the thing. The people who just bought my old farm come from Newmarket. I'm told their daughter dresses the same way as the girl in the woods and that she's a troublemaker. She's my stepsister's friend, and Beebee dresses like that, too."

"You're jumping to conclusions. A lot of girls dress in black. Not just in Newmarket." Officer Summers sounded cold and crisp, like when they'd first met.

"Well, yeah," Evie said. The police officer wasn't getting her point. "But she's missing, like the other girls, and she lives in Newmarket, and now her friend lives in Caledon."

Evie heard the police officer exhale. "That may be," said Officer Summers. "But people do move from Newmarket to Caledon. And vice versa." Now she sounded bored.

Wasn't it a coincidence worth noting? Evie felt frustrated. "But what about my stepsister? How can I not worry?"

"I understand. But here's another thing. You rode through police tape. It's an ongoing investigation."

So that's why she's so grumpy with me, thought Evie. That police officer must have told on her. "I'm sorry."

"Evangeline? I'm going to send a message to the OPP in Newmarket about your stepsister. What's her name?"

"Thanks! Her name is Beatrice Gibb. We call her Beebee."

"There are more reports of missing girls than usual in Newmarket, so no promises, but I'll send it out."

"Thank you very, very much. I'm really worried, and I don't know what to do."

"I do. Stay away from the crime scene. You must let the police do their job. I warn you, anything you do will be seen as interference. You'll be in big trouble, and worse, it might hamper the investigation. Do you hear me?"

"I hear you. I'm sorry."

"Good afternoon, Evangeline." With that, the call concluded.

Evie's spirits rose. Officer Summers was going to help find Beebee. This was a huge relief. And she was glad she hadn't mentioned that she was following the ATV's tire tracks. For sure, it wouldn't have gone down well.

Now, she could hear the unmistakable roar of a busy highway, steady and loud, as cars and trucks and transports sped along at a good clip.

The noise got more intense as they emerged from the woods. There, down the slope in front of them, was one of Canada's busiest thoroughfares. Definitely not a good idea to cross it, even if the horses at home weren't waiting to be fed.

"Magpie!" she called. The dog stopped and looked up. "Come. We're going home."

Magpie crouched and tilted her head.

"I'm serious. Come!"

Evie turned Kazzam and headed back toward Parson's Bridge. Reluctantly, Magpie followed. Her ears flopped and her tail drooped, dejected about being called off the trail.

"You're a good girl, Mags!" Evie told her cheerfully. Magpie glanced up at her with hurt eyes. "You'll get over it when we come back tomorrow, girl."

Evie's mind turned to the case. This was what she knew:

One. A fourteen-year-old girl was fighting for her life in the hospital after being dumped in the woods.

Two. The tire tracks led westward, toward Maple Mills.

Three. Maple Mills had been bought by the family of Beebee's friend, whom Brent considered to be a troublemaker.

Four. That friend had moved to Caledon from Newmarket, Beebee's hometown and where the first body had been found.

Five. There was an Amber Alert out for a Newmarket teen named Stacey Linn, last seen hitchhiking toward Caledon.

Six. Beebee was missing, and according to Jordie, she looked and dressed just like the girl in the woods, and she had bad friends, including the one now living at Maple Mills.

Why does this all look so suspicious to me but not to the police? wondered Evie. *Am I missing something?*

Officer Summers had said that coming from Newmarket was hardly a clue, and that lots of teenagers dressed like the girl in the woods. Evie knew that lots of kids were troublemakers. And the tire tracks could end up anywhere. There were lots of places on the west side of the highway besides Maple Mills.

Officer Summers might be right. Evie should let the police do their job. Beginning to feel stupid, she slumped in the saddle. She did always jump to conclusions, and she should learn to look at the facts and follow the clues.

But, still, where was Beebee? Should they just sit back and wait for the police to find her? Paulina certainly didn't seem to care. A wave of irritation went through Evie. *What kind of mother leaves for a week and doesn't know where her kids are?*

Then Evie caught herself. Her own mother had never known where she was or what she was doing — not just for a week, but for Evie's entire life. Since Evie was a small child, Angela had been living on the streets of Toronto, addicted to opioids. She hadn't cared how Evie was doing — or if she had, she hadn't done anything about it. Besides finding another hit to make herself feel better. Evie's irritation turned to bitterness.

And now, just when everything seemed to be going well with her rehab, Angela had tried to escape. Why? Were the opioids calling again? Like they had every other time before? Evie would find out when she and Gran Mary went to see Angela.

Evie's shoulders sagged. She dreaded that visit. She intended to keep that to herself, though, because it might hurt Gran Mary's feelings to know how Evie felt. She wouldn't hurt Gran Mary for the world.

Evie wondered if Gran Mary was still sleeping. Jordie's dragon movie would be over by now. She pulled out her phone and called home.

A small voice answered. "Hello?"

"Hi, Jordie. It's Evie. I'll be home soon."

"Okay. *How to Train Your Dragon* was *great*! Gran Mary had a big sleep and she feels a whole lot better. She's making me a snack right now so she can't talk."

"Tell her I won't be long, okay? And I'll feed the horses."

"Okay."

Comforted that all was well at home, Evie asked Kazzam to pick up a trot. The horse covered the ground between concessions easily. Evie smiled, feeling very lucky that she owned him.

Nobody had wanted Kazzam before he'd won the Queen's Plate. Evie was the only person who'd ever trusted him. In fairness, the small black gelding hadn't exactly been trustworthy, with his unfortunate habit of bucking jockeys off. She patted his neck as they trotted along the trails and promised him that he'd always have a home with her. She just needed to find his next career.

Soon they were back at the taped-off crime scene, and Evie wondered where her green quarter sheet might be. If it was just lying on the ground, why let it rot? She'd take a quick look.

Something caught her eye as they walked alongside the yellow police tape. A shiny object glinted in the snow under a bush. "Whoa, boy."

Evie backed Kazzam up, but she couldn't see the object. She slid down from her saddle and searched the area where she thought she'd seen it. Had it just been a flash of sun on the snow?

But no, there it was. She reached under the branches of a bush and retrieved a sharp piece of broken mirror. The unbroken edge was curved, indicating that the mirror had been round, about four inches in diameter.

She tucked it away in her coat pocket so no animal would step on it and get hurt.

Evie led Kazzam a bit farther to look for her quarter sheet, but the green blanket was gone. *Oh well*, she thought. *Worth a try.*

She put her left foot in the stirrup and got back up. Kazzam spun around to face the other way and went rigid. At the same moment, Magpie's ears pricked forward and her ruff went up.

"What is it, girl?" Evie whispered. Magpie's tail wagged briefly in response, but she growled softly and continued to point in the direction of the lane leading back to the road.

Seconds passed before Evie heard what Magpie and Kazzam had heard. It sounded like a car, and it was coming up the lane at a good speed.

Was it that sour-faced police officer? Or maybe Officer Summers, who'd told her not to return in no uncertain terms. How would she explain why she was here? Evie didn't want to try. She'd go home a different way, and there was no time to lose. She turned Kazzam and trotted briskly through the woods until she found the trail leading to the fields behind Parson's Bridge.

By the time Kazzam and Evie rode up to the barn it was 4:35 p.m. Not terribly late, but the three horses were milling around in the paddock, impatient to get their grain. *Horses are such creatures of habit*, thought Evie with a smile. *You'd almost think they wore watches.*

She quickly removed Kazzam's tack, rubbed him down, and led Christieloo, Bendigo, and Paragon into their stalls. She measured out their grain and supplements, checked their water buckets, and swept the barn floor. Soon, all the horses were bedded down for the night. She left the top of the Dutch door open to let in the fresh air, then she and Magpie headed up to the farmhouse.

When Evie entered the kitchen, a heart-warming sight greeted her: Gran Mary was on the couch with her arm around Jordie. She looked much better, just as Jordie had reported, and she was reading to him from a manuscript. Evie saw that it was a printout of her latest mystery, *The Boy on the Beach*.

> But her screams were drowned by the roar of the waves pounding on the sand. Thunder rumbled in the black skies, which were suddenly lit by a quick fork of lightning that evoked a gigantic serpent. The heavens opened. Cold, hard rain teemed down in sheets. Priscilla, alone and frightened and lost, had run out of options.

Mary looked up when she noticed Evie.

"Keep reading!" demanded Jordie. "You're very good at mysteries!"

"Agreed! Keep reading!" echoed Evie.

Mary put up her hand to silence them. "I'll mark my place, but first things first. Jordie told me that Paulina called. Tell me what's going on."

Jordie objected. "First tell me what happens to Priscilla after she escapes from Ed's car and runs away."

Mary smiled at the boy. "Be patient, sweetheart. Can I talk to Evie, please? Real life takes precedence. Fiction gets better with a little suspense."

Jordie folded his arms and pursed his lips. "Fine."

"Paulina was on a plane with Kerry, probably, because she said *we*," said Evie. "They were taking off and she didn't have time to say much, because the flight attendant turned off her phone, but she told me she couldn't reach Beebee. So Beebee doesn't know she's supposed to come here, and she doesn't have a key to their house."

"Oh, my," said Mary, her brow wrinkling. "So Beebee doesn't even know they're gone."

"She doesn't care," said Jordie. "Mom *never* knows where Beebee is or where she sleeps. What's the difference?"

"The difference is that we've been asked to look after her while they're away," Mary answered. "So we're responsible now."

"How do we look after her if we can't find her?" Jordie asked.

Mary nodded. "Very reasonable question, but we have to try. Let's start by calling all her friends."

"Jordie doesn't know her friends," Evie replied. "I already asked him. But Officer Summers said she'd report Beebee missing to the Newmarket police. What else can we do?"

"We can keep trying her phone. I don't know what else."

Evie sat down in the armchair beside the couch. "When she can't reach anybody at home, I hope she calls us."

Mary nodded. "I hope so, too."

"She won't, though!" said Jordie impatiently. "You don't believe me. Beebee doesn't want to be found!"

Mary said, "I don't like to think of her somewhere alone."

"Like Priscilla?" prompted Jordie. "On the beach in the rain? Lost and desperate?"

Mary chuckled. "Okay, Jordie. I'll read if Evie can make some dinner."

"Yes!" Evie jumped up. "I'll make a cold chicken salad while I listen in. Read loudly."

"But if the phone rings, we have to stop," Mary warned Jordie. "It might be the police."

Jordie nodded wildly. "Yes, yes, yes. Just keep reading!"

"So nice to have an appreciative audience," said Gran Mary, smiling. She nestled back, opened her manuscript, and continued to read.

"'Priscilla, alone and frightened and lost, had run out of options.'"

"You read that part already."

"I know. I'm trying to get us back in the story."

"Okay, okay. Keep going."

Mary chuckled.

She stumbled and lost her footing. The sand was rough and it tore a hole in her thin, wet party dress as she crumpled to her knees. She curled herself in a ball in an effort to stay warm, knowing that night was about to descend.

The wedding had been beautiful and the dancing a lot of fun, but now what? She was in a foreign place with no idea how to get back to her hotel. If only she hadn't accepted a ride back to the resort from that charming man, Ed.

The wind was relentless —

The phone rang. Evie picked it up immediately. "Hello?"

"Evangeline. Officer Summers."

"Oh, hello!" She turned to Mary and Jordie and mouthed *police*. "Is there any news?"

"I asked you to stay away from the scene."

Evie gulped. She went out to the hall to speak in private. "I didn't cross the police tape."

"I'm here right now. You can't deny you were here, and not very long ago. I'm looking at fresh tracks."

Busted, Evie thought. The car they'd heard must have been Officer Summers's. "Yes, but we didn't get close at all. Take a look! We stayed back from the tape."

"Why were you here at all?"

Truth time. "I wanted to find my quarter sheet."

She heard the officer breathe heavily. "We have the blanket and we will give it back to you when we're finished with it. I came back to follow the tire tracks to their origin to discover that you and your horse and dog have messed up the trail with prints."

"Oh." Evie couldn't deny it. "I'm sorry. Let me explain. I went there to tell you my stepsister was missing, and when you weren't there, I decided to see where the ATV tracks came from in case they led me to Beebee."

"Evangeline. The ATV is a key piece of evidence, and we need to find it. Do you understand? Your interference has made it more difficult to find it, not less. You're becoming a nuisance."

A *nuisance*? That was the last thing she wanted to be! "I only want to help! Is there anything I can do?"

"Yes."

Evie felt a rush of excitement. "What? I'll do anything!"

"Stay. Away."

All the adrenalin drained out of her. "Yes. Yes, I will."

"You said that before, yet still you came back, and by messing up the tracks, you've hindered the investigation."

"I'm sorry. Please understand, I found that girl, and Beebee is the same age, so it's extra emotional for me. I won't interfere again, but I still want to help and I want to find my stepsister and I want to know if the girl will be all right."

"I hear you, Evangeline. I'll call if we need your help. For now, there's nothing for you to do except stay out of the area."

"I get it." Evie was surprised to realize that her face was damp with tears. "Is there any news about the girl?"

"Nothing new. She's responding to medication but still in a coma."

"Have they figured out who she is?"

"She's Stacey Linn."

Evie gulped. "The Amber Alert from Newmarket."

"Yes."

"Thank you. And I'm sorry. Again. I'll stay away."

"Good evening, Evangeline."

Evie hung up.

"Are you okay, dear?" asked Mary. Evie nodded, despondent. "Tell me everything, Evie. Maybe we can figure this out together."

"But how? I'm just in the way. I didn't mean to be a nuisance, but that's exactly how they see me."

"Let me try. I'm very good at mysteries."

Evie smiled just a little. "Yes, you are."

"Sit down here." Mary nudged Jordie with her elbow. "Right between Jordie and me. Start at the beginning."

Evie told Gran Mary everything, including how she'd gone back to the scene of the crime and gotten into trouble with Officer Summers.

Jordie stopped sulking and began to take an interest. "This is a real mystery story," he said. "But I still need to know what happens to Priscilla."

Mary laughed. "We'll read more later."

She brought out some paper and took notes. Together, she and Evie drew a map of the trails and listed all the clues, big and small. They were engrossed in theories when Evie got a text.

She looked at her phone. "It's Mark. He's calling the farmhouse in a minute. Should I take it?"

Mary looked puzzled. "Why wouldn't you?"

"Because we're busy with this."

"It can wait while you talk to Mark. Jordie and I can finish making dinner."

"I forgot all about dinner," said Evie.

"I didn't!" Jordie declared. "I'm starving."

The phone rang. Evie grabbed it and went into the mudroom to talk. "Hey, Mark!" she said brightly.

She was answered by a high-pitched giggle. It definitely wasn't Mark.

"Hello?" said Evie. "Who's this?" The person whispered, but Evie couldn't make it out. "Speak louder. Who is this?"

There was more giggling. "Have it your way," said Evie. "I'm hanging up."

A female voice said, "Hey, Mary Parson. You're the first contact to answer." She giggled again.

Evie was confused. "Whose contacts are you calling?"

"Beebee's."

"You have her phone?"

"Yeah."

"Why?"

"She gave it to me." The voice was cheeky and bold.

"Where is she?"

"Here."

"Where's here?"

"Wouldn't you like to know?" The girl began to giggle again, and in the background Evie could hear others joining in. She listened for Beebee, her surprise giving way to hope.

"Put her on the line," she said as calmly as possible.

"She doesn't want to talk to you. Right, Beebee?" There was sudden hilarity in the background. Evie thought there must be at least four girls, but she couldn't hear her stepsister's voice.

"Then why'd you call?"

"To see who'd answer." The girl's singsong tone was mocking.

Evie decided to test her hunch that the Newmarket teens were gathering in Caledon. "How many of you are there at Maple Mills?"

There was silence on the other end.

"Hello?"

The call disconnected, and the phone went dead.

Evie entered Beebee's number. It rang once and then went to dial tone. She walked out of the mudroom in a daze.

Mary looked up from the sink. "Evie? Who called?"

"A girl just called. She has Beebee's phone. I think she's at Maple Mills."

Mary put down the peeling knife and dried her hands on a dishtowel. "Why do you think that?"

"When I asked how many of them were there at Maple Mills, she hung up."

"It's not exactly proof. Call her back."

Evie nodded. She pressed the Recall button and

waited. It rang, then disconnected. She tried again with the same result.

As soon as she hung up, the phone rang, startling her. She answered quickly. "Yes?"

"Hey, it's Mark! Six o'clock on the dot." He sounded jovial.

"I can't talk right now, Mark. Beebee's missing."

Mark's tone immediately became serious. "Wow. You go do what you gotta do."

"Sorry."

"No worries. Anything I can do to help?"

"Nothing. Any news?"

"Only that I miss you."

"I miss you, too."

"Good luck, and keep safe. Text me later?"

"I will. Don't worry." Evie ended the call.

Mary had been watching Evie sympathetically as she talked to Mark. "What do you want to do, Evie?"

Evie knew it was a long shot, but she had to ask. "Can we take a look around, just in case?"

"You mean drive to Maple Mills?"

"Yes. I won't sleep if we don't at least take a look."

Mary paused, then nodded. "Okay. We'll go. But don't get your hopes too high."

"I know. Thanks, Gran Mary. I mean it. Thanks."

Mary gave her a quick hug and said, "Call Officer Summers. She'll want to know about that phone call."

Evie dreaded doing it, but she pressed in the numbers. Officer Summers picked up on the first ring. "Summers here."

"It's Evangeline Gibb."

Evie heard a deep sigh before the woman spoke. "I gave you my private number for emergency use. Only."

"I understand, but you should know that I just got a call from somebody using my stepsister's phone. I think I know where she is."

"That is good news."

"I think she's near Maple Mills."

"Why?"

Evie answered, "I asked if they were at Maple Mills and the girl hung up on me." Knowing how weak her reasoning sounded, she grimaced. A few seconds passed. "Hello? Officer Summers?"

"I'm here." There was another pause. "We are trying to solve a murder, plus what appears to be an attempted murder."

"Yes, ma'am."

"We are remarkably short-staffed. Everyone is working overtime. Including me. We're getting a lot of leads and are trying to follow all of them. Understand?"

"Yes, I do. But this might be related."

"Because somebody used her phone?" Officer Summers didn't try to mask her irritation. "Evangeline, if you think you know where she is, go pick her up. Simple."

"Right. I won't call again."

Evie pressed End and turned to Gran Mary. "We're on our own."

6

The Search for Beebee

Absorb what is useful. Discard what is not. Add what is uniquely your own.

— Bruce Lee

While Evie was talking to Officer Summers, Mary had made sandwiches and packed them in a box with some drinks, cookies, and bananas. They all climbed into the truck. Jordie sat in the back with Magpie, who they'd brought along for her tracking skills.

"We have no time to lose," said Gran Mary as she turned north on the gravel road. "It'll be dark in an hour."

"Actually," Jordie corrected, "I checked Google. Now that it's Daylight Saving Time, the sun sets at 7:24 tonight. We have fifty-eight minutes from" — he stared at the dashboard clock — "*now!*"

"Thanks, brother," groaned Evie.

"Can I have a banana?" asked Jordie, his mouth full of cheese and lettuce sandwich.

"How can you eat like that when Beebee's missing?"

"She's always missing. No big deal."

Evie passed a banana to him, offered one to Mary, and took one herself. She took a bite, but her stomach was in knots, and she didn't feel hungry. That call had creeped her out. Was Beebee really at Maple Mills? And if she was, what else would they find there? How many others? Were they dangerous?

Within ten minutes, they were crossing the six-lane highway. It was busy with fast-moving vehicles of all sizes, and Evie was glad she hadn't attempted it on horseback earlier.

A couple of concession roads past the highway, Mary turned right. As they drove up the road to Maple Mills, Evie said, "Let's go up to the Fourth Line and check out the old caretaker's house."

Mary shrugged. "Good idea. Did you get the impression that the girl was calling from indoors or outside?"

"Indoors for sure."

"That'll make it harder to find her."

"Our old gates!" exclaimed Jordie as they passed the impressive iron entrance with three large initials, MMS. "Can we go in?"

"No. They're probably locked," answered Mary. "Anyway, we have a job to do."

"What do those signs say?" Jordie asked. "There are two, one big and one small."

"What signs?" asked Mary.

"Beside the gate, just ahead," said Evie. Mary slowed the truck as they passed. Evie took a look. "The small one is a missing dog poster." The picture showed a black-and-white-and-grey dog with a golden-brown ruff around its neck. "It looks like a shepherd and collie mix."

Jordie read the bigger sign aloud. "'March Madness Steeplechase! Support Heart and Stroke Foundation on March seventeenth! Sign up online at www.mmsteeplechase.com.'"

"That's St. Patrick's day," noted Evie.

"They might've called it the St. Patrick's Steeplechase," said Mary. "But then the initials would have been SPS, not MMS."

"Very clever," Evie said. "Brent Keir said they did an annual fundraiser in Newmarket. The tradition continues."

Jordie was excited. "I know what a steeplechase is! It's a horse race over jumps in a big field. Sometimes horses race together, and sometimes it's timed. Sometimes it's hedges and ditches, and sometimes it's a cross-country course."

"You're absolutely right," Mary said. "Good for you."

"You should do it, Evie!" Jordie exclaimed with admiration. "You and Kazzam would win for sure. You're so fast!"

Evie continued looking out her window for any sign of Beebee. "Thanks, Jordie, but a horse needs a lot of training to do that. Except for three logs on the trail, I've only jumped Kazzam in the ring, and the race is next Sunday."

"That's six whole days away." Jordie's expression was confident. "I'll train him! It's gotta be easier than training a dragon, and I know how to do that."

Mary laughed. "I like your attitude, young man. Never say never. You remind me of another great trainer, Jerry Johnston."

"Here's the Fourth Line," Evie said. "It's a dead end."

As Mary turned left, Jordie cried out, "There's another missing dog poster on that telephone pole there!"

"I see it, too. Go slow here, Gran Mary. That's the old caretaker's house, and that's the lane." Or what was left of the lane, Evie noted.

"Which is impassable," Mary said, looking ahead. "It's overgrown."

Evie agreed. "It sure hasn't been used for a long time."

They came to a stop across the road from the house. No lights were on. No vehicle was in the driveway. There were no signs of life whatsoever.

"It looks abandoned," said Evie.

"Indeed it does. Let's keep going." Mary drove past. "Keep your eyes peeled for any sign of her."

Evie and Jordie scanned either side of the dirt road for buildings or other places where Beebee might be hidden. They drove to the end of the road and back with no luck, then returned to the old caretaker's house.

Mary stopped the truck across the road. "This is our best bet. Why don't we wait here and watch, just in case."

"In case of what?" asked Jordie. His eyes were huge. "Ghosts?"

"No, silly!" said Evie. "In case somebody shows up."

Mary turned off the headlights. They waited.

Five minutes later Jordie asked, "How long are we going to sit here?"

Evie opened the truck door. "I'll go look."

"No!" Jordie cried. "You might be kidnapped!"

"I'll be all right. If anything happens, you can save me."

"Are you sure?" asked Mary. "It's almost dark."

"I know," answered Evie. "But we're here and I don't know what else to do."

Mary nodded. "If she's not there, we're going home."

Evie got out with Magpie and quietly closed the truck door behind her. By now dusk had fallen, and there was very little light. She crossed the road and circled the house. She listened carefully, but heard nothing. It did feel a little spooky, maybe because Jordie had mentioned ghosts.

There was a sharp bang. Evie spun around to see where it had come from. A breeze had knocked an old shutter against the window.

She put her right hand over her pounding heart and kept Magpie at her side with the left. "Holy," she whispered. "That really scared me."

Magpie put her nose down to the ground. Evie watched her work. It was fascinating to see how methodically the dog sniffed, back and forth and back and forth around the house, giving particular attention to the front door and the basement hatch.

Within a couple of minutes, the dog came to Evie and sat. She was very relaxed. Evie sighed. If Magpie had scented Beebee, she would've been whining and wiggling all over the place.

Just to be sure, Evie pounded on the door of the house and yelled, "Hello?" She turned on her phone flashlight and looked in all the windows. She saw dusty, vacant rooms with no trace of habitation. There were no footprints, smudges, fingerprints, leftover food, or even garbage anywhere in sight. She tried to open the windows, but it was clear that they'd been nailed shut.

No one was in there, and in fact it appeared to Evie that no one had been in the old house for years.

She went back to the truck and climbed in. Magpie sat at her feet. "A dead end."

"Just like this road," answered Jordie.

Mary snorted. "Exactly. Let's go home."

But Evie didn't want to give up so easily. "Could we check that old house around the other side first?"

Mary paused, then nodded. "I guess so. It used to be called the Douglas house. We can take a look."

She turned right at the road.

"You sure are brave, Evie," said Jordie with admiration.

"Hey," said Evie. "I was brave because you were watching over me."

"I would've protected you if somebody was there."

Evie leaned over the seat and rubbed his head. "Thanks."

Mary drove around the concession to the old house at the opposite end of the Maple Mills acreage and pulled over.

A chain-link fence six feet high had been erected across the front. Cement boulders blocked the entrance, with a huge No Trespassing sign right in the middle, and a notice of demolition from the Town of Caledon.

"It's all dark in there," Jordie said. "Talk about spooky."

"It sure isn't friendly looking," agreed Evie, eyeing the debris and broken glass lying around. The place looked deserted.

"Don't even think about it. You're not getting out," Mary told Evie. "It's condemned. You're not climbing that fence."

"Maybe there's a hole somewhere."

"No, Evie. It's hazardous." Noticing Evie's mood, Mary said, "Cheer up, dear. If you want, we'll come back tomorrow when it's light out."

"I do." Tears welled in Evie's eyes. "Poor Beebee."

Jordie said, "Like I keep saying, she's with her friends and doesn't want to be found."

Evie wondered if that was true. Maybe she'd been laughing with the others when that girl had called. But what about poor Stacey Linn and the dead girl from Newmarket? Could Beebee be in the same kind of trouble? "Even if Beebee doesn't want to be found, she needs us to get her out of here."

"That's probably very true." Mary put the truck in gear. "But there's nothing more we can do tonight."

Evie wasn't ready to accept that. "You didn't see that poor girl in the woods! Can we go back and drive up the lane at the old caretaker's house? What if she's in one of the grooms' cabins?"

"Honey, there's no way the truck can get up that lane without getting stuck. You saw it."

"We can walk."

"The cabins are far from the end of that lane. Do you think we could find them in the dark, anyway?"

Evie's head dropped. "I don't know."

"First thing tomorrow, we'll come back. I promise," Mary said. "We'll find her. We'll bring Kazzam."

In a deep voice, Jordie growled, "A horse and a dog are all you need to track a person down." He grinned. "That's from *Mantracker*. We should be on that show."

Evie was roused from her sleep by the sound of her phone. She grabbed it from her bedside table on the third ring. "Hello?"

"It's me." The voice on the other end was hushed and urgent.

"Beebee?"

"Yes. Come get me. I'm at the old farm." She was speaking quickly and sounded out of breath.

"Maple Mills?"

"Yes! In some horrible old smelly place. Just come!" There was a scuffling sound, then Beebee said, "Hey!"

The line went dead.

Evie jumped out of bed. It was just before six in the morning. She hadn't slept much at all. She'd been imagining all sorts of horrible situations that Beebee might be stuck in.

Evie pulled on her clothes and looked in Gran Mary's room. The bed was empty. She ran downstairs. Mary was making breakfast, a coffee mug in her hand.

"Gran Mary! Beebee just called. She's somewhere at Maple Mills. She wants us to come get her!"

Mary stopped what she was doing. "Wake Jordie up, then get Kazzam ready. We'll need him to cover all that ground."

Within thirty minutes, Gran Mary was hitching up the horse trailer while Evie put the other horses outside with the round bale.

She tacked up Kazzam and led him up the ramp. She stroked his nose as she tied the shank to the metal ring with a boat knot. "We'll find her. There's nothing the police can do that we can't."

She closed the ramp and fastened all the latches. Jordie had already taken possession of the passenger seat, so Evie climbed into the back with Magpie right beside her.

As soon as she began to drive, Mary outlined the plan. "We'll go back to the Fourth Line and unload Kazzam. Evie, you take Magpie with you and check things out. Good?"

"Yup." Evie nodded. "We'll ride up the lane beside the old caretaker's house. I'll look in the grooms' cabins first. If Beebee's there, we'll come right back."

Mary said sternly, "But if there's any hitch, you call me for help. We'll stay where we park unless you text me otherwise."

"Right," Evie said. "I have my phone with me. If she's not there, I'll keep going and check the old Douglas house."

"Okay. If you don't find her after one hour, come back and we'll go right to the front gate and insist on searching the premises."

Jordie yawned. "She'll change her mind, you know."

"About what?" Mary asked.

"About being found. We're wasting our time." Jordie looked miserable. "What am I going to do while Evie's out looking?"

"You'll wait with me," answered Mary. "I brought books and cards and some games."

Jordie's face brightened. "Video games? On your phone?"

"No. Checkers and Monopoly."

"Or ... I can go back to sleep for a while. You woke me up really, really early." He was still in his pyjamas, and he snuggled up into a ball with his blanket and pillow.

"We couldn't leave you home alone," Mary explained.

"Why not? Mom always does."

Evie and Mary shared a glance.

Mary stopped the truck and trailer along the dead-end road across from the old house, in the same place they'd parked the night before. Evie and Mary got Kazzam off the trailer. Magpie sat at attention, thumping her tail on the ground in excitement, while Mary gave Evie a leg up. The black gelding was nervous and hopped in anticipation.

"Last thing, dear," said Mary. "No heroics, you hear? If something isn't right, call me immediately. I'll call the police."

Evie sniffed. "Not that they've been helping."

"They will if we need them."

"We connect in one hour, regardless. Right?"

"Right. Or before. I'll be right here."

Evie set off down the rutted lane on Kazzam, followed by Magpie. Even though it was very early, the day was dawning more mildly than usual for mid-March.

Evie took a deep breath and tried to relax. She felt oddly uneasy trespassing on her old family farm, with no idea what she was about to face. She must be ready to think fast.

They trotted past the abandoned caretaker's house toward Maple Mills Stables, now known as MMS. At the end of the lane stood the chain-link fence with a padlocked gate. A little distance to the left was a hole in the fence that they used to get through. Luckily, the new owners hadn't fixed it, because she didn't have a plan B. They inched carefully through the broken chain-link.

The property stretched out before them. Evie was struck once again by the beauty of these rolling pastures. They were bordered by dense woodland and fenced by pristine white boards that eventually converged at the architecturally perfect stables over the next hill. The majestic main house was off in the distance, surrounded by the fabled century-old maple trees.

Evie asked Kazzam to canter. They sailed along the dirt trail between the fenced paddocks in the direction of the grooms' cabins. Gran Mary had been right. It was much easier to do this with a horse, and in daylight. Plus, the cabins were much farther than she'd remembered.

When she got to the top of the ridge, she was astonished at what she saw. She slowed Kazzam to a trot and then halted to take a good look.

Construction work was being done in the huge upper pasture. Evie counted six trucks and about ten workers. Truck tires churned up mud as the ground thawed. People were busy digging holes, measuring distances, and hauling lumber. A backhoe was digging up a lot of earth, and one of the trucks had a long flatbed piled with lumber and wooden structures that looked like coups and jumps.

Of course, Evie thought. They were building a cross-country course for the steeplechase! The new owners had arrived only last week, and already they were remaking the property.

She hadn't expected to encounter anyone out here, especially so early, but she knew what to do. *People think you belong if you act like you belong.* She'd learned that at school after being considered a loser for long enough.

Evie arrived at the cabins. Both cabins had three bedrooms with bathrooms attached and a shared living space. They had been occupied to capacity at the height of Maple Mills's prosperity.

Before dismounting, she watched Magpie for signs of excitement. The dog investigated all the smells with normal interest and then sat down to scratch her ear.

Not promising, Evie thought. Regardless, she slid down from Kazzam's back, threw the reins over his head, walked up to the door at the first groom's cabin, and knocked loudly. She was counting on the grooms being at work so she could snoop. If someone answered, she would ask if the new people were hiring.

Nobody answered, and the windows and doors were locked up tight. Evie peeked through the windows. The rooms were freshly painted in a crisp white. There were new beds and dressers, but no clothes or linens, and no signs of life.

The same was true of the other cabin. It looked renovated, but vacant. She walked around to the back to check for signs of comings and goings and found none.

Plus, Magpie showed only casual interest. Beebee was definitely not here.

Evie got back in the saddle and headed toward the Douglas house at other end of the estate. It had been the original farmhouse on this property, but now, abandoned and condemned, it might very well be what Beebee would describe as "horrible and smelly."

Straight ahead in the next field, there was a secret cave in the side of the hill where she and Jordie had used to hide from their parents. For old times, she'd ride by and check it out. Maybe the green curtain would still be hanging over the entrance.

Kazzam cantered across the rough ground. *It feels good to be back on these fields*, Evie thought as they ran. She remembered her exhilarating early-morning sessions training Kazzam. Everybody, including Jerry and Mary, had given up the idea of racing him, but Evie had been determined to keep him racing fit. She was glad that she had. She smiled, again replaying their victory.

Suddenly, Kazzam spooked sideways to the left, and Evie lost a stirrup. "Whoa, boy!" she called. He flattened his ears and kicked out to the right.

An ATV raced up beside them. She'd been so deep in her thoughts that she hadn't been paying attention. An old man was driving and waving and crowding Kazzam over. Evie couldn't hear what he was yelling, but imagined it was about her trespassing. She quickly made a plan and slowed Kazzam to a halt. The horse was agitated and wouldn't stand still. Evie decided to imitate Paulina at her most imperious. It had worked before.

"Don't you know anything about horses?" Evie demanded. "You scared my horse!"

The man got off of the ATV and stood with his hands on his hips. He was tall and close to seventy, Evie guessed, and he spoke with some kind of a European accent. *Norwegian?* she wondered. *Dutch?* "I have orders, yah? Nobody is allowed on this land without permission. Nobody."

"And who gave you those orders?" Evie challenged.

"The owner, Dr. Maris-Stapleton." The man began to look a little amused. "And who are you, young miss?"

"Who are *you* is the question." Kazzam was already edgy, but instead of trying to calm him down, Evie dug in her heels and pulled on his mouth, asking him to rear and look dangerous.

The man stepped back from the flailing hooves.

"Look what you've done!" Evie made her escape, pretending that she couldn't handle her horse. "Help!"

Off they galloped. She laughed aloud, thrilled with the success of her ruse. "Good boy, Kazzam! That was perfect!"

The horse did a small joyful buck in response.

Evie's heart was racing. She'd been lucky this time, but she wouldn't have too many chances. That man, whoever he was, would be looking for her, and time was running out. She had to find her stepsister before she was kicked off the property.

She pointed Kazzam in the direction of the old Douglas farmhouse, and they sped toward it. As they passed her old hiding place, Evie saw that the old green curtain was still hanging, tattered but intact. *I must tell Jordie*, she thought. *He'll be pleased.*

She looked over again. Magpie had stopped. She was howling and barking and wagging her tail at the entrance of the cave, excited and wriggling all over. Evie slowed Kazzam and circled back.

7

Piers Anders

Your time is limited, so don't waste it living someone else's life.

— Steve Jobs

Evie brought Kazzam to a halt beside the hideout entrance and slid to the ground. Magpie whined and jumped and raced back and forth from Evie to the curtain. Something inside the cave was getting her very excited.

"It's okay, Mags," Evie cooed. "Good girl."

She inched toward the cave, leading Kazzam. He was nervous and refused to move any closer, so Evie held the buckle at the end of the reins with her left hand, and with her right, reached out and cautiously lifted a corner of the curtain. She was ready to jump back if an angry raccoon or a mother coyote with pups was in there.

Magpie dashed inside. The dog disappeared into the darkness, making her funny throat noise. Evie couldn't see a thing.

She had to investigate. She tucked Kazzam's reins in the stirrups and said, "Don't go anywhere, please. I might need you to get me outta here fast."

She knelt down and lifted the curtain, allowing the daylight to pour in.

In the back corner, huddled against the earthen wall, was Magpie, nestled into the form of a slight, young person. As Evie's eyes adjusted to the gloom, she saw it was a girl dressed entirely in faded black, with a black hood obscuring her face. Then, the girl lifted her head.

"Beebee!" cried Evie. Her stepsister's face was oddly white. Black eye makeup streaked her cheeks. She looked terrified.

"Evie! It's you! You came!"

"We've been looking all over for you!" On her knees, Evie reached out her arms, and Beebee scrambled into them.

"Thank you so, so, so much, Evie! I've been so, so scared! It's been crazy. So much has happened."

"You can tell us all about it in the truck. Gran Mary and Jordie are waiting." Magpie nosed her way into the embrace, and Evie rubbed her head. "Good girl, Mags! Let's go home."

Beebee began chattering quickly. "This morning after I called you, I escaped. Nobody was up and my door was unlocked. It's been awful, Evie! I wanted so much to belong, but then things started happening and I don't anymore, so I came to the hiding place 'cause I thought you might look for me here …"

Beebee's eyes grew larger. She stared over Evie's shoulder. "Oh, no. Someone's coming!"

Evie looked behind her. That man was zooming toward them on his ATV. She needed to come up with another plan.

"You stay hidden. I'll get rid of him. Can you ride Kazzam back to the trailer with me?"

The younger girl nodded madly. "Now?"

"No, when he's gone. Don't let him see you. I don't know if we can trust him."

"Okay." Beebee nodded several more times.

Evie stepped out of the cave and dropped the curtain behind her, just in time to hide Beebee from the man's view. As casually as she could manage, she climbed back onto Kazzam, intending to lead the man on a wild goose chase, and then come back.

"You!" yelled the man. "No more tricks! Stop now!"

"What a cute little hideaway!" said Evie, channelling her stepmother again. "Whatever is it for?"

"You are not authorized to be on MMS property. I will escort you off the premises."

"Then I've gone to a lot of trouble for nothing!" Evie pouted, thinking as fast as she could. "I came to sign up for the March Madness Steeplechase."

The man stepped off the ATV and smiled the way a cat might smile at a goldfish. He spoke more slowly. "You want to sign up for the Steeplechase, yah?"

Evie was wary of his sudden change in manner, sensing a trap. "Yes. Can you tell me where to go?"

"The Steeplechase is a fundraiser. It's one thousand dollars per entry. Other classes are less. You did say the Steeplechase?"

Evie tossed her head, just like Paulina would. "Yes, that's what I said, and I know what it costs. No problem."

"You have the money with you?"

"I never carry cash!" she exclaimed with indignation.

"We take credit. But it's a tough course. You have done this before, yah? You are an eventer?"

"Of course!"

"What level?"

Evie knew only a bit about eventing. She knew it was a combination of show jumping, dressage and cross-country, but she wasn't at all sure about the levels. She remembered once hearing someone say that they'd gone Prelim. "Prelim," she said.

"On that horse? He's quite small for those big, solid jumps."

"Don't let his size fool you. He's amazing."

"You'll have to pass a little test before I believe you." The man appeared to be having fun at her expense.

"Why should I have to prove anything to you?" she sassed. Even to her own ears, the Paulina routine was getting old.

"As it happens, I am the person who takes the entries. I am also the person who decides who is eligible to compete."

Evie realized that she was in a pickle. She toned down the act. "Oh. What's the test?"

"Follow me." He got back onto the ATV and headed up the hill.

Evie called down, "Beebee? Did you hear all that?"

"Yes! Where are you going? What are you doing?"

"Getting tested, I guess. Don't go anywhere, I'll be back as soon as I can!"

"Can't we just go now?" she pleaded.

"We could try, but what if he chases us?" Evie said.

"I'll stay," Beebee answered quickly. With some of her old spunk, she demanded, "But Magpie has to stay with me."

"Good idea." Magpie's nose pushed back the curtain, and she looked to Evie for instruction. "Stay, girl. I'll be back."

Magpie disappeared again behind the cloth.

Evie and Kazzam cantered to the top of the hill, then trotted over to join the man on the ATV as he surveyed the evolving course, his hand shielding his eyes.

Evie was impressed at the progress. It looked like the course might be finished later that day.

Just then, a truck with an enormous water tank stopped at the dry bed of a newly dug water hazard, and the driver jumped out. He attached a hose and turned a crank. Water gushed out in a huge torrent, spooking Kazzam.

"Okay, we begin," said the man firmly. "What's your name?"

"Molly Peebles."

"Let's try again. That's the fifth lie you've told me."

Evie was taken aback. "What do you mean?"

"I know a rider when I see one. Your horse was not out of control when you ran away. That was the first lie." He counted on his fingers. "And, two, you're not here to sign up. Three, you don't have a thousand dollars. Four, you've never run that horse over a cross-country course. Five, your name is not Molly Peebles." He held up five fingers, one for each lie. "That is a fictitious name made up by the winner of last year's Caledon Horse Race. How am I doing?"

Evie didn't answer. So the man knew the Molly Peebles story. Evie had entered the Caledon Horse race under an assumed name. What else did he know?

"Let's start again. What's your name?"

"Evie Gibb."

"Very good."

"What's yours?"

"Piers Anders," he answered.

Evie gasped. Piers Anders. Now she recognized him.

He was famous. Not only had he won an individual gold medal in eventing at the Olympics, he was considered to be the best course designer and trainer in the world.

She was out of her league. Should she continue to bluff, or come clean? How best to get Beebee and leave the property? Her mind was spinning.

Piers chortled. "You seem not so haughty now. Is there a problem?"

"Yes, there is. A big one. I don't know if I can trust you."

"Trust *me*? Trust is in short supply here. When you are dishonest once, let alone five times, how do you expect anything you say to be believed?"

Evie was ashamed. She felt the heat on her face and knew she'd turned completely red.

"You have the decency to blush. Tell me the problem."

"It's an unbelievable story. I don't expect you to understand."

"Try me."

Considering that Beebee had apparently been held against her will on this property, it was hard to know who was a good guy and who was bad. But Evie decided to take a chance that a gold medallist had better things to do with his time than to detain children.

"My stepsister, Beatrice Gibb, is a friend of Cynthia Maris-Stapleton." Evie watched Piers's face for any sign of recognition. There was none, so she continued.

"Her mother asked my grandmother to look after her over the March break, but nobody knew where she was." She wasn't sure how much to tell.

"And? How does that bring you here?"

"She called me and said she was somewhere at Maple Mills, where we used to live."

"And so, you run around on your horse looking for her?"

"Yes."

"And you found her in that little hole in the bank."

Evie was startled. "You saw her?"

Piers sighed. "No. But your dog is no longer at your side. I believe you left it with her to keep her company."

Evie nodded. "I'm sorry I tried to fool you."

"I'm old and not so easy to fool. So now, what do you want to do?"

"I want to take Beebee home with me."

"Both of you on your horse?"

"Yes."

"Good idea." He smiled and nodded. "But, before you do, I want you to try out a few obstacles, to see how they ride, yes? Would you do that for me?" He looked at the evolving course critically. "I'm on a tight schedule, as you can see, and with the quick thaw and the muddy patches, I've had to adjust, yah? Before all the machines leave, I must know if we need to make changes."

"Does this mean that you believe me and you'll let me take Beebee home?"

Piers chuckled deeply. "Yes. Of course. You'll help me?"

"If I can, but I need to get Beebee away from here. There are people here who don't want her to leave."

"Yah, yah. This will be quick." He tilted his head. "You know, you're the first North American I've met who uses a horse to go places and would think to ride double. Most of you are so fearful of doing anything not perfect, it makes me crazy."

"Thank you," said Evie. She was genuinely touched by his praise. "But you were right. I lied about having evented. I don't even know what Prelim means. Kazzam knows how to jump in the ring, but he's only jumped three natural jumps ever, and that was yesterday. I'm not sure I can help."

"I'm sure you'll do fine. You're a rider, and he's an athlete. This is not a Preliminary course, it's a Pre-Training course, which is easier. The jumps are not more than point nine metres, or under three feet high. Yah?"

It didn't sound horribly high. Evie nodded. "I'll try." If she could be helpful, it was the least she could do.

Piers's face held a puzzled expression. "You remind me of somebody I know, or knew, long ago. But I can't think of who."

Evie shrugged.

"But now. Let's get to work." Piers studied the course. "Pick up a canter and drop down this bank into the water. Canter across the pond. Jump up the other bank. Circle back over the two wooden roll tops. Two strides in between. You can do this?"

Evie nodded, eyeing the rounded jumps. They looked enormous and very solid. But if Piers Anders thought they could do it, they could do it. She took a big breath and reviewed his instructions. Into the water and out, then over the two wooden obstacles. She patted Kazzam's neck. "We can do this, can't we, boy?"

Kazzam snorted and pawed twice with his front right hoof. And to show he was feeling good, he hopped in place and began to canter.

"Wait!" Piers threw up both hands. "No, no, not all at once! First, we ask the horse to do each part separately, from a walk. If there is a problem, we work on it, with no stress. *Then* we put them all together, see?"

Evie thought that made sense. She nudged Kazzam forward to the top of the bank and kept him walking until he got to the drop. He hopped down, walked through the pond, and up onto the other bank.

"Good! Very good! Now trot the roll top jumps. First try one, and then the other, and then both of them together. Yes? If there's a problem, we figure it out."

"Okay!" Evie did exactly as she was told. She trotted to the first, and Kazzam vaulted quietly over. She cantered him away, and then brought him back to a walk. Then, she trotted him to the second roll top, and he hopped over in the same calm way, without hesitation or any balking. Now, she asked him to canter them in a line, one after the other. Evie was astonished. Kazzam was great!

"Good! Good! Now you are ready to put it all together at a canter. Yes?"

"Yes!" Evie asked Kazzam to canter from a standstill. As if he'd done it a thousand times, the small black gelding dropped into the pond, cantered through at a steady pace, lifted himself up the bank on the other side, made his turn, and effortlessly sailed over the two solid wooden roll top jumps. He stopped casually at the surprised feet of Piers Anders, gold medallist.

Evie beamed from ear to ear as she patted Kazzam's neck. "That was fun!"

"You've done this before, yah?"

"No, but we really like it!"

"I see that!"

"Can I get Beebee now? I don't want to be gone too long."

"Very soon. She'll be fine. She has your nice dog for company."

"But I need to get her away from here."

Piers nodded. "Yah, I see that. Can I get your help with this one first, before I let the machines go?"

Evie looked over at the cave. An ATV was parked beside it, with a person sitting inside. "Who's that?"

Piers indicated his phone. "I asked one of my students to wait there. Just in case your stepsister tries to leave on her own. Or one of those people you mentioned comes to get her."

"Thank you." Evie was grateful and felt much more at ease.

"Now," Piers said. He pursed his lips and rubbed his chin in thought. "Take him away from here to my left at a canter. When you get past that grove, there is a vertical jump followed by a ditch, followed by another vertical jump. Altogether, it's called a coffin. It's a Preliminary obstacle, but this one is not as high. Jump it, then take the path to the right when you get to the fork, go over the giant goose, veer left, go down the drop in the woods, and back to me. Yah?" He indicated the direction and swept his arm as he spoke. "Got it?"

"Yes, I think so."

"Again, one piece of the puzzle at a time, then put them together, yah? Off you go."

As Evie and Kazzam cantered up the hill toward the coffin, she heard the roar of the ATV and glanced behind. Piers motioned for her to go ahead and ignore him, so she looked ahead and concentrated on the task he'd set her. The vertical jumps and ditch coming up looked large and airy and very close together.

Evie considered turning away, explaining to Piers that it was too tough, but Kazzam grabbed the bit and shook his head impatiently, then bucked a little as he cantered.

Evie got the message. "If you think you can do it, I'll stay out of your way, boy." She gritted her teeth and slowed him to a trot.

The jumps didn't look as big once she got closer. They consisted of posts in the ground with two plain wooden rails across. She asked Kazzam first to trot over each one calmly, then slow to a walk.

She pointed him toward the ditch next. Kazzam found it unsettling, maybe because the lumber surrounding the pit was bright and new. The first time, he stopped at the brink and nervously shuffled his feet. Evie asked him to do it again, and found that when she looked over it and not into it, he responded much better. The third time over the ditch was a breeze.

She put this part together, cantering over the first vertical, then the ditch, and then the second vertical. She patted his neck. "So, this is a coffin, Kazzam!"

They continued to the fork at a trot. The enormous wooden sculpture of a goose was spooky-looking to Evie, but no problem for Kazzam. He hopped over it easily. The last part of this assignment was the drop, which was difficult because it was in a shady patch and hard to see with eyes accustomed to the bright sunlight. Kazzam hesitated a little, but kept moving forward.

Now, they would put it all together. She asked Kazzam to canter and kept her hands and heels down.

He approached the coffin combination coolly. He landed the first jump, took a stride, cleared the ditch, took another stride, and jumped the second vertical jump with confidence.

"Good boy!" she praised, and steered toward the right fork at a canter, which brought them quickly to the giant goose, which the brave black gelding jumped in stride. They turned to the left and dropped easily down the steep, shaded bank, cantered a few strides, and slowed to a trot.

Evie was astounded by her horse's abilities. "Kazzam, you're a genius!" She stroked his neck and patted him.

Piers came up beside them when they halted, grinning broadly. "So. You must be my students. You and your horse. You have the special something. I've been looking for this, to teach, to make something great. Yah?" He gave Kazzam a firm pat on the neck and pulled a business card out of his back pocket. He handed it to Evie. "You call me today. We will make a plan."

"A plan?"

"Yah. It's your school holiday, yes?"

"Yes. For a week."

Piers laughed. "No holiday for you! Go now. Rescue your stepsister. I will turn the blind eye, yes?"

"Yes! Thank you!"

"Go quickly and stay out of sight. Call me today or I tell on you." He winked.

"I will!" Evie turned Kazzam toward the cave.

"One more thing!" Piers called. Evie stopped. "You did not lie about one thing. This small horse is amazing." He grinned broadly and waved goodbye.

Evie's heart was full of joy. This man was a legend in the horse world, and he wanted *her* to be his student! And Kazzam! This was very exciting. Jerry wanted Kazzam to keep racing, and Evie understood why, but now she was certain of one thing: Kazzam would become an event horse. Not a mediocre one, but a really good one!

It was almost an hour since she'd left the trailer. Gran Mary would be anxious for news. She called.

Mary answered on the first ring. "Evie?"

"I found Beebee. We're coming now."

"Thank heavens!" Mary's voice was full of relief. "That's great news!"

101

At the cave, Evie thanked the man who'd guarded it while she was riding. He waved and drove away.

Before Evie could dismount, Magpie came bursting through the green curtain, wagging her tail, followed by a very angry-looking Beebee.

"What took you so long!" she wailed. "I thought you were *never* coming back!"

"I'm glad you're back to your old self," chuckled Evie. She slid down and gave Beebee a leg up. Then she jumped back up in front of her. "Hold on to me, okay?"

"I know how to ride, Evie. Remember, *I'm* the one Kerry thinks is the best rider. I have perfect form."

Evie was too happy to care about Beebee's bragging. She had impressed Piers Anders, and she'd found her stepsister and was bringing her home. "I remember. Hang on!"

"Not too fast!" cried Beebee.

Off they went, with Beebee noisily complaining about the speed, the bumpiness, and the saddle hitting her in the wrong spot.

Evie steered Kazzam to the outer edge of the field, as far away as possible from the construction and all the people. She glanced back briefly to see Piers Anders waving. She thrust up her left arm to acknowledge him and continued galloping past the empty grooms' cabins and along the trail leading to the hole in the chain-link fence.

When they slowed to walk through the gap, Beebee yelled, "Let me down! I can't take it anymore."

"I thought you knew how to ride?" Evie said, poking fun.

"I do, just not like a cowboy, you moron! Remind me never to ride with you again!"

"Remind me never to save you again."

Once past the hole in the fence, they were off the MMS property and onto the rutted lane that led past the old caretaker's house to the road. Evie moved Beebee's skinny legs over to one side so she could slide down to the ground. Magpie jumped up and licked her face when she landed.

"Stop it!" Beebee whined, wiping her cheek in disgust.

Jordie came running. "Beebee! You're safe! You're alive!" Tears ran down his face.

In spite of herself, Beebee ran and hugged him. "I didn't know you cared!"

"Neither did I," he said. "Eww. You smell bad."

"*You* smell bad!" Beebee pushed him so hard that he fell to the ground. "And you're crying like a baby!"

"Hey!" called Evie. "Can't you two be nice for one minute?" She rode Kazzam ahead of the two kids at a walk.

Mary had turned the rig around so it faced homeward and was waiting at the lowered ramp. "Success! Well done!"

Evie jumped down. "Thanks. I sure was worried." She patted Kazzam's neck fondly, unbuckled the girth, and pulled off his saddle. Mary handed her the halter and shank and took the bridle that Evie had slipped off Kazzam's head.

"Be warned. Beebee's in a cranky mood," Evie whispered.

Mary laughed quietly. "I'd worry if she wasn't. I'm so glad she's safe."

They loaded Kazzam and latched up the ramp.

"Hi, Beebee!" called Mary warmly as Beebee and Jordie crossed the road to the truck. "It's so good to see you!"

The girl frowned. "Jordie says I have to stay with you. Do I?"

Mary was surprised. "Where else would you like to stay?"

"With my friends. In Newmarket. I'll hitchhike back."

"Told you so," said Jordie.

"Shut up!" snapped Beebee. She tried to shove him, but he got out of the way first.

Mary opened the passenger side door. She had a concerned look. "You ride up front with me, Beebee. Let's talk."

Beebee climbed in sullenly. "Later," she said.

"No, Beatrice. We need to talk now. You called for help, and we came. Are there other kids who need our help, too?"

"Why d'you wanna know?" Beebee's eyes narrowed.

Mary was firm. "So we can get them out of here."

"They wouldn't come with you."

"How many are there?"

"Stop asking questions! I'm done with all of you."

Evie stared at her. "Beebee, what changed? At the cave you were scared and dying to get out of here, and now you're mad at us for caring about the others?"

A tear rolled down the younger girl's face, but she refused to answer.

Evie, Jordie, and Magpie got into the back seat, and Mary started up the engine.

"I'm done," Beebee repeated. She folded her arms, and within a minute, her head dropped to her chest. She was fast asleep.

Mary gently covered her with a blanket and turned up the heat.

Trouble Brewing

There is no greater agony than bearing an untold story inside you.

— Maya Angelou

Beebee slept soundly on the way home, and Evie filled in Gran Mary and Jordie about how Magpie had discovered Beebee in their old secret cave, and how frightened she'd been. Evie told them about being chased and caught by an old man on an ATV, and how he'd asked her to try the new obstacles to see how they paced out.

"Gran Mary, have you heard of Piers Anders?"

"Of course I have. He won the gold in Sydney, in 2000."

"Cool!" exclaimed Jordie. "Bags of gold, like pirates find? Or a chest full of gold coins?"

"Neither," Evie explained with a chortle. "He won a gold medal at the Olympics. He's the man I was talking about."

"The man who chased you on the ATV was Piers Anders?" asked Mary.

"Yes. Did you know he's the course designer for the March Madness Steeplechase?"

"No! He's pretty high priced for a little fundraiser."

"He wants to be my coach."

Mary was quiet. "He's the top of the top, dear. He's likely over our budget. Considerably."

"I'll pay him out of my Queens Plate winnings."

"You're keeping that money in your savings account for your future and your education. That's very important, Evie."

"Anyway, I'm supposed to call him later. Do you think we could make this work?"

"Yes, we can." Mary paused. "If it's what you want."

"It is. I've been nervous about Kazzam racing after his injury, and I've been thinking about what he should do next. I had no idea about cross-country until today, but he loves it. And so do I."

Mary nodded. "He's brave, he's confident, and he's extremely athletic. It makes sense." She drummed her fingers on the steering wheel. "Well, we won't be able to afford regular lessons, but I'll pay for one or two — and I insist, Evie. It'll be worth it. I just got my royalty cheque in the mail, so this is very good timing."

"Money from all the books you've sold?" asked Jordie.

"Exactly," Mary answered. "You know, Piers Anders is known for his skill with horses all over the world. He was famous even before the Sydney Games."

"I didn't know that."

"Yes. Decades ago he came to Caledon to give a clinic. I attended, and he taught me a lot. Leave it with me."

Evie was thrilled to the bottom of her toes that Gran Mary approved. "Thank you! What I need help with is transportation."

Mary smiled over her shoulder at Evie. "I'll drive you. As long as I can watch sometimes."

"Deal!"

They pulled into the driveway of Parson's Bridge just as Jerry was driving out. He stopped his truck beside them and rolled down his window, eagerly motioning for Mary to do the same.

"There you are! Just the woman I came to see. You're looking much better than the last time I saw you!"

"When you woke me up, sick with a cold, and demanded we talk right that minute?"

Jerry avoided the question. "Good news! I have a spot at Rainbow Racing Stables. I can bring No Justice over this very afternoon."

"Jerry, you should've talked to us before making —"

"Is that him on the trailer? Drive him over! I can't wait to get started." Jerry quivered with excitement, reminding Evie of Magpie whenever she saw a squirrel.

In the back seat, Evie rolled down her window. "Hold on, Jerry …"

"No time to waste. You *know* you want him to race!"

"Remember how Kazzam is *my* horse, and *I* will decide what he does?" Jerry's eyes became suspicious. "Well, I've decided. He's not going to race. He's going to be an eventer, and my coach will be Piers Anders, Olympic gold medallist."

"You can't do that, Evie! Mary, talk some sense into her!"

Mary shook her head. "Sorry to disappoint you, J.J., but Evie has decided, and I back her up one hundred percent."

"Me, too!" yelled Jordie. "I back her up *two* hundred percent!"

"No Justice is the best racehorse I've ever worked with! You have to reconsider! I'm not even talking about all the money he'll make. Talk about gold ... there's no money in eventing. Not a cent!"

Beebee groaned. "Quiet! Let me sleep!"

Everybody ignored her except Jordie. "*You* be quiet! This is important!"

"Shut up, jerk!" Beebee pulled her hoodie over her ears.

Jordie lurched forward from the back seat and yelled in her ear. "You shut up!"

Without turning around to look, Beebee threw back her two fists and hit him squarely in the face.

"Oww! That hurts!" Jordie began to sob.

"We need to go," Mary said to Jerry matter-of-factly.

"You're a glutton for punishment," said Jerry. He had to shout to be heard over Jordie's wailing and Beebee's screaming. "Call me when you change your mind! And you *will* change your mind. No Justice is a talent, a gold mine, and he'll be wasted." Jerry gunned his truck and sped away down the lane.

He's angry, thought Evie. She was sorry about that, but Kazzam had already made him a lot of money, and she wouldn't change her mind just to please him. Kazzam had been a natural out there in the field.

Mary drove to the barn and turned off the engine. Her eyes were hard, and she spoke firmly. "Beebee and Jordie, that was unacceptable. You will treat each other with respect, and you will be civilized with everybody. I expect good behaviour. I will not tolerate rudeness."

Beebee mimicked her in a singsong voice. "I will not tol-er-ate rude-ness."

Mary stared at her. She curled her lip and growled, "Get out."

"What did I do?" the girl wailed.

"You get out of this truck this minute and walk up to the farmhouse. If you haven't sorted yourself out by the time I get up there, I will find somewhere for you to spend this week that you will not like one bit. Do you hear me?"

Evie was shocked. She'd never heard her grandmother talk like that. She looked at Beebee, who was slowly backing out of the truck, afraid to say a word. When the girl reached the ground, she turned and ran right up to the house, never looking back.

"I ... I ... I'll be good," babbled Jordie. "I promise."

Mary tousled his hair fondly. "Don't worry."

"Can I stay here and not go to the place I won't like one bit?"

"Yes, you can," Mary chuckled. "Jordie, I just needed to set the ground rules with Beebee. We must treat everybody the way we want to be treated ourselves."

Jordie stayed with Mary and Evie while they unloaded Kazzam, got him cleaned up, and put him out into the field. The other three horses came trotting up to the gate to meet him, and as soon as he was released, he raced away with the others right behind him, happy to be reunited. After a minute of prancing and playing, they were calm again, all munching on the round bale together as if he'd never been away.

After the trailer was unhooked, they moved the truck up to the house. Beebee was sitting on the step, glowering. She yelled, "The door's locked, just so you know."

Mary sighed. "Let's get something to eat. Beebee, since you've had a terrible time lately, you get to choose. Whatever you want, I'll make. And we're eager to hear your whole story from start to finish."

Beebee shrugged.

"We have a million questions," said Evie. "Like, who called me from your phone last night? And how many other people are at Maple Mills? And do you know Stacey Linn?"

Beebee glared at Evie with open hostility.

Mary put her key in the lock. "Evie, give the girl a chance to get settled. She must be starving. We have to look after her."

Beebee stuck her tongue out at Evie behind Mary's back and smiled secretively. She mouthed, *You'll never know.*

When Mary opened the mudroom door, Simon and Garfunkel came tumbling outside, full of energy and joy. Magpie and the two Labs circled the house a few times and then settled down to their normal calm. It reminded Evie of how the horses had greeted each other after Kazzam returned.

She wondered if people had a similar pattern, and thought about how Beebee and Jordie had hugged each other in greeting and then begun to fight. Maybe fighting was the normal state of their relationship. If so, there'd be no peace in the house at all.

Jordie called out, "Gran Mary? The light is flashing. Can I press the button?"

"Yes, dear. Please do."

"You have one new message. Message one."

"Hello, Ms. Parson. This is Madeleine Surrey from the Quest. Dr. Marshal asked that you come see him and visit Angela Parson Gibb this afternoon, anytime between noon and four. Please call us to confirm at 519-738-4109."

"End of messages."

Mary looked at her watch. "It's after ten o'clock now." She picked up the phone and left a message that

110

she'd be there around noon. "I haven't met Dr. Marshal yet. He must be new. I hope there's nothing wrong."

Evie could see how stressed she was. "It'll be fine, Gran Mary," she said. "I'd like to come, too, if that's okay."

"Yes. You should come." Mary looked at Beebee and Jordie sitting on the couch, searching for a television program to watch. "We'll have to bring them, too. I don't want to leave them alone together."

Evie agreed. "Beebee might hitchhike back to Newmarket."

Mary raised her eyebrows and nodded. "Too true. Let's have something to eat. We'll leave around 11:45." She turned to Beebee. "Have a nice hot shower, honey. Evie can lend you clothes until we get yours washed."

"No way I'm wearing Evie's clothes!"

"Will absolutely everything be a problem?" Mary asked.

Beebee said nothing.

Evie wasn't thrilled with the idea of Beebee wearing her clothes, either. "I'll throw your clothes in the washer and dryer. Forty minutes for the washer and forty-five for the dryer. Lots of time."

Beebee sniffed. "Whatever." She got up from the couch and stalked to the bathroom, slamming the door behind her. Seconds later she tossed her filthy clothes out into the hall. Black hoodie, black stretchy pants, black socks, black underwear, and black T-shirt. Evie scooped them up and put them in the machine with extra soap.

As soon as Beebee had scrubbed herself and was wrapped up in a housecoat, she chose pancakes and eggs for an early lunch. Jordie wanted bacon, too, so Evie sizzled some up in the pan.

When lunch was ready, they sat down around the kitchen table. Beebee was so busy eating that she forgot to be rude.

Evie watched her wolfing down her food. Just a couple of hours ago, they'd been worried that she'd come to serious harm. Evie felt grateful that wasn't the case. "I'm glad you're here, Beebee. We'll think of some fun things to do while school's out."

With her mouth full of pancakes and maple syrup dribbling down her chin, Beebee said, "What's your idea of fun, freak? Riding a horse? Shovelling crap?"

"Beatrice," said Mary sternly, "watch your language."

"Yeah, yeah, or I go to that place I don't wanna be."

Evie noticed that even though Beebee was talking tough, her lower lip trembled. "Tell us what happened. Somebody called Gran Mary's number from your phone last night. I tried to call back, but nobody answered."

"I lent it to a girl."

"This morning you said you were in a horrible place and needed to be rescued."

"I made it up. I was fine."

"That's weird. You didn't seem fine."

"You're calling *me* weird? Orange head."

Ignoring the remark about her hair colour, Evie said, "If you were fine, why did you tell me you escaped and ran to the cave because I might look for you there? Who did you escape from?"

"Leave me alone." Beebee put down her fork. "I don't want to be interrogated!"

Mary said, "For now, what's important is that you're here with us, and safe. But if there's anything that the police should know, you must tell us. We'll help."

"Whatever." The girl hung her head. "I don't have my phone. I have nothing to do. Can I watch TV?"

"Certainly." Mary patted the girl's hand. Beebee pulled it away hastily and shuffled to the couch.

"By the way, I hear you know Cynthia Maris-Stapleton," Evie said.

Beebee stopped in her tracks. "Leave Cyn out of this!"

Evie stared. "O-kay ..."

"Everything was great until her father forced her to go to Florida to look at a stupid horse!"

"So, why did you hitchhike to Caledon if she was in Florida?"

"She wanted us to come, so we came. She didn't know she'd have to leave. Me and another girl were going to be initiated."

Mary had been listening. "Initiated?"

"Forget it!" snapped Beebee. "It didn't happen!"

"Who took your phone?" Evie pressed.

"The mean one."

"Who's she?"

"None of your damn business! Leave me alone." Beebee turned on the television and began scrolling through the channels.

Evie shrugged. Beebee wasn't going to be helpful. That much was clear.

After she finished cleaning up the dishes, there was just enough time for her to make two phone calls.

The first was to Mark. She took the phone into her room and got caught up on all his news, which included his sunburn, his sister getting in trouble with their parents for staying out too late with friends, and the balmy weather. As they laughed and chatted, Evie felt her stress leaving her. She loved that Mark delighted in her sense of humour. He thought she was funny, and he made her feel appreciated.

"You be careful," said Mark. "It was brave, how you went searching for Beebee. But stay safe. When I get back, I'll help you solve this mystery."

"I know you will, like you helped last June. That was crazy."

"That was the most exciting thing I've ever been part of!"

"Which thing? The rescuing-my-mother thing, the racing thing, or the sending-my-father-to-prison thing?" asked Evie.

"All of the above. I wish I were with you now. I miss you."

"I miss you, too. But I have to hang up now."

"I don't want to hang up. I like talking to you."

"Me, too, but I have to call Piers Anders before we go to the Quest. Sorry, Mark."

"Amazing. You amaze me."

"Talk soon?"

"Tomorrow, okay?"

By the time Evie got off the phone, she felt like she could take on the world. She felt she could take on anything.

Cheerfully, she walked into the kitchen to return the phone.

"What are you so happy about?" glowered Beebee.

Evie took a deep breath and tried not to respond to the negativity. She vowed to stay cool. Beebee had been through something tough.

"Seriously. What could possibly make you so happy? If you could see yourself, you'd be depressed. Carrot top."

Mary looked up from her book. "Beatrice!"

"Sorry. I should've said *moron*." Beebee shot Evie a malicious glance before turning back to the television.

Evie wasn't at all sure how this new arrangement was going to work out. It was like adopting a porcupine. She tried to squelch her sense of foreboding and asked, "Gran Mary? Can we talk to Piers Anders now? I want to call him before we go see Mom."

"Sure. Hand me the phone when you're ready."

Evie felt nervous as she pressed the numbers.

"Yah?" Piers answered on the first ring.

"Oh, hello! It's Evie Gibb. You said to call?"

"Yes! So good. You will be my student, yah?"

"I'd love to be your student. When do you want me to start?"

"Tomorrow morning, same time, yah?"

"Yah! I mean yes! Can you talk to my grandmother? She'll be driving me."

"I look for you tomorrow. I talk to grandma now."

Evie passed the phone to Mary. Mary didn't say much, but she nodded and smiled a lot. It seemed to be a genial conversation.

Mary hung up and brushed her hair off her face. Her eyelashes fluttered. "Piers Anders! Who would've thought?"

Evie's eyes widened. She suddenly pictured Mary as a young woman. "Are you blushing, Gran Mary?"

"No!"

"Okay, if you say so. What did he say?"

"He has high hopes for you. He doesn't want to be paid."

"What? He'll teach for free?"

"He said his first coach did that for him, for the love of the sport, and it's time to pass the good deed forward. Someday you'll do the same, he said."

"Really?" Evie was confounded. "I'll work really hard and make him proud. I'll pay him back that way."

Mary hugged her granddaughter. "I know you'll make him proud. You make me proud every day." She wiped a tear from her cheek. "Now, let's get ready to go see your mother. Quick shower and off we go."

By 11:50 a.m. they were back in the truck and on the way to the Quest.

Beebee sat in the front again, where Mary could watch her. The girl and her clothes were clean, but she wasn't happy. "Why do I have to go to the funny farm? She's not my mother! This has nothing to do with me."

"Because I don't trust you to stay at home," answered Mary sternly. "You have to earn that privilege."

"You think I'll run away?" Beebee sneered. "Because I will."

"Which is why you'll stick with me." Mary wasn't happy, either. "I'm looking after you this week, and I intend to give you back in one piece."

Beebee snarled, "I don't need a babysitter. I'm not a baby."

Evie took a good look at her stepsister. Since the last time she'd seen her, Beebee had lost weight, and she'd been very slight to start with. It wasn't a healthy look. Without the black and white makeup obscuring her face, the deep, dark circles under her eyes and the pale, pasty hue of her skin were apparent. The skin around her finger-nails was raw and swollen.

"You didn't use to bite your nails, Beebee," she said.

"Screw you."

Mary bristled. "Beatrice! Watch your language!"

"Why is it always *my* fault! Evie should mind her own frigging business!"

Mary stopped the truck. "You listen to me. You will behave in a civilized manner —"

"I'm outta here," Beebee sneered as she tried the door handle.

Mary engaged the child lock just in time.

"Let me out!"

Mary was outraged, but she sat quietly, composing herself, waiting for Beebee's yelling and pounding to end.

Jordie whispered in Evie's ear. "I told you she was weird."

9

The Quest

If you don't like something, change it. If you can't change it, change your attitude.

— Maya Angelou

They arrived at the impressive black iron gates of the Quest exactly at noon. Evie felt nervous. She wanted to see her mother and hoped she was better, but she didn't want to be disappointed, either. She told herself to relax and go with the flow. There was nothing she could do but wait and see.

To distract herself, she noticed the high walls made of stone and how attractively they curved around the grounds. How long did it take to build those walls, she wondered, with how much rock and how many workers?

Beebee had fallen asleep again, much to the relief of the others in the truck.

To their right was a parking lot with an EMPLOYEES ONLY sign, and to their left was a steel pad with numbers built into a stone pillar. A discreet notice asked them to press 0 for assistance.

Mary pressed the button. It buzzed several times before someone answered.

"May I help you?" said a tinny female voice.

"Yes, thank you. It's Mary Parson. I'm here to visit Angela Parson Gibb."

"Yes, we're expecting you. Please park in the visitors' section to the left of the front entrance. Madeleine Surrey will meet you and escort you in."

"Thank you."

The gates slowly opened, and Mary drove her truck through. The driveway was long, half a kilometre at least. Evie looked along the wall and pictured her mother trying to escape. She saw an orchard, all the trees' branches still leafless. Was that the orchard where Angela had been caught? *Why had she done it?* Evie wondered for the twentieth time. Had she been looking for drugs? Evie would find out today, whether she wanted to or not.

As instructed, Mary parked in the section marked VISITORS ONLY. There were only a few designated spots, and they were all vacant. Evie knew the Quest had a very strict policy about visitors, but it was a little unsettling for theirs to be the only vehicle there. Mary put the truck in park.

A middle-aged woman had been watching them from the front entrance. She was dressed in a trim grey pantsuit with a bright-yellow blouse. Her short brown hair blew back, and her heels clacked hollowly on the cement walkway as she came over to greet them, smiling in welcome.

"Good day!" she said heartily. "I'm Madeleine Surrey. Dr. Marshal is waiting in his office to speak to you before we see Angela." She noticed the children in the truck. "My, who have we got here?"

Beebee opened one eye and spat out, "Just so you know, I'm not freaking related to the crazy lady." She shut both eyes tightly and pretended to go back to sleep.

Mary inhaled sharply and made the introductions. "The pleasant girl in front is Beatrice Gibb. She's not a relative by blood, as she so eloquently noted."

Madeleine smiled widely.

"In the back seat we have Jordie Gibb. He's Beatrice's half-brother. Their mother is Grayson Gibb's second wife."

Jordie waved. "Hi, Madeleine. A girl in my school has that name!"

"I hope she's nice."

"She totally is," he assured.

"And this" — Mary pointed to Evie — "is Evangeline Gibb. Angela is her mother."

Evie smiled at Madeleine. "Hello. Pleased to meet you."

Beebee mimicked Evie from under her hoodie. "Hel-lo. Pleased to mee-eet you."

Nobody commented.

Madeleine had a phone with her, and she stepped away to chat into it privately.

Jordie whispered, "Maybe she won't let us in now, because of Beebee."

"Fine," sneered Beebee. "Let's ditch this nuthouse."

Secretly, Evie wouldn't have been upset to turn around and go home.

Madeleine returned to the truck. "Shall we go in?"

"I'm not moving!" Beebee howled. "I'm tired and I'm staying in the truck."

"Not a problem," said Madeleine. "I've asked Bonnie Waters to stay with you."

"I don't need a babysitter!"

"Rules are rules. We don't allow unescorted visitors on the property."

As Madeleine spoke, a pretty young woman appeared beside her, a little out of breath. She looked to be in her midtwenties, Evie guessed, and had a sparkle in her eyes.

"Hi, Beatrice. I'm Bonnie."

"Go away," Beebee yawned. "Leave me alone."

Bonnie laughed. "Hate me all you like, and please yell and scream. Bring it on. It's good for my training."

Beebee looked shocked. "You're a psycho. Gran Mary! You can't leave me with a psycho!"

Madeleine ignored her and spoke to the others. "Can we go now? The doctor is waiting."

Mary, Jordie, and Evie did as they were told, leaving a screaming Beebee and an enthusiastic Bonnie alone to sort things out. Evie glanced back. Beebee was red in the face and yelling, but she had no doubt that Bonnie could handle her.

They followed Madeleine through the front doors and along a wide corridor, straight into the middle of the building, where there was a covered courtyard. *It's like a huge wheel*, Evie thought, *with four halls leading from a hub, like spokes.*

They stopped at a door that faced the round inner space. Evie noticed a big mirror beside it, built into the wall. She looked around and noticed three other offices that looked the same, all facing the glass-roofed courtyard, each one set between two halls.

Madeleine knocked lightly.

"Come in!"

She opened the door wide. They entered to see the back of a tall, white-haired man who was rummaging through the papers on his desk.

"Oh," Mary gasped.

"What, Gran Mary?"

Mary shook her head. Her face had turned pink.

Madeleine said, "Dr. Edwin Marshal, I'd like to introduce you to Mary Parson, and Evangeline and Jordie Gibb." She closed the door behind her as she left.

The doctor turned. Evie studied him. He looked intelligent and kind in a faded, bookish way. His steel-blue eyes rested on Mary and stayed there.

"Mary Parson. It's good to see you. It's been decades." He paused. "You look wonderful. Just the same."

"I'm in shock, Ed. I didn't expect to see you."

"I'm sorry. I had the advantage," Dr. Marshal said. "We will find time to catch up. Please sit, everyone." He walked to the far side of his desk and took his chair. "I've ordered hot drinks."

Mary sat between the two children as they listened to him.

"I'm here at the Quest on loan. They've used my services before and give me this office when I need it." Dr. Marshal sat down at his desk and continued looking for something among his papers. "Your niece, Angela, has been extremely helpful with a case I've been working on."

Judging by the heightened colour on both adults' cheeks, they knew each other better than mere acquaintances. Evie could sense a gentle tension in the air, and she stayed alert.

The doctor looked at her. "You look so much like your mother and your great-aunt. I'm sure people tell you that all the time."

"Yes, they do." Evie blushed, ignoring his mistake about Gran Mary. She hated blushing. She let her hair fall over her face.

"It's a compliment," said Dr. Marshall. "Red-haired beauty certainly runs in your family."

Jordie grinned. "Beebee thinks red hair is horrible."
Everybody looked at him.

"But I like it!" Jordie was defensive. "Just saying."

Dr. Marshal laughed. "I like it, too." He got down to business. "Now, you came to visit Angela. I'm happy to tell you that she's doing remarkably well. Everyone here respects her and likes her a lot. Including me. I can say that we feel positive about her chances of recovery from her opioid addiction."

"That's so good to hear," Mary said with relief in her voice. Evie felt her heart lighten.

"Now, before we go see her, I want to discuss another matter." Dr. Marshal picked up a sheet of paper. "Ah, here it is."

From where Evie was sitting, it looked like a photocopy of a police report.

There was a tap on the door, and Madeleine entered with a tray. On it were two mugs of hot chocolate and two of coffee, with a small sugar bowl and a milk pitcher. "I'm sorry to interrupt."

"Not at all. Thank you, Madeleine. Just what we need."

Once everyone had been served, Dr. Marshal spoke again. "Yesterday morning, Angela said she urgently needed to get to a phone. She didn't feel she could tell the staff what it was about, and therefore they wouldn't allow her to make the call. Rules, you know." His eyebrow lifted. "So she tried to escape."

Evie listened carefully to his every word.

"Normally, it would've stopped there. She would have been put in the secure wing, and the length of her stay would have been increased." He paused. "But a very astute young intern, Bonnie Waters, brought this matter to my attention. She was one of my students and knows my field."

Bonnie was the one out in the truck with Beebee, Evie remembered.

"I'll keep this short and simple." Dr. Marshal rested his elbows on the table. "Angela was tutoring a troubled young patient from the youth wing, and the girl shared some distressing secrets with her. That night, the girl committed suicide."

Evie inhaled sharply. Mary took her hand and one of Jordie's.

Dr. Marshal rubbed his temples. "After the girl killed herself, Angela felt compelled to break the confidence. She told Bonnie a little of what the girl had said. Bonnie got in touch with me, and I came here as soon as I could." He indicated the messy desk. "Angela has since told me more."

He put his elbows on the table and clasped his hands. "Her information gets us closer to exposing a society of young girls whose influence has resulted in one death, one suicide, and, most recently, one hospitalization."

Evie was utterly gobsmacked. "Stacey Linn."

Dr. Marshal leaned in closer. "Do you know her?"

"No, but I heard the Amber Alert yesterday, and then I found her in the woods when I was out riding, totally by chance. Actually, my dog found her. At first I thought she was dead. Later Officer Katrina Summers told me it was Stacey Linn."

"What else do you know? Any more names?"

"Cynthia Maris-Stapleton?" Evie whispered, then covered her mouth. Had she jumped to another conclusion?

Dr. Marshal squinted at her. "Tell me all you know."

"Okay." Evie blinked. "I found Stacey Linn in Caledon, but there's this Newmarket connection that keeps coming up, including with the other girl who died before.

Cynthia's family moved to Caledon from Newmarket. Beebee's involved somehow, because we rescued her today from MMS, the farm Cynthia's family owns now. And Doctor, my mother wouldn't be so desperate to get to a phone unless it was connected to our family."

"And Beebee is Beatrice?"

"Yes. Beatrice Gibb."

The doctor nodded. "You have a good picture of the situation, Evangeline, and your suspicions are not without merit. Your stepsister, Beatrice, could be very helpful to us."

"She won't help!" exclaimed Jordie. "She'll tell you to mind your own freaking business."

"Jordie!" said Mary.

"No, I mean that's what *Beebee* will say! Not me!"

They laughed at his earnestness, lightening the mood in the room. Jordie seemed quite relieved that they found him funny.

Evie asked, "How much does Beebee have to do with all this?"

"The fact that she called you for help indicates that she's new to it. She hasn't gone underground into their world."

"That's good," Evie said. "Cynthia is in Florida right now, looking for a new horse. Beebee likes her, but it seems there was a mean girl who took charge while Cynthia was away."

"There's a power structure," said Dr. Marshal. "That girl would be Cynthia's designated lieutenant, and she wouldn't do a thing without Cynthia's orders."

"So Cynthia seems nice, but isn't?"

Dr. Marshal exhaled. "Cynthia Maris-Stapleton has some very deep problems."

Evie put something together in her mind. "Is Bonnie Waters gathering information from Beebee now?"

Dr. Marshal smiled. "You're very smart. I want you on our team." He offered his right hand across the desk.

"I already am." Evie reached out with her right hand, and they shook. She felt ready to take on the world.

"Now, are we ready to see Angela?" asked Dr. Marshal.

They rose from their chairs.

"Doctor, you called my mother Gran Mary's neice," Evie said. "My mother isn't her niece. She's her daughter."

"Evie," Mary said, looking a little uncomfortable. "Dr. Marshal and I haven't seen each other in a long time."

Evie knew she'd spoken out of turn. "I'm sorry, Gran Mary. I didn't mean to …"

Dr. Marshal looked confused. "I thought Angela's parents were Ted and Alicia." He looked at Mary. "I wish I'd been able to get to your brother's funeral. I was interning at the Mayo and couldn't get away. It was terrible, that crash. Alicia was a wonderful person, and Ted was a great guy. He was my hero in school."

Then he tilted his head and turned back to Evie. "Why did you say that Angela is Mary's daughter?"

Evie blushed again. She repeated, "I'm sorry, Gran Mary. It's your story to tell. I shouldn't have —"

"No, Evie. Don't apologize. It's not a secret anymore. I would've told Ed anyway. Evie's quite correct. Angela is my daughter, I'm proud to say."

Evie watched Dr. Marshal process this new information. His brow furrowed.

"You would've been a teenager when she was born."

"I was."

126

"Was it the year my family moved to Vancouver?"

"Around that time, yes."

"We'd broken up."

"It made sense. Long-distance relationships rarely work."

"I wanted to be independent and free." He smiled. "But I wasn't free for long. I married the first girl I saw on campus. We had two daughters." His expression grew serious. "Lynn died of cancer in January of last year."

"I'm very sorry, Ed," said Mary.

"And I'm sorry, too, Mary. I never knew about your child."

Mary smiled softly. "Nobody knew. I was young and stubborn. Ted and Alicia really wanted a baby, but had a lot of trouble conceiving. It made sense to me."

"It makes perfect sense." He stopped speaking and plunked down in the nearest chair.

Mary and Dr. Marshal had dated in high school, Evie realized. The tension in the room was becoming tangible. She opened the door a little to let in some air.

"Good idea, Evie," Mary said. "Can you and Jordie wait in the hall? We'll only be a minute."

Evie and Jordie went out and closed the door behind them.

"Why did you do that?" Jordie whispered. "Now we can't listen to them."

"I know. I'm sorry."

Just then, they saw Bonnie and Beebee walking toward them. Beebee glowered when she recognized them, but only slightly. *Big improvement*, Evie thought.

"Hi. We're coming to talk to Dr. Marshal," said Bonnie.

"Ah," said Evie. "They're discussing something private."

"No problem," Bonnie said. "So far, so good?"

"Yeah," answered Evie, observing her stepsister. "But not as good as you. What did you do to her?"

Beebee was making faces at her reflection in the window. Bonnie laughed. "Hey, they can see you."

"No way," said Beebee, then halted. "I can't see in. How can they see out?"

"It's a one-way mirror. It's reflective on this side, but transparent on the other."

"So crazy people can't see what the doctors are doing?"

"No, to entertain the doctors when crazy people make faces."

Beebee laughed, forgetting to be cynical for a minute.

The door opened. Mary walked out first, followed by Dr. Marshal. "Bonnie, please take Jordie and Beatrice to the cafeteria. I highly recommend the french fries."

Jordie spun around. "Count me in! French fries with lots of ketchup!"

Dr. Marshal and Bonnie spoke briefly and then Bonnie took the kids down the corridor to the cafeteria. Jordie hopped and skipped along the hall while Beebee tried her best to be cool.

Evie followed Mary and Dr. Marshal down the hall to Angela's room. She felt her stomach tighten into knots.

Surprise awaited her when Angela opened the door. Evie's mother looked radiant and happy, calm and poised. Her copper hair seemed thicker and had been cut to an attractive chin length. Her eyes and skin gleamed with health. Evie was glad to see that Angela had gained a little weight, which ironed out some of her wrinkles. Gone was the haggard look of a person living on the street. Evie fervently hoped that look was gone forever.

"You look beautiful, Mom!" she said, awash with relief.

"I'm so happy to see you, my sweet Evangeline."

They hugged for a long moment.

Evie began to cry. She was surprised at the depth of her emotion, and she wiped her cheeks with her hand. "I miss you, Mom. Can you come home soon?"

Angela nodded. "I hope so. It's up to Dr. West."

"And me," Dr. Marshal interrupted. "I get a vote, too, and it's looking good."

"Thank you, doctor," said Angela. "I'm very grateful to you for believing me when I ran away to find a phone. I wanted to warn my mother about Beebee's involvement in the group."

Evie noticed that everybody had tears in their eyes, even Dr. Marshal, who was gazing at Angela approvingly.

Then it hit her. Could Edwin Marshal possibly be Angela's father? Was the timing right? That would make him Evie's grandfather. She'd never had a grandfather before.

She stared at him, looking for a family resemblance.

Dr. Marshal caught her staring and said, "Evangeline? Can we talk for a minute while your mother and grandmother catch up? I'll bring you back, I promise."

Evie nodded and followed him back down the hall to his office. Once they got settled, he said, "We need to make a plan and act before another child dies. Let's go over what you know."

Evie told him how she'd found the girl in the woods, what Brent Keir had told her, and the few details she'd gleaned from Beebee, including the fact that Cynthia had asked all the girls to come to Caledon and that Beebee had not yet been initiated. Evie confessed to having become a nuisance to the police.

Dr. Marshal nodded and encouraged her as she spoke. When she was finished, he said, "Good intelligence. And you say your friend is moving in as a groom?"

"Yes. Yolanda Schmits. She's totally reliable."

He made another note. "We couldn't have set this up so well if we'd tried. Anything else?"

"I think that's all. I'll tell you if I remember more."

"You're going to MMS tomorrow morning?"

"Yes. What would you like me to do?"

"The best thing for now is to just keep your eyes open."

"What about Beebee? You said she could be helpful."

Dr. Marshal rubbed his forehead. "I thought so at first, and Bonnie told me that she wants to help. But it's too soon for her. She might get swept back in. My instinct is to keep her hidden."

"Hidden? Is she in danger?"

"The danger begins when Cynthia returns. She cannot tolerate people leaving, and she will try to bring Beatrice back in. It'll be tough on the girl she left in charge, who allowed Beatrice to escape from their grip before being initiated. Very tough."

"How did you get Beebee to agree to help?"

"It was Bonnie. She showed Beatrice how she's being used by this group, and that these people are not her friends."

"And Beebee believed her?"

"You've asked the thousand-dollar question. Never underestimate the strength of a group mentality. Beatrice will likely want to go back to them at some point — but what works in her favour is that she got a taste of what they're doing and she didn't like it."

"When does Cynthia get back?"

"I understand that she's coming home to compete in the Steeplechase on Saturday."

"That gives me a good reason to watch the MMS. Not that I needed one. It looks like a really exciting day."

Dr. Marshal smiled. All the lines on his face smiled along with his mouth. 'You're a committed investigator, Evangeline."

"Thanks!" Evie said, pleased. "Now I have some questions."

"Fire away."

"You said that Cynthia has some deep problems. What exactly are they?"

Dr. Marshal sighed. "It's very complicated and not at all clear. I could speculate for days on her family history, her need for control, her hunger for attention, her yearning to belong, but until I have a chance to really probe, I'd only be guessing. Sorry to disappoint you. What's the second question?"

"What is Dr. Maris-Stapleton famous for?"

"He's one of the best heart surgeons in North America and has become an international leader in heart disease research."

"Part B of question two: Why is he so rich?"

Dr. Marshal whistled softly and raised his eyebrows. "He is very rich, you're quite right. He developed and patented a drug called Adenosinol, which slows the heart almost to a stop while a patient is in surgery. It's had an enormously positive effect on surgical outcomes." He paused and checked his watch. "Another question?"

"Yes. If you and the police know as much as you do, why not swoop in and arrest Cynthia now? Wouldn't that stop kids from getting hurt?"

"Ah. Let me explain our justice system. It's one thing to know something or have a good hunch about it, and it's another thing to prove it beyond a reasonable doubt. We must build the case and line up the evidence. We cannot get anything wrong, not one thing. If we do, it all comes tumbling down, and Cynthia will be free to do it again."

Evie nodded. "With another group of girls. I understand. And you and the police are working together to build the case?"

"The police are interested in the how, when, and where. I'm interested in the why. Anything else?" Dr. Marshal looked at his watch again and began to tidy his papers. Obviously, he needed to get back to work.

Evie badly wanted to ask if he was her grandfather, but the words stopped at her lips. She felt herself blushing again.

"What, child? I don't bite."

"I can't. It's too personal, and we just met."

"Then it can wait," Dr. Marshal said with good humour. "But my guess is that it's about me and your grandmother. We dated. That's all I'll say." He rose. "Now, back to the case. When you have something to report, use this." He handed Evie a phone. "Press 1, and it'll ring through to me. If I don't answer, leave a message. I'll get it, even if I don't respond right away."

"Is there anything special you want me to look for at MMS?"

"Gossip relating to Cynthia, her animals, and her friends."

Evie remembered Brent telling her that Cynthia had trouble keeping horses sound. "Her animals?"

"Yes. Her activities concern animals as well as people."

Evie's mind was spinning as she tried to think what that could possibly mean.

"Let's get back to your mother. I know she'll want to visit with you." Dr. Marshal opened the door for both of them. "A word of caution at MMS," he said. "Don't get ahead of yourself. Don't jump to conclusions until you've gathered all the facts. I learned that many years ago, and I have to keep learning it."

Evie nodded sheepishly. "I tend to do that."

Dr. Marshal laughed loudly. "I noticed."

Dark Secrets

The cruelest of individuals depend a great deal on the puzzlement of others.

— Javier Marias

On the way home from the Quest, Evie sat quietly in the back seat of the truck beside Jordie, who was busy with a game on Mary's phone. Up front, Beebee and Mary chatted amiably about their visit, a big improvement from the trip there.

Angela had looked wonderful, thought Evie. She seemed so much better in every way than before she'd gone to rehab. If everything continued to go well, she could come home later that week. And Evie would be very glad. She wasn't worried about it anymore. She crossed her fingers and made a silent prayer.

When they'd had a chance to talk privately, her mother had told Evie more about the girl who committed suicide, whose name had been Heidi Beale.

Heidi had told Angela that she'd been initiated into Cynthia's select group of friends, referred to as the Circle, and that it was a big honour. Her first task was to help dump the body of the girl who'd accidentally died in

Newmarket. That experience had scared her so much that she hadn't wanted to be part of the Circle anymore. She'd run away and gotten help. Two big no-nos in Cynthia's book, which caused Heidi to live in constant fear.

Heidi had firmly believed that Cynthia could enter her brain and force her do something dreadful to pay for her betrayal. Even kill herself in some ghastly way. Tragically, Heidi had made this prediction come true by committing suicide in the washroom.

A sinister picture was emerging, Evie mused. Cynthia Maris-Stapleton was small in stature, but wielded frightening clout. She was a few years older than the other girls in her class. They all believed that she possessed magical powers, and anyone who disobeyed her orders, no matter what vile thing she'd asked them to do, would die.

Evie shuddered.

"Why so glum back there, Evie?" asked Beebee.

"Just thinking."

"You're scowling like an old man."

Evie turned the tables. "Why so chipper, Beebee?"

Beebee's eyes narrowed. "Are you insulting me?"

"I'm complimenting you. It's nice to see you cheerful."

"I want to be a detective. Bonnie Waters said I'd make a good one. She gave me lessons in tailing a target."

Evie didn't want to dampen her stepsister's new-found sense of purpose by mentioning Dr. Marshal's reluctance to get her involved. "Who's your target?"

"That mean girl. Her name is Althea Presley, but sometimes they call her Thea, sometimes Al."

"So how would you tail her?"

"I can't divulge." Beebee made a zipping motion over her lips.

Whatever Bonnie had said to Beebee, it had changed her attitude for the better, Evie thought. She hoped it would last.

"This afternoon Beebee and I are going to train Paragon for the MMS show," Mary said.

"The Steeplechase?" asked Evie.

"No! That's another level altogether. The hack class. Maybe even the point nine hunters."

"That's great."

"Do you want to take Kazzam, Evie?" asked Mary. "You could do the metre jumper."

"Why not! We can go together. Beebee will love Paragon."

"And he'll love me," Beebee said. "I have perfect form."

"What am *I* going to do?" asked Jordie wistfully.

Mary laughed. "You'll be riding Christieloo."

"Yay! She's the prettiest one, with her white mane and tail!"

"Yes, she is. She's a very sweet mare."

"Can I ride in the show?"

"If you work hard."

"Cool! Wait 'til I tell my friends."

Beebee snapped, "You don't have any friends."

"I do, too!" he retorted.

"Do not!"

"Do, too!"

"Kids!" Mary spoke sharply. "Enough! I have little enough patience with this head cold. We won't do anything if you squabble. We're almost home."

Magpie and the Labs came bounding up as the truck stopped at the farmhouse. They all got out and went in the mudroom door.

"Evie, can you help me get the horses ready?" asked Mary.

"Sure," she replied. "Can I use your computer after that?"

"Homework?"

"Yes. If I'm going to start training tomorrow, I want to get all my work finished."

"Absolutely."

"And I want to do some googling, too," Evie admitted.

"Googling?"

"I want to find out about what Dr. Marshal does."

"Hmm." Mary nodded thoughtfully. "He's a psychiatrist and a criminologist, but I'm curious about his specialty, too."

As soon as everybody had changed into riding clothes, they went out to the horse field with halters and shanks. The day had warmed up so much that they wore sweatshirts and no overcoats.

"I've never done this before," said Beebee. "Gone into a field full of horses, I mean. Isn't it dangerous?"

Mary answered, "If you bring food, they might crowd you, but these horses are anything but dangerous. Don't worry." She pointed to the tall bay gelding. "That's Paragon. Go up to him quietly with your hand extended."

Beebee squeezed her eyes shut. "What if he bites me?"

"Why would he bite you?" asked Evie.

"My pony, Alphonse, always did."

Evie tried to choose her words carefully. "You had an unfortunate relationship with Alphonse. Paragon is gentle, and has no reason to hurt you."

"Alphonse had no reason, either."

Evie decided to tell the truth. "Come on, Beebee. You were horrible to him. You were impatient. He never knew what you wanted. You kicked him and hurt his mouth with your rough hands. He hated you, but you hated him, too. Admit it."

"He was stupid! Kerry made me ride him, but I would've won more ribbons on Casper."

"If you treat Paragon the same way you treated Alphonse, he'll become just as bad. And he's much, much bigger, so be nice to him."

Beebee stared at Paragon and made a decision. "Here, Paragon. Come to Beebee! Nice horsey."

Mary and Evie laughed quietly as they watched Beebee creep forward slowly. Paragon was curious. He stood and watched her, then put his nose right into the offered halter.

"There!" Beebee exclaimed. "Did you see that? He likes me!"

"You're off to a good start," Mary encouraged.

Jordie had put a halter on Christieloo and was waiting with her at the gate. "Are you guys coming or not?" he called.

Beebee and Jordie led Paragon and Christieloo up to the barn. Kazzam and Bendigo remained in the field, nosing around for grass that had been hidden under the snow all winter.

Mary showed the kids how to groom the horses and pick the dirt and stones out of their feet. The coats they'd grown over the winter were falling out, so there was a growing pile of hair on the stable floor. Evie helped them fit the saddle pads and saddles on the horses' backs, then she attached the girths and tightened them so the saddles wouldn't slip. Once the bridles were on the horses' heads and all the buckles were fastened, the two animals were ready to ride.

"I've never ever done that before," said Beebee. "Kerry always had Alphonse ready when I showed up."

"Maybe that was part of the problem," said Evie. "Alphonse had no idea who you were."

"He was so stupid he had no idea of anything," Beebee retorted.

Evie raised her eyebrows. "Oh, really?"

"Duh. Really. Dumb, dumb, dumb."

Evie felt the need to defend the pony. "Remember when you won the junior hunter class at Palgrave in the finals?"

"Yes. I had perfect form."

"As soon as you left the ring, what did Alphonse do?"

"He bucked me off. I hate him! It hurt."

"That shows you how smart he is."

"Smart? That's how stupid he is!"

"No. He's so smart he figured out how to behave in the ring, but outside the ring, his job was done and he could get rid of you."

"He knew that?" Beebee was skeptical.

"Absolutely. And then he got away from you when you were leading him back to the trailer. You were so mad."

"Yes, I was mad! In front of all those people? It was so embarrassing! I would've killed him if I'd caught him."

"Exactly. He knew that. That shows he's smart."

"But you walked right up and caught him! I'm still mad about that, Evie. You made me look bad."

Mary intervened before Evie could answer. "Beebee gets your point, Evie. Alphonse is a smart pony. Let's move on. Come outside, and let's get you up."

Beebee pouted. "Do I have to have a lesson at the same time as Jordie? I'm way advanced, and I have —"

"Perfect form?" Evie finished the sentence for her.

Mary shot Evie a glance. "Behave yourself."

"I've had lots of lessons with Kerry," said Jordie. "I can trot and canter and everything."

"Good." Mary held Christieloo at the mounting block. Evie helped Jordie into the saddle. She adjusted his stirrups and positioned his feet correctly so his weight was on the balls of his feet, then she led him away while Gran Mary helped Beebee.

"Kids, follow me into the riding ring," said Mary. "There's a bit of mud, so keep to this end. Evie, can you stick around for a few minutes until they get confident?"

"Sure." Evie sat on the top rail of the fence and watched.

Mary stood in the middle of the ring. She instructed them on correct posture and hand position as the horses walked around the fenceline. She asked them to halt and then reverse their direction.

Five minutes later, Mary asked them to pick up a trot. Evie was pleasantly surprised to see how well Jordie was doing. He appeared to have excellent balance and a feel for the horse. Beebee rode more awkwardly, bouncing a little with sloppy reins, but Paragon knew his job so well that it didn't matter.

Mary waved. "Off you go, Evie! Thanks for your help. I think we're good here, don't you?"

"Yes! You guys are doing great!"

"Who looks better?" asked Beebee. "Me or him?"

Evie grinned. "You both look good, but only one of you has perfect form!" She pointed at Jordie, which made him grin.

"Get out of here, Evie," warned Mary. "Google away!"

Evie went into the house and got herself set up at Gran Mary's desk with her school books and Mary's computer. Her plan was to do the French grammar homework first, and then write the essay on *Lord of the Flies*. She would work on the history reading before bed. If she read a little every night this week, she'd be able to finish the reading and get the questions done on time.

But her curiosity was burning. She wouldn't be able to concentrate on her schoolwork until she'd found out more about Dr. Marshal and his specialty.

Evie connected to the internet and typed in *Dr. Edwin Marshal*. Immediately the screen showed twenty-five hits. She scrolled down newspaper headlines and books he'd written, but first she went to Wikipedia. She learned that he was a medical doctor and had a Ph.D. in criminal psychology. Police forces called him when they needed his assistance, and he appeared in court to educate juries about cult psychology.

Cults, Evie noted with a chill.

The most recent newspaper story was about the girl who'd been murdered in Newmarket. Her name was Patricia Price. Dr. Marshal had suspected that the crime was connected to a cult. He'd insisted on doing a complete blood analysis, which had revealed that a drug available to medical practitioners only had been found in the girl's system. He'd predicted more deaths.

Turns out he was right, Evie thought grimly.

His published research papers were lengthy and detailed, and Evie scanned them for information.

He'd written an article about what makes a cult different from an ordinary club, religion, clique, or group of friends who think and dress alike. He addressed the controversy around the use of the term *cult*. Another article discussed the different types of cults and how some are more destructive than others. Even a family can be defined as a cult if there is a narcissistic parent who controls the family with an iron grip. A charismatic leader who demands total obedience creates a cult when other people are compelled to obey.

Why are people drawn to cults? she wondered.

Dr. Marshal wrote that nobody is immune, but some are more vulnerable. If a person feels unappreciated and neglected, they might search for a place to belong. Such people are easily spotted and drawn in by groups such as Scientology, the Solar Temple, and religious groups with reinterpreted scripture. Others who might have believed that they would never become a cult member can simply fall into the wrong group of friends and slowly be indoctrinated into the mindset without being aware of what's happening. They would, in fact, deny it strongly.

Evie read about different types of mind control. Through various tactics, sometimes harsh, sometimes loving, people are made to feel that they're thinking for themselves, when in reality, their thoughts are being programmed. Dr. Marshal warned against assuming all cults are the same, since there are as many types as there are personalities of leaders.

Interesting stuff, thought Evie. And what about the leaders? What kind of person started a cult? It came down to a combination of charismatic personality, fringe beliefs, narcissism, and a taste for violence.

She read:

What stands out about these individuals is that they were all pathologically narcissistic.

They all had an overabundant belief that they were special and that they had to be revered. They demanded perfect loyalty from followers, they overvalued themselves and devalued those around them, and they were intolerant of criticism. Above all, they did not like being questioned or challenged.

Another article caught her attention:

Almost always, a new member is required to submit to degradation that will be used as blackmail if he or she tries to leave the group. Humiliation with family and peers keeps inside knowledge from getting out. Documented initiation rituals are common as well, which bind the members to the leader in the same way.

In every case, secrecy, obedience, silence, and fear are paramount. The indoctrination happens in incremental stages, binding members more and more tightly until they feel they have no personal autonomy. There is a loss of freedom. They cease to think independently and feel they have no choice but to stay.

Evie sat in front of the computer, numbed by what she'd read. At the Quest, Dr. Marshal had told her two things. One, that Evie should watch out for anything unusual regarding people or animals, and two, that Cynthia's activities concerned both animals and people. How did animals fit in?

Evie let this percolate in her brain while she completed the fifty questions of the French grammar assignment. It felt good to check it off her list. One down, two to go.

Keep going, she told herself, and opened *Lord of the Flies*, written in 1954 by William Golding. The assignment was to write five hundred words explaining why the story was still relevant today. Evie's toes tapped under the desk while she thought.

She'd intended to write her essay from a feminist point of view and explore if this story would have gone the same way if it had been British *girls* whose airplane had crashed on an isolated island. She'd planned to argue that girls would've had a much better shot at self-governance, and that the whole thing wouldn't have deteriorated into such a horrible power struggle and ultimate mess.

But the situation with Beebee had changed her perspective. The Circle was a group of girls, and things had already deteriorated into a horrible mess.

So, why was the novel relevant today? Her new knowledge about cult dynamics gave her a different angle. The story was about a clash between two factions with two different leaders. Power politics between people, whether male or female, are the same today as they were all those decades ago, and human nature shows its ugly side when unchecked.

That would do the trick.

Evie went to work. It was difficult to condense her concept into five hundred words, but in an hour the essay was finished. With a grand flourish she checked it off. Done.

The history assignment was about Sir Winston Churchill, who was the British Prime Minister during the Second World War. She would begin her reading that evening.

Evie was putting away her books when she had a nagging thought about Cynthia Maris-Stapleton. Heidi had told Angela that Cynthia was a few years older than the others. Had she failed some grades? If not, where had she been?

She opened Gran Mary's computer again and googled her, not expecting anything more than her horse show results, which came up first. Cynthia had done quite well, but this was interesting ... there was a big gap in her attendance at shows. Then, Evie looked into her education. There were no records of Cynthia for two years, until she showed up again the previous year. Interesting.

Mary and the kids bustled in, chattering about how well they'd done and how Mary had made them clean the tack and do all the chores, including feeding and watering.

"I never knew that was how you did it!" said Beebee as she unzipped the chaps she had borrowed from Evie. "I thought bridles stayed that way all the time."

"And horses clean their own stalls?" Evie asked. "And they brush themselves 'til they shine?"

"Easy, Evie," said Mary. "Beebee is learning, so don't make fun of her."

"Sorry. I can't help it."

"Old habits die hard, just like old cowhands," said Jordie.

Everyone looked at him in surprise.

"I heard it on *Heartland*," he said. "Which reminds me. Can we watch television until dinner?"

"Sure," said Mary. "Take off your boots and go get cleaned up. Dinner will be very simple tonight. Tomorrow I really have to get groceries. And some more cold medicine. It's really helping."

While the kids were washing up, Evie and Gran Mary organized dinner. Mary quietly asked, "What did you find out about Dr. Marshal?"

"He specializes in cults."

"Really?"

"Yes. I thought cults were all the same. Witchy stuff. But there are lots of other kinds, like so-called religions and even families. I printed up some articles for you. It's all about a strong, dominant leader with followers who obey, no questions asked."

"Fascinating. I'll take a look."

"I knew Beebee was in with a bad crowd, but I'd never have thought of it as a cult."

"A 'bad' crowd?"

"You're right. It's a terrifying crowd. Kids form cliques all the time. This is much worse."

"*Cult* is a scary word. But not many cliques have fatalities."

The phone rang.

Beebee had just come out of the bathroom, and she picked it up. "Hello?" Her expression hardened. "You don't care about me anyway, Mom, so why are you mad?" she snapped. "Go back to your Pinot, or whatever you're drinking, okay? I'm fine without you. Better, in fact!" She shot a look at Mary. "Yeah, she's here. Unlike you."

Sullenly, Beebee passed the phone to Gran Mary and stomped over to the couch.

"Hello, Paulina?" Mary looked startled and then said, "Yes, of course you're right. We should've let you know. I'm sorry." There was another pause while Paulina spoke. Mary replied, "You can call here anytime, too, Paulina. Again, I'm very sorry."

146

Evie stopped listening. Instead of thanking Gran Mary for looking after Jordie and searching for Beebee *and* rescuing her, Paulina was blasting her for not having called earlier!

As soon as Mary hung up, Evie whispered, "Beebee was already missing and in a cult when Paulina left the country. She's the one who should apologize!"

Mary made a frustrated grunt. "I don't pretend to understand Paulina, but she was very worried about Beebee, and we forgot to call her. She has a point."

"You are so reasonable," grumbled Evie.

Beebee had curled up on the couch with her scrawny arms wrapped around her bony legs. She looked unhappy and small. Evie had only the slightest idea of what Beebee was going through. The conversation with her mother could only have made things worse.

Feeling sympathetic, Evie sat down in the chair beside her. "Hey, Beebee. How're you doing?"

Beebee glowered at her and rolled her eyes sarcastically.

"Right," said Evie. "I guess things look pretty bad."

"Why did you come get me?" Beebee blurted harshly. "What's in it for you? It's not as if you like me or anything."

Evie thought about that. "You're my little sister, and you needed me. You'd come for me if I called you."

Beebee's eyes overflowed with tears. "I'm not sure about that. That's just it! I'm not very nice."

"I'll need you one day, and you'll prove yourself wrong."

"Maybe. I don't know. I try. I was nice to all my friends in Newmarket. That turned out great. Phuh."

"And they were nice to you?"

"Yeah. We were a really tight group. It was great."

"You were new. And, I guess, glad to make friends."

"Hey, I'm not embarrassed or anything. They're the cool girls. Everybody wanted in."

Evie could see how dangerous and appealing that group might have looked, especially to a new kid at school. "Who's your best friend?"

"Stacey."

"Stacey Linn? The girl I found in the woods?"

Beebee nodded. Her mouth formed a sad pout. "We hitchhiked here together."

Holy, Evie thought. "Do you know what happened to her? How she got to the woods?"

Beebee didn't answer, but her eyes welled again. She murmured, "I ... I ... I hope she's okay."

"She's doing better. I think she'll be fine," said Evie kindly. "I didn't know she was a friend of yours." She glanced at Mary, but her grandmother was busy in the kitchen, not listening.

"She is. I met her the first week of school. She's how I met Cynthia. It was a big deal. Like, huge. She pulled strings for me."

"Really," Evie said. The structure of the cult was becoming clear to her. It was an honour to become part of this clique, just like Heidi had told Angela. "How well do you know Cynthia?"

"Not well. She's kind of like the queen. Her clothes are the coolest and so-o-o expensive. And she's beautiful. Everybody thinks so."

"I've never met her."

"Trust me. Mirrors are her friends." Beebee put her left hand to her lips to hide a smile. "In more ways than one."

Evie remembered the tattoo on Stacey's inner wrist and tried to check Beebee's arm, but couldn't see. She

148

said, "I googled Cynthia. She was off the radar for a couple of years."

Beebee shrugged. "She talks about learning things at juvie."

"Juvenile detention?"

"Yeah. Voodoo magic and crazy cool stuff. We call ourselves the coven."

The coven? Evie thought. "Is Cynthia a witch?"

"Nah. It just makes us look badass and freaks people out."

"So, are you part of the coven until you get accepted into the Circle?"

Beebee's eyes flew wide open. "I never said anything about the Circle!" Evie noticed how frightened she looked. "Who told you?"

"Heidi told my mother about it at the Quest."

"Heidi talks too much. *Talked.*" Beebee's eyes became slits. "Just so you know, everyone who Cyn *invites* is part of the Circle, including *me*, before and after initiation. Duh."

"Oh." Then Evie asked, "So why do you call yourselves the coven?"

"Hey, stupid, enough of your stupid questions. I told you already. It's what we call ourselves to sound badass." She pointed at Evie with a shaking finger and lowered her voice. "Nobody knows about the Circle, so you keep your bloody mouth shut. Go away." She covered her head with her arms.

"Stacey has a tattoo. Do you?"

Beebee's head shot up and her mouth dropped open in shock. "She was initiated and I wasn't! Shut up! And go away!"

I guess that's all for now, Evie thought with certainty. Dr. Marshall had warned her that Beebee's loyalties might be conflicted. Evie saw that she'd pushed the limit, and she hoped it hadn't been too far.

The phone rang again. Evie jumped up. "Hello?"

"Is that my babe?"

"Hey, Mark! Just a minute." She turned to Mary.

Mary smiled and answered Evie's question before she asked it. "Dinner will wait. Say hi to Mark from me."

Evie took the phone into her room and got settled into her pillows. "Mark, you'll never guess what's going on here, and you'll never guess what I'm doing tomorrow."

Training

False words are not only evil in themselves, but they infect the soul with evil.

— Socrates

At a quarter to eight the next morning, they loaded Kazzam into the trailer, fully tacked. Evie was excited and nervous about her lesson with Piers Anders. Beebee and Jordie sat in the back eating orange slices and toast with peanut butter and honey.

"If Piers thinks Evie is a good rider, he'll be amazed when he sees me ride," Beebee said with her mouth half-full.

Jordie grinned. "He'll be amazed … that you don't fall off!"

Beebee shoved him so hard that Jordie lost his grip on his gooey toast. "It's your fault! You clean it up!" he yelled.

"Children!" Mary scolded. "Enough!" She rubbed her forehead with her right hand as she drove.

Evie remembered that Gran Mary still had a cold and wasn't used to having kids around. "Hey, guys," she said to distract them, "when's Gran Mary going to give you another riding lesson?"

"Today?" Jordie asked hopefully.

Beebee retorted, "I don't need lessons. I have perfect form."

"Right," said Evie. "But you and Paragon have to get used to each other before the show."

"Well, if Paragon needs lessons, that's different."

Mary smiled and said, "He does, so we'll have lessons later at Parson's Bridge."

"Yay!" cheered Jordie.

"Bor-ing." Beebee yawned theatrically.

They reached the imposing iron gates of the old Maple Mills Stables. Mary pressed the call button and waited.

A reverberating voice answered, "MMS."

"Hello, it's Mary Parson. I'm here with Evie Gibb to —"

"Yes! Piers is expecting you. Drive right up past the barn and follow the lane to the upper field. You can park there."

"Thanks."

Mary glanced at her passengers in the back seat. "We're back at Maple Mills." She drove through the gates and along the tree-lined, paved driveway past the lower paddocks and sand rings.

Beebee blanched. "I made a mistake. I shouldn't have come. I don't feel so good."

"What's wrong?" asked Mary.

"My tummy hurts."

"You probably ate too fast."

"No, I think I'm really sick. I want to go home."

Evie thought she knew her stepsister's problem. "This is the first time you've come back through those gates since Dad went to jail."

"I don't care about what happened last year. I care about what'll happen today, when Althea sees me!"

"Is Althea here?" asked Evie.

"Yeah. She and the coven live in that old house at the back. She'll capture me and punish me for running away!"

"The coven?" asked Mary.

"That's what we call it."

Mary stated slowly, "A coven is a group of witches."

"Duh, I know. Cyn's a witch. There, Evie, I said it! She's a witch! Happy now?"

Evie said, "You sound like a real badass, Beebee."

"Beebee, there's a difference between calling yourself a witch and actually practising the occult. Which is she?" Mary asked.

Jordie laughed. "That's funny! *Witch* is she! Get it? Which witch?"

"Shut up, Jordie! It's not funny," Beebee barked. "Just don't let her see me!"

"We won't," reassured Evie. "And she won't come around with Gran Mary here."

Beebee ignored her and spoke to Mary. "Can we just go home?" The girl looked agitated. "I'm scared."

Mary nodded firmly. "We'll go home as soon as we drop off Evie and Kazzam. Duck down on the floor and keep quiet. Nobody will see you."

Beebee crept onto the floor and crouched into a ball. She stayed silent as they drove past the barns and paddocks and up the hill. They parked the rig beside another truck.

As soon as Mary cut the ignition, Beebee hollered from the floor of the back seat. "Don't stop!"

Patiently, Mary said, "I won't let anybody harm you."

"Thank you," Beebee sniffed.

"Stay close to me," cooed Jordie. "I'll protect you."

Beebee reached up and punched his leg hard. "I can look after myself, idiot!"

Jordie wailed. "I don't care if they kidnap you and torture you with witchcraft!"

Mary turned around in her seat and glared. "Children! Stop fighting before I go barking mad."

"We wouldn't want that, yah?" said a man with a European accent.

Evie saw Piers Anders standing beside Gran Mary's open window. His hands were on his hips and he had a big grin on his face.

When Mary twisted around to look at him, he stared. His face registered genuine shock.

Neither spoke.

Evie noticed how red Mary's face was getting. What was going on? Thinking the adults might be able to talk if they were alone, she got out of the truck while still keeping an eye on them.

"Beebee, Jordie," whispered Evie, "come on."

"No!" Beebee whispered back. "They'll see me!"

"Suit yourself. Then we'll never find out what's going on here."

Beebee reconsidered. "The coven sleeps late. I'll stay low."

The kids tumbled out the back door on the far side and the three of them hid behind the trailer, as close as possible so they could listen.

"Who's that?" asked Jordie quietly. "And why is Gran Mary so upset?"

"That's Piers Anders, stupid," answered Beebee. "He's famous. Don't you know anything?"

"Shh," said Evie. "I can't hear what they're saying."

They hushed and listened to the adults' conversation.

"You're the grandmother I talked to yesterday?" Piers asked.

"Yes."

"Why did you not tell me it was you?"

"I guess I thought you knew."

"How could I know? Evie's name is Gibb, not Parson."

"I didn't think you'd remember me, Piers."

"Not remember *you*?"

"I didn't know what you'd think of me now, a little old lady with a bad cold." Her voice was subdued. Evie strained to hear.

"My, my, Mary. How could you say such a thing! Am I not a little old man myself?"

Mary and Piers chuckled together.

Jordie asked, "Were they married once, or something?"

"Hush, idiot," said Beebee.

Jordie was indignant. "I can talk if I want."

"If they hear us, they'll stop talking," Evie said.

Jordie nodded and covered his mouth with both hands.

Mary spoke next with an upbeat tone. "Well. Now you know. Evie's my granddaughter and I'm her grandmother."

"Yes, now I know." Piers paused and then said softly, "The oddest thing, Mary. When I saw her ride, when I first saw her face, she reminded me of someone, but I couldn't think who it was. Now I know. It was you."

"She has talent, Piers. Much more than I ever did."

"Let's not compare! You were intuitive and gentle and brave, just like Evie. Always the same, on a horse or not."

"Thank you." Evie heard the pleasure in Gran Mary's voice.

"So? I will not lose you again, now that you are here?"

Evie couldn't make out what was said next, only murmurs and mumbled words. She sidled closer to hear better, when Piers loudly said, "So, we begin? We get your granddaughter up in the saddle!"

Mary's door slammed shut. Evie and Jordie scurried to the back of the trailer and dropped the ramp, trying to look like they hadn't been eavesdropping.

Evie backed Kazzam out, put on her helmet and gloves, and hopped up into the saddle. She was ready to go by the time Piers had walked around the rig.

Beebee folded her arms across her chest. "Piers Anders, I'm Beatrice Gibb. I have much better form than Evie. My trainer says so, and everybody knows it. I want you to train me, too, for the March Madness show."

Mary gasped. "Beatrice! You're asking too much!"

Piers laughed heartily. "No shy children here! But I must get permission from the owner. He's very strict about his privacy."

Beebee held her ground. "I know the owner's daughter. I'm sure he'll let me."

Piers's eyes narrowed as he observed her. "Ah. You are the little sister that was hiding in the cave."

Mary said, "Piers, I apologize. We will not intrude on anyone's privacy. Jordie, Beebee, back in the truck. We'll have a lesson at Parson's Bridge."

"Why should Evie get the best trainer?" Beebee exclaimed. "It's not fair!"

"Beatrice Gibb." Mary sounded firm. "Get in the truck."

"Do you think I'm a better trainer than Mary Parson?" Piers asked Beebee. "My, my. You are very wrong. If you do as she says, you'll win the ribbons, yah?"

Beebee opened the truck door and climbed in. She said, "She makes me ride with Jordie. I'm much better than him. Plus, I'm a detective."

Piers raised one eyebrow. "A detective. Intriguing. Anyway, listen to your grandmother. You need no training help from me."

"She's Evie's grandmother. She's not *my* grandmother."

Piers threw his head back and laughed. "That, I guessed."

Jordie got in beside his sister. "She's not my grandmother, either, but I wish she was. She's my Cran Berry. I want to live with her and Evie forever, if my mother lets me."

Beebee gave him a dismissive look. "Our mother wouldn't miss us if we never came home. You know it's true."

From atop Kazzam's back, Evie explained to Piers, "Jordie and I have the same father, but different mothers. My mother is Angela, and theirs is Paulina."

"Ah. Mary's daughter is named Angela?"

Evie nodded. Piers turned to Mary. "You must tell me all about your life since you broke my heart."

"I broke your heart?" Mary's eyebrows were raised. She let out a small laugh. "You are chivalrous."

Piers looked puzzled. "Why? It's true."

"All the women loved you, Piers. I was just one."

"No, Mary. You were *the* one."

Evie sat quietly on Kazzam, incredulous. Dr. Marshal yesterday, and Piers Anders today. Her grandmother had secrets! Evie vowed to find them out. Most importantly, could one of these men be her grandfather?

Mary blushed and looked uncomfortable. "What time should I come back for Evie?"

"We need two hours today, not more. Good?"

"Yes. I'll come back at ten." Still flushed, Mary got behind the wheel and started the truck. Piers stood watching as she drove down the hill with the horse trailer. He seemed lost in thought.

Evie waited. Finally, she cleared her throat. "Ahem?"

Piers was startled and turned quickly. He laughed, flustered. "Sorry! We begin now?"

"I'm ready!" said Evie.

"So! Yesterday we did the coffin, the drop, the roll tops, the bank, the water, and the goose. Yes?"

"Yes!"

"Today we do the Normandy bank, the stone wall, the shark's teeth, the corner, and the skinny — where the mud has dried and the ground is good. Tomorrow we do the hedge, the bounce, the Trakehner, and the hanging log fence. Good?"

"Good!" Evie answered without hesitation, even though she had no idea what he was talking about. All she knew was that she had great confidence that Kazzam could handle anything.

Piers got onto his ATV and headed to a different area than the day before, over the hill to the south. Evie followed on Kazzam, relieved that the earth-moving machines were all gone.

At the top of a rise, a young man held a powerful-looking bright bay gelding without any white markings, tacked up and ready to ride. He was gorgeous looking, long and sleek and sinewy. Evie guessed he must be at least seventeen hands high.

Piers got off of the ATV and strode up to the horse. The man gave him a leg up, adjusted the stirrups, and tightened the girth.

From the rise, Evie could clearly see the old Douglas house. The windows were covered with newspapers and cardboard. Access from the road was blocked by a tall chain-link fence. She stared at it, thinking again how creepy and forbidding it looked.

Mounted, Piers walked over to her. "Stay away from that place, Evie. No good is there."

She was startled. "Why? What's in there?"

Piers shook his head. "Evil."

Evie felt a chill throughout her body. "It looks abandoned. Does somebody live there?"

"Evil lives there."

Evie saw how serious his face was. She didn't know Piers at all, yet she felt she could trust him. "Can I ask you something?"

"Yes. I may not answer, but you can ask."

"When my stepsister said she knew Cynthia, you looked odd. Can you tell me why?"

Piers picked his words carefully. "I've worked for Dr. Manfred Maris-Stapleton for almost two years. He's a kind man, and highly intelligent. His wife had cancer and died when Cynthia was young. He never remarried, and he travels the world with his important work. He tries his best with his daughter. He moved here in hope of getting her away from a bad influence. Sadly, she *is* the bad influence, and she brings it with her wherever she goes. I've said enough."

Evie nodded. "Does Dr. Maris-Stapleton know who's living in that house?"

"There are things that fathers cannot accept."

She wasn't sure what to make of Piers's words, but knew to leave it alone for now. She changed the subject. "You're training a horse for Cynthia to compete in the Steeplechase?"

His eyebrows raised in surprise. "This is the horse. His name is the Chancellor. I call him Chance. How do you know this?"

"I was told," Evie said evasively. "Chance is very beautiful."

"Yes. But also very talented and kind. He's a good one."

Evie could see that. "When will Cynthia get back from Florida?"

"Tomorrow night."

"Can we train together? I'd like to meet her."

"No, Evie. We will train in private, according to her father's wishes. This is why we must learn everything today and tomorrow, and then you must rest Kazzam on Friday, before the big day Saturday. Yes?"

"Yes." Suddenly, she understood. "Are you saying that I should compete in the March Madness Steeplechase?"

"Of course! Why else are we learning these things so quickly?"

"I ... I ... for fun?"

Piers grinned so widely that his face was transformed. "Fun is what happens when you are well prepared. You want to know about fun? You'll never have so much fun as you're going to have on Saturday. So! We will prepare!"

After their horses were warmed up, Piers led her to the Normandy bank. "This looks difficult, but it rides well," he called.

He's right, it looks difficult, Evie thought. *Very difficult*. She just wasn't sure how well it would ride.

A deep rectangular ditch lay in front of a steep bank built up with planks. There was a solid jump on top of the bank. A raised lip protruded from the opposite end, followed by a drop. *How the heck?* She wondered if Kazzam could figure it out.

Piers observed her concern. "I show you."

He gathered his reins and gently patted the neck of his horse. He cantered a circle and quietly directed Chance toward the combination. The gelding's lovely face showed eagerness as he willingly jumped over the ditch and touched on top of the bank. Without a pause, he hopped over the wooden jump and landed lightly on the ground on the other side of the drop.

"Wow," said Evie. "You made it look so easy."

"With experience and a good horse, everything is easy. And this is a very good horse." Piers rewarded Chance with a sweep of his right hand down the smooth neck. "Now. Again, we do this in pieces, but you must listen carefully."

Evie nodded.

"Walk him up to the ditch. Let him look. When he's calm, let him jump up to the top of the bank, good?"

Evie did what she was told. Kazzam planted his feet in resistance at the base of the ditch, so Evie waited. "When you're ready, boy. Take your time."

With little warning, Kazzam leapt the ditch, and Evie found herself at the top of the bank, stopped in front of a sturdy log raised on posts.

"Good, Evie! Now, turn him around and jump down across the ditch from where you are."

Kazzam and Evie turned around and looked down into the ditch. Evie nudged him with her heels gently, asking him to go forward. The horse had different ideas. He spun back around, jumped the log, and sailed off the other end of the Normandy bank to the ground below.

Evie stayed balanced, with her heels jammed down and her arms extended to allow her horse to stretch out his neck and land safely.

"What are you doing?" yelled Piers. "Come here!"

Evie rode Kazzam over to the unhappy man. "I'm sorry!" she said. "I didn't mean to do the whole thing! Kazzam did it himself, I promise."

Piers began to laugh heartily. "I see, I see. He copied Chance. Well, do it again now. And please, do it just the same, with your weight exactly right, over the feet. So good, Evie!"

"You're not mad?"

"How can I be mad? Most times, the Normandy bank takes all day to learn. That's why we started here." He reached across Chance's withers and patted Kazzam's neck with a firm touch. "Such a horse. Go in slow, girl, with propulsion and confidence."

Evie collected her horse into a slow canter, just as Piers had done with Chance. She circled toward the Normandy bank, coming in straight for the last three strides. She looked over the ditch and up and felt Kazzam's muscular action as he sprang with agility to the top of the bank. Maintaining minimal contact with his mouth, ready to give him the reins, she rode with her leg firm but not urging. Kazzam hopped lightly over the log. Evie kept her heels down and looked forward across the lip.

It felt like they were flying. By the time they landed and cantered away, Evie couldn't stop laughing with elation.

"He seems to know how to do this already!" she exclaimed.

Piers nodded. "Sometimes the good ones do. And he watched what Chance did. That helps a lot." He raised a finger to his head to make a point. "But, I believe it is the trust between you, Evie. He has talent, yes. He's athletic, yes. But he trusts you and knows you will never hurt him with your hands or your heels or your voice. Be proud, Evie." Piers wiped a tear from his eye. "Now we go to the stone wall. Come."

Down the hill to the west was a group of jumps that Evie hadn't seen before. Piers rode ahead of her and stopped in the middle of the field. He motioned for her to bring Kazzam closer.

"After the Normandy bank, these might look easy. Kazzam is a good horse, yes, but he needs to see these things before Saturday, yes? There will be enough distractions even so."

Evie nodded. "Can you do them first, and we'll follow?"

"Yes. I can train Chance and you at the same time." He grinned broadly and pointed. "We'll trot over that wall both ways. Remember to look over all obstacles, Evie, never at them. Then, we go next to the shark's teeth."

Evie tightened her calves, and they followed Chance toward the wall. It was thick and crumbly, with large cracks and loose stones, obviously very old. *Odd*, she thought. In all the years she'd lived there and ridden through the fields, she'd never noticed it. When they got closer, she could see it was made of preformed plastic. Amazingly lifelike, but fake.

Chance cantered forward, and Evie kept Kazzam three strides behind. Chance cleared the wall, then Kazzam followed over with ease and landed at a slow canter.

"Circle him and come from the other way!" shouted Piers. He stopped Chance to watch them. "On his own!"

Evie nodded. She kept Kazzam cantering with the pressure of her legs and circled him around to face the wall from the opposite direction. Kazzam floated to it and flowed over, landing with a pat on the ground. Evie praised him. "Kazzam the Wonder Horse! That's your new name."

Piers sat watching. Evie rode up to him for instructions.

"I tell you what you do, young Evie. I keep asking myself, why is this so easy for you? Why? The answer is so simple."

Evie waited, unsure of what this great coach might say.

"You are always balanced. Your weight is always in your feet, not forward or backward, but always centre. Your feet are always under you, and your hands always give him the right amount of rein. This gives such confidence to your lovely horse. He knows you are with him, and he's free to do his job. Marvellous. Marvellous."

"Thank you, Piers. I have confidence in him, too. He never lets me down."

"You see? It must work both ways. Now!" Piers pointed to another group of jumps. "The shark's teeth. There are three strides between them. It's nothing bad, but a little scary to a horse the first time. We do one at a time. We go over both ways and then come back, and then we do both together. But first, take him close to the first one so he can look."

Evie trotted up to the first strange-looking jump. There were triangular wooden pieces that looked like the upper jaw of a huge shark. She could imagine why a horse might not want to get near.

Piers called, "Come, follow us now!"

She pulled Kazzam in behind Chance and they cantered toward the crazy, scary-looking jump. Chance jumped it, but Evie was still studying it and forgot to look over the fence. Kazzam suddenly stopped. Evie slipped forward onto his neck and almost fell off.

"My fault, boy!" She pushed herself back into the saddle, expecting Piers to start yelling at her.

He didn't.

She turned back at a trot, this time thinking about what she was doing. Over Kazzam went, landing with a little buck as if to give her a slap on the wrist. Evie laughed. She brought him back to a trot and circled around to approach it from the other side. Again, the little black gelding boldly jumped it.

"No need for me to preach at you, Evie. You knew what went wrong and you fixed it. Now, we do both with three strides in between. Follow me, and count out loud!"

Once the jump was completed successfully, Piers called, "Now, on to the corner!" He indicated a solid wooden jump with a flat triangular top held up with poles. A pot full of bright flowers sat on the widest part of the triangle.

"How do we jump that?" asked Evie. "It makes no sense."

Piers laughed. "Forget to make sense! Just jump it!" He directed Chance to the flat edge of the triangle and calmly leapt. "Like this, yah?"

Watching them, how to ride the corner jump became clear. Evie trotted Kazzam closer and said, "Okay, boy. If Chance can do it, we can, too." She let him take a good look, then brought him to it from a canter. Over he went!

"Amazing!" she yelled.

Piers clapped his hands, holding the reins. "Good! Do it again so you are sure of it, then we'll come to the last one of the day, the skinny."

Evie and Kazzam flew over the corner and cantered along to catch up with Piers and Chance. He pointed at an unusual sight. A child-sized table with two small chairs at either end was set for a doll's tea party, complete with plastic tablecloth and tiny china.

"Why's that here?" asked Evie.

"That's the skinny. You are to jump over it."

"No, not really?"

"Yes, really. It's all glued down. Isn't it clever? I designed it myself."

"Is that a real skinny? It doesn't look like a jump at all!"

"A skinny can be anything narrow, to test the horse and rider's bravery, skill, and accuracy. This will be on the Steeplechase course. Understand, on Saturday it will be flagged."

"What do you mean, flagged?"

"Notice that there are sticks on both sides of each jump on the course? Yah? A white flag will be on the left side and a red flag will be on the right. Always jump with the red flag on your right. Then you know you're jumping from the correct direction."

"Good to know," said Evie. "Red on the right. R and R."

"Good. So? Give it a try?" said Piers with a smile.

"Are you going first?"

"Not this time. See what Kazzam will do. We have lots of time."

"No time like the present," said Evie. She'd learned her lesson at the shark's teeth and kept her eyes over the tea party. It was such an odd thing to jump that Evie didn't want to look at it, anyway. They trotted up and over it without a problem. She turned and jumped over it from the other direction, as Piers had always instructed.

"Why do you always say to jump it both ways?" asked Evie.

"I think you know already."

Evie thought about it. She'd noticed before that a horse might spook at something coming home, even though he'd already seen it on the way past. "Does it look different to them from different directions?"

"Yes! Exactly so. It looks like an entirely new thing. Now, Chance and I will do the skinny. Can I confide? I wasn't sure if Chance would like it at all!"

Evie laughed, pleased that Piers had asked them to go first. She felt proud.

Chance and Piers cantered toward the tea party jump. Evie watched as Chance slammed on his brakes at the very last second. "You see?" grinned Piers.

He slowed Chance to a walk and patted his neck to reassure him that he wasn't in any trouble. They picked up a trot and headed for it again. This time Chance hesitated but leapt.

Evie laughed. He'd jumped twice as high as necessary. Piers asked him to canter the skinny both ways, and this time it looked effortless.

They trotted up to Evie. "That will do very nicely," Piers said and looked at his watch. "Now, I want you to put all this together and then walk the marvellous horse out until your beautiful grandmother comes to get you. Yes?"

"Yes, for sure." Was this the time to ask? "Um, Piers? Did you and Gran Mary used to go out together?"

"Mary." Piers breathed in slowly and nodded. "I saw Mary and fell in love with her. There was someone else in her life, someone who'd moved away, and her heart wasn't ready for me. But I tried. I would've married her. We had many good days back then." He sighed. "Many good days."

"What happened? Why didn't you get married?"

Piers laughed the laugh that Evie had come to enjoy. "It's not always like the movies, my girl. I competed in Europe and got involved in my career, but Mary was always on my mind. Time passed. I heard she was happily married and had a child. I couldn't barge back into her life, could I? I'm not one to wreck a marriage. So, I stayed away." He looked sad. "But I never forgot her."

Evie was tempted to tell him the story of how Mary had had a child alone and unmarried, and had given her daughter to her brother to raise as his own, but she stopped herself, not wanting to make this mistake twice. It was Mary's story to tell, not hers.

Instead, she asked, "Did you get married? Have children?"

"No. I never did. It never seemed the right time or the right person." Piers's face changed. "I answered your questions, Evie. Will you answer mine?" he asked humbly.

"Yes, of course."

"Is Mary married? Or with somebody?"

"No. She's alone." The image of Dr. Marshal came into her head. "But I think there's one guy who'd like to change that."

"No doubt! This time I will not let that happen." Piers spoke assertively. "So? Let's put it together, shall we? The stone wall, then the Normandy bank, the shark's teeth, the corner, and end with the skinny. Yes?"

"Yes!"

168

"You do it first, alone. Then I do it alone. Then we do it together, horse beside horse."

Evie nodded. Kazzam had had a little rest while they'd chatted and was keen to get started. She looked at all the jumps that Piers had mentioned and made a plan about how to approach each one.

"Let's go, boy. Let's get this done," she whispered.

Kazzam tossed his mane and squealed with impatience. The stone wall was first.

12

Beebee

It's in the ability to deceive oneself that the greatest talent is shown.

— Anatole France

Evie walked Kazzam down the hill after completing the course without a fault. She pinched herself. Piers had been thrilled, especially at how well Kazzam had behaved when he and Chance did the course together. He'd told her that most horses couldn't handle the stimulation of jumping beside, behind, or in front of another horse, and that in Europe, Steeplechase horses began as foxhunters so they could get accustomed to riding in groups when they were young.

Piers had set up a lesson for the same time the next day. He would call Gran Mary to make plans for the Steeplechase.

The welcome breeze cooled Evie's hot face and dried her sweaty horse. "You're such a good boy," she said as she rubbed his mane. In fact, he was astonishing, she thought. Considering that he'd been bred as a racehorse and trained only to run fast, it was amazing that all these new skills came to him so quickly.

Kazzam had been intelligent and focused throughout the lesson. Those were the traits that allowed him to learn so well, Evie concluded, plus his confidence and his courage to try.

It was ten o'clock, time for Mary to pick them up. Evie would keep Kazzam moving until she arrived. He'd had a good workout, and she didn't want his muscles to stiffen up.

Her head was full of new information, yet there was much more to know, and more types of obstacles to figure out. She needed to think it all over and replay Piers's instructions for each obstacle again and again, so she wouldn't forget.

As they walked along on a loose rein, she noticed a blond woman waving to her from behind the big white barn trimmed in dark blue. It was Yolanda Schmits.

"Yoyo!" Evie called, happy to see her friend.

Yolanda put her finger to her lips and quickly shook her head. *Something's wrong*, Evie thought as she rode toward her.

Yolanda looked around furtively, like she was afraid.

"What's up?" asked Evie quietly. She looked around as well, uncertain what was causing Yolanda's nervousness, dismounted, and ran up her stirrups. "Tell me."

"I arrived today. I unpacked my stuff." Yolanda paused to find the right words. "There was a dead cat in my cupboard."

"Horrible!" said Evie.

"It was awful." Yolanda looked pale.

"I'm so sorry. It must've been a shock."

"It was! It kind of spooked me."

Evie nodded in agreement. "No kidding. Are you living upstairs, like before?"

"Yeah. All five of us. It's temporary. I'm the last to arrive, so I got the worst bed."

"Five people? There are only two rooms! Why can't you live in the grooms' cabins?" Evie thought of the freshly painted rooms she'd seen.

Yolanda grimaced. "That was the plan — they're all fixed up with new beds and everything — but the plan changed. Dr. Maris-Stapleton said maybe next week."

"Hope so." Evie would let Dr. Marshal know about the dead cat. He'd said to watch for irregularities with people and animals. "How long had the cat been dead?"

"Hard to say. Less than a week."

"Did it belong to anyone?"

"It was Herman, the barn cat. You remember him. He was here when you lived here."

"Of course I remember." Herman had been handsome, with a black and white coat. Evie felt a wave of sadness for his death. "I loved Herman. Have any more animals died?"

Yolanda took another look around to be sure they were not overheard. "No, but we found a starving dog in the other room. He'd been there for several days, like the cat."

"How did he survive?"

"By drinking from the toilet. No food, but at least he had water. He tried to claw his way out. I saw his bloody paws."

"That poor dog! Who does he belong to?"

"I don't know. He's some kind of shepherd mix."

Evie remembered the posters around the property. "Yoyo! Did you see those missing dog posters?"

"No."

"In the picture it looked like a shepherd mix. Where's he now?"

"My friend's looking after him. She's a vet tech."

"I'll call the number on the poster and tell them to talk to you." Evie had a thought. "Poor Herman must have stunk to high heaven. People must have noticed!"

Yolanda sniffed and pursed her lips. "He was wrapped in plastic."

"What!" Again, Evie was shocked. "Somebody killed him on purpose?"

Yolanda began to shake. She tried to keep it together. "It's horrible. I don't know what's going on. Nobody does."

Mary's rig had turned up the driveway, but Evie had more questions. "How did Herman die?"

"That's another weird thing. He looked peaceful. No tooth marks or signs of struggle. No obvious cause of death." Yolanda noticed Mary's rig, too. "Evie, I shouldn't have said anything. I don't want to lose my job."

"This is totally strange. I'd like to help."

"Thanks," Yolanda said. "But if anybody hears that I've talked, I'll be fired. We had to sign contracts to keep everything said and done here confidential, on threat of immediate dismissal."

"I won't say a word. And just in case you need it, the apartment over the garage at Parson's Bridge is vacant."

"I'll need it if you get me kicked out again," said Yolanda with a sparkle. "Like last time."

"I didn't mean to, Yoyo!" Last June, Yolanda had been fired for doing Evie a favour.

Yolanda grinned. "I know, Evie. Just kidding. Everybody was fired in the end, anyway."

They were surprised when Mary's truck and trailer drove right past them and up the hill. It didn't even slow down.

"Didn't she see you?" asked Yolanda.

"She didn't even look," said Evie. "If I want a ride home, I'd better follow her." Evie walked Kazzam to the nearby mounting block and got back up. "I'll be back tomorrow. Let me know if anything else weird happens."

Yolanda sighed deeply. "It will, I can feel it. I just don't know what."

The two friends said their goodbyes, and Evie and Kazzam retraced their steps up the hill. At the crest she saw Piers and Mary deep in conversation.

Evie needed to call Dr. Marshal. She pulled out the phone that he'd given her and pressed number one.

"Edwin Marshal here."

"It's Evangeline — Evie."

"I've been waiting for you to call. What's happening?"

As factually and precisely as she could, Evie told him Yolanda's creepy news about Herman and the dog and what Piers had said about Cynthia and his suspicions about the Douglas house.

"Thank you, Evie. Good work. Will you be training again on the property tomorrow?"

"Yes, that's the plan, but not on Friday."

There was a pause. Dr. Marshal said, "We need somebody on the inside. Can we get Yolanda Schmits on board? Beatrice cannot take part in this."

"I agree," said Evie. "Beebee panicked as soon as we drove onto the property."

"And Yolanda?"

"She'll tell me things, but she doesn't want to lose her job. She signed a confidentiality agreement."

"Of course."

Evie glanced over to the rig. It seemed that Piers and Mary were beginning to argue.

"I'll need a blood sample from the cat. Can you ask Yolanda to put it in a freezer until I get it?"

"Sure. I'll call her."

"So, Evie, I have news."

Evie was intrigued. "What?"

"Stacey Linn has come out of her coma. She's too frightened to talk to the police, and they've called me in. I'll see her shortly."

"That's great! Do you think she'll survive?"

"Yes, I do. It was helpful that the doctors knew what drugs to look for in her blood."

"I'm very glad. What should I do now?"

"Keep doing what you're doing. I can't give you firm instructions, since it's hard to know where anything will lead. Report to me as often as there's news."

"Okay." Evie inhaled. "Ah, Dr. Marshal? You know how I told you that Officer Summers thinks I'm a nuisance?"

"Yes?"

"Could you let her know that we found Beebee? I should've called, but I'm afraid to. I'll admit it."

"Actually, we're working together. She knows about Beatrice, and she knows that you're helping me. In fact," he said, a smile in his voice, "she thinks you'll be an asset precisely for the reason that she found you irritating."

"What's that?"

"Your persistence."

Evie grinned as they disconnected, feeling better about Officer Summers. She left a message on Yolanda's phone about putting Herman in the freezer and rode Kazzam over to the trailer.

The adults were still engrossed in their discussion. Mary saw Evie coming and pretended that nothing was

175

amiss, but her colour was high. "Why, Evie! Piers told me that you and that little Thoroughbred of yours had a brilliant day."

Evie nodded. "He was amazing. Thanks, Piers."

Piers smiled. "You are most welcome. Thank you, Evie, and thank you, little horse. We see you tomorrow, same time, yes?"

Mary gave him a look. Piers looked decidedly unhappy.

"What's wrong?" Evie asked as she slid down from the saddle. "I'm not totally oblivious. I can see there's a problem."

"Yah. Your grandmother is worried about the Steeplechase on Saturday."

"I certainly am!" blurted Mary. "Especially now that I know it's to be run as a group!"

"Only the four finalists! It's a crowd pleaser, and a big part of the fundraiser. It won't be a crazy scene, I promise."

"You can't promise that, Piers. Anything could happen. And I didn't know until today that the intention was for Evie to compete at all. You said you were coaching her for the love of the sport."

"Please," Piers said earnestly. "I know what I'm doing. Please bring Evie and Kazzam tomorrow. Can we talk more, yes? Maybe later today?"

Evie realized how badly she wanted to compete and that she really, really wanted to win. "It's no different from riding a race, with horses galloping all together. I can do that. Kazzam can do that. It'll be fine."

"That just shows how ill prepared she is!" Mary exclaimed to Piers. "Jockeys are trained professionals! Riding with amateurs is another world altogether.

Amateurs make huge mistakes, and at high speed, those mistakes can be disastrous."

"I select the riders. I will prepare her, Mary. I promise. Can we talk later?"

Mary dropped the ramp. "Load him, Evie. We must hurry. I left the kids watching a movie."

Once Kazzam was on the trailer and Evie was in the truck, Mary drove over the grass and around to the driveway. Her mouth had become a rigid line, and her wrinkles were exaggerated. Evie said nothing, waiting for her to speak.

After a few minutes, Mary said, "He wants to drop by to see me later, Evie. Hah."

"What's the problem, Gran Mary?"

"Piers is the problem. He thinks he can waltz right back into my life after all these years. Hah!"

This was a new person altogether, thought Evie. *Gran Mary's human after all!* "He's a really nice man."

"He swept me off my feet, then disappeared. I was in love, and I thought it would be forever. But he left. I never heard from him again after that summer." Tears welled in her eyes.

"But he told me today that he was in love with you, but he heard you were married, so he stayed away. He didn't want to show up and wreck your life."

"So I should run to him? And have my heart broken again?"

"No! I'm saying there's no harm in letting him explain, that's all. From his perspective."

Mary kept quiet. Evie knew there was no point in arguing and looked out the window at the passing scenery. "Oh, there's the missing dog poster! I need to call the owner." She took out her phone and began to enter the number.

Mary slowed the truck. "Did you find it?"

"There was a mixed-breed dog found in the grooms' quarters. It was starving. It might be this one."

"I hope this story has a happy ending," said Mary.

The call was answered on the first ring. "Yes?"

Evie said, "I saw the poster about your missing dog."

"Yah? Have you seen him?"

Evie was startled. She recognized the voice. Unsure of how to break the news, she continued. "No, I haven't seen him, but you should talk to Yolanda Schmits at the main barn at MMS."

"Who is this?"

"It's Evie, Piers."

"Evie!"

"Yolanda found a dog at the barn."

"She found Loewe?"

"Uh, I'm not sure it's him. That's the thing. He might not be yours, but a shepherd mix was found upstairs in the barn. In an empty groom's apartment."

"What are you not telling me, Evie?"

"The dog was starving. He's in bad shape. Yoyo took him to her friend who's a vet tech."

There was a pause. "This Yoyo, she is at the main barn?"

"Yes. She's there now."

"Thank you, Evie. I will go now. Thank you again." He hung up.

Mary sighed. "Poor Piers. Let's hope the dog survives."

When they drove up the lane at Parson's Bridge, Magpie raced up to the truck. Evie rubbed her ears and gave her a good petting. Magpie stayed at her side as Evie unloaded Kazzam, groomed him, and walked him outside to be with the other horses.

Since they'd left MMS, Mary had been very quiet. Now, she said, "You must think I was very harsh about Piers. I'm sorry I exploded like that."

Evie was surprised. "No, I understand. You don't want to make yourself vulnerable again."

Mary exhaled and smiled. "Your wisdom impresses me, dear, and at such a tender age."

"I still think you should hear him out. He might be my grandfather."

"Evie!" Mary swatted her granddaughter with a glove. "You say such things!"

"Is he?"

"Why would you ask such a question?"

"Why do adults answer questions with questions?"

As they walked toward the house, Jordie came running out in his socks. His eyes were wild. "Gran Mary! Evie! Something's wrong with Beebee!"

"What is it?" Mary asked.

"I don't know! I found her a few minutes ago!"

They all ran into the house.

"Where is she? What happened?"

Jordie was extremely agitated. He said, "Somebody phoned her, then she didn't want to watch the movie, so I turned it off and put in the dragon movie, and I called her but she didn't answer, and I looked around the house and then I found her in her room."

Mary and Evie bounded up the stairs and threw Beebee's bedroom door wide open.

She was lying on the bed, face up, her legs and arms spread wide apart. Her face was pale, and her tongue hung out one side of her mouth. Her eyes were open and glassy.

"Evie," commanded Mary, "stay with her. I'll call for help."

Evie nodded and sat beside Beebee on the bed. "Beebee? What did you do to yourself?" she asked quietly. She held Beebee's limp hand and stroked her cheek. Her stepsister looked drugged.

Jordie crept into the room. "What's wrong with her? Is she dead?" His face was as ashen as Beebee's.

"No, she's alive. Did anybody come over?"

"No, I don't think so. The dogs would've barked."

"Yeah, you would've heard them," Evie agreed. "Do you know who called her?"

He shook his head. "No."

Evie thought she knew. The giggling girl who'd called before.

Mary came back into the room with her phone. "I called 911 and an ambulance is on its way. I texted Dr. Marshal as well, just so he knows."

A thought nagged at Evie. "Is there any medication in the house, Gran Mary?"

Mary's eyes widened. "Yes. Cold and sinus and flu medicine, aspirin, ibuprofen, sleeping tablets ..." She ran to the bathroom.

Evie followed. The medicine cabinet was open. Small empty bottles littered the sink, counter, and floor.

"She poisoned herself," said Mary. "I didn't think ... I should've known better."

Evie rushed back into the bedroom and turned Beebee so her head was hanging over the side of the bed. She stuck her finger down the girl's throat to make her vomit.

Beebee gagged, but nothing came up. Evie tried again with no luck, and continued trying.

Sirens wailed up the driveway. Mary ran downstairs to let them in.

Quickly and efficiently, two paramedics entered the room, placed Beebee on a stretcher, and carried her down the stairs and into the ambulance.

"I'm going with her," said Mary. "Stay here and don't open the door for anyone." She put on her coat and boots and grabbed her handbag. "Everything will be fine. I'll call you."

They watched the ambulance drive away, listening mutely as the siren got more and more quiet, until the forlorn sound disappeared altogether.

Jordie began to cry.

13

Rivals

The easiest reading is damned hard writing.
— Thomas Hood

As soon as the ambulance left, Evie dialed *69 to see who'd called last. The number that came up was Beebee's phone. Evie's suspicion was confirmed. The girl who'd taken Beebee's phone had called again. No wonder she had panicked.

An hour passed. There was very little food in the house, but Evie thawed a frozen lasagna in the microwave for lunch. Neither she nor Jordie had much of an appetite.

Evie stayed close to the phone and tried to keep Jordie's mind off his sister. There was nothing on television that he wanted to watch, and *How to Train Your Dragon* didn't interest him. "How about a game of cards?" she asked.

Jordie shook his head.

"Monopoly? You always win."

"No."

"Trivial Pursuit?"

"No. *You* always win."

"Why don't we read more of Gran Mary's new book?" asked Evie. "*The Boy on the Beach*?"

"Yes! Priscilla is alone and cold with a ripped dress and she's lost."

Evie found the manuscript beside the couch, and they settled in to continue where Aunt Mary had left off.

"Okay, Jordie. Here we go." She began to read.

> Priscilla's only thought was to stay alive until morning. Hopefully, she could find her way to civilization when the sun came up, if she lived through the night. With numb fingers she began to dig a nest in the sand for protection from the relentless wind. Busy at her task, Priscilla didn't observe the shadowy figure that crept up behind her.

"No!" yelled Jordie. "Priscilla can't take any more awful things happening to her!"

"Don't worry," Evie said. "Gran Mary won't kill her off."

"Okay. Keep reading." Jordie snuggled in closer to Evie.

> "Hello," said a voice. Priscilla thought she'd imagined it. "Hello!" the voice repeated more loudly.
>
> This time Priscilla knew it was real. Had Ed tracked her down? Was he angry that she'd fought him off and escaped from his car? With fear in her heart, she froze.
>
> Slowly she found the courage to turn and

face the person who had spoken. The person who stood behind her in the dark.

It was a teenaged boy. He was tall and thin, wearing only shorts and a ragged shirt.

"You're shivering," Priscilla said.

The boy didn't make eye contact. "We saw you from our house. My mother told me to bring you home, out of the storm. Follow me." He turned away from the beach and began to walk."

"Hooray!" cheered Jordie.

"I told you Gran Mary wouldn't kill her off."

The phone that Dr. Marshal had given her started to ring. "Jordie, I have to get this in case it's about Beebee."

"I need to hear, too."

Evie put the phone on speaker. "Hello?"

"Hi, Evie. I'm here with your grandma. Beatrice will be fine."

Jordie thrust his fists in the air. "Thanks, Dr. Marshal! That's so great," said Evie.

"She overdosed on cold medication and soporifics and required gastric irrigation. They're going to keep her overnight, possibly longer. She's resting now. I haven't spoken to her yet."

"The person who called Beebee right before she overdosed is the same girl who took her phone. My guess is Althea. The call came from Beebee's cell."

Dr. Marshal didn't speak for a few seconds. "That means they're looking for her. I'm sending Mary home now. Look around the house to make sure that there's no other medication lying around that Beatrice could consume. She's at risk of repeating this behaviour."

"We'll do that."

"And don't let anybody in the house."

"I won't." Evie had goosebumps. Had the girls found out where Mary lived? If not, it was only a matter of time.

"I spoke to Stacey Linn today," Dr. Marshal said. "The good news is that she'll recover fully."

Evie sat up straight. "That's great!"

"Yes, it is. Her parents haven't left her side."

"What did she tell you?"

Dr. Marshal paused. "She didn't want to give me any details. She fears for her life if she does. She only admits to hitchhiking from Newmarket to Caledon with Beebee to meet friends. She says they're in a club with an initiation ceremony, but that it was all friendly and nothing bad happened. She has no memory of what happened between meeting her friends and waking up in the hospital."

"And her parents? Do they believe her?"

"Yes. According to them, she's a good girl, has never been in trouble, and has lovely friends."

"Do they know how lucky she is to be alive?" asked Evie. "If Magpie hadn't found her and you hadn't known the drug to test for —"

"I know. But she insists that it couldn't have been her friends. That they would never harm her."

"Oh, right."

"And her parents agree. They want the police to track down the homicidal maniac who did this to her."

Evie said, "That's what we're all trying to do."

Dr. Marshal sighed. "I'd hoped she would give us something useful."

"We'll figure it out."

"I like your attitude, Evie."

They hung up. The landline began to ring. Jordie jumped up to answer it. "Hello?" His face darkened. "Yes, Mom. I'm fine."

Evie couldn't hear what Paulina was saying, but she listened to Jordie's end of the conversation.

"Beebee's in the hospital … she had gassy irritation … I didn't hide it from you, Mom! It just happened! Yeah, she'll be okay … she ate all of Gran Mary's pills … no! They weren't just lying around. They were in Gran Mary's bathroom, high up in a cabinet … She went to the hospital with Beebee … okay, she'll call you when she gets home … okay, okay. You call back later."

He hung up.

"You okay, Jordie?"

"She thinks Gran Mary was negligee."

"You mean negligent? That means careless."

"But she wasn't! Beebee did it herself!"

"I know, I know. And she had *gastric irrigation*. That means she had her stomach pumped."

"Then why didn't he say that? And why does Mom blame Gran Mary and not Beebee, anyway?"

"Don't you worry, Jordie. There are things that mothers can't accept." As the words came out, Evie realized that she was almost quoting Piers Anders.

There was a knock on the door. The three dogs leapt up from their beds and began to bark.

Jordie said, "Gran Mary said not to let anybody in. Dr. Marshal did, too."

"I'll just see who it is." Evie put her finger to her lips and crept over to take a peek at who was at the door. Standing there was Piers. Relief flooded over her. "It's only Piers. Hi," she said to him as she threw open the door. "Come in!" She glanced at Jordie to reassure him.

Jordie shrugged and mouthed, *Don't blame me.*

"Thank you." Piers Anders stepped inside the mud-room. "Is your grandmother home? I wish to speak with her."

"She'll be back soon," said Jordie. "She was at the hospital with Beebee."

Piers's eyebrows rose. "The hospital? Is the girl all right?"

"She'll be okay," answered Evie. "She overdosed on all of Gran Mary's cold medication."

"Oh, dear." Piers shook his head sadly.

"She'll be okay," Evie repeated. "They're going to keep her for a day or two to be sure."

Piers nodded. "Good. Good." He stood there awkwardly.

Evie wondered what Gran Mary would have done in this situation. "Uh, come in if you'd like to wait for her, please, and, um, can I get you a coffee?"

"Yes, yes. That is wonderful. I take a bit of sugar and a dash of milk." He took off his riding boots and placed them together on the mat, then carefully hung up his coat. "May I sit?"

"Yes." *This is awkward*, Evie thought. Piers seemed very uncomfortable, too, but she had no idea why. "Did you talk to Yolanda about the dog?"

Piers nodded. "Yes. It's Loewe. I'm grateful. So grateful. I picked him up from her very nice friend, and he's in the truck."

"Bring him in!" said Evie.

Piers indicated the dogs and shook his head briefly. "He's not in good shape. He needs quiet. I cannot stay long, at any rate."

Evie suggested, "Why not bring him into the mud-room? We'll close the door so our dogs will leave him alone."

Piers brightened. "Yes, yes. He'll be very happy to stay with me. I'll do that now." While he fetched his dog, Evie and Jordie organized a bed of old towels and some water and kibble.

She knew he'd been starved and locked up for days, but Evie wasn't prepared for the sight of Loewe as he staggered in with Piers's help. His coat was drab and his torn paws were bandaged. He looked exactly like his picture — black, white, and grey with a golden-brown ruff — but he'd lost his glossy shine and keen eyes.

"Oh," was all she could say.

Piers shook his head. He gave his dog a gentle pat on the head. "I don't know how this happened. He's at my side all the time. I was giving a lesson, he chased a squirrel, and he never returned."

"Which way did he run?"

"Toward the Douglas house."

Piers and Evie looked at each other. "Are you thinking what I'm thinking?" Evie asked.

"That somebody from that house captured Loewe and left him to die in the barn?"

Evie nodded and asked, "But why? It makes no sense."

Piers stood up straight. "But now, I have him back. He'll get healthy soon. I will not let him out of my sight."

"Herman the barn cat wasn't so lucky. Yoyo found him when she moved in this morning. The body was wrapped in plastic."

"The black and white cat? He's in the back of my truck."

Evie was confused. "Who's in the back of your truck?"

"The black and white cat. Yoyo gave him to me. She doesn't have a freezer he'll fit in. You want the body, yes?"

"I guess. Dr. Marshal wants to get a blood sample."

Piers smiled sadly. "That black and white cat was a funny one. The horses liked to rub his back with their noses. He and Loewe were friends, and Loewe doesn't usually like cats."

"Herman was one of the greats."

"So," said Piers, "we must be watchful of all the animals."

Loewe settled onto the soft towels and yawned. He placed his head on his bandaged paws and closed his eyes.

"Good. We leave him to be quiet now, yes?"

Evie and Piers closed the mudroom door behind them. Piers sat on the couch with Jordie while Evie went to the counter to make Piers a coffee.

"Can you read, Piers?" asked Jordie. "I mean, in English?"

Piers chuckled deeply. "Yes, I can. Can you?"

"Yes, but I like it better when somebody reads to me. Can you read me *The Boy on the Beach*? Gran Mary wrote it and it's really good."

"What a good idea," said Piers. "She's a good writer, yah?"

"Yes! She's the best! This is her newest one and it's not even in the bookstores yet."

Piers opened the binder. Jordie showed him where Evie had left off, and Piers began to read in his deep voice.

Priscilla did as she was told and followed the tall boy away from the gusting wind and swirling sand. He didn't look behind. He walked slowly but steadily across the beach and through the waving sea grass. Far ahead, Priscilla saw a small light flickering.

Evie brought the coffee and sat down on the couch beside Piers.

"Thank you, Evie," he said. He took a sip.

"You're not going to stop reading now?" asked Jordie.

"No! Absolutely not." Piers smiled. "This is a good story."

An hour passed as Piers read Mary's story to Evie and Jordie, with the three dogs at their feet. Loewe was content by himself, and they were all engrossed. Things got serious when Priscilla was abducted by the boy's mother and tied up in the basement.

Priscilla sat on the cold cement with her arms tied behind her back and her mouth covered with sticky duct tape. The boy stood in the far corner under the stairs and stared at her, expressionless. The only light in the damp darkness came through a tiny barred window set high on the slimy wall. The sound of a rat scurrying across the floor, its long tail swishing behind it, made her shudder.

She looked at the boy. He had not moved in all the hours that had passed. His face was still blank. *There's a story here*, Priscilla thought.

"What's your name?" she asked. The boy appeared not to have heard. "Where are we? And why am I tied up? Do you think I'm a criminal?"

The boy sat still. Perhaps he was deaf. Perhaps he was deathly afraid of his mother. *Perhaps*, thought Priscilla, *he's also a prisoner*.

The dogs lifted their heads and thumped their tails in unison as Mary's head poked around the door frame from the mudroom.

"Well, hello!" she said. "Now I know who belongs to this poor dog!"

Piers jumped to his feet, disturbing Jordie and dropping the manuscript, which Evie caught before the pages fell apart and tumbled to the floor.

"Mary! I came to speak with you."

"First, can someone help bring in the groceries? I had to stop on the way home. The cupboards were bare."

"Yes, yes!" Piers answered. He put on his boots and rushed out to the truck before Evie and Jordie had even gotten up off the couch.

"Eager, isn't he?" Evie joked.

"I'm not so easily impressed," sniffed Mary.

"Playing hard to get?"

"Bring in the bags, smarty-pants!"

Evie, Piers, and Jordie carried in the shopping bags full of groceries and put them on the counter while Mary put them away.

Amid the chaos, another person entered the room holding a small briefcase. "Hello, everybody!"

"Dr. Marshal!" said Jordie. "What are you doing here?"

"Now, Jordie," chastised Mary. "Be polite. Edwin, good to see you. Is everything okay with Beebee?"

"Yes, yes. I'm here about the cat. I called Yolanda and she told me she sent it to you. I came right over."

"Yes," said Piers. "It's in my truck. I'm Piers Anders." He put out his right hand.

"Good to meet you. I'm a long-time fan. Dr. Edwin Marshal." They shook hands firmly, each man checking out the other with narrowed eyes and a clenched jaw.

Evie smiled to herself. One of these men might be her grandfather. Which one? Both would have been handsome in their day, she could tell, and both were successful and accomplished.

She noticed Mary looking at her with alarm. Evie held back laughter and whispered, "Don't worry, Gran Mary. I won't say what I'm thinking."

"You'd better not," the older woman warned quietly.

"My dog was locked up in the barn and starved," Piers said. "I just got him back. Do you want blood from him also?"

Dr. Marshal nodded. "Might as well. We'll see what we find." He and Piers went into the mudroom to get the sample.

With the men out of the room, Jordie said, "Gran Mary, what's going on?"

"With what, Jordie?"

"Dr. Marshal and Piers. They talk nice, but they don't like each other."

Evie couldn't help herself. "They're rivals. They both like Gran Mary and want to win her heart."

"But they're old!"

"Watch yourself, young man," chuckled Mary. "Youth is a condition that only time can heal."

"What?" Jordie looked puzzled.

"Nothing. It's a saying. But one day, if you're lucky, you'll be as old as Piers and Edwin. And me."

Jordie rolled his eyes. "I hope not."

"It's not that bad, you scamp!" Mary rubbed the boy's hair fondly. "Evie, can you go start the horses' feed? I won't be long."

"Sure." Evie paused. "I didn't think Beebee would do that. Search for pills, you know?"

192

Mary looked at her seriously. "Neither did I."

"Should she get help? Like Angela?"

"Yes, for sure, but I'm not her legal guardian. I'll call Paulina now and tell her what happened."

Evie remembered. "Oh! Paulina called and talked to Jordie. She said she'd call back later."

"She thinks you were negligee."

"Negligent, Jordie," corrected Evie.

Mary looked sad. "I don't blame her. She'll be very worried."

The men came out of the mudroom.

Jordie said, "Piers, can you read me some more of Gran Mary's book?"

Piers's eyes twinkled. "Of course, Jordie, my man! It would be an honour." He sat down on the couch, stretched out his arms, and crossed his legs, making himself very much at home.

Dr. Marshal sniffed, looking displaced. "Well. I must be going."

Piers said heartily, "Yes. It was good to meet you, Edwin. Let me know what you find in Loewe's blood, will you?"

"I will." But Dr. Marshal wasn't about to be dismissed. He turned to Mary. "I noticed the farm next door is for sale. Tell me about it."

Piers sat up. "The farm next door? For sale?"

Trying to look innocent and keep a straight face, Evie said, "It's over twenty acres of scenic rolling hills, in move-in condition, and with really nice neighbours."

Dr. Marshal looked at Piers. "I saw it first."

"Actually, Jerry Johnston is looking at it," said Evie.

Mary was putting the lettuce in the crisper. "J.J.? I didn't know that."

"He said he'd love to live next door to you."

Both Dr. Marshal and Piers looked so concerned that Evie couldn't contain her merriment. Jordie joined in.

Mary sneezed and threw up her hands. "Kids! Get outside and bring in the horses. It's feed time."

14

March Madness

Great ideas need landing gear as well as wings.
— C.D. Jackson

It was finally Saturday, March 17th, the day of the Steeplechase. Evie and Kazzam stood on a hill overlooking the grounds in the warm-up area adjacent to the parking field. She was wearing Angela's silks over her protective vest. Bright-pink polka dots on a white background, with periwinkle-blue stripes on the sleeves. The matching helmet cover had pink polka dots on one half and blue stripes on the other. Also wearing the white breeches that Imogene Watson had given her for the Queen's Plate last June and her mother's racing boots, Evie felt lucky. And the luck of the Irish had prevailed as well, for the weather was mild and sunny.

More than a hundred horses would be on the grounds today, the majority of which were entered in jumper, hunter, and equitation classes. It was a charity event with steep entry fees, but there was prize money for each class, giving people hope of recouping their costs. The goal was to raise money for heart disease research, Dr. Maris-Stapleton's specialty.

Twenty horses had qualified to compete in the March Madness Steeplechase. It was one thousand dollars to enter, and the purse was five thousand, leaving fifteen thousand dollars for the cause. Each entrant would do the cross-country course alone, and then, based on time and faults, the top four would race together at two o'clock that afternoon. The head-to-head race of the final four was the most anticipated and talked-about event of the day.

Evie hoped that she and Kazzam would make the final four.

They'd gotten to the grounds early so that Kazzam could get acclimatized to the fairground atmosphere, but Evie soon realized it was more for her sake than for his. So far, Kazzam had taken everything in stride, from the striped tents to the pony rides. Golf carts, motor scooters, colourful balloons — even the Ferris wheel on the infield of the practice racetrack hadn't spooked him.

She patted his neck. "You are possibly the best horse that ever lived in the entire history of horsekind."

From the rise, they watched the steady stream of horse trailers, trucks, and cars coming up the lane and parking on the next hill. Gran Mary had been among the first to arrive. She'd chosen the perfect spot under a shady tree beside the water tanks. The portable toilets stood in a row discreetly behind a nearby hedge.

They'd had to lock the dogs in the barn that morning, because Magpie had insisted on following the truck and trailer. They'd had to bring her back home twice. Evie knew the dogs would be fine. They had water and kibble and blankets to sleep on. Still, Magpie would rather have run free. She didn't like being locked up.

Jordie would be grooming Christieloo by now, guessed Evie. His class was the first of the day, and he was very nervous. She chuckled fondly as she pictured his white, pinched face that morning, properly dressed in the stock tie, jacket, and breeches that Gran Mary had bought him especially for this day. He'd hardly slept and couldn't eat any breakfast. He worried that he might be sick. Gran Mary had packed an egg and bacon sandwich for him to eat when his stomach settled. He'd gobbled it up on the drive over.

He had asked a few times whether Beebee might be well enough to come to the show. Not to compete, but for moral support. *They argue all the time*, thought Evie, *but they really do love each other.*

As soon as Kerry had heard about Beebee's overdose, he'd insisted that Paulina book a flight and go directly to the hospital to be with her daughter. *Good for Kerry*, Evie thought. It'd be a big relief for Gran Mary. Paulina could make the decisions now. Beebee's condition had improved, which was very good news.

The bad news was that Evie hadn't heard from or texted with Mark since they'd spoken on Thursday night. It was strange, since they'd been in contact throughout the spring break, and Mark had been a constant source of support. She'd left several messages yesterday. She tried to put it out of her head. Maybe his phone battery had died. Regardless, she would've loved to hear him wish her good luck.

Kazzam's pointed ears pricked up and almost touched each other. He sniffed the air and spun to his left. Eve looked to see what interested him. At the far side of the warm-up area, a young man was getting Chance warmed up for the trials. Kazzam nickered.

Horses started in order of when they were entered. Chance had been entered first, so he'd do the course first.

Kazzam had entered last, and therefore his would be the twentieth and final round.

Kazzam nickered again, and Chance returned the greeting. *He's such a good-looking horse*, thought Evie. He might just be their biggest competition. Everything depended on the ride that Cynthia Maris-Stapleton gave him, and Evie was very curious to see how they got on together.

On Thursday, Piers had given Evie a lesson on the remainder of the obstacles that might be on the course: the arrowhead, the brush, the bullfinch, the bounce, the Trakehner, and the hanging log fence. He'd finished satisfied that Evie understood how to approach them and that Kazzam knew what to expect.

Friday had been the gelding's day off. He'd enjoyed loafing with Paragon, Bendigo, and Christieloo. Jordie had insisted on practising for the hack class one more time, and Evie had watched him. She was startled at the improvement he'd made in just one week under Mary's guidance. He'd worked very hard. Evie hoped he'd win a ribbon, as Piers predicted any student of Gran Mary's would.

Friday had also been when Gran Mary, Officer Summers, Dr. Marshal, and Evie met at Parson's Bridge for a meeting. The police had gathered enough information to get a search warrant for the Douglas house. After much discussion, they were satisfied with their plan and asked Piers to keep people away from that area.

Evie's eyes focused on the condemned house across the field. The Circle would be broken, and the innocent girls returned to their worried families. Not one more person would be left to die in the woods. Goosebumps formed on Evie's arms. Stacey Linn's slight form lying face down in the snow would forever haunt her.

While she'd let her mind wander, several horses had been mounted and ridden to the practice area. Chance was warmed up and ready. His rider trotted him up to a vertical, and they jumped. *Yes*, thought Evie. *Chance is the competition.* Bold, forward, fluid, with tons of scope. The other horses paled next to him.

She was startled out of her reverie by a loud comment. "What's a pony doing in this competition?"

The man who'd spoken was riding an enormous black Percheron cross. Kazzam was only fifteen hands, and Evie imagined that being looked down on from a height would dwarf him further. She was prepared to ignore the comment, but the man added, "I'm calling a steward. You shouldn't be here."

"He's entered fair and square. And he's a horse, not a pony. Measure him yourself."

"If you say so. Just don't ask me to scrape your body off the Normandy bank."

"Deal. As long as you don't ask me to share the five-thousand-dollar prize." Evie moved Kazzam into a trot and left the man howling with sarcastic laughter.

She was reminded of all the other times that people had underestimated her horse due to his size. It still bothered her! Evie scolded herself for letting that man get under her skin. *Focus*, she told herself. *Breathe. Turn his judgmental nastiness into motivation to kick his butt.*

She looked over at the Parson's Bridge trailer. Jordie was getting up on Christieloo. The mare's golden coat shone brilliantly in the sunlight. Her flaxen mane was braided tightly, and her tail plait gave her hindquarters a nice shape. Gran Mary held her as Jordie mounted, and then she rubbed his boots with a cloth. She straightened his jacket and tie and gave him a big smile, lending him some last-minute confidence, Evie knew.

Jordie and Christieloo headed in the direction of the front ring, where the children's flat class would be held. There, they would warm up with the nineteen other contestants.

Evie checked her watch. In five minutes, Chance and Cynthia would go on course.

And in five minutes, the first part of the plan would begin.

If all went well, while Cynthia was riding in the qualifier, a police team headed by Officer Summers would raid the Douglas house and take the girls there to safety.

Evie's job was to text Dr. Marshal the second Cynthia was on course. She was also to alert him if they were disqualified, went off course, or had two refusals on the same obstacle — anything that would change the four-minute time frame. Their plan would go much more smoothly without Cynthia's interference.

Evie looked out over the huge course. The topography was rolling and scenic. All the jumps were marked with big white numbers on kelly-green backgrounds in honour of St. Patrick's Day, and just like Piers had said, a red flag waved at the right and a white flag at the left of each jump.

While she waited for Chance to start, Evie reviewed the course in her mind and traced her route with her finger. She'd memorized it thoroughly, but was nervous enough that she worried she might forget where to go next. She wanted to do the best she could and make Piers proud. But most of all, Evie admitted, she wanted to win for herself and for her horse. She was going for it.

Now Chance was being led into the starting gate with a girl on his back. The normally calm gelding showed white in his eyes, and his neck was lathered. He was anxious.

Evie unzipped her fanny pack and pulled out her phone. She got the text ready to send to Dr. Marshal.

This was the first time she'd ever seen Cynthia Maris-Stapleton. Evie observed her with interest. She was as beautiful as Beebee had said and small in stature. *Overly thin*, Evie thought, but from this distance she looked pretty in a fragile way, with long dark hair tied into a ponytail under her helmet. She was wearing the latest and most expensive in equestrian apparel. Her Irish tweed jacket was cut in a flattering style and lined in pale-purple satin that matched the bows in her hair. Even her cross-country vest was purple! Her boots and saddle looked to be the same Hermès designs that Evie had seen in a magazine. If you didn't count her icy expression, she was the picture of wealth and innocence. It was difficult to imagine this delicate girl with enormous eyes as the master manipulator that Dr. Marshal had described.

The timer held up his arm and counted down. "Ten! Nine! Eight! Seven! Six! Five! Four! Three! Two! One! *Go!*"

Chance leapt out of the gate and powered down the hill to the first hurdle with ground-eating strides. Concurrently, Evie pressed the Send button on her phone. The text was sent.

Cynthia aimed Chance toward the two natural hunt coops in the woods with four strides in between, and Chance obliged. *What an honest horse*, Evie thought. And Cynthia was a fine rider. Her hands were quiet and her legs still, and she stayed out of Chance's way and let him do his job, which Piers had taught him well. Evie was reluctantly impressed.

She watched them navigate the coffin, often called the rails/ditch/rails combination, and disappear into the woods, where the giant goose jump stood, followed by the drop. They had no problems, because in good time Chance re-emerged and squarely jumped the wide stone wall.

He was jumping over the ditch and up onto the Normandy bank when Evie's phone pinged. She watched Chance leap down the other side and gallop past the secret cave where Beebee had hidden, and then she read Dr. Marshal's text.

Police found next to nothing.

Evie texted back. Nothing?

Burned-up garbage and signs of recent habitation.

No girls?

No.

What should I do?

Text if you see anything unusual.

Okay.

Evie felt numb with disappointment. She wondered where the girls had gone and what would happen next.

Her focus was split as the elegant Chance ate up the ground and easily cleared the two shark's teeth jumps set three strides apart. Cynthia rode with quiet authority. Chance headed up the hill and turned to his left to jump into the pond, canter through, and leap up the other bank, then he made a sharp right toward the roll top jumps. He handled each combination and obstacle well.

Evie's mind raced. The Circle had vacated the Douglas house. Somebody must have tipped them off. Why else would the garbage be burned? But who? Where had the plan gone wrong?

They urgently needed to find these girls. The longer the leaders had them in their thrall, the more danger they were in. One girl was dead, one had committed suicide, and one was recovering. And that didn't take into account poor Herman the cat and Loewe the dog, and all the other unknown animals that had been killed in the name of this cult.

Distracted, Evie noted that the second horse was now on course. He had trouble with the first coop and was whistled out on the second. The third entrant started.

She watched Chance and Cynthia handle the corner and the skinny, continue across the driveway over the log, the bounce, and the Trakehner, double back across the driveway, and head over the final hurdle, a hedge with a ditch in front.

The growing crowd in the centre of the racetrack cheered wildly, and Cynthia pumped her fist in the air. Evie looked at the huge scoreboard next to the food tents and shops. It read, CYNTHIA MARIS-STAPLETON ABOARD THE CHANCELLOR. DOUBLE CLEAR. They had completed the course within the specified time — not too slow and not too fast — and had cleared all the hurdles without refusal and in the correct order. And they'd made it look easy.

There were seventeen horses left to go before Evie's turn. Each trip took a maximum of four minutes, and a horse left the starting box every two minutes. Evie calculated that she'd have just enough time to join Jordie's cheering section. Beebee couldn't be there, but Gran Mary would be. And Evie, too.

Evie and Kazzam trotted quickly. The course crossed the gravel driveway twice, and there were barriers and attendants to hold traffic until the way was clear. They had to stop once to let a horse through on course. The attendant waved them on, and they reached the ring just in time to see the second half of Jordie's class.

Ten horses had been dismissed, and ten remained to compete for the ribbons and prize money. Jordie was still in the ring! Evie saw Gran Mary giving him a wave and a grin. She and Kazzam stood watching quietly, ready to dash back for their turn on the Steeplechase course.

There were two women in the centre. One was the judge and the other held a clipboard. The judge was a tall, elderly woman with a regal bearing and a patrician face. The scribe was younger but looked very much like the judge. Evie wondered if she might be her daughter.

"Slide your numbers to your left side," the judge said through her microphone.

All the junior riders obeyed, adjusting the strings around their waists so that their numbers were visible to the judge. Jordie was number seventy-two.

"Now, on your left diagonal, trr-ot!"

Five horses and five ponies began to trot. Jordie had a big smile on his face. He was enjoying himself, unlike most of the kids, who seemed either stressed or downright terrified.

"On your left lead, can-ter!" the judge ordered.

Christieloo easily transitioned from a steady trot to a light, rhythmical canter. Evie's eyes were drawn to her. Her distinct colouration might have something to do with that, Evie observed, but the mare had very nice movement, and Jordie was riding her well.

"Hand gallop!"

Did Jordie know what a hand gallop was? As she watched, she realized that very few of the kids did. Some continued to canter exactly as before, while others

204

galloped, hell bent for leather. Jordie leaned forward in a two-point position, with his hands light and slightly farther up Christieloo's neck. He increased the mare's speed but remained in complete control.

Where had he learned that? Evie turned to look at Gran Mary. She was absorbed in Jordie's ride. Her face held a look of rapt attention and unmistakable pride.

"Trr-ot!"

The riders slowed their animals to a trot. A couple of them yanked on their ponies' mouths, but not Jordie. His hands remained quiet and gentle.

"Wa-alk and re-verse!"

Jordie quietly slowed Christieloo to a walk, then turned her to the wall and continued in the other direction. He slid the number to his right side.

Evie was amazed. While she'd been learning how to ride the cross-country jumps, Gran Mary had made Jordie a polished rider!

They trotted, cantered, and hand galloped on their right leads. Not only were Jordie and Christieloo the best suited to each other and the most responsive, they looked the best and seemed to be having the best time. *If I were the judge*, Evie thought, *for sure Jordie would win first prize. Hands down.*

The judge conferred with her scribe. One long, tense minute later, she asked the contestants to come to the middle, side by side.

"Seven and forty-four, please leave the ring. And thank you very much." The judge gave the disappointed juniors a gracious, warm smile as they walked out. "Sixty-five, thirty-three, eighty-seven, twelve, fifty-one, ninety-six, twenty-six, and seventy-two, please line up in that order."

Evie was stunned. Jordie was in the ribbons, but just. He had come in eighth. How was that possible? He and Christieloo were miles above their competition. She looked over at Gran Mary, expecting to see shock and dismay. Instead, her grandmother was beaming and cheering!

Mary caught her eye and gave her a big wave. She parted the crowd to join Evie. As she came through, she yelled, "He did it!"

Evie's brow furrowed. "Eighth?" she yelled back.

"No! He won!" Mary stood beside Kazzam and gave his ebony neck a stroke. "The winners were listed in reverse order. Jordie won first!"

Suddenly, the loud speaker squeaked and sputtered. Kazzam's ears flattened and his body tensed.

"The last rider for the Steeplechase qualifier, please! Number twenty! Kazzam and Evangeline Gibb, come to the starting gate!"

Evie inhaled sharply. She'd underestimated how much time she had. She looked over at Jordie. He saw her and grinned more widely than she'd ever seen him grin. She raised her hand and gave him a salute and a vigorous thumbs-up. She was so proud that she felt tears coming.

Gran Mary grabbed Evie's leg. She spoke firmly. "Do this, Evie. Have a great time."

Evie snapped into real time. "I will!" She turned Kazzam to face the hill, and off they galloped.

15

Jockey Girl

Float like a butterfly. Sting like a bee. His hands can't hit what his eyes don't see.

— Muhammad Ali

The attendants on the driveway held people back as Evie and Kazzam hastened to the starting gate.

The timer was pacing. He looked at his watch and yelled to a woman, who pointed at Kazzam and Evie as they hastily approached. The man threw up his hands in a frustrated gesture.

Evie and Kazzam arrived, pumped up and ready to go. "I'm sorry I'm late!" Evie called out. "My little brother won first place in children's equitation!"

"We've been waiting for you!" the timer yelled. "Most unprofessional. I could disqualify you!"

"I'm very sorry. I thought I had five or six more minutes at least. I'm so sorry! I'd be so happy if you let us compete."

Kazzam began to paw the ground. He shook his head and neck and pranced. Evie placed her right hand on his neck. "It's okay, boy. Easy, Kazzam."

"Four horses off course, three whistled out for refusals — two on the Normandy bank — and two riders with involuntary dismounts, both at the skinny. It's a gong show."

"I promise we'll do the best we can."

"Why not? You can't be worse than some of the others."

"Thank you!" Evie tried to position Kazzam in the start box to wait for the countdown, but he reared up and walked on his hind legs. Her little horse wanted action.

"Keep your horse under control!"

She managed to back him in. He stood, but he quivered madly with anticipation.

"Ten! Nine! Eight!"

Evie prayed under her breath. "Dear Lord of creatures great and small, please, please, please, help Kazzam fly over the hurdles today and keep him safe, and I promise to be good for the rest of my life. Amen."

"Two! One! *Go!*"

Kazzam stopped quivering and stood still. Evie waited.

"For crying out loud! You're being timed!" the man hollered.

Still, Evie waited. She knew only too well that Kazzam needed to start at the time of his own choosing, usually three or four seconds after the bell. In his racing days, he'd regularly bucked jockeys off for digging in their heels or urging him with a crop. Evie's secret with this outlaw horse was patience.

She sensed the timer coming closer. "Stay back!" she yelled.

"He needs a smack!"

"No! No, please, he doesn't. You'll see."

Despite her warning, the timer made the mistake of reaching out to give Kazzam's backside a slap. Quick as lightning, the black gelding shot out a hind hoof and warned him away.

Evie hoped that the man wouldn't change his mind about letting them go. Kazzam appeared to have the same thought. He took off like a small, shiny black rocket and headed straight down the hill toward the first of the two coops in the woods.

As the first jump loomed ever closer, Evie feared that his speed was too intense. This was a problem. When Kazzam was in this mood, he hated being told to slow down and would fight the reins if she pulled. She put all her weight in her heels and sat down in the saddle, keeping her hands as light as possible.

Just as she was certain that they would go crashing out of control through the solid wooden coops and into the dark woods, Kazzam figured it out and settled back on his haunches. He set up the first jump just right and hopped over, then took the full four strides and handily jumped the second coop out into the sunlight.

Evie's pulse was racing. "Don't do that again, Kazzam. You scared the pants off me." Kazzam shook his head eagerly from side to side and then up and down. They turned right. The coffin combination was the next on course.

Kazzam snorted with confidence as he picked up speed. Again, Evie pushed down her heels and hoped for the best. The gallop to the starting gate had revved him up, she knew. She also knew that once revved, Kazzam would most likely stay revved.

She steered him to the centre of the first set of rails. Over they went, bounding over the ditch and leaping the second rail fence.

The giant goose was around the corner to the right, and Kazzam wasn't daunted by the huge wooden sculpture. Over he flew, then cantered around the trees to the left and down the drop, no problem. *Whew*, Evie thought.

The wide stone wall looked imposing and solid, even though Evie knew it was fake. She remained as still as she could and let Kazzam find his spot. She followed his neck with her arms as he stretched out and leapt much higher than he needed to. He landed farther than was comfortable for the left turn ahead. But turn they did, heading to the Normandy bank, where two other horses had quit.

Evie looked up at the top of the landing, as Piers had instructed, not down at the ditch. Kazzam leapt up without flinching. Once on the crown, he took one stride and then lifted off into the air over the vertical jump at the lip of the drop.

"We're flying!" Evie hooted out loud. She laughed in glee. They were airborne! When the gelding finally landed, he gave a quick, joyful buck.

They were having the time of their lives. Evie felt like she and Kazzam were the same animal; he was the power, and she was the brains.

They passed Evie's cave at a gallop and climbed up the slope to the shark's teeth jumps. Evie remembered her mistake in training and looked over them, not at them. Over they leapt.

It was time to slow things down, she thought. If their time was too fast, they'd get points taken off and wouldn't make the final four. Kazzam didn't seem the least bit tired. He wanted to go faster, not slower, so to use up a little time Evie rode him in a much larger circle to the left than required as they headed toward the pond.

They approached the drop into the pond straight on. Kazzam splashed right in, cantered through, and sprang out of the water and up onto the far bank. Again, Evie made a wider circle than necessary as they made for the two roll tops, hoping to add a few seconds to their time. Over the first roll top they went. They landed, took two strides, and sprang over the second one.

On they ran, down the hill toward the corner jump. Evie remembered it as an odd-looking triangular thing, but it looked even odder now, with flags on both sides. She felt unsure of where and how to jump it, but by following the deepest hoof tracks, she figured it out in time to steer Kazzam to the correct spot. Over he went in stride, as if he did this every day.

"I love you, Kazzam!" shouted Evie with a grin. "I'll love you even more if you don't spook at the skinny!"

The skinny was mere strides away. The skid marks on the ground all around it were a testament to how many horses had had difficulties with the jump. There it was, the table set for a children's tea party, with a chair at either end, facing inward. To Evie, it was right out of *Alice in Wonderland*, bearing no resemblance whatso- ever to a jump.

Evie tried to settle Kazzam so he could take a better look. "Easy, boy!" she said. But he had different ideas. He grabbed the bit, sped up, and leapt, leaving a lot of air between himself and the strange obstacle. Evie was sure they'd jumped three feet higher than they needed to.

They landed close to the driveway and crossed the gravel at a quick pace as two attendants held back the pedestrians and traffic. Evie was grateful that they were on the job.

As they galloped past the grooms' cabins, an intense flash of light startled her. She glanced over her right shoulder to look. There was nothing out of the ordinary, just empty cabins. It must have been sunlight glancing off a window, but her eyes needed a second to readjust.

She looked ahead to see the hanging log. The top rail was tied to thick hemp ropes suspended from an overhead beam, and anchored with ropes to the rails below. Kazzam lifted his chin, tucked his hindquarters under him, and pushed off with ease. Up and through they went, landing lightly and carrying on.

The bounce was next, farther down the field and to their right. As they approached it, the entire fair became visible, with tents and rides and people everywhere. Bright colours, joyful noises, and salty, sweet food smells assaulted their senses. Evie kept her concentration on their task. "Kazzam, stay with me, boy."

The bounce consisted of two sets of rails with no strides between them, just room enough to land and take off. Evie felt Kazzam's confusion for the first time that day. She rubbed the crest of his neck with her fingers as she held the reins. "Easy, boy. It's two jumps, not one."

Kazzam slowed. He hopped. He snorted. But he kept moving forward. He bounded like a rabbit on all four legs, then vaulted over the first set of rails. He landed so close to the second set that it seemed to Evie that there was no room for his front legs to touch the ground before he sprang over on hind legs, just like a kangaroo.

What just happened? wondered Evie. *Did his front feet touch down? Is that even possible?* She hoped they wouldn't lose points for his not putting four feet on the ground, but she marvelled at his athleticism. How many other horses could do that? "You're a superstar, Kazzam!"

The Trakehner loomed. Evie had googled it and learned that this was not a Pre-Training jump. It was used in Training level and higher. But here it was, regardless.

Evie closed her legs on Kazzam's sides, put her weight in her heels, and looked over the ditch with the rails set in the middle. Kazzam had no trouble jumping it at all.

"One more to go, boy," she cooed.

Ahead on their left was the paddock holding the jumper classes beside the practice ring. Horses were everywhere, either showing over colourful fences or getting warmed up. It was a bright blur with moving objects, but Evie refused to be distracted and tuned it out, willing Kazzam to do the same.

Behind the big barn was the practice racetrack, and the infield was packed with fair-goers. A huge cheering section sat in the bleachers. A lot of people were dressed in green for St. Patrick's Day, and they were in a party mood, waving banners, stomping, and making noise.

Straight ahead was the driveway, followed by the last jump on the course: the long hedge jump with a narrow ditch in front.

Evie made an effort to slow Kazzam, but once again the little black gelding refused to listen. He shook his head *no* and spurted forward. All she could do was go along for the ride.

Abruptly, Kazzam slid on loose gravel and went down.

His front knees hit the driveway, and his hind legs skidded sideways to the right. Evie's helmet slid over her eyes. She let the reins slide through her hands so his neck could stretch forward in an effort to maintain his balance. She sat as lightly in the saddle as she could and lifted her feet so they wouldn't get crushed or drag him down.

The world switched into slow motion.

Kazzam never stopped his forward momentum. He gathered his hind legs under his body and thrust himself up from his knees and back onto his front feet. He took two strides from the driveway to the hedge and sailed over. He landed lightly, then triumphantly made a dash across the finish line.

With her helmet over her eyes, Evie couldn't see anything but the ground. She'd lost her reins, and her entire body pulsed and throbbed with adrenalin. Tears ran down her cheeks. She threw her arms around her brilliant gelding's neck. "Good boy! Good boy!" She patted his neck in firm strokes. "Kazzam, you did it! Don't ask me how. But you scared the bejesus out of me."

When she pushed her helmet back, she saw Piers Anders clutching Gran Mary's arm. Jordie stood beside them with his mouth wide open as he held Christieloo's reins. The same expressions crossed each of their faces: awe, fear, wonder, and relief. Even Christieloo's big brown eyes had widened in shock.

Kazzam's sides were heaving. Evie slowed him to a walk and kept him moving until his breathing became normal. She circled back to where her family and Piers were standing and slid down to the ground to check Kazzam's knees. They were only slightly scraped, and a drop of blood trickled down his left shin. His left thigh had been scraped, too, but only the hair had been rubbed off.

Yolanda came running from the barn with soapy water splashing in a bucket. She sponged Kazzam's legs gently and pulled a couple of gravel chips out of his left knee as Evie replaced his bridle with the halter Gran Mary had brought.

"He'll be fine," Yolanda said, "but bring him over to the barn and we'll cold-hose him."

"Thanks, Yoyo," Evie said. "Did you see him slide?"

Yolanda snorted. "No, but I heard all those people cry out at once. It sounded like a tidal wave!"

Piers hadn't said a word until now. "Evie, you are my little Jockey Girl. I am speechless. And my hair is now grey, yes?"

"It was grey before!" Evie began to laugh and couldn't stop. She knew it was nerves and tried to control herself, but that just made her laugh harder.

A long black snout pushed her thigh hard. "Mags?"

Evie fell to her knees and hugged her sleek black dog. Magpie made her gulping noises and licked Evie's face. She couldn't stop wiggling and wagging her long skinny tail. "How the heck did you get here, girl?" Evie wondered aloud.

She was still patting Magpie when she heard Gran Mary say, "Disqualified?"

Evie stood up and stared at the three people who'd appeared beside them. One was the man who was acting as the timer. Another was the elegant older woman who'd judged Jordie's class. The third was a short, sturdy man of about fifty-five or sixty, with intelligent eyes and an approachable demeanour.

She looked up at the big scoreboard. It read, EVANGELINE GIBB ABOARD KAZZAM. DISQUALIFIED.

"Disqualified?" Evie repeated. Was it the bounce, she wondered? Or the extra wide turns? Had they gone off course? "For what?" she asked.

The timer spoke smugly. "If you haven't read the rules and regulations, you should." He shot Evie a look full of distain.

Piers smiled with his mouth but not his eyes. Evie remembered that look from when she'd first met him and

215

he'd caught her out in a lie. Well, lies. "Jeffery," he asked politely, "which rule are you speaking of?"

"Rule ten. A rider must never touch the ground."

Piers nodded wisely. "Just so. That's an important rule. But Evangeline Gibb never touched the ground, yes?"

"Wrong! When the horse fell, her left heel touched the gravel, sending dust up in the air as proof. I saw it." Jeffery glared at Piers, ready for a battle.

Evie glanced at the other two judges. The woman was not happy, and the man looked very sorry about the situation. Evie assumed that they were unwilling to contradict someone who seemed so very certain about the facts.

"Jeffery," Piers stated firmly, "her horse did not fall. He slid. And both of her feet remained up."

"And do you have proof?" asked Jeffery. "If not, we three judges have the ultimate authority to disqualify Kazzam and Evangeline Gibb. They will not be in the final four."

Evie suddenly felt exhausted. "I'm going to let Kazzam cool down. He did his best and I'm proud of him."

"We all are," said Gran Mary loudly. She removed the saddle and threw a sheet over the gelding's back. Evie, Kazzam, and Magpie started walking across the field.

"Just a minute!" called Jeffery. "All dogs must be on a leash!"

Evie turned to face him. She unsnapped the lead shank from Kazzam's halter and fastened it to Magpie's collar. Then she resumed walking, her dog on a leash and her horse loose by her side. "Your rules, not mine."

They walked across the field, away from the crowds and the noise. Evie felt drained. Kazzam walked with

216

his head low, as if he knew they'd been disqualified. "It's not your fault, boy. You slipped on loose gravel. It was bound to happen to somebody." She rubbed the soft skin behind his left ear. "Maybe we should have gone a bit more slowly there. What do you think?"

It was not yet noon, and the cross-country course would be clear until two. Evie wandered toward the fields near the old caretaker's house to get some peace and quiet. "Maybe it's better this way. We've had the best day ever. Right, boy?" Kazzam simply plodded along beside her. He'd exerted himself and seemed happy to have a rest.

Magpie began to strain at her leash. Evie figured they were far enough away from the judges that she could let the dog go. As soon as Magpie was free, she dashed straight northward.

Evie sighed. "I'll never catch up to that dog on foot." She buckled up the dangling chinstrap of her helmet, clipped the shank to the left side of Kazzam's halter, and tied the loose end to the right of it, making reins. Then she hopped up onto the cooler covering his bare back. "Good thing you're small," she said.

They trotted in the general direction that Magpie had gone, past the skinny and over the driveway as it curved west. Magpie made a tiny yelp. She was at the grooms' cabins.

Interesting, Evie thought. She watched her dog carefully, remembering the flash of light she'd seen when they were on course. Was somebody in there? More specifically, were the Circle girls in there? Dr. Marshal had told her they were no longer in the Douglas house.

She urged Kazzam closer. Magpie was agitated. Her nose was on the ground and her body twitched with energy. She made her little throat noises and wouldn't stop moving from place to place all around the far cabin and then back again.

Evie slid from Kazzam's back and tied the lead shank in a knot so it wouldn't fall forward and trip him. She hid behind an old maple and peeked out.

Magpie had too much interest in the cabins to ignore. Something or someone was in there. Evie took the phone from her fanny pack and pressed 1.

Dr. Marshal answered on the first ring. "Evie?"

"I'm at the grooms' cabins," she whispered. "Magpie is going nuts at the one farthest from the barn. Are you here?"

"No, I'm testing some material. What's up?"

"I'm not sure, but Magpie is onto something. I think the Circle might've moved here."

"Do you see something? Or is this just based on your dog's behaviour?"

"Just on Magpie's reactions, but she doesn't make stuff up."

"Maybe it's a raccoon."

Evie exhaled. Dr. Marshal wanted proof. "Maybe."

"Watch the cabin, and if you see anything concrete, call me back. Don't go near it, just watch. Can you do that?"

"Yeah."

"Stay safe."

Evie pressed End. He didn't believe her, but why should he? He didn't know how Magpie worked. And maybe Evie had jumped to conclusions. *It wouldn't be the first time*, she thought with a grimace.

She checked on Kazzam. He was past the trees, grazing, and safely out of the sightline of the cabins.

She turned back to watch the cabin. Magpie had stopped moving. Her right ear lifted, and she cocked her head. One paw came up in the bird-dog position.

What was she listening to? Evie was curious.

A blond teenager crept out of the cabin. She had a sallow complexion and was dressed in all black. The girl furtively looked to her left and to her right, then crouched down. "Here, doggie," she cooed to Magpie in a baby voice. "Here, doggie. Come to momma." She held out her hand. In it was a large cube of raw meat. "Here, doggie."

Magpie sniffed, then cowered. She growled softly and backed up.

"Come here!" the girl commanded. She made a lunge for Magpie's collar, scaring the dog further.

Not wanting this to escalate, Evie stepped out from behind the tree. "Hi!" she said, as if she'd just arrived.

The girl looked up at her, startled and flushed. "Hey!" said the girl, recovering. "This your dog?"

Evie nodded. "Yeah. I'm just cooling out my horse and let her off the leash, sorry. Is she bothering you?"

"No! I thought she was lost. I'd adopt her in a second. She's so cute." The girl stepped closer to pat the dog.

Magpie's ruff was already up on the nape of her neck, and now she showed her teeth. She didn't like this girl.

"Come, Magpie," said Evie.

"Is she dangerous?" asked the girl.

"Only sometimes," said Evie as a warning. "Come on, girl." Magpie obeyed and sat, watching the blond girl with complete focus. "Do you live here?" Evie asked casually.

"Yes. It's great! All painted and new stuff and everything."

"So, you're a groom?"

"No-o-o …" The girl's head tilted in confusion. "But I might be a bride one day!" She laughed. To Evie's ears the laughter sounded false.

"I mean, do you work at the barn?" said Evie, ever more suspicious. "Aren't these cabins for barn staff?"

"Oh, yeah, I do! I was kidding. See you." The girl abruptly turned and re-entered the cabin.

Just then, Jordie came galloping up on Christieloo. "Hey, there you are! Gran Mary says we're leaving now."

"Okay," Evie called. "You go, and I'll be there as soon as I can. But walk her, Jordie! Christieloo can't get on the trailer huffing and puffing."

"I was looking all over for you. I had to go fast," Jordie explained, as he and Christieloo walked away sedately. He turned back and gave her a look. "Walking. See?"

Evie waved him away and pressed 1 on the phone again.

"Evie?"

"Yes. A girl came out of the cabin. She says she works at the barn, but I don't believe her."

"Why is that?"

"Because she doesn't know what a groom is."

"Not everybody does," Dr. Marshal sighed. "I need more proof than that. There's nothing more to do today. You might as well go home."

The Grooms' Cabins

Impossible is just a word thrown around by small men who find it easier to live in the world they've been given than to explore the power they have to change it.

— Aimee Lehto

With a lot of backing up and going forward inch by inch, Gran Mary tried to ease her truck and horse trailer out of the packed parking lot. They'd arrived early that morning and had since been hemmed in on all sides. Mary was getting angry.

Evie stood outside directing her. "Stop! Too close!"

"Don't people have any consideration?" Mary sputtered out the window. "Or common sense? They put their own vehicles at risk when they park so close. This is crazy!"

Jordie quietly sat in the passenger seat, proudly holding his first-place ribbon. The smile on his face made Evie smile, too.

"What's so funny?" Mary snapped.

"Nothing! Jordie's happy, so I'm happy."

Mary frowned. "And *I'll* be happy when we're out of this place."

The black truck beside them was the biggest problem. The owner showed up just as Evie was directing Mary to come forward one more inch.

"Hey! Careful there!" The man yelled.

"Oh, am I glad to see you," said Evie. "We have to leave, and if you could move ahead just a little, we'll be good to go."

The man looked over the situation and agreed. "It's the only way you're getting out." Then he did a double take. "Hey! You rode in the qualifiers. I'd know you anywhere with that crazy pink and blue shirt and your red hair."

"Yeah. Kazzam and I went last."

"Ho-ly. That was a ride for the history books, I'll tell you."

"Thanks," said Evie. "It was fun. But I was disqualified for touching the ground."

"Before the last jump? On the gravel lane?"

"Yeah. It happened so fast I can't remember if I touched or not."

The man shook his head. "Too bad. You were great. Hey, let me move my truck so you can get out."

"Thank you so much," said Mary. "We really appreciate your help." Evie noticed that her grandmother was back to her polite persona.

"No problem." The man added, "Wait 'til I tell my wife. Her money was on you and she got the whole thing on her phone."

Evie thanked him and got in the back seat beside Magpie. Once the black truck was out of the way, it became much simpler to make an exit. Soon they were out of the field and onto the driveway, passing the tents and crowds.

Kazzam and Christieloo hadn't kicked or even moved during all the to-ing and fro-ing of the trailer. They contentedly munched from the hay nets that hung on either side of their standing stalls. Kazzam's knees looked good, too. There was no swelling at all.

Evie relived her wild ride. She'd had so much fun with her plucky horse, in spite of the hair-raising moments and the slide on the gravel. Maybe Piers could continue giving her lessons, she thought. She really hoped he could. She'd be absolutely heartbroken if he couldn't.

As her thoughts drifted, she absently rubbed Magpie's silky black ears. Suddenly, the penny dropped, and she stared into her dog's brown eyes. "You crossed the highway! You followed the trail that we found that day, didn't you Mags, and then you crossed the highway to get here. There's no other possible way!"

"What are you mumbling about back there?" asked Mary.

"Magpie. She ran here from Parson's Bridge. I know how she got out of the barn 'cause she's done it before, but I just realized that she had to cross that huge, busy highway!"

"Gee," said Jordie. "She could've been hit."

"No kidding." Evie didn't want to think about it.

Mary said, "She's remarkable."

"She sure is!"

"Just like her owner," Mary added.

"Thanks, Gran Mary. I was disqualified, though."

"You rode amazingly well. You should have heard Piers the whole time. He was riding along with you."

"Yeah!" Jordie shrieked. "He used his hands and arms, and every time Kazzam jumped, his leg came up. He counted strides between jumps, too. He thinks you're marvellous!" Jordie imitated Piers's accent. "Mah-va-luss! Yah?"

Evie was glad of Piers's praise. She remembered him calling her his Jockey Girl. "I wanted to win."

Gran Mary chuckled. "Of course you did, dear, but honestly, I'm glad you're not riding in the final four this afternoon. Anything can happen when horses compete side by side."

"Maybe you're right. I learned a ton today. Kazzam proved himself, and we're going home in one piece. Not bad."

"Hear, hear. Not bad at all. I'm proud of you, Evie. Very proud." Gran Mary drove out of the MMS gates and turned right.

Jordie held up his red ribbon with a big green shamrock on the rosette. "I'm proud of *me*, too!"

Evie and Gran Mary laughed. "You were great," Evie said. "The best by a mile. I'm glad I saw your class."

"It was fun. I wasn't scared. Some of the others were."

"You're right, they were scared," Gran Mary agreed. "Hey, Jordie, what do you say about showing Christieloo this summer? You could have a lot of fun, and it'd be fun for me, too."

"Yeah! Super cool!"

"You were the only one who knew what a hand gallop was," added Evie.

"Gran Mary taught me. She's a great coach. Beebee says she isn't, but she is." His face fell. He said quietly, "I wish she were here. She should've seen me go. I hope she's okay."

Evie reached into the front seat and gave his left shoulder a squeeze. "We all do."

"We sure do." Gran Mary took a deep breath. "Well, that was a good day. Jordie won first with Christieloo, and Kazzam and Evie showed that they have a great future in eventing."

Gran Mary's phone rang. "Jordie, can you answer that for me?"

"Sure." Jordie found the phone in Gran Mary's purse. "Hello? Jordie, the first-prize winner, here."

Evie and Mary chuckled.

"Oh, hi, Piers ... no, she's driving ... uh, what?... Super!... I'll tell Evie ... yeah, we'll come right back ... hey, can you find a parking spot for us?... see you soon!" He pressed End with a flourish.

"What was that?" asked Evie. "Why did Piers call?"

"Why'd you say we'd come back?" Gran Mary asked.

"Evie and Kazzam made the final four! They can race!"

Gran Mary sped up and turned right. She entered a circular driveway on the concession and used it to double back.

"Gran Mary," said Evie, "I know you'd rather I didn't race, but —"

Mary interrupted her. "When you get a second chance, girl, you take it."

Evie felt excitement build up inside her. Things were so much better with Gran Mary on her side. "Thanks. I will."

A few minutes later they drove back through the impressive steel gates of MMS. Piers was waiting for them. He waved with both arms and ushered them into the elite parking area reserved for sponsors in the front field, across from the jumper ring. His face was flushed, and he looked out of breath. He'd likely run down the driveway to meet them.

"Evie!" called Piers. "This is marvellous news! Yah?"

225

Jordie winked at Evie and mimicked him in a whisper. "Mah-va-luss! Yah?"

"How did it happen?" asked Mary as she put the truck into park and they all got out. "How did Evie get requalified?"

"A man and a woman came into the show office in the barn. They had a video of Evie's slide on the gravel. I saw it, too. It was amazing. Her feet stayed right up. In fact, she was holding them up, yah, Evie?"

Evie nodded. "I tried to, because I didn't want to pull Kazzam over, but I couldn't be sure whether they touched or not."

"They didn't, and now we have proof," Piers enthused. "Jeffery wanted to keep you out of the race, but the other judges insisted. There would have been hell to pay. That man was angry!"

Jordie said, "I bet it was the man who moved his truck for us. He was twice as big as Jeffery!"

"It had to be him," agreed Evie.

Piers opened the front door of the trailer. "First we take a look at Kazzam. If his knees are puffed up we will change our plan."

Piers inspected Kazzam thoroughly. He was satisfied that the gelding could race. "I go now," he said, checking his watch. "Be at the start box area by 1:45, no later, and have this good horse warm and ready to go. Yah?"

Evie grinned and gave Piers a high-five. "Yah!"

Piers headed up the hill, and Mary and Jordie got back in the truck with the windows open.

Jordie had brought along Mary's manuscript. "Cran Berry? While we wait can you read some more from *The Boy on the Beach*?"

"How can I resist?" Mary found where they'd left off and pulled Jordie closer to her.

Evie stood and listened for a minute as Mary read.

There was something about the boy, Priscilla thought again. *He never moves, and he only stares. Perhaps he's drugged.*

To test his reaction, with her foot she sent a stone scuttling toward him. The boy's eyes focused.

"My mother will never let you go free," he said. "She made a trade."

Priscilla was startled when he spoke and confused by his words. "A trade?"

"Yes. You for me."

"Who did she make the trade with?"

"To the people who sell people. They will be here to get you very soon."

"Is it some kind of slave trade?"

The boy didn't answer.

So, Priscilla concluded, *I'm here alone. This boy can do nothing for me, but he can't stop me, either.*

Even from the depths of the basement, she could hear the wildness of the storm outside. She looked at the tiny window high up on the wall. *Better to brave the elements than to wait for whatever will happen here*, she thought.

That's good advice, Evie told herself, thinking of the strange girl in the grooms' cabin. *Better to check things out myself than wait for others to act.* She pulled out her phone and texted Yolanda.

Are you guys moving into the grooms' cabins? The message sent with a swooshing sound.

Immediately, there was an answering *ping*. Not yet.

Is anybody there now? *Swoosh*.

Ping. No. Busy. Talk later?

Just as she'd suspected. Sure. *Swoosh*.

Evie made a decision. First she checked that the horses were content. She gave them a big drink of water until they refused to drink any more, then added more fresh hay to the hanging nets. Gran Mary had parked under a tree so the trailer would remain cool.

Evie put Magpie in the back seat and told her to stay. "Okay if I leave her with you?" she asked her grandmother.

Mary looked up from the manuscript. "Where are you going?"

"To find a porta-potty. And the jumper finals are starting, and I want to watch. I'll be back with lots of time."

"Be sure you are. I don't want to have to send Jordie galloping around the countryside to find you again."

Jordie wagged a finger at her, making a funny face.

"Right." Evie grinned.

She had only a loose plan as she set out toward the grooms' cabins. She felt sure that the Circle had moved there, but Dr. Marshal needed proof, and she intended to get it.

She walked up the driveway past the growing crowds. Many more people had arrived, making this the biggest event that Evie had ever witnessed in the neighbourhood. Kids, teenagers, adults, and seniors were all outside for a day of fun after a long, icy winter. Kids were on bikes, dogs were on leashes, and it seemed that everyone was eating hot dogs and drinking sodas.

Minutes later, she found herself facing the two grooms' cabins. They were very basic structures, freshly painted. With mature trees to the north, they looked welcoming and homey. If she hadn't known better, she would have thought this the least likely place in the world for anything bad to happen.

Evie took a deep breath and marched up to the cabin that the girl had come out of earlier. She knocked at the door.

There was no answer. Evie pressed her ear to the door, but heard nothing. She knocked again.

Suddenly, she heard a familiar growl behind her. Magpie! She must have jumped out of the truck! Evie spun around just in time to move out of the way of a leaping body. The blond girl had silently crept up behind her and hurled herself at Evie in a tackle.

The girl crashed against the door. She turned to face Evie, anger oozing out of her features, along with blood from a cut on her forehead. "What are *you* doing back here!" she spat.

Magpie growled louder.

Evie stuck with her plan. She straightened up and spoke decisively. "Welcoming you to MMS because you're new. But if you're going to be like this, I take it back."

The girl squinted, trying to think of a good response.

"Let's start again," Evie said. "My name is Anne. What's yours?"

"People call me Al."

Al as in Althea. Cynthia's second in command. The girl lifted her hand to check her forehead, and Evie caught a glimpse of her left wrist. The tattoo of a jagged circle. Proof for Dr. Marshal. "Why were you so nice when I saw you before, and so nasty now?"

Again, Evie watched emotions flit across Althea's face as she decided how to answer. "You scared me. I thought you were breaking in."

"Why would I do that?" asked Evie. "I bet the doors aren't even locked." To prove her point, Evie turned the door handle. But it was locked. "Oh. Guess I was wrong."

From inside came the sound of feet pounding on stairs, then it stopped. Magpie whined and sniffed at the door. She dug with her paws as if trying to burrow under it. She whined louder when the series of thumps came again.

"Who's that?" asked Evie innocently.

"Who's what?" answered Althea. Her eyes were blank.

"Never mind. Anyway, you said everything was new. I'd love to see inside."

"I'm busy, okay? You came at a bad time."

Evie smiled brightly. "Okay. Anyway, welcome to MMS. I hope you and the others enjoy working here." She slapped her thigh to call Magpie and began to go.

"Why do you think there are others in there? And why are you welcoming me? You don't own the place. I know who the owner is."

"I'm just being friendly."

Althea's eyes shifted back and forth. "You go now, okay? And take your filthy fleabag with you."

"Yeah." *Exit stage left*, thought Evie. She and Magpie began to walk away. She turned back, pretending to wave goodbye, just in time to catch Althea opening the door. A set of frightened eyes peeked from around the doorway.

Evie's heart raced. She was halfway back to the trailer before she managed to compose herself. She took out her phone and pressed 1.

"What is it, Evie? I'm working."

"Althea is in the north cabin, and there's at least one more person there."

"How do you know she's Althea?"

"She has the circle tattoo, and she called herself Al."
There was silence. "Dr. Marshal?"

"I'm here. I'm thinking. You were right."

"Yes. I repeat, Magpie never makes stuff up."

"I'm calling Katrina right now."

Evie looked up ahead and saw some people standing
with Gran Mary around the trailer. As she got closer, she
recognized the three judges and hurried over.

"Hi!" she said, a little out of breath.

The judge named Jeffery scowled. "What did I tell
you about your dog being off leash? It's not too late to
disqualify you again. I have every —"

Mary interrupted him. "The dog was in the truck.
She climbed out through the back window and followed
Evie. It's not her fault. It's mine. I called Magpie and
she wouldn't come."

Jeffery inhaled as if about to speak, but the elderly
woman put her hand on his arm. "We're pleased to have
Evangeline in the race. We came to tell you that official-
ly, dear."

Jeffery inhaled again. "I was about to say —"

"And," the short judge quickly added, "to apologize for disqualifying you in the first place." He glared
at Jeffery. "Right?"

"I understand," said Evie. "You didn't know."

"We're grateful those nice people came forward with
the video," said the woman. "There's no justice like true
justice." Her bright-blue eyes twinkled.

Evie took another look at her. "You know my horse's
racing name?"

"Yes. The story of you and No Justice is a legend.
My great-granddaughter wants to become a jockey because of you."

"Wow," said Evie. "It definitely was an adventure."

"I should say so." The judge smiled and offered Evie her hand to shake. "We've been rude from the beginning. My name is Dorinda Brickenden."

Evie stared. This woman was famous! She'd been a top international jumper and had established the Canadian Sport Horse Association, as well as having bred horses that competed in the Olympic games. Evie stammered, "I-I'm so happy to meet you. I'm Evangeline Gibb."

Dorinda smiled warmly as they shook hands.

The short, stocky man introduced himself with an impish grin. "Steve Clifton, huntsman for the Caledon Hounds. You ride like a champ! I'm excited to see you in the final." Evie liked his soft, rural British accent, and she shook his offered hand as well.

"Jeffery Bush," said the timer roughly, hands in his pockets.

Evie saw how difficult it was for him to admit he was wrong. She tried to make peace. "We got off on the wrong foot when I was late to the start box."

He sniffed. "And when your horse tried to kick me, and when you had your dog off leash. Twice. And you had your horse loose, too. I have to say, people like you make it impossible for people like me to do our jobs."

Suddenly, Evie found this man with all his complaints and negativity hilarious. She couldn't help herself and began to laugh. When the other two judges joined in, Evie guessed that they felt exactly the same.

A young voice came from the truck. "Cran Berry? Can you keep reading, please? I need to know what happens!"

"Just a minute, Jordie," answered Mary. "I'll be right there."

The judges said their goodbyes, got on an ATV, and drove away. Evie watched them go. "Is that really Dorinda Brickenden?"

"Yes, it is. She's a role model to us all," said Gran Mary. "Now, it's time to get your horse ready. Need a hand?"

"No, I'm fine. Jordie needs you to keep reading." Evie smiled. "But can you keep Magpie from following me this time?"

"I'll keep her on a leash, I promise."

"Any word about Beebee?"

Mary shook her head. "Let's hope that no news is good news."

17

The Final Four

The brave man is not he who does not feel afraid, but he who conquers that fear.

— Nelson Mandela

Evie got to the top of the hill before any of the others, feeling eager but also very nervous. Every rider in the final four badly wanted to win, and it would be a race from start to finish. If she could stay on course and clear every jump with no refusals, speed would win — and Kazzam had the speed. It was the unexpected that she felt nervous about.

The starting box had been removed, and there was a long yellow ribbon stretched across the starting area. Evie assumed it would drop to the ground after the countdown. She wondered if a horse might trip on it or spook at it.

Don't worry about it, she told herself. *Breathe.*

The weather had been beautiful for the last few days, but reports predicted it was about to change and become more seasonal. Evie looked at the grass that had started to green and the beginnings of buds in the tree branches.

It was hard to believe that snow was forecast. Not surprising for this time of year, though.

She breathed deeply, in and out.

The new course was posted on a board beside the fence, and Evie studied it carefully, thinking of ways she could adjust her ride. The pond was the first obstacle. The Normandy bank was second, riding in the opposite direction from the qualifying round. They'd taken the log off the end of the bank to allow this to work. The number of hurdles was reduced from seventeen to six.

She looked down the rise and traced the new course with her finger. The pond, the bank, the wall, the hanging log, the Trakehner, and finally, the hedge. She noticed the spots where heavy horse traffic had churned up the mud and made a mental note to avoid them if possible, or at least to avoid sliding.

She was curious as to who had made the final four. The Chancellor was a given, with Cynthia aboard. Their trip had been flawless, and Evie shivered a little in anticipation.

She spotted an ambulance parked beside the practice track, directly across the infield from the stable. Another one was on the hill overlooking the pond. They had to be on the premises by regulation, Evie knew, in case of an accident, but the sight of the two ambulances reminded her that things could go very wrong very quickly.

Thoughtfully, she stroked Kazzam's neck and savoured the solitude before the event. "You are my one and only horse. Just so you know, if Gran Mary is right and this race is super crazy, we're pulling out. I don't care what you think, I'm telling you how it is." She dug her fingers into the roots of his mane and massaged his crest. "We're a team. I'll never have another partner like you."

"Good luck, Red."

Evie looked around to see who'd spoken. The man who'd been riding the big black Percheron was sitting on the fence.

"Hey, thanks."

"Kingston and I crashed at the Normandy bank." He chuckled ironically. "I said you shouldn't ask me to scrape *you* off it, remember?" Evie nodded. "Well, I'm not asking to share your winnings. I'm here to say I was a jerk. That was mean, what I said about your horse."

"Don't worry. He's small, I get it. And you weren't the only one who crashed at that bank."

"Thanks for that. I've got money on you, Red. Win for all the underdogs out there."

"Don't bet all your money. I just told my horse we're pulling out if things get crazy."

The man nodded. "Be safe. That's far more important." He climbed down and began to walk away, then turned back. "Kingston bruised his knees, and I bruised my ego. I won't be so cocky next time."

"That's good. I mean, I'm sorry." Evie wasn't sure what to say. "I mean —"

"I know what you mean." The man laughed in a jolly way. "Go out there and have a good time."

"Thanks!" Evie was glad he'd found her to apologize. She'd put it behind her, but it still made her feel better.

Chance was trotting toward them now, coming up the hill with his signature smooth athletic stride. Kazzam whinnied a friendly greeting, and Chance returned the courtesy. *Funny*, thought Evie, *how horses know which horse is a friend and which horse is a foe. It's so simple for them. With people it's different. Maybe because people find ways to disguise their true intentions, but horses don't.*

236

Chance's rider was the same young man as before. Evie wondered why Cynthia never warmed Chance up, even now, before the final four, where establishing mutual trust was paramount.

Another horse was coming their way: a dappled-grey mare with a black mane, tail, and legs. Evie really liked her fancy look, but she was skittish. She tossed her head and sidestepped, trying to get over to where the trailers were parked. She neighed loudly. Another whinny, likely from her trailer mate, echoed hers franticly. Evie guessed the mare's rider had his hands full.

It was getting close to two o'clock, and the last of the final four hadn't appeared. Evie looked around to see Piers driving Cynthia up the hill in his ATV. Evie was struck again by her delicate prettiness and the coldness in her eyes.

Jeffery Bush walked stiffly to the starting ribbon to check things out with great importance. His eyes darted around, looking for someone or something to criticize. He strutted and preened and looked exactly like a large bird wearing a vested suit, thought Evie. She tried hard not to giggle.

The fourth horse was arriving now, at a gallop. Evie was glad it wasn't her racing up the hill like the harried-looking young man on the lovely chestnut mare.

"It's about time! Riders up!" called Jeffery. "Line up in this order." He peered at a list in his hand, stretching his arm farther away from his eyes before he could read it.

"On the far left, facing the course, are Mon Amie with Justin Wills. Next are Ruby Tuesday and Harry Singh. Kazzam and Evangeline Gibb, and then at the far right are … the Chancellor! And Cynthia Maris-Stapleton!" Jeffery sounded like he was giving a royal proclamation.

He smiled broadly at Cynthia and mouthed the words, *Good luck*.

Evie couldn't help it this time. Her nerves were on edge. She let out a short, snorting laugh at his obsequiousness.

Jeffery spun toward her, his face dark with disapproval, but before any words could be exchanged, Piers Anders stepped forward and addressed the group.

"You are the final four. Congratulations to each of you!" he declared, with jovial, authentic authority. "I am Piers Anders, and I designed the course. We have a few rules, yah? Stay out of kicking distance, stay on course, and stay out of trouble. There will be elimination for interference. We have jump judges at all obstacles, like before, wearing green jackets with reflective vests. And they have smartphones to record you as you go." He grinned. "The crowds are contained at the stables and track. Nobody will interfere with your ride, yah? Good luck and good rides to you all!"

He looks so happy, Evie thought. *He loves his work, even after all these years.* His enthusiasm was contagious. Evie saw the two riders who'd had such worried faces relax and begin to smile. Only Cynthia's face remained unchanged.

The mood switched back to stressful as Jeffery spoke. "Get in the correct order! I told you already, now do it!"

Evie refused to let him bother her. With leg pressure, she asked Kazzam to move next to Chance. The two horses nickered their hellos, and Evie felt a surge of affection for the bay horse.

She looked at Cynthia, sitting on Chance beside her, looking every inch a doe-eyed beauty. Here was the heartless cult leader who had created the horrific and mysterious Circle. Evie said, "I really like your horse. He's a beauty."

Cynthia seemed annoyed to be spoken to. Her eyes turned stone cold. "Beauty is as beauty does. As in winning."

"Oh." Evie was caught off guard. Did Chance have to win to be considered worthy? *Poor horse*, she thought. "Have a good ride."

Cynthia turned away and said nothing more.

There was something incredibly odd about her. *Hollow* was the word that first came to mind. Distant? Unfeeling? Disinterested? Empty? That was it, Evie thought. Empty. Like there was no humanity in her.

Then she put Cynthia out of her mind and focused on the race.

"I will count down from ten!" announced Jeffery. "As soon as I cut the ribbon, you go!"

Evie breathed deeply as she positioned her reins and stirrups.

She balanced her weight over the balls of her feet to be ready for Kazzam's gigantic starting leap. "Kazzam," she whispered in his ear. "We're in this together, come hell or high water."

Kazzam threw up his head and shook his whole body. He pawed with his front right hoof, then sat back on his haunches and rose on his back legs. Evie reassured the other riders. "Don't worry, it's just his way of saying he's ready." The other horses understood, but the riders looked at her warily, making Evie laugh. "Seriously!"

Jeffery said, "Evangeline, control your horse or you're disqualified. Again. This is your last warning."

"Yes, thank you. I understand," she said, settling down. Kazzam relaxed as soon as Evie did.

"Ten! Nine!"

Evie said her little prayer quietly. "Dear Lord of creatures great and small, please let us soar together and bring us home safely. And if it's not asking too much, we'd like to win. Amen." Then she added, "And I promise to be good for the rest of my life. Amen again."

"Three! Two! One!" Jeffery cut the ribbon with a huge pair of dangerous-looking gold scissors. "*Go!*"

Three horses sprang forward at the same time and dashed down the rise toward the pond. Evie sat waiting for Kazzam to feel the urge to run, ready for his powerful launch.

Jeffery did not step forward to smack Kazzam's rump this time. *At least he's learned*, thought Evie.

Zoom. Kazzam vaulted forward with such an enormous spring that Evie was caught off balance, in spite of her preparation. But she still had the reins in her hands and her feet in the stirrups, so she was quickly able to regain her composure.

Evie delighted in her horse's quickening rhythm as he followed the others down the hill toward the pond. He closed the gap and splashed in, right behind the three horses riding side by side.

Kazzam's speed increased. He hit the water and caught up to the others, and they galloped out the other side, four abreast.

Being in the middle of this race is utterly amazing, Evie thought. The riders wanted to win, but so did the horses, and they were challenging and sizing each other up, just like their riders were. Kazzam was fast, Chance was experienced, and Mon Amie and Ruby Tuesday were dominant mares with high self-esteem. To sense the horses' battle underneath the human battle made this a totally different experience than when they'd ridden the course one at a time. It had become a contest on two different levels.

The Normandy bank was just ahead. The horses hadn't yet jumped it from this direction, and Evie felt them all suck back slightly in apprehension. Kazzam was the first to figure out how to do it. He boldly jumped up on the platform, with Mon Amie on his heels. Together they leapt off the top and over the ditch.

Ruby Tuesday and Chance landed a second later, but they cut the corner hard on the right turn and crowded Kazzam and Mon Amie on the approach to the stone wall.

To get ahead, Mon Amie's rider used his whip. She raced forward and charged the wall, jumping it from too long a distance and knocking it hard with her hind legs. The hollow noise of plastic being thumped was a surprise to the chestnut mare. She spooked sideways and almost lost her footing on the landing. Now she was angry. She bucked and shot out her hind legs.

Kazzam had been surprised by the hollow noise as well, and he shied away from the mare's back feet. Snorting, he kept his distance and let her go, then jumped the stone wall at an almost leisurely pace. Evie knew his temperament. She'd learned from experience not to try to influence his speed. Even a little extra leg pressure might elicit a rebellious buck.

The three other horses raced ahead. Evie was determined to let Kazzam run his race. She rode patiently, but began to wonder if he didn't care enough to win. She was so tempted to urge him on!

The two mares and Chance had made the turn and were now quite a distance ahead on the straight stretch of the course, with Chance in the lead. Evie estimated that she and Kazzam were half a football field behind.

Just as Evie was sure they could never catch up, Kazzam's astonishing speed kicked in. He went from first gear to fourth in less than a second, digging in with his head down. It was exhilarating! This was the speed that Evie remembered from the Queen's Plate. This was what she dreamed of! *This* was what he was named for. Alakazam! Evie grinned like a monkey and chirped, "Yeah!"

Kazzam's strides lengthened and quickened as he ate up the distance, his feet barely touching the ground. Air whistled through Evie's helmet and caused tears to run down her face. She gripped his sides tightly with her calves and clutched his mane for dear life.

The backsides of their three competitors grew bigger and bigger as Kazzam sped forward, almost as if they were standing still. He overtook the mares at the corner and was neck and neck with Chance four strides from the skinny. The small black gelding passed the big horse handily, jumped the skinny, and was well in the lead as he crossed the gravel driveway.

The next jump on course was the hanging log, and Kazzam was now five strides ahead of the competition.

To their right were the grooms' cabins. Evie closed her right eye, in case the bright light flashed again. She was ready for that, but was not ready for what lay ahead.

The top rail of the hanging log, suspended by thick ropes from an overhead beam, began to move a little. Evie knew it was designed to not move at all. Was she imagining it?

Evie calculated that they had fewer than ten strides at most to figure it out.

A slight figure dressed in black stepped out from behind the thick post at the left side of the jump. It was a girl with a hood over her head. She grabbed the rope with both hands and with a great deal of effort, made the log slowly zig and zag.

Evie was not imagining it. The ropes that secured the top rail to the base must've been cut.

Six strides away. If Evie pulled Kazzam up, they'd be off course. If they went for it, they might crash.

Evie sat up. She pushed her heels into the stirrups. Keeping her weight centred and her hands on his neck with her fingers grasping his mane, she let Kazzam go. If he wanted to, he would.

Three strides away. Evie warned him, "Easy, boy. I'm going to yell." She hollered at the top of her lungs, "Interference!"

With one stride left, Kazzam made his decision. Gathering all his strength under his hind haunches, he hurled himself between the moving log and the overhead beam. Evie flattened her back as low as she could and ducked her head down beside his neck.

They landed. They were through. *It's a miracle*, Evie thought. To avoid the rocking log, Kazzam had jumped so high that Evie had felt the overhead beam graze her back.

She glanced behind to check on the others.

Chance had landed safely, and the others were right behind.

Evie looked ahead, set their path to the Trakehner, then peeked back to see Ruby Tuesday rearing up and Mon Amie dashing sideways. The log was still moving.

She and Kazzam rode on. The race had become a farce. The interference at the hanging log would nullify the Steeplechase altogether. Should she keep going or pull up?

Her indecision caused Kazzam to slow. He was waiting for instruction. She felt Chance nearing them on their right as they approached the second-last hurdle.

"Hey!" Cynthia called, "let's do the last two together!"

Evie was surprised. She felt a wave of suspicion, but couldn't think of any possible motive, since the race was over.

"Why not?" she yelled back. Coming in together might make the best of a bad situation for the waiting crowds.

Together, Chance and Kazzam cantered. They found a length of stride that fit them both and stayed close together. Their ears were pricked forward, and it seemed to Evie that the horses were quite content to move in tandem.

Three, two, one, and over the Trakehner the two geldings went, one small and ebony black, the other tall and bright bay.

Evie and Cynthia were exactly in sync as well, leaning forward and releasing pressure on the reins just the right amount as the horses stretched their necks in harmony.

They landed exactly together, on the same lead, and cantered onward toward the final jump, the hedge with the ditch in front.

Evie found herself changing her opinion of Cynthia. Arriving at the finish line together spoke of a desire to create harmony, and it was Cynthia's idea. Maybe there was a bit of good in her, Evie thought. Maybe she wasn't totally devoid of humanity after all.

To their left, the crowds had gathered for the grand finish. As well as filling the stands and covering the infield, they were all over the driveway and pushing against the attendants and barricades along the route. There were hundreds of spectators, Evie estimated. The noise had grown astonishingly loud. Tension was building, and emotion was very high. People were waving betting slips and cheering madly.

Evie felt great.

Halfway to the hedge, Chance bumped Kazzam. Evie rode on, assuming it had been a mistake. Then Chance began to crowd Kazzam over to the left, close to the wire barricade.

"Cynthia, move over, okay?" demanded Evie.

Cynthia didn't appear to have heard. Chance put his ears back and tossed his head, but Cynthia drove him with her reins, heels, and whip, and continued to bump Kazzam with her unhappy horse.

Evie knew what to do, and so did Kazzam. Speed up and leave them behind. They began to accelerate. But, quick as lightening, Cynthia moved her whip from her right hand to her left and poked Kazzam in his right flank.

Kazzam leapt up in the air. His right leg shot out in reaction and missed kicking Chance by a mere inch. Evie was stunned by the enormity of his response and held on tight.

Now, Kazzam was angry. He clenched the bit in his teeth and prepared to make a dash for the final fence. Cynthia reached out to grab his bridle, but Chance put his head down and veered to his right at that exact moment. Cynthia's hand grabbed empty air instead of bridle.

Kazzam flew over the ditch and the hedge and dashed through the finish line tape. They were first.

She heard hundreds of people gasp as one. Then dead silence.

Some people were covering their mouths. Others were hiding their eyes. Evie saw shocked faces all around her, all staring at something behind her. She forced herself to look.

Cynthia lay crumpled on the landing side of the hedge. She began to move, and when she lifted her head she looked furious.

Evie's attention went from Cynthia to Chance, and she gasped aloud. He was stuck in the brush on top of the jump, with his front legs on one side and his hind legs on the other. His soft brown eyes shone with distress and confusion as he struggled and lurched to get free.

He whinnied a high, anguished sound of pure agony.

Kazzam nickered. He snorted and pawed the ground, then turned and trotted back to the hedge. The only sounds in the uneasy silence were the clip clops of his hooves.

He stopped in front of Chance. The bay gelding made a deep, throaty noise. His entire body shuddered. His finely sculpted head reached out to nuzzle Kazzam, who gently massaged the crest of Chance's neck with his teeth. Chance took comfort in Kazzam's presence, Evie saw, and he began to relax and slowly stop struggling, even as the sound of sirens wailed louder and louder as an ambulance came for Cynthia.

This beautiful horse had been honest and brave, and his elegant movement was stunning to watch.

This beautiful horse had disobeyed Cynthia to avoid hurting his friend Kazzam.

And this beautiful horse had a broken leg.

It was obvious for all to see. His front left leg dangled uselessly, the bones below the knee shattered.

Evie's heart sank. She slumped in the saddle. There was no doubt about what would happen next. He would be given painkillers. He would be euthanized. Humanely. Immediately.

Evie slid to the ground and held Chance's head in her arms while Kazzam continued to massage his neck, easing the pain.

The bay gelding's eyelashes fluttered against Evie's wet cheek.

It isn't fair! Her insides screamed. *Cynthia did this!* Evie should never have trusted her! If they hadn't ridden in together, this never would have happened. The Chancellor did not deserve to die. His career had just begun, and if he'd had any other owner than Cynthia Maris-Stapleton, he would've had a wonderful, long life. It wasn't fair.

Chance breathed out a quiet groan that spoke of insufferable pain. Evie held his head to her chest as tightly as she could and said her prayer. "Dear Lord of creatures great and small, please, please, please, take this pure soul to that river in horse heaven where he can frolic along the grassy bank with Black Beauty and Ginger and Merrylegs and I promise to be good for the rest of my life. Please please, please, please …"

The veterinarian approached with four assistants who carried a collapsible tent and medical supplies. Kazzam refused to move away, and Evie held her ground when an assistant tried to grab her arm. Chance needed them, and Evie was prepared to resist. The veterinarian waved him off. "Let them be," he said.

Together, they waited with Chance until the heavy sedatives kicked in and his eyelids drooped, then closed forever.

18

Mysteries

It's one thing to say, "You liar," but there's a person who lies and a person who believes the lie. Perhaps that is the most interesting thing of all, the other half of the equation, and where we fit into all of this.

— Alex Gibney

It was over. The Chancellor was gone. Evie sobbed. It wasn't fair.

Cynthia had been placed on a stretcher and was being loaded into the ambulance. Evie was disgusted that she hadn't even looked at Chance, nor seemed to care that he was euthanized. Now Cynthia screamed, "Daddy! Daddy! Come now!"

Evie jolted out of her fog and realized that people were shouting at her to clear the area. The ambulance was ready to go, and the sirens started up again. She was numb. Her ears refused to register the chaos around her.

She needed to get away from the noise. To think. To make sense of the unthinkable. She climbed onto Kazzam's back and they walked away.

Kazzam began to trot, then to canter. The faster he went, the less her brain hurt. Kazzam felt the same, she knew.

"Run it out!" she hollered to her horse. "Run for Chance!"

They ran up the hill along the fenceline past the starting gate, then south beside the concession road. They finally came to a stop beside the old Douglas house.

Magpie caught up with them, panting hard and dragging a leash. At least Gran Mary had tried, Evie thought.

"Good girl, Mags!" Evie said as she dismounted. "You found me." She knelt down beside her faithful companion, grateful for her comfort, and held the worried dog's head in her arms. She hugged her until the panting slowed.

She unsnapped the leash. Evie had ceased to care about rules. Cynthia played by her own rules, that much was clear, and she had literally destroyed a good horse. *A very good horse*, Evie amended. *An incredibly good horse.*

She wiped her wet face. "I'm so mad I can't think straight," she said to both Magpie and Kazzam.

Kazzam was breathing hard, so the three of them began to walk. Evie needed to stay away from the crowds and all the fuss. They stayed where it was most quiet, around the old Douglas house.

A quick movement at the back corner of the house caught Evie's attention. She froze.

There! Was it animal or human? She led Kazzam closer, toward the rear of the house. Again! A quick motion. Evie couldn't see clearly through the scrub and debris, so she got closer.

Magpie wagged her tail in excitement and looked at Evie for permission. "Go, girl," she said. Magpie made a small throat noise and dashed off.

A girl's voice scolded, "No! Bad dog!" Then Evie heard a yelp. Magpie ran back to her, tail between her legs and ears low. That girl had kicked Mags! Evie and Kazzam hurried to interfere.

Suddenly, the girl darted for cover, and Evie recognized her.

"Beebee!" she called.

Beebee stopped running and slowly turned around. The look on her face puzzled Evie. She'd expected her stepsister to be happy to see her, or at least relieved that she wasn't being stalked by someone from the Circle, but instead Beebee had a guilty look about her eyes and mouth — the look of someone trying to think fast.

"It's not what you think!" Beebee yelled. "I'm working undercover!"

Evie called back, "Then don't tell the world!" With Magpie and Kazzam at her side, she walked up to her stepsister. "What's going on?"

Beebee's eyes widened with feigned innocence. "Paulina thinks I'm fine, so I got out of the hospital, and I wanted to help, so I called Dr. Marshal, and he told me to come here to gather evidence and join up with the Circle again so I could tell him everything they do."

Evie had strong doubts about Beebee's story. Dr. Marshal had been against getting Beebee involved again, and the police had gathered whatever evidence they could find from the house earlier that day. Plus, Evie was very angry about her dog. "Why did you kick Magpie?"

"So she wouldn't give me away! Nobody's supposed to know I'm here! And I only sort of pushed her with my foot."

"I can't believe you'd kick her." Evie kept her dog securely by her side. "She did nothing wrong."

"A detectives does her job at any cost."

Evie looked pointedly at Beebee. "We were worried about you, and thought you'd be staying in the hospital to get treatment."

"I don't need treatment! I'm fine! Mom says so!"

"But you overdosed on pills, and that's wack. And if you're here undercover, why didn't I know about it?"

"Because! Dr. Marshal said if you knew, you'd maybe act different and give it away, and you had a race to run."

Evie was skeptical. "Is that true?"

"Why would I lie? Why else would I be here? They want to kill me!" Beebee was red in the face, and she looked truly upset.

"Yes, they do. Or at least to scare you," agreed Evie. "Who called you at Gran Mary's farm, before you took all the pills?"

Beebee's eyes flickered back and forth. She said nothing.

"Was it Cynthia? Or Althea? Who, Beebee?"

"I can't say because I'm undercover."

"You're still protecting them? The person who called you scared you so much that you tried to kill yourself!"

"That was my decision, not theirs!"

Evie opened her eyes wide. "That's so weird I don't know what to say."

"That's your problem, not mine."

"Somebody warned them that the police were coming this morning. Who did that? Was it you?"

Beebee mimed locking up her lips and throwing away the key. She stared at Evie with open defiance.

"Let's see what Dr. Marshal has to say." Evie pulled out Dr. Marshal's phone, and watched Beebee's expression become nervous as she pressed 1. He'd always answered on the first ring, but this time he didn't pick up.

Beebee laughed harshly. "Give it up, Evie!" She turned away, "Now, I have work to do."

"What are you looking for?"

Beebee quickly spun around and said, "Evidence."

"Let me help."

"No! Go before anybody sees you. You'll blow my cover. If your mutt hasn't already." She disappeared around the corner.

Evie continued to stare at the Douglas house, unsure of what to think or do. She was spent. She'd raced twice, Chance was dead, and she couldn't think straight. They should go home. Beebee wouldn't listen to her anyway.

Magpie wagged her tail and pushed Evie with her nose.

"What do you know that I don't, Mags? What does your long nose tell you?"

Magpie looked into Evie's eyes with adoration. Evie rubbed her ears and called Dr. Marshal again. Again, there was no answer. She continued walking Kazzam, heading toward the warm-up ring and horse trailer parking. Her day was done.

A tall, athletic young man came running toward them. He waved his arms and called to her, but the breeze took his words in another direction.

He looks a lot like Mark, thought Evie. *Wait! Not possible — it is Mark!*

Magpie rushed down the slope and jumped up to lick his face. Mark hugged the dog and gave her a good pat. Evie and Kazzam met them halfway.

"Evie!"

"Mark! I can't believe you're here! I tried to call you all day yesterday and this morning, and —"

"I dropped my phone in the ocean." Mark took her

in his arms and kissed her on her mouth. They held each other tightly, completely engrossed in each other, totally oblivious to the outside world.

Then Kazzam nudged Mark hard with his big, solid head, sending the teenager stumbling backward to get his balance.

Evie and Mark looked at each other, stunned. They began to smile, then grin, and then they broke into laughter. They laughed until they had to hold their sides.

"A jealous horse?" exclaimed Mark when he caught his breath. "Who knew?"

"He was here all break. Where were you?"

"I get it. I'd feel the same. Hey! You were amazing in that race."

Evie's joy disappeared with a thud in her gut. "Then you saw what happened."

Mark nodded. "It was a horrible thing, that accident."

Evie slowly shook her head.

"What are you saying? It wasn't an accident?" Mark asked.

"Wasn't it obvious?"

"I couldn't tell. It happened so fast. Your grandmother recorded it, so the judges are examining the video now."

"Good. They'll see for themselves."

"And what happened at the hanging log when those horses went off course?"

"Somebody was there swinging the log. The riders must've complained by now."

"Yeah, they did, but the jump judge came up and said that nothing was wrong. She said that you and Cynthia went over no problem, but the others just refused and then retired."

"That's a big fat lie! That's not what happened at all. The jump judges each recorded their assigned jumps, so the video will show the truth."

Mark shrugged. "She didn't get anything. She was aiming at the ground the whole time by mistake."

Evie was outraged. "Seriously?" Then she remembered. "What am I saying? The jump judge wasn't there. The only person I saw was a girl in a black hoodie. I'll go down and tell them!"

"For sure you should," Mark agreed. "I'll keep Kazzam walking, unless he still hates me. The judges are at the office now. Oh, and J.J. is here somewhere."

"Really? Jerry's here?"

"Yeah. He came to cheer you on. He bet a whole whack of cash on you and Kazzam."

"They'd better refund it," Evie said with a grimace, but she was pleased that Jerry had accepted her decision not to race Kazzam, for now, at least. "Oh, can Mags stay with you, too?"

"For sure. At least *she* loves me." Magpie leaned on Mark's leg and looked up at him with melting eyes, proving his point.

"Seriously," Evie said, "I wish you'd been here this week."

"Me, too. Next time I'm staying home where all the action is, I swear." Mark leaned down and kissed her again.

Evie kissed him back and sighed. "I need to go."

"You go. I'll be here with your dog and your horse." Mark looked at Kazzam. "Right?"

Kazzam threw his head and snorted, covering Mark with wet droplets of horse snot.

"That's what *he* thinks," laughed Evie. She blew Mark a kiss and started down the hill to talk to the judges.

The crowds had thinned quite a bit since she and Kazzam left the finish line, and those who remained were gathering their things and departing quietly. The earlier gaiety of the day had vanished completely. Even the weather had changed from sunshiny to overcast. Evie shivered. It was March, after all. She was glad that her jacket was in Gran Mary's truck.

The judges' office was at the rear of the barn in the room facing the practice track. Jerry Johnston had used it back when Maple Mills was up and running, so Evie knew it well. She walked right in, ready to explain what happened at the hanging log.

The three judges were in the far corner peering at a phone. Beside them stood a short man wearing thick glasses with heavy black frames and a blue cap with *MMS* embroidered in gold. She looked for Gran Mary and didn't see her, but Piers Anders was there and Evie was glad to see him. He turned when she entered and studied her face solemnly. He didn't smile.

"What's happening," she asked, suddenly concerned.

"We're trying to find out," he answered sadly. "Maybe you can explain why you did what you did."

Evie was confused. "Me? Doesn't the video show what happened?"

Piers's mouth turned down. "It shows that Kazzam kicked the Chancellor and that you bumped him to the right, which caused him to lose his balance." Piers's face hardened. "It wasn't worth it, Evie. Chance losing his life. Nothing is worth it, especially not winning a race."

"That's not what happened." Evie felt hot tears fill her eyes. Her throat constricted and she squeaked, "It was over by then, so there was nothing to win, because

255

of interference at the hanging log. I can't believe you think I ... I'd never do anything like that."

"The video tells the story." Piers was as emotional as Evie. "I'm disappointed in you."

She gasped. His words felt like a knife plunging into her heart. She sank into a chair, not trusting her legs.

The man with the black-rimmed glasses approached. He pointed a finger at her nose. "My daughter told me you shoved her horse. The video proves it. I warn you, I am taking legal action. I talked to my lawyers, and you will pay. Cynthia will likely be released from the hospital today, but that horse was valuable. We need a replacement."

This must be Dr. Manfred Maris-Stapleton, Cynthia's father. Was this a nightmare? Evie wondered. How could they have it so wrong?

The door opened and two young men entered. They were the riders whose horses had been spooked by the swinging log. Evie leapt to her feet. "You tell them!" she pleaded. "Tell them what happened at the hanging log!"

They glanced at each other and shrugged. The man who'd been riding Mon Amie spoke. "We tried. Nobody believes us."

Ruby Tuesday's rider added, "We came back to get our registration fees refunded. The race was rigged."

"You're right, it was rigged! Somebody was swinging the log," said Evie loudly, facing the judges.

"Impossible," said Piers. "It's secured firmly with rope."

"Go and check!" Evie said. "Somebody must've cut it, because the top rail was swinging for sure."

Mon Amie's rider agreed. "It wasn't safe."

Evie continued. "A girl was there, wearing black with a hood on her head, so I couldn't see her face. She was rocking the log. Kazzam jumped it anyway. I saw Chance land, but it was rocking when the mares refused, and I don't blame them!"

Jeffery Bush responded. "By our rules, the jump judge was the only person allowed to be there, and she would do no such thing." He spoke dismissively. "I don't believe it."

"Was the jump judge wearing a black sweatshirt with a hood?"

Jeffery smiled condescendingly. "Hardly. The judges all wore reflective vests over green MMS jackets."

Evie asked the riders, "What was the person who rocked the log wearing?"

"A black hoodie," they answered simultaneously. This caused the judges to start talking again.

"The jump judge at the hanging log was a respectable young woman, and a good friend of my daughter," interrupted Dr. Maris-Stapleton.

Ruby Tuesday's rider said, "We told you what happened. This girl says the same. We're not here to cause trouble. It wasn't a fair race, and we want a refund."

Mon Amie's rider nodded his agreement. "Interference."

Dr. Maris-Stapleton exploded. "I don't give a damn about the hanging log! I care about what occurred at the last jump."

Dorinda Brickenden stepped closer. "Evangeline," she said quietly, "please tell us what happened at the hedge."

"Can I see the video?" Evie asked.

"No," Jeffery said sharply. "Tell us your version first."

Evie inhaled and tried to remain calm. "Okay. This is what happened. Cynthia and I rode the Trakehner together. It was her idea to ride in together, because the interference at the hanging log nullified the race. But then she steered Chance into Kazzam to cut him off. She did that twice, but Kazzam kept going. Next, Cynthia poked him with her crop, hard, and he kicked at it. Then, just before the hedge jump, Cynthia tried to grab Kazzam's bridle, but Chance moved away before she could get ahold of it."

Tears flowed down Evie's face as she finished her story. "Then Kazzam jumped the hedge and we crossed the finish line. When we looked back, poor Chance was hanging on the hedge and Cynthia was on the ground."

Nobody spoke. Dorinda took the phone from Jeffery and showed Evie the footage.

As Evie watched, her spirits sank further and further. She could understand from the footage why they thought the worst. Especially since Cynthia had told them she'd been bumped. The video showed Kazzam leaping over the hedge and Chance making a huge swerve to his right at the same time.

"There must have been people who saw it from the other side?" she said desperately. "Or from the horses' point of view?"

Piers shook his head gravely. "Nobody was allowed on the other side. It was roped off and guarded."

"You're in trouble, young lady," said Jeffery. Self-righteousness shone in his eyes. "I knew from the start that you were a problem. A real troublemaker. I hope you have a good lawyer."

"This whole thing is sad," said Steve, the stocky judge. "I like you and your horse. Would've bet on you, too, if I weren't a judge." He gave her a friendly but concerned look.

"I'm sorry, Evangeline," said Dorinda. "Without other evidence, it appears like you're at fault."

Piers stood tall. "Cheating is unacceptable, Evie. You were my student. I had high hopes."

Evie was devastated. She felt wronged and misunderstood and powerless. "Piers, it's not what —"

Jerry Johnston burst through the door, his face intense and glowing. "I've got it!" He waved a smartphone in his left hand. "Proof!"

"Jerry!" cried Evie. "I've never been so happy to see you in my entire life!"

Jerry was out of breath. "I asked everybody I saw if they had footage. I almost gave up, but I finally found this man. He sent it to my phone. *This* is it." He held up the device and pressed Play.

They all crowded around. The recording had been made from the farthest end of the designated crowd area, near the Trakehner. It showed the horses from behind as they ran away from the camera, toward the hedge.

From this angle, the video confirmed Evie's story from start to finish.

It showed Cynthia forcing her horse to crowd Kazzam, not once, but twice. It clearly showed Cynthia poking Chance in the rear flank with her crop. And with crystal clarity, it showed Cynthia's hand reaching out to grab Kazzam's bridle. As Evie had described to the judges, Chance veered away, but lost his balance and stumbled.

What Evie hadn't seen came next. On the small screen, she watched Cynthia prodding the off-balance horse with the end of her crop just as he was about to refuse the jump.

Evie covered her mouth in horror, and plunked back into her chair. There was no way Chance could have cleared that jump. If he hadn't been forced to take it, he would still have been alive.

"There's more," said Jerry "The man's wife started filming earlier in the race. It's a little blurry — an older phone — but watch this." He played another video.

When it began, Evie and Kazzam had already cleared the hanging log, and Chance was in mid-jump. After he landed, the log began to rock, and the two mares spooked to the side. A figure in black wearing a hood could be seen beside the jump. It confirmed the riders' stories.

Before anybody could speak, Jerry said, "And there's one more thing." In his right hand, he held up a whip. "I found this on the ground after Cynthia was taken away in the ambulance. This is her crop." He pressed it against the table. Sparks flew and sizzled.

Everyone gasped and jumped back.

"It's a cattle prod, and it gives out very nasty shocks." With a dramatic flourish, Jerry unscrewed the end and dumped out three C2 batteries onto the table. He placed the crop beside them.

Evie whispered, "So that's why Kazzam reacted like he did."

Jerry nodded. "And that's why Chance tried to jump the hedge even when he knew he couldn't make it."

Piers knelt beside Evie. "I'm so sorry." His face was stricken with guilt. "Can you forgive me?"

Evie tried not to cry. "I wish you'd believed me. I really, really do. I'm not a cheater! And I'm devastated that Chance died, and I'm so angry that Cynthia caused it!"

"How dare you say that?" Dr. Maris-Stapleton said. "That's slander!"

Piers stood up. "Evie is right. Cynthia needs to answer for her bad behaviour, Doctor." He looked down at the shorter man. "Althea, too. She was the jump judge, yah?"

"Piers, you're on dangerous ground here. Apologize and I'll forget you said that."

"I speak the truth. For her own good, Cynthia must not get away with this."

"I'll talk to her. Meanwhile, she'll need a new horse. Look after that, will you?"

Piers was flabbergasted. He shook his head and sputtered, "My god, man."

Then Dr. Marshal strode into the office. "Ah, I see I'm interrupting. Sorry to barge in." He looked around, then his eyes rested on Evie. "Yolanda said you'd be here, Evie. You called my phone twice. Is it important?"

Evie blinked. For a second she drew a blank, then she remembered. "Yes. Did you ask Beebee to come here?"

"No." Dr. Marshal looked puzzled. "Why?"

Evie felt like she'd turned to ice. She muttered, "Oh, no."

Dr. Marshal stared at her. "What's going on?"

"Beebee's at the Douglas house. She said you told her to go undercover and become a member of the Circle again."

Dr. Marshal looked shocked. "I have to get on this, fast. Excuse me. You stay right here, Evie. I may need you."

19

The Secret Tunnel

Courage is contagious. When a brave man takes a stand, the spines of others are often stiffened.
— Billy Graham

Dr. Marshal stepped outside where he wouldn't be overheard and began to make a phone call. Meanwhile, the three judges put their heads together in the corner to discuss how to sort out the mess caused by the race.

Evie felt buffeted with emotions. She wished Gran Mary was there and wondered where she was. She'd been exonerated by Jerry's footage, but she didn't care anymore what the judges decided. Rules and regulations wouldn't bring Chance back. And she was curious about what Beebee was doing and knew it couldn't be good. She thought about Mark, back with Kazzam and Magpie. He'd be worried about what was taking her so long.

Piers sat down beside her. He looked so old and troubled that Evie couldn't stay upset with him. She said, "It's okay. Really. Just from that first video, I would've thought the same."

"I should have known you better than that. You're not a cheater, as you said. I know Cynthia, and she is one.

I'm ashamed. My only excuse, Evie, is that I was overly emotional, mourning for the Chancellor." He looked down. "It hurts me."

"Me, too."

"He was rare. Talented, yes. Handsome, for sure. But so kind. So safe. Rare to have all this in one animal."

Evie nodded in agreement. "You were training the Chancellor for the race. Are you Cynthia's coach?"

"No. Kerry Goodham trains Cynthia, and I train her horses."

"I guess that makes sense." Something else had puzzled her, and she decided to ask. "Why didn't Cynthia ever ride him, except in the race? She didn't even warm him up."

"Yah." Piers paused, searching for words. "She makes horses sour, even Chance, who was so forgiving. I had to keep her time in the saddle ... limited."

"That doesn't make sense. She rides really well."

"Yah. But she has no feel. They know that. Something about her upsets them. She should be riding a motorcycle. This is the difference, Evie, between good and great." He patted Evie's hand. "Now, you — you connect with the horse's mind."

"Thanks, Piers." Evie felt herself blush with pride.

"So. I am resigning my job today. My heart cannot be in it."

"Really?" Evie was startled. "What'll you do?"

"There's always a job for a horseman who knows how to work."

"That's what Jerry says, too."

"I've saved up a nice little amount." Piers's eyes twinkled. "I'm glad you care, but don't worry about me, yah?"

Dr. Marshal got off the phone and joined Piers and Evie. "I've let the police know. May I sit?" he asked as he sat down with them.

"Of course," glowered Piers. "But you already did."

Evie chuckled. "Hey, you two, don't be mean. Gran Mary likes nice people."

Dr. Marshal and Piers looked like two boys caught sneaking cookies. Evie was amused by their expressions.

Dr. Marshal got down to business. "The blood results are in. Piers, your dog was poisoned with the same substance that killed the barn cat."

"Herman," said Evie.

"How is your dog?" asked Dr. Marshal.

"Loewe is getting stronger every day," answered Piers. "Thank you for being concerned."

"It was a medical question," said Dr. Marshal. "I'm interested in his symptoms."

"Ah. I should have guessed. So far, he's eating, drinking, and evacuating normally. His energy is still very low, and I'm keeping him confined to my house to rest."

Dr. Marshal nodded curtly. "Good. His lethargy is to be expected."

"Was the same substance found in the girls?" Evie asked.

Dr. Marshal pursed his lips. "I must be very careful here, since it reacts differently in humans."

"So that's a yes?"

Suddenly, Evie caught a movement outside the window. It appeared to be a loose horse with flapping stirrups. Then, the door swung wide open, and a tall black dog shot into the room.

"Mags?" Evie jumped to her feet and looked outside again. The loose horse was Kazzam! "Gotta go!" she yelled and sped out the door.

Evie and Magpie raced across the track and up the hill in the direction she'd seen Kazzam running. Where was Mark? And where had Kazzam gone? He might break a leg if he tripped on his reins, especially if his flapping stirrups spurred him on.

Remembering how she'd called him from the field back when they'd been training secretly for the Queen's Plate, Evie scooped up two blades of grass. The wind was at her back, which gave her an advantage. She held the blades close together, held them to her lips, and blew hard, making a noise like an out-of-tune oboe.

Over the hill, two black pointed ears appeared, followed by a white heart on a black face.

"Kazzam!" Evie shouted, and kept running. The black horse ran to her and stopped at her side. He was breathing heavily and was quite distressed, blowing with enlarged nostrils and showing white in his eyes.

Evie held his bridle in one hand and put her other hand on his forehead. He leaned into it for comfort. "It's okay, Kazzam. Everything is all right."

Except it wasn't. The smell of smoke reached her nose and made her cough. Fire. Smoke was coming from the southwest corner of the estate. The Douglas house. Where Evie had last seen Beebee.

Panic rose in Evie's chest. Her knees felt weak. *Keep it together*, she thought. *This is no time to collapse, like when I found the girl in the woods. I need to find Beebee. And Mark.*

Evie mounted Kazzam and urged him to head toward the Douglas house. He resisted, but then reluctantly obeyed. Magpie stayed close, watching for a way to help.

Sure enough, as they crested the rise, she saw the Douglas house engulfed in flames. Could Mark and

Beebee be somewhere in there? If they were, how could Evie possibly find them?

Kazzam snorted. He didn't want to get any closer to the fire. Evie fully understood his fear. His heart was thumping so hard that she felt it through the saddle flaps. She stroked his neck reassuringly, thinking that they should turn back and run for help.

But then, Magpie began to bark urgently.

Through the smoke, Evie saw a human figure. She blinked, and when she looked again, it was gone. Coughing in the sooty air, she forced her stinging eyes open and searched for it. Suddenly, the figure emerged from the smoke. It was a man carrying a large sack over his shoulder.

No. It was Mark, carrying Beebee!

Magpie ran toward them through the thickening smoke.

"I need you to be brave, Kazzam," Evie said. "We must help them, and we must do it now."

Kazzam seemed to understand her urgency. He followed Magpie, galloping toward the flames.

"You rock, Kazzam!" she cried.

As they got closer, Mark stumbled and fell to his knees, gasping for air. Beebee rolled off his shoulders and didn't move. The fire was intensifying. The heated grass around the house was catching fire, and it was spreading fast. There was no time to lose.

"Kazzam, you've carried two people before. Now, you must carry three."

They pulled up right beside Mark and Beebee, and Evie slid down to the ground. Wordlessly, Mark and Evie dragged, shoved, and pushed Beebee until she was balanced on her belly over Kazzam's withers. Evie got up next and sat behind Beebee, as far to the front of the saddle as she could. Coughing badly, Mark put his left foot in the stirrup. Evie reached down, and they clasped left arms. On the count of three, he jumped, and she hauled him up to sit behind her, over Kazzam's kidneys.

Evie held Beebee tightly with her right hand and steered with her left. Just as they turned away from the heat, a bush ignited beside them. Kazzam spooked sideways. Everyone was jolted, but they managed to stay on. A near miss. Once they were sorted, they walked a few steps, and as Kazzam adjusted to their weight, he began to trot. Kazzam was determined and strong, thought Evie, but he was small, and this was a very large load.

They moved directly across the field toward the big barn, where they would find help.

Piers, Mary, and Jerry came bumping up the hill on Piers's ATV. They met near the secret cave. Mark slid down first, still coughing, and helped Evie get Beebee to the ground. "I heard screaming at the Douglas House," he gasped. "It was Beebee. Help her."

Mary said, "I flagged down the ambulance when I saw the loose horse. It's coming now!" She waved both her arms as the white truck came speeding across the field.

Evie was grateful that there had been two ambulances on the grounds for the day, and that the second one was still there. She watched as the two medics quickly and gently lifted Beebee onto a gurney and slid it into the rear of the vehicle. They secured an oxygen mask over her mouth and nose.

Mark began to cough again. He sank to the ground.

"You should go, too," Evie said to him.

"No, no." He shook his head and held up a hand. "I just need a breather. I'm fine."

One of the paramedics knelt beside him. "You come with us, son. You've inhaled a lot of smoke."

"No, I'm fine, really!" Mark said, but then he had a coughing fit that he couldn't control.

"You're coming with us," said the other paramedic firmly. The two men helped Mark get to his feet and hooked him up to oxygen in the back of the ambulance beside Beebee.

"Mark?" called Evie before they closed the double doors at the back. "You're a hero. Big time!"

Loaded with its patients, the vehicle drove over the uneven ground toward the driveway, sirens screaming.

Piers, Mary, Jerry, and Evie stood on the hill as the sound got fainter. The smell of smoke permeated the air.

Mary looked down the hill toward the road. "The fire trucks are coming."

Evie said, "It's at the Douglas house. Mark went in to get Beebee."

Piers put a hand on her shoulder. "And you went into the smoke to get them out of danger. I'm so proud of you."

Evie shook her head. "It was Kazzam who did it." She patted his neck. "You're Kazzam the Wonder Horse," she said. Magpie looked up from where she lay beside them. "And you're Magpie the Wonder Dog, so don't be jealous." Evie then looked at her grandmother. "Where have you been? And where's Jordie?"

Mary hesitated for a split second. "I'm not totally sure."

Evie tensed. "What do you mean?"

"I don't want to worry you just now, dear. He's probably fine."

Dread filled Evie's chest. "When did you see him last?"

"About an hour ago. I've been looking for him. He went to check on Christieloo in the barn, where Yoyo gave her a stall so she wouldn't have to wait on the trailer. One of the new grooms took Jordie under her wing, so at first we weren't worried, but he's been gone for too long."

A new groom? Evie was now fully alarmed. She thought of Althea luring Magpie with a piece of meat in her hand. Jordie's funny little face flashed in her mind, and a pang of fear shot through her body. "What if he's been kidnapped?"

"By who?" asked Jerry.

"By Althea or one of the other girls in the Circle."

Piers said, "It couldn't be Althea. Dr. Marshal called your police officer friend. She took Althea in for questioning, and Dr. Marshal's there now."

"But still! We have to find Jordie!"

Magpie had been sniffing around and had followed her nose over to the secret cave. She pushed open the faded green curtain with her long snout and wagged her tail slightly. Her ears were limp as she looked back at Evie and made her gulping noises to get her attention, then she began to whine loudly.

"What's up, Mags?" Evie crouched down and looked inside the cave. A crumpled piece of paper lay on the ground in the middle of the space. She reached in and brought it out. She read it aloud. "'Jordie will be returned alive if you stop hunting us.'"

Evie held up the note and cried out, "That new groom was one of them!"

"Why would she leave the note here?" Gran Mary asked. "We might not have found it."

"It must've been Beebee," Evie said. "Nobody else knows that we'd look for Jordie here." Her mind raced.

"When the police found Althea at the cabins, did they get the others?"

"What others?" asked Jerry.

"The other girls in the grooms' cabins. The Circle."

Piers shook his head. "Dr. Marshal said only Althea was there. No one else."

There had been at least one girl in the doorway behind Althea, Evie was sure. If they hadn't fled already, they'd still be in that cabin. And possibly Jordie was there, as well.

Evie hopped back up into the saddle. "I'm going to find him." Her plucky black horse whinnied and pawed the ground, ready again for action. He reared and hopped impatiently. She said to the startled trio, "Meet me at the cabins."

"Yah!" Piers responded.

"And call Officer Summers. Magpie! Come, girl!" Evie rode Kazzam directly across the fields to the grooms' cabins, with Magpie right behind.

They got there fast. Evie observed Magpie as she sniffed the walls and the area around the cabin. She appeared calm and unexcited. *Maybe I'm wrong*, Evie thought. But she didn't think she was. She'd seen activity earlier, with her own eyes.

Magpie howled softly. She became agitated as she moved farther away from the back of the cabin into a small grove of bushes. Now whining loudly, she dug furiously with her front paws. Then she sat down and stared at Evie intently.

"What, Mags?"

Three short barks and a gulping noise was the answer.

"I'm coming." Evie slid to the ground. She removed Kazzam's saddle and bridle and dumped them at the base of a tree. Kazzam immediately dropped to his front knees, thumped his body to the ground, and rolled on the rough brown grass to give his back a good scratch.

Magpie started digging again with even more determination. Evie rushed to join her. There was a rusted metal handle firmly screwed into a partially buried wooden door. Dirt had been thrown over it, and it had been crudely camouflaged with leaves and sticks.

She tried to lift the door, expecting it to be heavy, but it was spring-loaded. It popped up easily, surprising her and sending her staggering. A deep hole was revealed.

Evie crouched at the lip. Magpie came up beside her, and together they peered down into the darkness. The air was dank and cold. It smelled like foul earth, and they both recoiled. The hole was deep, with an old makeshift ladder leaning against one side.

Evie took her phone out of her pouch and turned on the flashlight. She immediately wished she hadn't as a rat scampered out of sight.

Should she wait for the others? No. Jordie was missing. Somebody had to go down and see if he was there, and it had to be now. Every second counted.

Evie turned around onto her belly and began to lower herself down the rickety ladder. The rough walls were dripping with condensation, which made the ladder wet and slippery. The second rung broke under her weight. After her heart had stopped pounding, she continued downward, testing each rung for strength as she went.

At the bottom, she looked up to see Magpie's concerned black face staring down, her ears drooped forward, whining. "It's okay, girl. You stay."

Evie shone the light around her and took a good look. She wondered if this might be an old cold storage.

The ground was rock sediment, and there was an opening in the wall straight ahead. It looked to Evie like it might be a tunnel connecting the cabins.

She went through the opening. Magpie whined louder and began to dig at the top of the hole. "It's okay, Mags. You stay," Evie repeated. She had to admit, Magpie's presence gave her comfort. Also, the dog would point Gran Mary and the others to where Evie was.

The tunnel was roughly two feet wide and five feet tall, making Evie feel claustrophobic as she made her way through. She was careful not to stumble on the uneven footing and tried not to breathe the rancid air too deeply.

Another rat skittered for cover, and Evie jumped. She forced herself to calm down and continue. The need to find Jordie was the only reason she didn't run back to the daylight.

Her flashlight flickered on the sweating walls and rested on an empty feed sack held up with wooden boards, curtaining off the end of the tunnel. She gathered her faltering courage and pulled the curtain aside, revealing a hidden room. It was hard to make sense of what her flashlight lit up.

Large lumpy burlap sacks were piled in the far left corner of a tiny, windowless room. In the corner to her right was a pile of garbage — empty tin cans, potato chip bags, banana skins, rotting food, and broken bottles. The stench assaulted her nostrils, and she breathed through her mouth.

That's why the rats are here, Evie thought. But where were the people who had created all this trash?

One of the sacks moved just a little. Evie shuddered, expecting another rat.

The burlap moved again and grew taller. Horrified, Evie backed away, ready to flee, but stopped when an arm emerged from the bag, followed by the face of a girl.

"What's the password?" the girl whispered fiercely.

Evie willed her legs to keep standing and ordered herself to remain calm. "Althea sent me."

"No password, no go. Get out!"

Evie thought hard. What could the password possibly be? "There was no time for Althea to give it to me, but people are coming. It's urgent."

"Okay." The girl spoke quickly. "Skill-testing question. What are Althea's other names?"

"Al and Thea." Evie hoped this would do.

"Right. Okay. What's your name?"

"Evie. What's yours?"

"None of your business."

"Where are the others?"

"Come out," the girl commanded.

A face popped out of one of the burlap sacks, and then another. In the light of Evie's phone, they appeared to be in their early teens and were unkempt.

"Any more?" asked Evie, hoping to see Jordie.

"Just us three," answered the girl who'd shown herself first.

"Can you turn that thing off before you blind us?" the middle one asked.

Evie turned off the flashlight. It immediately became pitch black, and she hoped they wouldn't try to escape in the dark. She couldn't capture them alone. "Althea told me to bring you to her."

"Where is she?" asked the first girl.

"I'll show you. You can't stay here."

"We know that," said the middle girl. "Our old house is gone." All three girls snickered. "Gone up in flames." They giggled harder, showing no sense of urgency.

Evie was beginning to make out their outlines as her eyes adjusted. These girls didn't seem to think they were in any danger, and they certainly did not picture Evie as their saviour. They appeared to be quite content to remain in their current situation.

But did they know how serious things were? Evie said, "Beebee got burned in the fire. She's in the hospital." The girls looked away. Thinking they might have a conscience after all, Evie added, "It didn't go so well."

"So? Things happen," smirked the first one. "She proved her loyalty." The others nodded with assurance.

"At least she lived," said Evie, attempting to smirk like them. "And Stacey's still alive, too. Not like Patricia."

"And Heidi," said the second girl.

"Yeah!" said the third.

"Yeah!" piped up the first girl. "She squealed like a pig."

Evie took a chance. "So. Who's going to be next to die?"

That got a reaction. The three girls cowered and the middle one said, "Not us. Cynthia won't hurt *us*."

"Or Althea," said the first. "Our mirror will never break."

Mirror? What was that all about? wondered Evie.

All three girls nodded nervously in unison. Gone was any sign of their former bravado.

A memory of something Beebee had said about Cynthia surfaced. She'd said mirrors were her friends, in more ways than one.

"Your mirror will never break," Evie prompted. "It'd be bad if it did."

"Not just bad." The middle girl's eyes grew huge. "But *death* to she who betrays. You know how it goes."

Again, the girls nodded with synchronized motions. In a singsong style, they chanted, "Death to she who disobeys. Death to she who betrays. Never shall we make mistakes. Never shall our mirrors break."

This is getting seriously weird, thought Evie.

She heard someone calling her from above ground.

20

The Broken Mirror

There are all kinds of courage.... It takes a great deal of bravery to stand up to our enemies, but just as much to stand up to our friends.

— J.K. Rowling

"Evie!"

At the sound of the voice, the three girls covered themselves back up in the burlap. Evie turned her flashlight back on and studied the walls around them for a possible escape hatch. This cave must be connected to the cabins, but she couldn't see how.

"Evie! Answer me!" called Gran Mary. She sounded frantic.

"I'm coming!" Evie yelled.

The three girls had become motionless, just like they had been when she'd first arrived.

"Don't move," Evie said. "I'll be right back. You hear me?"

Not one of the girls answered. *They're well trained*, Evie thought. *And afraid to step out of line.*

There was a sudden movement in the garbage pile.

Evie flinched at the sight of scurrying rats. A tin can fell off the pile and rolled away, and then a bag full of rubbish. As she backed out of the room, another can tumbled from the pile. She stopped.

She shone her light on the trash and stared. Was that a mop of brown hair? It looked like the top of Jordie's head. Was it her imagination? Then it moved.

Evie stood rooted to the spot, her entire body covered in goosebumps. She had to find out. She decided on a desperate act. "These rats are horrible!" she cried as she kicked at the garbage. "How do you live like this?"

When she was sure that none of the girls was going to respond, Evie reached into the pile. Her arms immediately found the sturdy shape of a little boy. She grabbed him around his middle and pulled him out. His arms and legs were bound with rope, and his mouth was covered with duct tape. He was shaking and fighting to breathe.

Evie hoisted his small body over her shoulder and carried him through the tunnel to the bottom of the ladder. She gently placed him on the ground and slowly pulled the duct tape away from his mouth. Jordie gulped in air.

"It'll be okay, Jordie," Evie whispered. "Stay quiet."

She looked up. Magpie stared down at her from the top of the hole and began to whine and bark frantically. Mary's face appeared beside the dog's.

"Evie, come up here right now! You should've waited for …" Then she saw the bundle at Evie's feet. "Is that Jordie?"

Evie nodded and put her fingers to her lips.

Mary immediately began to descend the ladder.

"Be careful," Evie murmured. "Look after him. I have to go." She raced back to the interior room, praying that the girls hadn't fled.

In a stage whisper, she announced, "Hey! Somebody's coming down the ladder. Now! We have to go out the other way."

The first girl poked her head out from the burlap. "Let's go." She slapped the bag of the second one.

The third girl emerged from her sack and pushed hard on the wall behind her. A large square hole opened up, and the cellar was flooded with light. Right in front of them was an old wooden staircase.

Evie had expected a connection between the cave and the cabin, but she was still amazed. "You go first. I'll follow."

Seeing the girls in the light, Evie was appalled at the dull condition of their skin and hair. They were unhealthy and malnourished. Their black tattoos stood out against their sallow skin. She wondered how long they'd been under Cynthia's spell.

The leader of the three headed up. At the top of the stairs, the girls crouched down on all fours.

"Why are you crawling?" asked Evie.

"The windows. We can't be seen," answered one girl. Evie was beginning to differentiate them. The first girl who'd spoken was the leader. The second girl was her deputy, and they both ordered the third girl around.

Evie looked out the window to check on Kazzam, who was calmly grazing.

Outside on the driveway, a police cruiser was parked. Evie felt a wave of relief. Her problems were solved. Officer Summers was sitting in the front, staring at the cabin. A male sat in the passenger seat.

Evie was glad the girls were crouched below the windows and couldn't see all the action.

There was a wild scratching at the front door.

"What's that noise?" asked the second in command.

"It's just my dog," answered Evie. Magpie's worried face popped up in the front window.

"Wait a minute!" exclaimed the leader, standing up. "I know that dog! You came here before. Althea told you to go away!"

"Who are you?" the second girl demanded. "You're no friend of Althea's! What do you want?" She stood up as well.

"I ask the questions!" challenged the leader. "You shut up!"

Evie saw Officer Summers get out of the cruiser and approach the cabin door, leaving the other officer in the car.

The two standing girls saw her coming, too.

Before Evie could react, all three scrambled back down the stairs and into the cellar. The wall slammed shut.

Evie opened the front door and pointed. "Quick! They went out the back way!" she cried. "Follow me."

She and Officer Summers dashed around the cabins in time to see Piers struggling with two of the girls, who'd just scrambled up the ladder. The third was running north into the grove of trees, with Jerry in pursuit. Magpie ran faster and headed her off. The girl screamed, and Evie saw that it was the leader.

Piers was gripping the arms of the two other girls as he tried to avoid their flailing legs. He was having significant trouble holding on to them. One girl was about to squirm her way out of his grip.

Suddenly, Mark appeared and grabbed the girl's arms from behind. Just in time.

Evie's jaw dropped. "Mark?" she yelled. He grinned. It wasn't a backup officer in the cruiser. It was Mark!

Officer Summers called out, "Everybody, stop where you are!" Evie was startled at how quickly the action froze.

Holding both arms of the struggling leader, Jerry pushed her toward the others. Officer Summers efficiently marched them all to her vehicle, with Jerry, Piers, and Mark flanking them, and Magpie ready to nip a heel.

"You're coming with me," Officer Summers said as she opened the back door of the cruiser.

The leader started to object. "You can't do this! We have powerful friends! You're going to be in so much —"

"Enough!" Officer Summers firmly cut her off. "Remain silent."

The girl immediately clamped her mouth shut. Officer Summers put them all in the back seat and locked the windows and doors. There was a sturdy partition between the front and back seats.

Jordie. Evie raced around the cabin. Gran Mary was kneeling beside the boy. She'd removed the ropes and cleaned away the remnants of duct tape. His head was propped using Mary's sweater as a pillow.

"He's breathing," Mary said. "And he's conscious. But he hasn't said anything."

"Jordie," pleaded Evie. "Jordie?"

He groaned softly. Evie held his limp eight-year-old body close to hers. The little boy turned his head and looked at her. "Evie? What happened?" His voice was scratchy and weak.

"Jordie!" Evie hugged him and shook with emotion. "You're going to be okay."

Jordie opened his other eye and looked around. He saw Mary. "Cran Berry, hi. The girl said there'd be pizza. Can we have pizza?"

"Yes!" Mary and Evie said in unison. Behind them, Piers, Mark, Jerry, and Officer Summers had gathered. They began to laugh with relief. Jordie was back.

Evie wiped her eyes. "Let's go home."

Officer Summers cleared her throat. "We'll need to get him checked before he can go home. I've called the paramedics back."

"Thank you," said Mary. "That saves us a trip to emerg."

"Gran Mary," asked Evie, "how did you get him up that slippery, broken ladder?"

"It's amazing what an old lady can do when she needs to." Mary smiled at Piers. "With a little help." Then she added, "You're very strong."

"For an old man." He smiled gently back at her.

Jordie's lip trembled. "Was I going to die?"

"Oh, my dear boy," said Mary. "No. We would've looked for you until we found you. We're all here with you now."

The ambulance came to a stop beside them, and two paramedics appeared. After checking Jordie's vital signs and taking some blood, they declared him fit to go home. They told Mary that they'd email the results of the blood test to his mother, Paulina, and then instructed her to take him to the family doctor if there were any concerns.

"He'll be fine," one of the paramedics said. "But he's been through a stressful event. Make sure he gets lots of rest."

"We are all very grateful," said Mary. "Thank you for coming, and for the important work you do."

The paramedics left as quickly as they'd arrived, on to the next emergency.

Piers gently picked up Jordie. The little boy rested his head on the man's shoulder and closed his eyes. They all walked together around the cabin to the front.

"You turned up right when we needed you," Evie said to Mark. Aren't *you* full of surprises."

He laughed softly and took her in his arms. "So are you." They hugged. Evie's entire world lightened. She felt Magpie leaning on her leg and freed a hand to rub her dog's ears.

"How is Beebee?" Gran Mary asked Officer Summers.

"She'll be fine. Smoke inhalation is her most serious injury. Her mother is with her. Dr. Marshal is talking to Cynthia and Althea now." Officer Summers gave her head a small shake. "I have to say, with dogs finding fugitives and horses coming to the rescue, this has been the oddest case I've ever worked."

"Is it over now?"

Officer Summers lifted an eyebrow. "All that's left to do is collect enough evidence to prove our case in court." She got in the cruiser with her unhappy passengers securely locked in the back seat and drove away down the lane, past the stables.

Piers stepped up beside Gran Mary, Jordie still nestled in his strong arms. "Such adventure."

"Where you are is always an adventure, Piers." Mary carefully brushed some hair from Jordie's forehead.

Evie saw them share a loving look and felt happy inside.

Jerry started walking toward the barn. "Not needed here," he mumbled. "Gotta get back."

"Hey! Gran Mary!" said Evie. "That's our rig!"

Sure enough, the Parson's Bridge truck and trailer were heading in their direction, with Yolanda driving. Evie waved with both arms and called, "Yoyo!"

Yolanda stopped in front of them and hopped out. "Hi! I need that stall I put Christieloo in, and your keys were under the mat, like always."

Christieloo's pretty brown eyes stared out from the trailer window.

Jordie beamed. "Christieloo!" he sighed. The mare nickered to him. *This is the start of a beautiful friendship between boy and horse*, Evie thought.

Mary said, "We're ready to go. Thanks so much, Yoyo, for everything. For the stall, for looking for Jordie, and for bringing us the trailer, too."

"My pleasure! Christieloo was no fuss at all." Yolanda looked at Jordie and examined his dishevelled clothes and filthy face. "I see you turned up, young man. A little worse for wear." A concerned look crossed her brow. "I'm sorry I let you go off with that girl. I thought she was one of the new grooms."

"She said she had a nice horse, like mine," Jordie mumbled. "And that I could have a piece of her pizza." He closed his eyes.

Mary said, "It wasn't your fault, Yoyo. You couldn't have known. Can you come over for dinner? Jordie wants pizza."

"I'd love to," Yolanda said. "Can I bring my boyfriend?"

"Boyfriend? I didn't know! Of course you can." Mary checked her watch. "It's already five, and we need a bit of time to get the animals looked after. Six-thirty?"

"See you soon!" Yolanda headed back on foot toward the barn.

Piers placed Jordie in the front seat of the truck and tucked his jacket around the boy for warmth.

Evie walked over to Kazzam where he grazed under the tree. She rubbed the perfect white heart on his black forehead and said, "Time to go home, boy. It's been a very, very long day."

Gran Mary dropped the ramp, and Kazzam quietly followed Evie up onto the horse trailer to stand beside Christieloo, who nickered softly in welcome. Mary closed the door behind them.

"Such a good boy you are, Kazzam," cooed Evie, rubbing his forehead again. "No other horse is as brave or good. I'm sorry about your friend the Chancellor."

Kazzam dropped his head into her arms. They quietly communed until Kazzam broke the moment by taking a bite of hay from the hanging net. Evie rubbed his right ear and Christieloo's left. "Travel well, horses. We'll be home soon."

When she stepped out of the front door of the trailer, she suddenly felt chilly. The weather had turned for real.

Mary was already behind the wheel. Jordie was cuddled up in the front with the heat on. Evie climbed into the back seat with Magpie and Mark.

Piers started his ATV. He looked at Mary wistfully, *Like a dog being left behind*, Evie thought.

She put down her window. "Piers! Come over for pizza, okay?"

His face brightened. "Yah! For sure I'll come!" Then he added, "Can I bring Loewe? If he's well enough?"

"Certainly," Mary yelled out Jordie's window. "See you later."

"Thank you, yah? I am very, very happy," he said. Evie thought she saw a glistening in the old man's eye.

"You're shivering," said Mark. He handed Evie her jacket and helped her get her arms into the sleeves.

"Thanks. It sure is a lot colder than this morning."

"Snow is forecast for tonight," said Gran Mary as she turned the rig around and boosted the heater.

"That's Canada for you. Spring comes when it's good and ready."

They drove toward the stable and saw Jerry getting into his truck. Mary put her window down and called to him, "Coming over for pizza, J.J.? It's turning into a party!"

Jerry grinned broadly. "Never miss a party! I'll bring beer."

"Great," responded Mary. Then she turned to Evie. "Can you order the pizzas on your phone?"

"Sure. Spirit Tree?"

"Yeah," mumbled Jordie. He lifted his head. "Ham and cheese and onion and tomato and bacon and ground beef."

"Yum!" Mark seconded the idea. "Feeling better, Jordie?"

"Pizza always makes me feel better!"

"Good man! I'll pick them up later if I can use your truck, Ms. Parson."

"Done," said Mary. "How many do you think, Evie? Four large?"

"Maybe five, just in case." Evie took out her phone and put in the order, adding a jug or two of cider with Mary's approval.

When she was done, Evie put her phone back in her pocket. "Youch!" She pulled her hand back out quickly. There was something sharp in there.

"What is it?" Mark asked.

Evie put her hand back in her pocket carefully and pulled out the piece of broken mirror that she'd found near the crime scene in the woods. She studied it and noted again the rounded edge of the unbroken part. It'd been just five days since she and Kazzam and Magpie had come upon the unconscious girl in the woods. So much had happened since then.

What had the girls in the cellar said? Evie thought hard. Something about how their mirror would never break, and if it did, it meant that they would die. And something about betrayal.

And in her hand she held a piece of a broken mirror.

"Seriously, Evie, what's wrong?" asked Mark. "You're freaking me out."

"I'm just trying to remember what those girls said."

"Girls?"

"I've got it! 'Death to she who disobeys. Death to she who betrays.'" Evie looked at Mark. "That's what they chanted. There's more, but I can't remember the rest."

Mark stared back at her. "Are you all right? Do you have a fever?" He put his hand on her forehead.

"No, I'm fine."

Jordie had been listening. He asked, "How does that go? Death to the she-bays, death to the she-rays?"

Evie enunciated carefully, this time using the same cadence as the girls. "'Death to she who disobeys. Death to she who betrays.' Oh, I just remembered the rest! 'Never shall we make mistakes. Never shall our mirrors break.'"

"Where did you hear that, Evie?" asked Gran Mary.

"The three girls who were hiding in the basement of the grooms' cabin said it in kind of a chant. They think that if their mirror breaks, death will follow." She showed Mary the mirror fragment in her hand. "I picked this up from the ground the day we found Stacey Linn."

"You'll have to show Edwin," said Mary. "It might be connected somehow. Where did you find it?"

Evie answered, "It was close to the crime scene, but not in it. Who knows how long it'd been buried in the snow."

Mary said, "But still. It could mean something."

"Like that Stacey Linn was meant to die?" Evie asked.

"Now that's just creepy," said Mark.

"Not as creepy as being hidden in a smelly basement," said Jordie. "It was just like in Gran Mary's book, when Priscilla gets put in the basement with rats. Yuck. At least there weren't rats!"

"Yes, there were," Evie said, continuing to study the broken mirror.

"What do you mean?" asked Jordie.

"There were rats down there. I saw at least five."

"Yuck-y! I wish you hadn't tell me that. It was horrible enough without the rats."

"Sorry," said Evie. "I thought you knew. If it wasn't for the rats digging in the garbage pile, I never would've found you."

Mark stared at her. "Run that by us again?"

"Jordie was completely covered in a pile of garbage. There was no way I would've known he was down there, except that rats were crawling around looking for food, and they knocked over some cans and stuff. *Voilà*! Jordie uncovered."

Jordie groaned. "That's so sick I feel like I'm going to vomit."

Mary pulled the truck and trailer over to the side of the road and stopped. She quickly reached across Jordie and opened the door. "Go ahead, sweetie."

Jordie's eyes widened. "I wasn't serious, Cran Berry. It was an analogy. We're learning about them at school."

Mark and Evie began to laugh. Mary shook her head and closed the door. "Next time, use a different figure of speech."

They started off again and soon turned onto their road.

Evie had been thinking. "How did Officer Summers get to the cabin so fast?"

Mary answered, "She wasn't far away. She was at the Douglas house with the firefighters."

Evie nodded. "Okay. And when did you show up, Mark? Last I saw you, you were in the ambulance with Beebee."

"The oxygen worked. I was fine once I stopped coughing," he said. "I convinced them to let me out before we left the property, and Officer Summers picked me up along the lane."

"Well, that was lucky. Without all of you, those girls would've escaped."

"All in a day's work." Mark pulled her close.

"Such a man," kidded Evie.

Magpie, Mark, and Evie huddled together in the back until they drove over the bridge at Gran Mary's farm.

In the front field, two horses lifted their heads from the round bale of hay. Paragon and Bendigo began to trot toward the trailer and follow it along the fenceline to the gate at the little barn.

As soon as the truck stopped, Evie heard the dogs barking. She got out and hurried to open the barn door. The two Labrador retrievers shot out and joined Magpie, all of them wagging their tails so hard it seemed like they'd knock themselves over.

Jordie stepped out of the truck and they instantly surrounded him, creating a joyful pile of boy and dogs.

Mark dropped the ramp. Gran Mary unsnapped Christieloo's side tie, and Evie freed Kazzam. Once Mark unhooked Kazzam's rear chain, Evie backed the gelding down the ramp. As soon as he was on solid ground, Gran Mary did the same with Christieloo.

"Hey, Jordie!" called Mark, "are you okay?"

"Yup!" the boy answered. "Nothing like a little dog therapy. Cesar Millan says."

"Of course. Are you feeling well enough to help me bring in Paragon and Bendigo?"

"No, Mark," Mary interrupted. "Jordie has to rest. Evie will come back to help you as soon as Kazzam's in the barn."

"I can do it!" Jordie disentangled himself from the happy dogs and hurried out to the paddock gate before Mary could stop him. Mark fastened lead ropes to their halters. He led Bendigo and Jordie led Paragon into the stalls.

"See? I could do it." As soon as Paragon was in his stall, Jordie plopped down on a bale of hay, looking a little white.

Gran Mary rubbed his head. "Stay there, sweetie. Rest."

Mary prepared the evening meals in the feed room, and Evie filled the pails with fresh water and put hay in each stall. Mark brought in the bridles, girths, saddles, and saddle pads from the trailer and put them in the tack room to be cleaned the next day, as Gran Mary instructed.

Soon, the horses were fed and bedded down. Evie gave Kazzam and Christieloo each a large scoop of hot bran mash and mixed some bute into Kazzam's mash to reduce any swelling caused by his slide on the gravel. She gave Paragon and Bendigo a bit of bran mash as well, since it was well past feeding time. Plus, horses liked to be treated exactly the same, or they'd feel it was unfair. *Like people, really*, thought Evie.

She stopped at Kazzam's stall. "I'll give you a full bubble bath tomorrow, if it's not too cold out. Are you good with that?"

"And you're getting a full bubble bath right now, young man," said Mary to Jordie.

Jordie nodded heartily. "As soon as we're in the house, I promise."

Evie chuckled. "And throw your clothes in the laundry, too." She touched the heart on Kazzam's forehead one last time and whispered, "See you later, sweet horse. Thank you for a totally amazing day." Her glossy black horse continued slurping up his mash and merely glanced at her. He was tired, she thought, and very hungry. He'd have a good sleep in his fresh, clean shavings.

"Just a minute," said Evie aloud. "We left the barn a total mess this morning. Somebody mucked the stalls. But who?"

Jordie spoke in a deep, sinister voice. "The shadow knows."

To Evie and Mark's surprise, Gran Mary spoke in the same low voice. "Who knows what evil lurks in the hearts of men?"

Jordie was gleeful. "You know it, Gran Mary! Nobody else does!"

"It was a radio show way back," she said.

"In 1930," Jordie proclaimed.

"How do you come up with all these random sayings?" asked Evie.

"Television. I watch a lot."

They unhooked the trailer from the truck and piled in, dogs and all, to drive up to the farmhouse.

As they opened the mudroom door, Jordie asked, "Gran Mary, can we read some more from your book? I mean, after my bath? We left Priscilla trying to escape from the basement, and the bad people were coming to get her. After today, I know how she feels, and I need to know what happens before I go to bed."

Gran Mary said, "In a perfect world, I'd crawl into bed right now. But we've invited over a mess of people."

"And we have lots of food," said a familiar voice from the kitchen.

"Angela?" cried Mary.

"Mom!" exclaimed Evie.

Evie and Mary rushed into the kitchen. Angela met them halfway, and the three of them hugged and wept happy tears.

Mary said, "It's so good to have you home, sweetheart."

"It's wonderful to be here," Angela said. "I moved into my lovely apartment over the garage this afternoon and got all unpacked. And this time I'm serious about staying healthy. I'm not going back."

Evie looked at her mother through teary eyes. She thought Angela looked radiant. Her heart swelled. "I hope so, too, Mom. I don't have much childhood left."

Then she noticed that they weren't alone. Dr. Marshal was sitting on the kitchen sofa, smiling. Beside him sat Bonnie Waters.

Bonnie said, "Hi, Evie. You've been busy!"

Evie nodded. "I guess we all have." She wondered briefly if Bonnie had brought news about the girls from the Circle. "Oh, this is Mark Sellers. Mark, this is Bonnie

Waters. She works at the Quest, where Mom is. Was. This is Dr. Edwin Marshal, he's a psychiatrist and investigator."

They all shook hands.

"On the way home, we stopped at Howard the Butcher's," Angela said. "We have chicken potpies and salad, with homemade carrot cake and ice cream. I've been dreaming of this for months!"

Mark asked Gran Mary, "Should we cancel the pizzas?"

"Not a chance. Two potpies as delicious as these won't feed the entire hungry pack. Can you pop over and pick up our order?"

Mark nodded. "Absolutely!"

Evie said, "I'm coming with you. We'll be back soon!"

21

Deductions

Fear is a reaction. Courage is a decision.
— Winston Churchill

By the time Mark and Evie returned with the piping hot pizzas, apple cider, and a dozen kitchen sink cookies for good measure, there were several vehicles parked at the house.

"Now, this is what I call a party," said Mark as he looked for a spot to park.

"Did Gran Mary invite all these people?"

"It was you who invited Piers, don't forget."

"He was so sad. Did you see his face?"

"You did the right thing. I think there might be something up between him and your grandmother."

"You think?" she asked with an impish grin.

"I'm a little slow, but not totally clueless." Mark made a face at her and handed over the keys to Mary's truck. "When are you going to learn to drive?"

"It was on my list for March break but it didn't happen."

"Instead, you won a Steeplechase and solved a crime. You crazy girl." He looked at her proudly.

"I didn't win."

"You would've won if it'd been fair."

"If it'd been fair, Chance would still be alive."

Mark leaned over and pulled her head to his shoulder. "I know you're sad, Evie. I wish I could make it go away." He turned her face to his and kissed her gently on her mouth.

Evie kissed him back, but not gently. And then again. She threw her arms around his neck and squeezed him hard. All the day's worries evaporated in a splendid haze of blissful, hurried, teenage love.

Suddenly, there was a tapping on the truck window.

Mark and Evie froze.

Jordie's eyes appeared. "Hi. Gran Mary sent me to help!"

Evie burst out laughing.

"Timing is everything," whispered Mark. He opened the truck door and said, "Great! You can carry the cookies as long as you don't eat them all before you get to the house."

They carried the food into the noisy farm kitchen now packed full of friends. Yolanda and Jerry chatted at the fridge with Piers. Loewe leaned against Piers's leg, getting his ears scratched. Dr. Marshal, Bonnie, and Gran Mary were sitting on the couch.

Angela came over to take the pizzas while they removed their shoes and coats. "Wonderful! Oh, Katrina Summers is coming, too," she told Evie. "And Yolanda's boyfriend is on his way."

"Should we get more?" Mark asked. "We could go right now. No trouble at all." He glanced at Evie and squeezed her hand. "Really. We'll get right back in the truck."

Evie felt her face flush.

Angela answered, "Thanks, but we should be fine. Glad you got two jugs of cider. And these cookies look incredible!"

Mark and Evie gave each other a wistful look. "Too bad," Mark whispered.

Through the laughter and chatter, they heard the shrill sound of the phone ringing. Gran Mary picked it up. She waved at Evie across the room, signalling for her to come over. *For you*, she mouthed.

Evie took the receiver from Mary and walked around the corner into the hall so she could hear. "Hello?"

"Hello, Evie. This is Dr. Maris-Stapleton. I hope I'm not disturbing you."

Evie was startled. "Not at all!" She had not expected this.

"I'm calling to apologize for what I said, and to apologize on behalf of my daughter. What happened today was unacceptable, and of course I will not be pressing charges. I won't keep you, now. It sounds like you've got guests. Goodbye."

"Don't hang up! Please. I'm really glad you're not suing me." Evie put her hand over the mouthpiece and popped her head back into the kitchen. She asked Gran Mary, "Can we invite Dr. Maris-Stapleton?"

Mary looked at her quizzically, then nodded.

Evie said into the phone, "Can you come over to Mary Parson's for pizza tonight? You'll know the people here, and we'd love to have you."

There was silence on the line.

"Dr. Maris-Stapleton?"

"Yes, yes, I'm here. I'm thinking."

"You must be very busy. It was just an idea."

"No. I'm not busy at all. I'm here alone in this big empty house, feeling … well … feeling very confused. Just give me directions and I'll come right over."

Evie gave Mary a thumbs-up and told the doctor how to get to Parson's Bridge.

Mary was getting out plates and cutlery. She asked Evie, "So how many are we're feeding?"

Evie counted on her fingers. "You, me, Mark, Jordie, Angela, Yoyo, her boyfriend, Piers, Dr. Marshal, Bonnie, Jerry, Officer Summers, and Dr. Maris-Stapleton. That's thirteen. Anybody else?"

The dogs started barking as somebody entered through the mudroom door. Yolanda rushed over and disappeared from sight.

"That must be the boyfriend," said Mary.

"You must be a detective," Evie sassed.

Yolanda came back into the kitchen smiling, arm in arm with her boyfriend. Evie did a double take. It was the farrier from Newmarket. "Brent!" she exclaimed. "Why didn't anybody tell me?"

Brent Keir chortled, and Yolanda's cheeks reddened. She said, "It's new. We haven't told anybody yet."

"Too late to keep a secret now!" said Jordie.

"How're you doing, little buddy?" asked Brent.

"Awesome. I was the champion today on Christieloo, and the Douglas house burned down, and Beebee's in the hospital again, but Mark saved her, and Evie and Kazzam did awesome, but their race was all messed up, and a nice horse died, and I was buried in garbage in the secret tunnel at the grooms' cabins, and —"

"Whoa, Jordie, my good man," laughed Brent. "One thing at a time. My head is spinning."

"And there's a whole bunch more!" Jordie concluded.

Angela spoke up, excited. "You mentioned the grooms' cabins, Jordie. There's some history to that secret tunnel. It was dug in 1837, and I'm told that William Lyon Mackenzie hid there when he planned to overthrow the governor and set up a provisional government."

"Wow!" enthused Jordie. "That's so cool!"

Everybody had stopped talking to listen, and Angela became flustered at the attention. "It's just a little piece of local history," she said, her voice trailing off.

"And very interesting, too." Mary put an arm around her shoulder for support.

There was a knock at the door, and Mary opened it to find Officer Katrina Summers. "Dr. Marshal invited me. I hope that's okay."

"Of course! Come in, let me take your coat." Mary turned to her other guests. "This is Officer Summers, everybody."

"Please, call me Katrina," she said shyly, looking around at all the faces looking back at her.

Magpie came up and nudged her in the leg with her long black snout. "She remembers me!" Katrina said. As she bent down to pat Magpie, the dog sprang up and licked her mouth.

Everybody laughed, and the ice was broken.

Evie, Angela, and Mark had been busy in the kitchen arranging the pizza, potpies, salads, the plates, napkins, and cutlery along the middle island. "Dinner's ready!" Evie announced. "Take a plate and help yourself!"

Mark indicated the sideboard and said, "Beer, wine, and apple cider right over here!"

"Hooray!" yelled Jordie. "I'm starving!" He raced over to Brent and pulled him toward the food. Brent didn't let go of Yolanda's hand, and they were the first in line. Everybody else followed. Soon, glasses and plates were full and people found little groupings to sit, chat, and eat with.

The room was warm and inviting, Evie thought as she took a look around. The fire burned cheerfully in the hearth, the food smells were mouth-watering, and the friendly chatter in Gran Mary's yellow kitchen never ceased. People seemed very happy to get together and share a meal. Evie was glad that Jordie had started this by talking about pizza.

There was another knock at the door. Evie opened it to reveal Dr. Maris-Stapleton holding an enormous bouquet of bright-yellow daffodils.

"For you, Evie," he said. "To apologize."

"For me? They're gorgeous!" Evie gushed when she found her voice. She took them in both hands.

He handed her an envelope, which she managed to tuck under her arm. "It's your entry fee," he said. "I'm returning it to all four of the finalists. It's only fair."

Evie nodded. "Thank you. It belongs to Gran Mary."

"Due to the interference at the hanging log, there will be no prize money. It'll all go toward heart research this year." He stepped inside. "At least something good will come out of this."

Mary walked over and took his coat. "I'm very pleased you could come, Dr. Maris-Stapleton," she said. "My, these are beautiful. Evie, the vases are in the mud-room. Get the big one on the far right of the top shelf."

Evie passed her the envelope and went to get the vase. As she put the flowers into water, she watched Gran Mary graciously introduce the latecomer around. Evie noticed that Piers never took his eyes off her grandmother. But then, neither did Dr. Marshal.

Jerry came up beside her. "What're you so serious about?"

"Nothing. I'm just thinking how glad people seem to be here."

"They are. It's good to get together, especially after all the trouble today. And everybody's hungry." Jerry helped himself to another slice of pizza. "Did you know that the farm next door has a SOLD sign on it?"

Evie looked at him. "Sold? Who bought it?"

"Search me. I thought you'd know."

"What time did you see the sign?"

"Around noon."

"When you mucked out our stalls?"

Jerry laughed. "Yeah. Four stalls is nothing. Sometimes I do nice things for the heck of it."

"Thanks, Jerry. We left such a big mess."

"My way of saying I'm proud of you, Evie. Kazzam is a splendid horse. He was a top racer, no doubt about it, but he'll make a top event horse, too."

Evie was touched. "You mean it?"

Jerry nodded. "Yeah, I do. Anyway, if you won't race him, nobody else will. And nobody will buy him, either, the way he bucks off everybody but you. You might as well do what you want with him and have a little fun."

Mary interrupted the various conversations in the room and loudly said, "Please everyone, help yourself. There's plenty of dinner left!"

Dr. Marshal stood. "And when you're ready, folks, I need some help regarding our investigation."

His announcement caused a stir. People quickly rose to get more food and cider, or another beer, then sat back down expectantly.

When all was quiet, Dr. Marshal said, "Everybody in this room has been impacted recently by an urgent situation, some more than others." He looked at Dr. Maris-Stapleton. "The doctor and I spoke about this just now, and he encouraged me to have an open discussion."

Dr. Maris-Stapleton nodded for him to continue.

"Evie found Stacey Linn in the woods last Monday, five days ago. If she hadn't, Stacey would be dead. Bonnie Waters and I have been collaborating for months on this case, and we're very close to putting the pieces together, but we need your help." He paused as if to find the right words and then continued. "As you know, this case concerns what we've determined to be a cult involving teenaged girls. Bonnie Waters is an expert. I'm sure you'll want to hear what she has to say." Dr. Marshal sat down.

Bonnie stood. "Full disclosure: I'm a trained psychologist, but my real expertise comes from personal knowledge. Not that many years ago, I was a member of a cult."

An audible gasp emanated from around the room.

"Not this cult, of course, but I understand these girls, because I was once like them." She smiled. "I know my stuff."

Evie studied Bonnie. Now it made sense how quickly she'd connected with Beebee when they'd met. Bonnie hadn't judged.

"Thanks to some quick thinking," Bonnie said, indicating Evie with a nod and a smile, "Althea is isolated, and the missing girls are safe. Their families are with them now. Some of them had begun to give up hope." She paused. "This cult is responsible for one death, one suicide, and one life-threatening injury. The missing girls were in jeopardy. Big time."

The room was silent for a moment as people absorbed the gravity of the situation.

Jordie fidgeted and then spoke in a rush. "I met those girls. They're nice. I want to help, but I don't know how."

"You can help by telling us anything out of the ordinary that comes to mind. It might seem irrelevant, but turn out to be the missing piece."

"What do you need the most to solve the case?" asked Jordie earnestly. "Top ten."

"Great question. At the very top is the ATV that was used to carry Stacey's body into the woods." She shrugged. "It seems to have vanished into thin air."

Jordie nodded seriously. "I'll try my hardest to help."

"We'd appreciate that, Jordie," Bonnie said. "Thank you." She continued. "Now that the leaders are in custody, we hope the girls will feel safe to talk, and the whole story will come out. But it's not over for them yet. These girls will be looking over their shoulders for some time." She looked around at the attentive faces. "I'm happy to answer any questions."

"Bonnie," Dr. Manfred Maris-Stapleton said, looking friendly and interested, "what is your definition of a cult?"

"A cult is commonly defined as a small group of people who exhibit excessive and undue devotion to a charismatic leader who demands complete obedience and engages in strange and sinister practices."

"I see. And tell me, why does a person join a cult?"

Bonnie answered carefully. "There are many reasons, but the underlying one is simply that people gravitate toward groups or families. When these groups are not our blood families, we call it fictive kinship. We need to belong somewhere, to feel a part of something, and any group is better than no group. The reality of isolation can be unbearable."

Jerry asked, "Is that why you joined a cult, Bonnie?"

"Yes. But I didn't think of it as a cult at the time," she answered. "Nobody does. It was a group of kids who wanted me to hang out with them. I felt flattered." She paused. "Every story is different, but in my case, my mom and dad were getting a divorce. They couldn't relate to me because they were so busy hating each other. I was miserable. I felt shunned by my family and my old friends, and I shut them out."

"So you needed new family?" Evie said.

"Right. Being shunned is a life sentence in nature. Imagine a young elephant alone on the Mara. Lions are smacking their lips. That elephant will keep trying to join a herd until he finds one that allows him in, or he'll form his own herd. People need to join up in exactly the same way."

Jordie asked, "Is that why Beebee burned down the Douglas house? She thought she'd be eaten?"

Bonnie laughed along with the others. "We don't know exactly why she did it, but that scenario makes sense. If she was desperate to be allowed back in, that would've been a good way to convince them."

Dr. Maris-Stapleton spoke up again. "And why does a person become the *leader* of a cult?"

Evie thought she knew why he was asking, as did everyone else.

Bonnie was forthright. "You and I will get into specifics after we've interviewed Cynthia this evening, but often it's a quest for validation and attention, and a way of owning personal power."

Dr. Maris-Stapleton stood. He inhaled deeply and then began to speak in a quiet voice. People had to listen carefully to catch his words. "My daughter Cynthia is guilty of cheating in the race today. I'm profoundly saddened by it." He looked around the room. Evie saw the depth of emotion in his dark eyes. "But there is no proof *whatsoever* that she has anything to do with this so-called cult. I resent the implication." He drew his shoulders back and sniffed. "I will contact my lawyers."

People stopped moving. The room seemed to freeze. Bonnie's mouth opened, but no sound followed. Evie looked at Dr. Marshal and saw curiosity in his eyes.

Evie wondered how it would feel to have your only child accused of such a horrendous thing. It was understandable that Dr. Maris-Stapleton wanted to deny it, but he'd also denied that Cynthia had cheated in the race until it had been proven beyond any doubt. Possibly, Evie mused, he'd protected Cynthia all her life and covered up her crimes. Maybe she'd never had to account for her actions.

Headlights illuminated the driveway as a vehicle approached the farmhouse and stopped. The lights went out and car doors slammed. Not wanting to interrupt this discussion, Evie quietly circumnavigated the room and opened the kitchen door before they could knock and set four dogs barking.

Two very unhappy-looking people stood on the stoop.

"Paulina, Kerry," Evie whispered, "come in!"

Paulina spoke through tight lips. "We won't come in. We want a word with Mary."

Paulina was tanned and seriously peeved. Evie looked over at Mary, who was approaching the door.

"Hi folks," Mary said pleasantly. "Please join us."

Paulina nudged Kerry, whose face wore a sheepish expression. He said, "Mary, this is not a social visit."

Paulina urged him on. "Go ahead, Kerry. Tell her." She looked at Mary defiantly.

Kerry cleared his throat. "Well ... well, Paulina's very upset about how you neglected Beebee, and she wants Jordie to come with us now."

"Right now." Paulina jutted out her chin and stamped her foot. "As in this minute."

Mary looked like she'd been slapped. "How *I* neglected ..."

Evie felt hot anger bubbling up inside her. She could not remain silent. She looked directly into Paulina's eyes. "*You* were the one who got on a plane without even knowing where Beebee was! *You* were the one who sat by the pool in Florida while Gran Mary, who was suffering from a head cold, looked after Jordie and tracked down Beebee and rescued her from a cult! You didn't even know that she'd hitchhiked to Caledon before you left!"

"You can't talk to me like this," whimpered Paulina, shaken.

"Why not?" Evie was just getting started. "It's the truth!"

Mary put a hand on Evie's shoulder. "It's okay, we can discuss all this later."

"It's not okay!" Evie sputtered. "Paulina neglects her kids! She always has! She doesn't deserve to have them, and they don't want to be with her, anyway! Beebee joined a cult and Jordie ran away from home to stay with us. And she says that *you* neglected Beebee?"

Paulina began to shake her head. "You're lying! What cult?"

Evie saw that the woman couldn't process this all at once. She felt her anger subside, to be replaced by a creeping sense of embarrassment about scolding Paulina within hearing range of a house full of people, even if she *had* meant every word. "I'm sorry, Paulina. I just got mad when you blamed Gran Mary."

Paulina couldn't speak. A tear fell down her face.

Piers joined them at the door with the faithful Loewe at his side. "So, lots to talk about, yah?" He put an arm around Evie and squeezed her shoulders. "Welcome back from Florida, folks."

Evie felt hugely grateful to Piers for coming to her aid.

Kerry glared at him. "So, Piers, what's up with cancelling the purchase of Starchild? I spent a lot of time on this deal. He's perfect for Cynthia."

Before Piers could respond, Dr. Maris-Stapleton stepped up. Kerry's face showed surprise at the sight of his client.

"And Starchild might yet be perfect for her. It would take just one phone call." He made a sweeping motion with his arm, inviting them in. "You'd best come inside and close the door. The entire house is getting drafty."

Very reluctantly, Kerry and Paulina entered the house. They refused to take off their coats and turned down the offer of dinner. They stood against the wall just inside the door, making it obvious that they didn't want to be there.

Everyone else remained seated, unsure of what was happening.

Dr. Marshal broke the silence. "Let me introduce myself. I'm the psychiatrist who's been looking into the case of the Newmarket cult called the Circle with which your daughter, Beatrice, has been involved."

Dr. Marshal had been blunt, and Evie wasn't surprised when Paulina staggered. Kerry helped her into a chair. Paulina had heard more than she could bear from both Evie and Dr. Marshal.

Then, Evie remembered the mirror fragment. "Speaking of things out of the ordinary, I have something that might be helpful. Or not." She went to get her coat in the mudroom and came back with the broken piece of mirror. She held it up. "I found this in the snow the day Magpie came across Stacey Linn in the woods."

Dr. Marshal's spun around to look, and Katrina sat up straight. "Where exactly did you find that?" she asked. Her tone was brisk.

"It was under a bush along the trail. I looked for more pieces, but it was the only one."

"Was it within the taped-off area?"

"No! I didn't dare go in there. I knew how mad you'd be."

"And why did you keep it all this time?"

Evie answered honestly. "I totally forgot about it. I only put it in my pocket so no animals would cut their feet."

Dr. Marshal said, "This might be important." He stood. "Officer Summers, please come with me."

Katrina carefully slid the broken mirror into a small plastic bag, then she and Dr. Marshal put on their coats.

Evie felt terrible. "I'm sorry. I forgot all about it until I wore that coat again today and put my hand in the pocket."

"Don't worry." Dr. Marshal smiled at her reassuringly. "We'll take a look at it. It might be nothing at all." He looked at Dr. Maris-Stapleton. "Would you come along with us? We have some questions, and you could be helpful."

Dr. Maris-Stapleton stood up. "Yes, along with my attorney. I'd like to speak to Cynthia, anyway. I'll follow you in my car."

"And Paulina?" Dr. Marshal said, "could you come and talk to Beatrice with us? We will explain everything more fully."

Paulina's mouth dropped open. She looked at Kerry, then at Dr. Marshal. "Can Kerry come with me?"

"Yes, of course." Dr. Marshal turned to Mary. "Thanks for a wonderful dinner, Mary. Sorry to take away so many of your guests."

Mary smiled. "First things first, Ed."

Bonnie, Katrina, and Dr. Marshal led the way, with Paulina and Kerry close behind.

Paulina found Evie with her gaze as she left. She looked sad. "You hurt my feelings, Evie. But you're not totally wrong."

Holy, thought Evie. *She really heard me.* They were gone before she could think of what to say.

Dr. Maris-Stapleton put on his hat and said tersely, "Thank you for including me." He slammed the door behind him.

After a stunned pause, Mary asked, "Cookies and coffee, anyone?" To Evie's ears, her cheerfulness sounded forced.

Jerry and Piers jumped up and made a show of getting dessert and having a good time. Yolanda and Brent did as well, but Evie knew the party was over. She began carrying dishes to the sink.

Mark came up beside her and put his arm around her waist. "It was a nice party. I have to get going, though. My mother and sister are swinging by to pick me up on their way home from soccer practice."

Evie turned to him. "See you tomorrow?"

"You bet." He looked like he wanted to kiss her, and Evie wanted to kiss him back. "Hey," he said, "you did the right thing with Paulina."

"Hope so."

"You did. She had to hear it. Might even make a difference. Look, I gotta go, but see you tomorrow. Can't wait. Say goodnight to Jordie for me. Poor kid. I couldn't find him."

Evie looked around the room. "He probably went to bed. I don't blame him. See you tomorrow." She blew him a kiss.

As expected, Evie found Jordie in his room upstairs. His light was off, but she saw his outline under the covers.

"Jordie?" she whispered. "Are you okay?"

"No."

"You've been through an awful lot today."

He lay there quietly and didn't answer.

She said, "You must've been scared when that girl took you."

"She didn't take me, I went with her. She was nice. That's the thing. I wasn't kidnapped like everybody says. She said Christieloo was the prettiest horse she'd ever seen, and she is, so I liked her."

"I would, too."

"And she said she had some pizza I could share, and she wanted me to see her horse. And then ..." He paused, and then a look of confusion passed over his face.

"And then what?"

"Then I was tied up like Priscilla in *The Boy on the Beach*. Everything was fuzzy until Cran Berry woke me up."

"The girl must've drugged you."

"Maybe. She gave me a piece of candy and I ate it."
He buried his head in his pillow. "I was hungry!"

Evie sat beside him on his bed and put her hand on his
shaking shoulder. "You didn't do anything wrong, Jordie."

"Yes, I did. I took candy from a stranger. And I went
with a stranger. You're not supposed to."

"I know. Don't worry. We all make mistakes."

"I won't do it again. You had to come looking for
me. I'm glad you did."

Evie sat with Jordie in comfortable silence until he
spoke again.

"I was thinking about Dad. He's in jail, and nobody's
looking for him."

Evie was surprised. "We don't talk about him much,
do we?"

"No. He made mistakes and was locked up, just like
me."

"Jordie, it's not at all the same. He did illegal things
on purpose, things that hurt people. He was dishonest.
You trusted somebody you shouldn't have, but it was
an honest mistake." Evie put her arm around her little
brother and held him close.

"He scared me. Dad did. I never knew what he'd do."

Evie nodded. "He scared me, too. He's a scary guy.
Maybe that's why we don't talk about him."

"He was fun sometimes." Jordie smiled a bit.

"Yeah, he was. The way he laughed made everybody
else laugh."

"Yeah. Maybe we should visit him sometime? In
prison."

Evie thought about it. "Maybe we should."

"Will Beebee go to prison, too?" Jordie's lip trembled.

Evie was shocked. "Why would she?"

"Because she did a lot of bad things." Jordie began to cry. "I don't want Beebee to go to jail!"

"I don't think she will, Jordie. She joined a group of kids who did bad things, and bad things happened, but she won't go to jail."

"She burned down a house."

Evie nodded. "She did. And she'll have to face up to that. But she might still be able to help make things right."

Jordie didn't respond.

Evie spoke gently. "You have a lot of things on your mind, don't you?"

He nodded and wiped his face. "Tell Mom I'm sick and I can't leave here."

Evie chuckled. "That's why you're in bed? You heard what they said? That she came to get you?"

"Yeah. I won't go with her. I want … I want to stay here forever. Can I, Evie? I'm your only brother." His eyes were wide and pleading and brimming with tears.

Evie squeezed him tight. "I want you to stay here forever, too. Paulina and Kerry will have their hands full with Beebee for the next little while. Maybe it'll all work out."

"It has to! I can't go back."

"But maybe your mother will smarten up. You guys have given her a real shock."

Jordie looked unconvinced. "Maybe."

"What about school? It starts in a couple of days."

"Can't I go to Abergrath? Where I used to go?"

Evie sighed. "I have no idea. Let's go talk to Gran Mary."

"No!" Jordie pulled the covers over his head. "I'm not going downstairs. I'm staying here."

"You can stay in bed if you like, but your mother and Kerry are gone. They went to see Beebee at the hospital."

Jordie sat up straight. "They're gone? Really?"

"Really."

Jordie's face brightened, and he hopped out of bed. "Are there any cookies left?"

Evidence

Kindness is the language which the deaf can hear and the blind can see.

— Anonymous

All the guests were gone. Jordie came downstairs for dessert and then snuggled up on the couch with a video game while Mary and Angela chatted and tidied the house.

Evie went outside to do night check with Simon, Garfunkel, and Magpie. The dogs raced off into the dark in all directions, enthusiastic to help.

Evie was glad to get outside. There was a nip in the air, and snow would be coming soon. The warmth they'd had over the last few days would not return for another month or so. Evie flared her nostrils and inhaled deeply, then watched the frost puff out on her breath as she exhaled. She allowed the peace of the night to embrace her.

The horses nickered as she entered the barn and looked at her over their chest-high stall doors. All the horses but Kazzam.

Oh, no. Is he colicking from all the exertion? Did he tie up? Evie rushed to his stall and peeked over the door. Kazzam was lying flat with his legs outstretched. He opened one eye and looked at her, then gathered his legs under him, popped up, and shook himself all over like a dog just out of the water. Evie exhaled with relief. Kazzam moved over to his door for a pat on the nose.

"I hope you feel better after your nap, boy. *I'm* sure as heck ready for bed."

Evie walked her tired black horse out of his stall and into the aisle to check his knees. Apart from very minor scrapes, there was no damage and no sign of swelling. She spread some furasine ointment on the scrapes and then put him back in.

Soon the buckets were full of water, and each horse had two flakes of hay to munch on. Evie gave Kazzam one more. "You burned up a lot of energy today. Knock yourself out."

Chores were done. Evie put one foot in front of the other and dragged herself toward the house. She yawned and then yawned again. The dogs followed her inside and flopped onto their beds.

Evie hardly acknowledged her family as she made a beeline for the stairs. "Night night," she muttered.

"But it's not even eight-thirty!" exclaimed Jordie.

"I know," answered Evie. "I'm done with this day."

From the kitchen Angela called, "Have a good sleep, Evie."

Evie stopped and turned. "Mom, I'm so glad that you're home." She opened her arms.

Angela stepped into her daughter's embrace. "This time it's forever. I love you so much I can't bear it."

"I love you, too."

"Tomorrow starts a brand-new day."

Evie brushed away a tear and began to climb the stairs again. "G'night, Gran Mary. Thanks for everything today."

"Good night, my dear," answered Mary. "Sleep in late. Angela and I will do the horses in the morning."

"And me, too," added Jordie. "I know how to muck stalls."

Evie was asleep almost as soon as her head touched the pillow. The last sound she heard was Magpie creeping into her room and turning in circles on the mat before settling in for the night.

It seemed mere minutes later that she dreamed that her phone was ringing. *La di dah, la didah didah di-daah.* It rang and rang, and then it stopped. In the dream, someone left a message with a *ping* and then called back. *La di dah, la didah didah di-daah.*

Evie lifted her head. This was no dream. She looked at her phone on the nightstand beside her. It was lit up with an unknown number.

"Hello?"

"It's me. Beebee."

"Hey," Evie whispered groggily.

"You wouldn't answer!"

"I was asleep."

"They let me have one call. You're it."

"Why me?"

"Because. You're a good person."

Evie blinked. She hadn't expected that. "What time is it?"

"This is important!"

Evie sat up in bed and looked at the clock beside her. "It's ten to five in the morning, Beebee."

"Just listen. I need you to do something."

"I'm listening."

"I know where the ATV is."

Now Evie was fully awake. "The ATV that left Stacey Linn in the woods?"

"Of course that ATV."

"Did you tell the police? And Dr. Marshal?"

"Yeah. They don't believe me."

Evie was surprised. "Why not?"

"Maybe I didn't totally one hundred percent tell the truth."

"They won't even look?"

There was a slight pause before Beebee spoke. "They looked where I told them three other times and it wasn't there."

"So why would it be there now?"

"Because this time I told them where it *actually* is."

Evie sighed. "Okay. I think I understand. Where is it?"

"Before I tell you, you have to promise to do exactly as I say. This is very, very important, and you have to do it before anybody else takes it, which might be any minute. They know the police are looking for it."

"By *it*, you mean the ATV?"

"Of course I do!"

"And by *they*, you mean the Circle?"

"Too many questions! Evie, you have to help. I need Cynthia where she can't get me. Like in jail! If they let her go, my life is over. And she's saying that she's completely innocent, that it was everybody else's fault, and her father has very expensive lawyers!"

"First, tell me something," said Evie. "Why did you get Jordie kidnapped? He's your brother."

"Half-brother. But I didn't think they'd really do it." Beebee spoke very quickly in a shallow, breathy voice. Evie could hear that she was trying not to cry. "I told them how to catch him and where to leave the ransom note, but I knew they wouldn't hurt him."

"They drugged him. They duct-taped his mouth. They buried him in garbage."

"Oh. I didn't know. I got carried away. I'm sorry!"

"I believe you."

"You do? Will you help me?"

"Maybe. Another question. How did you know about the police raid at the Douglas house on Saturday morning?"

"My mother told me. Jordie had told her something exciting was going to happen there. I put it together."

Evie remembered that Jordie had been watching a movie while they were planning. He'd obviously overheard and hadn't realized it was a secret. "Okay, I'll help. *If* you come clean about everything — I mean *everything* — and stop protecting them."

"I will. So you'll do it?"

"Yes."

"See, I told you. You're a good person!"

Evie sighed. "Tell me what you want me to do."

"Promise to do exactly as I say."

"I promise."

"On a stack of bibles?"

"On a stack of bibles."

"And you have to do it now. It can't wait."

"Beebee, enough!"

"Okay, okay. But do it as soon as we hang up."

Evie let out the dogs and left a note on the kitchen counter just in case she wasn't back home before Gran Mary and her mother woke up. Then she and Magpie went out to the barn.

316

The horses blinked rapidly when she turned on the lights and looked at her questioningly. "Don't ask," she said in response.

Just as Beebee had instructed, Evie tacked up Kazzam and rode down the driveway, followed by Magpie.

"This might actually be good for you, Kazzam," she said to her horse. "It'll stretch out your muscles after all the work you did yesterday."

Kazzam was not impressed. He was still tired, Evie thought, and so was she. The sun wouldn't be up for another couple of hours, but there was enough light in the sky to see their way up the gravel road toward the woods.

Had Beebee sent her on a wild goose chase, like she'd done to the police three times? It was certainly possible. Beebee had lied about most things lately, and even before that, she hadn't really been trustworthy. Evie began to feel a little stupid, but she'd made a promise to fulfill her stepsister's request. *Because I'm a good person*, she thought with a smirk.

She turned Kazzam up the lane from the road and into the darkness, listening to the sounds of her horse's quiet hooves on the underbrush and Magpie scooting into the bushes to follow a scent.

Evie thought she heard the quiet crunching of a car driving slowly up the gravel road. Was her imagination playing tricks?

"This'd be spooky if I was alone," Evie whispered. A twig snapped loudly in the forest, startling her. "Deep breath," she told herself aloud. "Deep breath."

Magpie leapt out onto the trail, chasing a frightened rabbit.

Evie chuckled in relief and started looking for the path that Beebee had told her about. Was that it there, on their left?

It was hard to see in the dark, but Evie took a chance. She steered Kazzam in that direction. If Beebee had told the truth, the shed wasn't far.

The trees opened into a small clearing. Surprise! A shed stood right in front of her, just like Beebee had said. *Why have I never noticed it before?* thought Evie. It was very old and was attached to the fenceline of the Tuerlings' property. The roof was half-caved-in and covered with moss, fully blending into the forest.

She dismounted, pulled out her phone, and took pictures of the shed and the ground around it, just as Beebee had directed.

"Magpie!" Evie called. The dog appeared instantly, eager to please. "I need you here for moral support."

Slowly, she opened the shed door. The hinges were rusty and the wood was pulpy. As she pulled, the top hinge came away, and the door sagged open on a slant.

The shed was full of dry garbage. Black garbage bags, burlap sacks, old plastic feed tubs, empty boxes. She took more pictures. The flash on her phone lit up the interior. Evie saw a glint of metal.

She carefully crept in and pulled the boxes and garbage bags aside. Aha! Under the pile of debris was the ATV, as promised.

When she'd gotten a few good shots of it, she tried to arrange things as they were before and prepared to leave.

Just as she hoisted the shed door back into place, Magpie began to bark a serious alert.

Someone was coming! This was exactly what Beebee had feared. She'd been right about not waiting until daybreak.

Just in time, Evie scrambled up on Kazzam's back and urged him deeper into the woods and out of sight, away from the approaching person, but with a good vantage. There was no way out.

Footsteps neared. From the long strides and the heaviness of the step, Evie surmised it was an adult man.

"Sit, Mags!" she ordered. Magpie did as she was told and stopped barking. Evie kept her finger to her lips to instruct her dog to remain still and placed her right palm softly on Kazzam's neck. Gently, she scratched his withers. "Please," Evie murmured. She hoped her animals would understand her plea. "Please don't move or make a sound."

The man came into sight. He wore a bulky black coat and a woollen cap. He pulled the shed door open roughly. The lower hinge came loose, and the whole door collapsed to the ground. Evie heard him muttering and swearing. There was another crash as he tossed aside the heavy door. Boxes and bags tumbled noisily as he hastily cleared them away.

The ATV engine came to life loudly, further shattering the stillness of the early morning. Headlights flashed on.

Evie was ready. As the man drove the ATV out of the shed, she snapped a picture. He didn't react, possibly because the flash went unnoticed in the brightness of the headlights.

Something nagged at her. The man had looked familiar. She glanced down at the picture she'd taken. "Holy," she whispered.

Evie waited until the ATV's noise was well away before she exhaled. "Good girl, Mags. Good boy, Kazzam."

Kazzam relaxed, and Magpie wagged her tail. Evie put a little pressure on her horse's sides, and they went back to the main trail the same way they'd come, following the newly made tire tracks.

Evie heard the metallic sounds of the ATV being loaded onto a trailer at the road. "Let's go!" she urged Kazzam.

Quickly, the horse picked up a trot. They got there just as a truck was moving off. Evie managed to snap one more picture from the side of the road: the licence plates of the truck and the trailer.

Beebee had told her the truth.

One more thing to do, and Evie's promise would be honoured. She texted her stepsister a thumbs-up.

It was almost seven when Evie got back to the farm. As she passed the kitchen window, she saw Mary deep in thought at her desk, typing on her computer. Evie watched her for a moment before entering. Her heart filled with love. Gran Mary was always there for people whenever they needed help, and she always had the best advice at the right time. If not for Mary, Evie had no idea what her life would be right now. Gran Mary had taken her in and helped her find her mother, and she was the prime reason Evie and Kazzam had won the Queen's Plate last June.

And who else would've opened her door so willingly to Jordie and Beebee, of no relation to her except through Evie?

Evie opened the back door. "Hey, Gran Mary!"

"Evie! You startled me!" Mary swung around on her chair.

"Is anybody else up?"

"No. Just us chickens. Thanks for leaving that note. Did you put the horses out?"

"Yup. They're fed and outside. I'll do the stalls later."

"Thanks," Mary said. "I'll help. What got you up so early? I thought you'd sleep late this morning."

Evie pulled up a kitchen chair and sat beside her. "Beebee called."

Mary closed her computer and looked at her quizzically. "And?" She tilted her head.

"And she told me where the ATV was hidden. Kazzam and Magpie and I found it."

"Where was it?"

"That's a good question."

"Tell me everything. Talk while I make another cup of coffee. I have a feeling I'll need it."

Evie nodded slowly. "Yeah. I think you will."

Thirty minutes later, Dr. Marshal and Katrina Summers were sitting at the kitchen table with Mary and Evie. Angela and Jordie were still asleep. The table was set with juice, coffee, fruit, bacon, toast, and cereal.

Dr. Marshal asked Mary directly, "I'm sure you didn't invite us over for breakfast. Why were we needed so urgently and so early?"

Mary nodded to Evie. "Evie will tell you. I'm just the cook."

Evie silently showed Katrina and Dr. Marshal the series of pictures on her phone, starting with the shed and ending with the licence plates. "Is this at all helpful?" she asked slyly.

Katrina and Dr. Marshal were stunned.

"Dr. Maris-Stapleton," said Katrina. "I wouldn't have believed that he was involved."

Dr. Marshal added, "Up to his eyeballs."

"That's why Beebee asked me to show you the pictures," said Evie. "She thought you wouldn't believe her."

"We wouldn't have," agreed Katrina. "She's told more than a few whoppers and wasted our time."

"But for Manfred to get the ATV himself and take it away ..." said Dr. Marshal. "That shows how desperate he is. Send us the pictures, Evie."

Evie typed in their email addresses, pressed Send, and lifted her head. "He must've gotten worried last night when he heard Bonnie telling us how important the ATV is as evidence."

"You're right. At the hospital, he probably asked Cynthia about it. If she told him that all the girls knew where it was, he would've become worried that someone would break their silence. I'm speculating here, but he might've then told her he'd look after it," added Dr. Marshal. "We gave each girl one call. Cynthia would've told one of them, and so on."

"Which is how Beatrice would've heard about it," nodded Katrina. "And she made her one call to Evie when she realized that the house of cards was falling in."

Dr. Marshal sat back. "Our little network worked exactly as we'd hoped."

"There's one more thing," Evie said. "Beebee told me that she found another piece of mirror at the Douglas house before she lit the place on fire. She saved it. It's in the pouch of her black hoodie at the hospital."

Dr. Marshal pulled out his phone and called Bonnie. He asked her to retrieve the piece of broken mirror.

While he was doing that, Katrina was on her phone in the other room getting the licence plate tracked. When she came back, she said, "The truck and trailer belong to

Piers Anders. I'm glad you have the picture of Dr. Maris-Stapleton driving the ATV, Evie. Otherwise the finger would have pointed at Piers."

"Which wouldn't have made any sense," Dr. Marshal cut in.

Evie hesitated. "But Dr. Maris-Stapleton doing this *does* make sense?"

Dr. Marshal nodded. "He's not the first father who was so protective that he ended up supporting and condoning, even exacerbating, bad behaviour.

Mary spoke up. "But surely he's not part of this cult?"

"Likely not," answered Dr. Marshal. "And he likely doesn't know the extent of what went on. But we need him to fill us in on some details, like how the girls had access to his drugs. We'll visit him now."

"Officers are on their way. They'll meet us at the front gates of MMS," Katrina informed him. "That ATV will have traces of blood and dirt on it, even if they scrubbed it down. If we're lucky, we'll find traces of the drug they've been using."

"Adenosinol?" asked Evie.

Dr. Marshal and Katrina stared at her.

Evie shrugged. "When I met you that day at the Quest, you told me Dr. Maris-Stapleton was famous for developing it. I googled it. Stacey Linn seemed dead when I found her, but she was alive with an almost undetectable heartbeat."

Dr. Marshal smiled. "You are a very smart girl. I'd love to take credit for it, but DNA doesn't lie."

It was Evie's turn to look surprised. "What are you talking about?"

"All I'll say is that you come by your skill with horses honestly."

Evie jumped to a conclusion. "Piers is my grandfather? *Piers* is Angela's father?"

"I can neither confirm nor deny because of my Hippocratic oath."

"Gran Mary? Is it true?" Evie hoped that it was.

Mary looked extremely uncomfortable. "I'm sure that Dr. Marshal and Officer Summers have a lot of police work to do."

Katrina finished her coffee in a gulp. "Ready when you are."

Dr. Marshal stood. "Right. We should go. Because of these pictures, Manfred has no choice but to tell us where the ATV is, and then we'll get it to the lab. If things go as they should, we'll have an airtight case by the end of the day."

Happy Trails

Happiness [is] a butterfly, which when pursued, seems always beyond your grasp; but if you will sit down quietly, may alight upon you.

— L.

It was late morning on Saturday, March 31st. After mucking the stalls and taking a leisurely hack, Evie and Kazzam walked along the path in the woods toward home. Magpie had fully enjoyed the morning, following along until she sniffed a scent that needed tracking. Many times, she'd disappeared and then shortly reappeared with renewed energy and a sense of accomplishment.

A lot had happened in the two weeks since the March Madness Steeplechase. Evie patted the sleek black neck of her horse. "You really did win that race, you know," she said. "Everybody knows it, even if your name isn't on the trophy."

Dr. Edwin Marshal had gone back to where his daughters lived with their growing families and continued his important work. He promised Mary he'd keep in touch now that they'd reconnected after all these years.

Evie knew that he'd hoped for more than friendship with Mary, but he seemed to understand. Or at least to accept it.

Bonnie Waters would carry on counselling Beebee. Beebee had gone through a period of denial, but now seemed to understand how important treatment was, and she finally admitted that she needed help.

No surprise Beebee searched for another family, thought Evie. Grayson was in jail, and Paulina mostly ignored her. And, as far as Evie knew, Beebee's biological father had disappeared completely when she was just a baby. There was a story there, but Evie had no idea what it was. Maybe one day she'd find out.

She absently patted Kazzam's neck as her thoughts turned to Piers. After a lifetime of bachelorhood, Piers had been thrilled to learn that he had a family. He'd become a fixture in Mary's kitchen, popping in daily for a coffee or for lunch. Mary seemed quite happy about it, too. Evie smiled. She'd noticed that her grandmother was taking a bit more care with her hair and makeup these days.

It had been good to get back to school. Evie smiled. A rest, really, from all the adventures that had taken place during the March break. It was great to reconnect with her friends, but the best thing of all was seeing Mark every single day. Thinking about him made her heart do a little happy dance.

Her English teacher had loved her essay on *Lord of the Flies* and had given her an A+. He'd had no idea why her essay was so impassioned and personal until the news about the Circle made a big splash in the press. The story was international news because Dr. Maris-Stapleton was famous for the advances he'd made in medical science and for his philanthropy. The police had charged him with being an accessory after the fact and for obstruction of justice. His illustrious career was over, and he was looking at time in jail.

Evie felt sad for him. And sad for all the good work that he would no longer be able to do for heart research. She shook her head. He'd tried to help his daughter, but he'd broken several laws.

His daughter, Cynthia, was in much worse trouble. She'd been charged with the second-degree murder of Patricia Price and the attempted murder of Stacey Linn. There was evidence that she'd stolen drugs from her father's locked cabinet and injected Adenosinol into several girls.

There was a lot of proof. Traces of blood and Adenosinol had been found on the ATV, as well as dirt that matched samples from certain articles of clothing. A used hypodermic needle laden with valuable evidence had been discovered among the ashes at the Douglas house. The piece of mirror that Beebee had taken from the Douglas house and the one that Evie had found on the trail both had particles, and partial fingerprints, that proved they were from one of the mirrors given to members of the Circle by Cynthia.

Dr. Maris-Stapleton's lawyer claimed that Cynthia had had no knowledge of any cult and was not connected in any way, and that all the evidence was circumstantial. But the jagged circle tattoo on her arm told the truth.

When the three girls who'd been hiding in the grooms' cabin were shown the shards of broken mirror, they panicked and began to talk. Individually, they told the police everything they could remember and connected the whole story together.

They told them that Cynthia had demanded the girls prove their obedience by each catching an animal and killing it. The offering was to be wrapped in plastic, and the presentation documented with pictures and a signed confession. This became collateral for Cynthia to be used as blackmail if the member ever wanted to leave.

Evie winced at the thought. It made her sick. Herman the barn cat had been a victim. Loewe had been lucky. Timing had worked in his favour.

With her subdued parents by her side, Stacey Linn had changed her story and finally recounted what really happened. She and Beebee had hitchhiked to Caledon together on Thursday, March 8th. They met up with the Circle in the old Douglas house and began preparations for their joint initiation ceremony, which was to be on Sunday the 11th.

The plan changed when Cynthia's father insisted that she go to Florida to try out Starchild. The ceremony was to be delayed until the following Sunday, but because Stacey had already injected Herman with a high dose of Adenosinol to kill him as proof of her loyalty, Cynthia decided to proceed with Stacey's initiation on the morning of the 11th and to wait to initiate Beebee after her return.

Beebee had already caught Loewe and put him in an empty groom's apartment, but thankfully, she heard about the delay before killing him. Even in all the ensuing panic, she had made certain that a groom found him. Evie didn't believe her stepsister would have been capable of killing an animal, anyway.

During her initiation ritual, Stacey was given too much Adenosinol and didn't regain consciousness. Cynthia thought she was dead. Beebee panicked and tried to call for help, so Althea was ordered to take away her phone and guard her.

When Cynthia left for Florida that Sunday afternoon, she left Althea in charge of disposing of Stacey's body, which she did on Monday morning.

That was when Evie found Stacey's seemingly lifeless body in the woods where Althea had dumped her.

Wow, thought Evie as she rode along the trail. *Double wow.* Beebee had been living in a snake's nest. And there was more.

Mirrors had been a pivotal part of Cynthia's reign of terror. Her beauty was celebrated. She constantly checked herself in mirrors and asked the girls to compare their beauty to hers. Nobody dared question that she was far more beautiful than anyone else.

Once the girls were accepted into the group, they would be tattooed with the jagged circle and receive their own circular mirror in a solemn ceremony. They were told that by means of these mirrors, Cynthia could see into their brains and know all their darkest thoughts. The girls were convinced that if their mirror ever broke, either by accident or on purpose, they would die an agonizing death.

A mirror that allows another person to see into your brain? thought Evie. *And that could lead to your death? Why had the girls believed it, and why the heck had they accepted this strange gift?*

The girls told the police that Cynthia would do unexpected and shocking things to keep them in line, like leaping into a room through a window, or hanging upside down over a doorway when you walked in. If her followers ever waned in their devotion, she'd reduce them to fearful jelly with disturbing threats of mutilation and death, rendering them too scared to talk about it to each other or to anybody else.

Their mantra came to Evie's mind. *Death to she who disobeys. Death to she who betrays. Never shall we make mistakes. Never shall our mirrors break.* Evie got goosebumps all over.

She understood a person's need to be accepted as part of a group. She understood the fear of isolation and loneliness. But had this cult really been better than being alone? Had it really seemed worth harming themselves and others, and killing innocent animals? Had these girls been so desperate to be accepted that they'd let Cynthia coerce them into doing horrible things? Apparently, so.

Beebee was a good example. She'd known how bad the cult was and had even tried to escape from it, but she still couldn't stand being shunned from the group. She'd sought redemption and inclusion and had therefore warned them about the police raid on the Douglas house. She'd tried to prove herself worthy by burning it down and coming up with the plan to kidnap Jordie.

And what had driven Cynthia? Had she been seeking to create a family, too? To belong somewhere? Evie remembered the icy coldness in the girl's eyes. She wondered if a part of Cynthia had died long ago, making her empty. Had she craved something to fill that hollow space? Maybe. Cynthia had thrived on dominance, not caring about the damage she caused. In fact, she'd seemed to relish it. Could she change? Did she want to? Evie had no idea.

Dr. Marshal certainly held out hope. He didn't think it was too late for Cynthia to find a purpose for her life and to replace her destructive urges with empathy for others. But it was up to her, he'd emphasized. Nobody could do the work for her, not even her father. No matter how much he wanted to help.

Dr. Marshal told Evie that his study of this case had just begun. He would examine Cynthia's motivations, as well as the long-term psychological effects her actions had on herself and on her victims. And he would try his best to help those victims regain their self-worth.

Cynthia had certainly ruined the self-worth of the young girls who'd become slaves to her. She'd been the undisputed boss of the cult and the unquestioned authority, terrifying the girls into submission.

Evie thought about it as they continued along the trails. There were two parts to this picture: the fooler and the fooled. *There's the person who controls and dominates, and the people who obey and submit. One can't exist without the other.* If Cynthia had had no followers, she wouldn't have had any power. If the followers had had no master, they wouldn't have gathered together to form a cult.

Magpie suddenly began to bark loudly. Kazzam spooked sideways, and Evie was jolted back into reality.

"Easy, boy!" she said as she gathered her reins and righted her helmet. "You'd think there was a wolf or something! Sheesh."

Garfunkel popped out of the underbrush, his tail wagging so madly that it looked like it might send him flying. Simon's happy Lab face immediately followed. Both dogs were so delighted to see Magpie that they couldn't contain themselves. All three wiggled and played right underneath Kazzam's belly.

"Hey, careful there, pups! What are you doing so far from home?"

She didn't have to wait long for an answer. Gran Mary came trotting around the bend in the woods, riding her old chestnut racehorse, Bendigo.

"Gran Mary!" called Evie.

"Hi! We hoped we'd bump into you." She slowed the gelding and stopped beside Evie.

"I'm just heading home."

"Can you join us on our hack, dear? I have news."

"Sure."

Jordie appeared just then, riding Christieloo and smiling from ear to ear. Right behind came Paragon, with Beebee in the saddle. She seemed happy, too, but clearly didn't want to appear uncool. *Her recovery from the fire had been speedy*, thought Evie. *Her recovery from the cult would take much longer.*

The biggest surprise for Evie was seeing her mother on a familiar-looking Thoroughbred. Angela's face was flushed, and she looked very comfortable on her horse.

"Mom!"

"It was too nice a day to sit at home while everybody else was having fun."

"Who are you riding?"

"Three guesses."

Evie took a good look. The clean, long legs and the elegant lines of the beautiful, bright bay were unmistakable. "Holy smoke! It's Thymetofly!"

"Yes! I should've known you'd get it in one."

"How did you find him, and where has he been?"

"Well, I never actually sold him. J.J.'s been looking after him for me."

"Really? I didn't know that. Is he moving into Parson's Bridge?"

Angela and Mary looked at each other and laughed.

Evie was confused. "What's so funny?"

Jordie answered for them. "Don't worry. It's a long story."

"That's okay, I have lots of time," Evie said.

They walked along, and Beebee began. "First of all, your mother, Angela, is the mystery buyer of the farm next door."

"Really?" This was news to Evie. She hadn't even known her mother was looking for a farm to buy.

"And she's renting it to my mother and Kerry."

"What! Really?"

Jordie piped in. "Mom says she's turning over a new leaf and she'll be the perfect mother now, but we can come visit Cran Berry and you all the time. And we can go to Abergrath School, which is totally awesome. My friends are there, and I love it so-o much."

"That's great!" Evie hoped that Paulina's promise would come true.

Beebee continued. "*And* Angela bought back Maple Mills Stables this morning while you were out riding."

"Maple Mills?" Evie was stunned. "Just now? Really?"

Gran Mary nodded. "She's talking to Piers and J.J. and Kerry about starting a first-class training operation, with Yoyo as the stable manager and Brent as the farrier." She twinkled. "I told you there was news."

"Really!"

"Stop saying 'really'!" Beebee chirped. "It's so annoying!"

"I don't know what else to say." Evie's head was spinning. "Mom? Is it all true?"

Angela laughed. "Yes. It all happened so fast. I bought the farm next door to have a place to call my own and be near Mary. But then I began to wonder if I'd made a mistake. If I'm to stay sober, I'll need something challenging to do. I can't just sit at home all day. When Maple Mills came up, I jumped at it." She spoke with enthusiasm. "I'm looking forward to working with J.J. again. Kerry will add so much as a coach, and I'm going to get to know my real father for the first time in my life. It's all rather perfect, isn't it?"

Her mother sounded alive and energized, but Evie felt an empty space in her stomach and couldn't figure out why. "It sounds exciting," she said.

"It *is* exciting!" Angela said. "I can't wait to get going. Piers is already organizing staff and schedules, and Kerry is looking at horses. The Thoroughbreds J.J. was looking after will be returning to Maple Mills to be retrained as jumpers or eventers. No Justice is the model, Evie! We'll do what you did with him!"

Glowing, Angela looked at everyone and said, "Race you to the windmill!"

Beebee, Jordie, and Angela cantered away on their horses. Mary waited to see if Evie was coming, then waved goodbye when she saw that she wasn't. Simon and Garfunkel barrelled after her.

Evie turned Kazzam around. She wanted to go home. She needed to think.

Quietly, she patted his neck. He was a special horse. What he'd accomplished was unique. What she and Kazzam had done, they'd done as a team. First the Queen's Plate and then the Steeplechase. They'd done it together. She was as important to him as he was to her, and the trust they had in each other made it possible to jump big fences and tackle difficult riddles. Did her mother really think it was so easy, that there was a cookie-cutter formula? Did nobody understand?

As they turned up the lane, it came to her. The reason she was feeling low was simple. She'd been completely left out of all the plans.

Everything had suddenly changed, and she wasn't a part of it. Nobody had included her. She hadn't known about anything. Paulina, Kerry, Beebee, and Jordie were moving in next door to Gran Mary. Angela was moving back to Maple Mills.

What about me? she thought. Would Gran Mary expect her to move out and live with her mother? Mary did have her own life to live, especially now that Piers was back in it.

And what about Kazzam? "Wherever I go in the whole world, you're coming with me, boy." Evie fought back tears. "You, too, Mags." Magpie wagged her tail and looked up at Evie lovingly. "Maybe we should find someplace else, anyway."

Everything was turning out great for Beebee and Jordie. Great for Angela. Great for Mary and Piers and Jerry and Paulina and Kerry and Yoyo and Brent.

It's great for everybody but me, she thought. *I should be happy for them. But I feel sad and alone. Where do I fit in?* she wondered. *Do I fit in at all?*

As she neared the barn, she saw that the door was wide open, and there was a shadowy figure inside. And then another one. She stared. Suddenly, the men slid back into the gloom against the door frame. She gasped. They'd seen her.

Should she call 911?

She didn't have her phone with her! Magpie and Kazzam would protect her, and if those men were burglars, hopefully they would run away.

She gritted her teeth and asked Kazzam to trot. She called Magpie for reinforcement. When they reached the barn, she slid down and boldly called out, "Hello? Who's there?"

There was no answer. She called more loudly, with as much aggression as she could muster. "Who's *there*?"

Magpie went right into the barn with her tail wagging, and Kazzam was quite relaxed. The animals' reactions were odd, Evie thought. Very odd. Warily, she threw the reins over her horse's head and led him in.

Piers and Mark stepped out suddenly.

"You scared me!" she yelled.

Piers grinned. "Yah! It's good for the heart!"

"What a dirty trick!"

Mark took her in his arms and said, "I'm sorry. But we have a surprise for you."

"Isn't scaring me out of my wits enough of a surprise?" She was still feeling low, and now she was annoyed at having been frightened. "Can I at least look after Kazzam first?"

Piers took Kazzam and quickly untacked him while Mark brushed him down. Once Kazzam was in his stall with fresh water, Mark took Evie's arm and seated her on a bale of hay.

"Close your eyes," commanded Piers.

Reluctantly, Evie did as she was told.

"Now, open them!"

Mark and Piers stood together holding an enormous homemade trophy carved out of wood. It was lacquered and shiny with a brass plaque on the base.

"For me?" asked Evie, her eyes widening.

"Yes, for you, my own dear granddaughter and daring Jockey Girl." Piers looked very proud. "Mark made this himself. He did a fine job. Read it, Evie."

As Evie read the inscription, she was overcome with emotion. Her eyes welled up and her throat constricted. She shook her head, unable to speak.

Mark said, "Let me read it for you." Then he had another thought. "No, Piers should do the honours."

Piers cleared his throat. "'To Evangeline Gibb and Kazzam, a.k.a. No Justice, true winners of the March Madness Steeplechase.'" He pointed. "Under here, in the small print, it says, 'And in honour of the Chancellor, may he rest in peace.'"

Evie let the tears roll down her face. "It's perfect. Thank you. You made it, Mark?"

"I did. I finished it today and couldn't wait, even though the last coat of lacquer is still tacky. Piers had the plaque done, and we met here to surprise you."

"You certainly did."

"Do you like it?" Mark asked.

"I love it!"

"So why are you crying?"

"Just stop talking and hug me."

Mark and Evie held each other in a tight embrace.

Piers cleared his throat again. "Ahem? I'll just take Kazzam out to his field and let Loewe out of my truck, yah? I thought if you saw him he'd give us away so I … er … anyway, I'll wait outside on the bench."

A few minutes later, Piers, Evie, and Mark sat in a row on the bench outside the barn. Loewe and Magpie lay at their feet beside Evie's wooden trophy. Kazzam foraged in the round bale for the best pieces of hay as Evie listened to Piers outlining the plan for the new equestrian centre.

"So. I've given you a thumbnail sketch, yah?" said Piers. "Will you help us in the training program?"

Evie paused thoughtfully. "As much as I can, but the only horse I've ever trained is Kazzam, and I wouldn't call that training. We sort of figure everything out together."

"Ah! But that is the secret with training! Training is removing fear from new experiences. It is letting horses get used to new ideas, and allowing them to accept!"

"That makes sense to me," agreed Evie.

"Where are you going to live?" asked Mark. "With your mother or your grandmother?"

"I don't know." Evie felt her stomach knot. "Until a few minutes ago, I didn't know I had to choose. But I'll have no say in it, anyway." She heard the tinge of bitterness in her own voice.

"Hey, Evie, don't be upset," said Mark. He took her hand in his. "It's all going to work out. Like training a horse. You need to get used to new ideas."

Against her will, she saw his logic. "I guess."

Piers held her other hand. "You must stay with Mary. She wants you here with her — she told me that — and Angela needs to sort out her new life, yah? She has much work to do."

Evie felt better knowing that she could stay with Gran Mary. She'd never lived with her mother, never in her life. She needed time to get to know Angela. And the thought of living in the big house at Maple Mills again held no appeal for her. "You're serious, Piers? Gran Mary said that?"

"Yah, for sure." He chuckled. "If I have my way, someday we'll live together as a big, happy family." He sounded gruff, but Evie knew that emotion had tightened his throat.

Evie squeezed Mark's hand on her left and Piers's hand on her right. "You've cheered me up, you two. Just think. I didn't have a grandfather until you showed up, Piers."

The old man snorted. "That first day I met you, I wouldn't have wanted you as my granddaughter." His eyes sparkled. "But I changed my mind."

"I'm the opposite," Mark said. "I wanted to be Evie's boyfriend the first day I met her."

"And you changed your mind?" Evie asked with mock alarm.

"No!" Mark blurted. "I didn't say that!"

The three of them laughed.

Kazzam abruptly lifted his head from his hay. He looked toward the road at the same instant that Magpie and Loewe began to bark. The handsome black racehorse let out a mighty neigh.

Answering nickers filled the air.

They watched the four riders walk their tired, happy horses up the lane. Kazzam trotted to meet them and accompanied them along the inside of the split rail fence.

Mary led the way on her faithful old Bendigo, chatting merrily with Angela on Thymetofly close behind.

Even from so far away, Evie saw a strong family resemblance in their smiles. She felt a surge of belonging. Less than a year ago, she hadn't known either one of them. If Gran Mary hadn't sent her a card on her sixteenth birthday, Evie would never have known of her mother's existence, and would never have found her on the streets of Toronto. Now, she couldn't imagine life without either of them.

Jordie rode Christieloo side by side with Beebee on Paragon. They were laughing about something they both found hilarious. They poked each other and fooled around, confident in their well-behaved horses. Evie made a wish for both of her siblings to be okay. She suddenly felt hopeful.

The black Labrador retriever, Simon, and the yellow Lab, Garfunkel, trailed at the rear of the cheerful procession, completing the tableau. They were muddy and fulfilled, with their tongues hanging out and their tails wagging low.

"Here comes our family," said Evie.

"There is not a more beautiful sight in the entire world, yah?" asked Piers hoarsely.

Evie fully agreed. Her heart swelled with happiness.